PRAISE FOR THE

NAPOLEON'S PYRA
a leader among historical novelists."
—Library Journal

THE ROSETTA KEY: "The action in nearly
nonstop, the humor is plentiful, and the intrigue is
more than enough to keep the pages turning."
—School Library Journal

THE DAKOTA CIPHER: "Fast, fun and fill of
surprises ... rich in intrigue and impressive historical
detail."
—Publishers Weekly

THE BARBARY PIRATES: "An action-filled romp
that's both historically accurate and great fun."
—Library Journal

THE EMERALD STORM: "A breathlessly exciting
adventure."
—Booklist

THE BARBED CROWN: "Description of war on the
high seas is rarely better than in this novel."
—San Antonio Express-News

THE THREE EMPERORS: "An especially
interesting underlying tension of mysticism and
science."
—Historical Novel Review

THE TROJAN ICON

February, 2016
ISBN 978-0-99066-21-6-7
Burrows Publishing
www.williamdietrich.comm

Book Cover Design/Interior Design by VMC Art & Design

To Henry Mills, just beginning to explore the world.

NORTH SEA

LONDON ·

· BERLIN

WAR

· VIENNA

· PARIS

MUNICH ·

ADRIATIC SEA

· ROME

TYRRHENIAN SEA

EASTERN EUROPE, 1806-07.

Ethan Gage travels from St. Petersburg,
Russia, to Jelgava in Latvia, Pulawy
in Poland, Balbec in Transylvania,
Constantinople in the Ottoman
Empire, and the Plains of Troy.

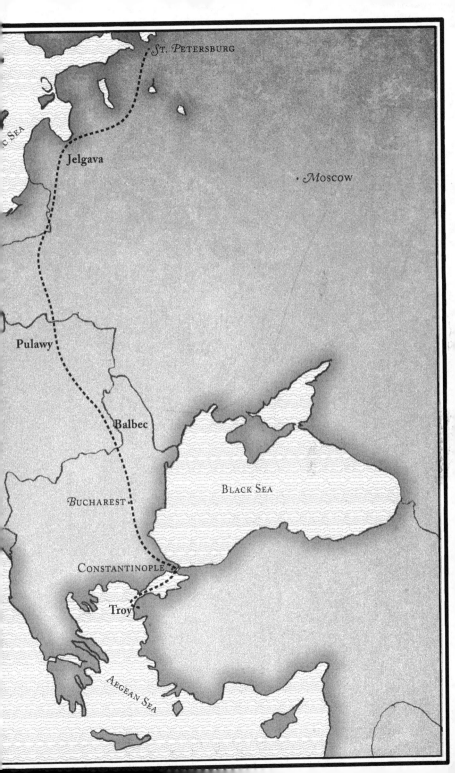

AN ETHAN GAGE ADVENTURE

THE
TROJAN
ICON

WILLIAM DIETRICH

I ran from the wolf and encountered the bear.
Russian proverb

THE GANTLET

English cannon barked and jumped, the crash of their carriages so severe that it rattled the chains of my manacles. I was blind to the battle on the deck overhead, but I could hear it. A cry of command, a tense pause while the touchhole was lit, the roar of the 24-pounders, the snap of restraining tackle as the guns recoiled, and then their heavy slam to the planking. Next a rumble of feet as cursing men sponged and reloaded. Howls if an Ottoman ball hit home. Cheers if the Turkish forts were hit. The slap of a bosun whipping frightened sailors back to duty.

The smoke of the fight descended to the orlop deck where I was miserably confined, my only light a single lantern. The haze choked like vile fog. We were sailing into a trap, a gantlet between two forts that I myself had engineered. What a surprise I'd prepared! How ironic that I was about to get a taste of my own deviltry!

I shouted again to be allowed to come to the quarterdeck to give warning. "Shut up, Gage!" the marines snapped back from where they guarded the powder magazine farther aft, taking care that no spark came near it. "To the devil with your tongue!" I could just make out the dim forms of powder monkeys scurrying up the companionways to bring fresh shot and sack. How I longed to be with the gun crews! Yes, put me in the midst of the blood-splashed tumult, far more exposed to cannon fire than here below the waterline—put me up there because I dreaded far more what lurked in this awful hold.

Another passenger—titled, cursed, silent, and implacable—was segregated in a wood and iron cage closer to the bow. Perhaps he was confined. Perhaps he'd demanded solitude. Perhaps he slept. Certainly he waited with the patience of a creature with endless time.

Waited to stalk my family.

This sea fight had many smells. The saltwater of the Dardanelles, of course. The scent of gunpowder, the sand spread to give traction in the blood, the blood itself, iron, grease, tallow, sweat, and even the ammonia of the piss buckets. When shots strike home and splinters fly, you can whiff the sweetness of raw wood. Stand with the marines and it's wool and gun oil.

These were not the smells that haunted me, however. I remembered all too vividly the rock dust of the gigantic granite cannonballs I'd help the Turks roll into place, and that was fearful enough. But now my nose was filled with a darker stench, an odor that made the British seamen avoid this orlop as if it was the womb of the plague.

It wasn't just the usual bilge water and rat droppings. This putrefaction was a reminder of the must of the tomb, the corruption of gangrene, the rot of spoiled food, and the pulp stench of worms. It was the smell of the world's darkest and deepest places, vents of sulfur, bones of gnawed flesh. It was the horrible stink of fundamental evil, a twisted hostility to everything good. It was the reek of secrets hidden and forbidden. It was the smell of the man, or thing, or monster, in the iron cubicle ten paces from me.

A bulkhead prevented me from seeing what the creature was doing. This alone inflamed my imagination.

Boom! Crash! Sound punched my ears, the ship shook from the pounding, and I was bounced an inch by every report of the artillery. What I dreaded was a far bigger impact, however, and what it might set loose.

The weight of the granite cannonballs I'd contrived could cause enough damage to set loose this fellow traveler. He lusted for Astiza's heart like a demented lover, and desired my son Harry for pitiless revenge.

I heaved against chains that wouldn't yield. My hands and ankles were raw. My throat was sore from protest and pleading. I had to protect my family and didn't even know if they were vulnerably unprotected in a foreign embassy or entangled in the world's greatest harem. They were in grave danger outside the seraglio and in terrible peril within it, given that the sultan's house was a pit of intriguing concubines, eunuchs, dwarves, mutes, and sultanas who conspired to elevate their rival sons.

So I tortured my imagination while tensing for imminent impact. The ship would reel when one of the massive cannonballs hit. Ribs could buckle, the hold could fill with water, I'd fight fruitlessly against my chains, men would wail prayers, and the evil one would burst from its dark quarters to roam like a beast.

How had I come to such desperation, after so many schemes?

As I told the British, one thing led to another …

PART ONE

CHAPTER 1

"You teeter on the lip of Vesuvius, Ethan Gage," warned the Russian foreign minister as I calculated my surroundings. To Adam Czartoryski's cautionary eye, I was a political opportunist leaning too far over the precipice.

"If so, it's a volcano of gold."

Indeed, I felt that I was inside a treasure chest in the gilded ballroom of Catherine the Great's former palace outside St. Petersburg. The occasion was a reception for Tsar Alexander, seeking public reassurance after his recent defeat by Napoleon at Austerlitz. I'd not only survived that battle, I was smartly dressed, comfortably dry, and flirting not just with nobility, but the chance to become noble myself.

"Not all that glitters is gold, my American friend. That's a Russian proverb."

"Fortune sides with him who dares. That's a Roman one." I'm ever the gambler, as well as a treasure hunter and go-between. The latest St. Petersburg craze was whist, and I could converse, flatter, and lose at cards when it was socially strategic to do so.

"Ah, Virgil," Czartoryski recognized. "You have a classical education?"

"No, I simply prefer concise wisdom to the windy. Napoleon says the key to communication is brevity. He can issue five orders in the time it takes most generals to clear their throat."

My patron laughed. Czartoryski's caution was well meant, but he was as indulgent of my ambition as I was impatient to exercise it. Russia didn't just seethe with opportunity, it glowed. The snow outside the palace was diamond bright, its reflection bouncing from window to mirror to candle, setting afire the gold leaf that climbed wedding-white walls like vines. The result was dazzle that would honor heaven, and it seemed an appropriate place to congratulate myself. If my life to date has been a catalog of frustrations, I still believe—like all Americans—that I deserve to be lucky someday.

Maybe that day had come.

Catherine the Great's palace in the outlying town of Tsarskoe Selo has a Great Hall the size of a cow pasture. One bank of windows looks out on a vast courtyard crowded with expensive sleighs, horses pissing craters in the snow and bundled teamsters smoking pipes around a bonfire. The other side views vast and empty gardens, their beds ermine white this February of 1806. The floor of the ballroom is intricate parquet, and the ceiling has a painting bigger than a circus tent called "The Triumph of Russia."

Nor is that all. Through arched doors I spied another gold room, and another and another, in infinite reproduction, until one reached a room paneled in orange amber, as cloying as honey and soothing as a womb. There were golden statues on the roof, marble statues in the garden, and crystal chandeliers big enough to hold a troop of monkeys. In other words, everything in Russia was grander than I'd dreamed.

And here I was, a ragtag American adventurer, wayward protégé of Benjamin Franklin, spy, soldier of fortune, and family man, with the world's most beautiful woman as wife. I frankly can't decide on the truth of Christian miracles, but I felt the devil's luck here in St. Petersburg. Less than three months before I'd been treacherously shot in the back. Now I was flattered as a military expert in surroundings sumptuous enough to sate a congressman. The place made Thomas Jefferson's new President's House seem like a log cabin.

I glanced at Astiza. At thirty-five my wife is no innocent ingénue. Her recent underground imprisonment has inevitably left lines in the corners of her eyes, just as I've detected the first gray on my temples. But we still have the ambition of the young. Moreover, Astiza does not just display the silken hair of Cleopatra, the face of Helen, the wisdom of Minerva, and the curves of Venus, she has presence wrought by character—or so is my opinion. She's also brilliantly eccentric, not least in the astounding fact that she married me. "Impressive, no?" I meant the palace, but was fishing for a compliment.

"If all the poor of Russia could come inside."

Such an attitude is sedition in St. Petersburg, but part of my wife's charm is candor. Lest she expand dangerously, I turned back to Czartoryski. "Yes, I heard you climbed Vesuvius above Pompeii while a diplomat in Italy. But I don't see the resemblance between that sulfur pot and this." The palace halls were jammed with five thousand of the rich and striving, including a crush of Prussians, Poles, Swedes, English, Austrians, Persians, and Ottomans. There were gigantic Circassian servants with russet beards and scarlet sashes, waiters "of color" (the new Parisian euphemism) in yellow jackets, and serving girls dressed like nymphs. The male European guests were booted, the women bejeweled, and the place had that reek of sweat and perfume that beclouds every royal gathering. Laughter pitched high because of anxiety. Dresses were cut low to command attention.

We were the only American couple, or rather half-American, since my Greek-Egyptian wife has never seen the United States. Today's occasion was Maslenitsa, the last week before Lent and the seventh before Easter. Russia, I'd learned, has more religious holidays than a banker in Jerusalem.

"Hell below, and Italy's blue vault of heaven above," Czartoryski said of the famed volcano. "One can slip, or ascend. That's life in the Russian court. In America you can afford to be naïve. In St. Petersburg, never."

I rotated my head. "I only see the heaven part. But I rely on you, Adam, to keep me from falling." My wife squeezed my arm, prudence in every finger press.

"And I rely on you to help me keep rising." His smile was that of a conspirator.

What fools our egos make us.

The Pole and I had struck up an unlikely alliance. He was fascinated that I'd known Franklin and dined with Jefferson, since Polish patriots admire the American Revolution. He hoped any military advice I gave might include reconstituting Poland as a buffer state between the French and Russian empires.

I was happy to oblige. While it's true I have the blemishes of ne'er-do-well, opportunist, cardsharp, and sycophant, I can sell myself as an expert after my misadventures with Napoleon, since the French emperor and I are both idealistic rascals with biographies in need of edit. Foreigners hold a third of the highest jobs in the Russian capital and are called *dvorianstuo*. Adam was my best chance to become a *dvorianstuo* myself.

The Russian government had given my family an apartment on Nevsky Prospect, a burly and gruff butler named Gregor so mute you'd think I'd cut out his tongue, and a stipend of five hundred rubles a month. All this when a Russian soldier could be fed with nine! I'd already acquired a sleigh, a fine new Jaeger hunting gun, a fur-coat for Astiza, and lead soldiers for my five-year-old son Horus, or Harry. It's gratifying to be a good provider—and if there's one thing that money guarantees, Franklin quipped, it's the desire for more.

"When will I have an audience with Tsar Alexander?" I knew a courtier could rattle around for months. "I can explain how the French army is different from the Russian."

"Yes. Frenchmen are allowed to think." Czartoryski had wit.

"And your own rise, foreign minister, is evidence such reform will be encouraged." I smiled at my wife, wishing she were more impressed by my flatteries. But wives know husbands too well, and she'd experienced just how catastrophic my partnerships with Bonaparte had been. Yet her gaze was determined too, her lips set in a necessary smile. Even sage and skeptical Astiza saw chance in our gleaming surroundings.

"Perhaps you can catch Alexander's eye today," Czartoryski said. "But don't be disheartened if such favor eludes you. You'll see a tsar's dilemma, thousands of people vying for his attention. Part of surviving Vesuvius is luck. You must time your visit between eruptions."

"And time your broadsides," boomed Vice Admiral Dmitry

Senyavin, commander of the Russian Adriatic fleet. He was on winter leave and tacked our way like a slim frigate, having been fascinated by my account of Trafalgar. "I believe you called the English smashers, did you not, Monsieur Gage?"

"Napoleon too," I told them. "Strike first, split the enemy, and annihilate each fragment in turn. I think Nelson and Napoleon might be twins separated at birth, one staying on land and the other going to sea."

"But Nelson dead."

"He had the genius to die at his greatest triumph. We'll see if Bonaparte's timing is equally adept."

"And our timing must include other guests." Czartoryski bowed and the minister and admiral turned. Astiza and I weaved our way to the groaning appetizer tables to snack on cheese, caviar, wintered fruit, and Russian teacakes, me slipping a few of the latter into my green frock coat pockets. I estimated getting from one end of the palace to the other was a good day's march, so I'd draw proper rations.

"I think we should heed the minister's friendly warning," Astiza murmured, nibbling as I chewed. "Politics here is treachery."

"Franklin said people should jump at opportunity as quickly as they do at conclusions." It's peculiar I still believe that, since so much treasure has slipped from my grasp. However, it's the most desperate who play the lottery most recklessly. When you have little chance, even the slimmest becomes compelling.

"Everyone here is dependent on the tsar and jealous as children."

"Czartoryski thinks that with your help I could get my own title." My wife wins invitations with her beauty and mystic reputation as a seer. Russians are as superstitious as sailors, their Christianity painted onto Slavic paganism.

"Certainly your wife's charm is your only chance, Ethan Gage." We turned. A uniformed Prince Peter Petrovich Dolgoruki bowed to Astiza with flirtatious flourish, his white glove fluttering this way and that like a moth. He surfaced to smirk at me. "I'm astonished you married so well."

"Ethan saved me," Astiza said.

"I cannot think of another explanation. Now: Does this reception not eclipse the court of Bonaparte?"

Dolgoruki demanded flattery even when he disdained me. The prince had reluctantly escorted us to this capital under the tsar's order, despite a mutual contempt forged shortly before Austerlitz. He was a dashing warrior of twenty-nine; I was a skeptical forty and still striving for the kind of fortune Dolgoruki was born to. The nobleman stood like a rooster, chest out, head high, his waist bearing a golden sword of the Order of St. George that had been awarded by Tsar Alexander to his losing officers to obscure defeat. While I thought Dolgoruki the epitome of highborn arrogance, he thought me the nadir of lowborn irreverence, a man who confused cynicism with intelligence.

Fate had kept us in orbit around each other.

"Well, both courts speak French," I replied. Seeking reassurance of Russian superiority was absurd since every noble in St. Petersburg dressed in French fashion, danced the polonaise, and did their best—which was not very good—to copy French manners. Russian men clumsily bobbed and weaved as they tried to master kissing both cheeks. Their women were worse, first evaluating each other's dresses, then bussing four to six times, next promising eternal friendship, and finally speculating on the preening males. I recognized the ritual, but you have to be born to that peculiar mix of grace and wit that the French bring to their palaces. I just play the sharpshooting American and neutral diplomat.

"I'm impressed by all the gold," I went on. "For a nation sustained by millions of serfs, imperial Russia has accumulated more than its share of precious metal." The country must have a mine somewhere, though it would be crass to ask for directions. "Best paint job since the Sistine Chapel. Not as holy, but damned inspiring in its own way. But it's not the court you have to equal, Prince Dolgoruki, it's the French army. Isn't it?"

He scowled. "Which you claim to know how to beat."

"I've absorbed the precepts of Napoleon."

"And when is this secret to be shared with our tsar?"

"I'm awaiting Alexander's invitation. Foreign minister Czartoryski suggested I might catch his eye here." I dropped the name of Dolgoruki's rival to remind the prince I was fortified with my own powerful allies. "I anticipate the tsar will want my perspective on America, too. Jefferson is my old friend, and the two leaders have written each other." As often as I can, I mention the President and Franklin, in hope their luster will rub off. Talleyrand, Fouché, Nelson, Pitt. I'm shameless.

"Stay away from Czartoryski. He cares more about Poland than Russia."

"Well, the tsar's wife seems to like him." It was common knowledge that Elizabeth and Adam had been lovers with Alexander's permission, since the tsar was besotted with beautiful Polish mistress Maria Narayshkina. One needed a chart to keep track of who was sleeping with whom in St. Petersburg.

"And the empress consort has gone on to another lover, at that fool's peril." Dolgoruki meant dashing Captain Alexis Okhotnikov, who strutted while the nobility quietly made bets on how long he'd live before an accident ended his unsanctioned romance with the tsar's wife. "Make no mistake, Gage. Be useful or find yourself out in the snow. Or in Siberia, should you really displease him."

I smiled brightly. "I'm sure the same admonition applies to you."

"I was born to this. You, like Bonaparte, are a scrambler."

"I'm honored by the comparison. He's an able fellow."

"We'll have our revenge on him someday. Perhaps I'll bring your wife his famous hat."

"I'd suggest trying peace. He's a difficult friend, but a terrible enemy." And I steered Astiza away, confident that Dolgoruki was simply jealous of my influence. St. Petersburg was stuffed with foreign military officers, architects, artists, gunners, chemists, diplomats, and explorers. Even the tsar's doctor was an Englishman named Sir Alexander Crichton, which was prudent given the Russian tradition of poison and quackery.

"You shouldn't antagonize the noble who brought us here," Astiza murmured. "Never humiliate a prince."

"The title is an honorific, like a knighthood in England." The Dolgorukis were an old and noble family, but heredity guarantees little in Russia. A good chunk of the aristocracy is chronically bankrupt from poor soil, worse weather, absentee management, and tsarist disfavor. "Word is that Dolgoruki will be promoted to save face and sent south to fight the Turks. Good riddance."

"You have a dangerous flair for insult, husband."

"I've had much practice."

Dire circumstance has made me a periodic spy for both the French and British, with and against the French army in war, and tangled up with Red Indians, pirates, slave revolutionaries, gypsies, savants, secret societies, and seductresses. None of this has proven very profitable, but it has taught me a great deal about human nature. People will go on scheming and shooting no matter which nation hires me.

"I understand you're willing to betray all sides, Monsieur Gage," said someone with a Prussian accent, as if reading my mind.

A ruddy German as sturdy as a stump barred our way, his boots planted apart. He had blond hair, a crimson eye patch, a Teutonic cross at his throat, and enough other medals to bedeck the coin belt of a belly dancer. "You've served France, America, and Britain in turn."

"Which simply means I'm a diplomat. And you are?"

"Count Lothar Von Bonin. I'm here to foster friendship between Berlin and St. Petersburg. I couldn't help noticing you conversing with Minister Czartoryski."

"I'm his advisor. A confidant of President Jefferson. And did you hear that I'm a Franklin man?"

"I'm a Freemason myself, and understand Franklin was a member. You as well?"

"Missed a few meetings." It was disquieting that odd strangers felt enough familiarity to strike up unwanted conversations. I don't recommend having a reputation; you never know whom it will attract. "I'd have assumed Prussians too hard-headed for Masonry."

"Not at all. The Illuminati and Rosicrucians have their

roots in Germany. Our King Frederick-Wilhelm is one of the latter. The Russians are enthusiastic Masons too, ever since the Scot James Keith introduced it. All of us mad for the occult, I suppose, to balance the tyranny of rationalism. Remarkable adventures you've had."

I tried self-deprecation. "Misadventure."

"And now both of us are in a place that combines science and mysticism. St. Petersburg is the head and Moscow the heart, the saying goes. The Enlightenment and Old Russia. Savants and saints."

"The marriage of our times," said Astiza, who'd make a far better Mason than me. Don't know why the fraternity won't permit women since her gender improves any gathering. I'd add them to an infantry regiment if it were up to me. They'd lend some sense, temper the language, and clean up the camp.

"Indeed, Madame, indeed!" His smile, however, was tightly sewn. "Something Czartoryski doesn't entirely understand; he urges the tsar to modernize too quickly. But Slavs are different than the West. Russia is moralistic without morals, and powerful without purpose. Alexander employs liberal advisors and yet recently imposed press censorship and a secret police. So I take lesson, and adjust my advice." He extended his arm. "I actually admire the flexibility of your allegiances. It means we might be friends."

I reluctantly reached to take his hand, and was startled when I was met with an upraised ivory stump. I paused in confusion.

There was a click, a snap, and a wicked blade a foot in length popped from the prosthesis, the candlelight catching the blade's edge. I started. The stump had a muzzle hole as well.

Von Bonin laughed. "Or enemies. It is your choice."

CHAPTER 2

I was saved from this display of bad taste by a blare of trumpets that announced the royal family. This custom is not as pompous as Americans might assume, since a buzzing crowd needs to know to quiet down, brush off crumbs, and turn the right direction. The French had told me that elaborate etiquette was invented to avoid embarrassment, not be the cause of it.

Certainly one needs skill for a palace soiree. The trick is to be seen, to meet useful people, and to avoid unpleasant ones like this one-handed, one-eyed Prussian. A dash of cleverness doesn't hurt, but flippancy is frowned upon. One must never arrive too early or too late, never laugh too much or not enough, never refuse a toast, and never drink past one's capacity.

The source of all favor stepped into the room with his imperious mother on one arm, his unhappy wife two steps behind, and his saucy mistress right behind her. Tsar Alexander is not just a king but god on earth, his empire stretching from the Baltic to Alaska. Its mongrel-mix of more than forty million is Europe's largest, twice that of France and eight times that of my own United States. The tsar owns everything and a system of *chin,* or rank, has kept the aristocracy in harness since 1649. 'The tsar will give' is recited with hope and resignation.

Von Bonin watched me watching Russia's ruler. "Alexander could lose a hundred battles and still be the planet's most powerful counterweight to Bonaparte," he whispered as we straightened, his blade snicking back into concealment like a naughty trick. "Limitless manpower. Just as England rules the seas, soil is the Russian ocean. And St. Petersburg is a European outpost in what is really an Asian nation. The Mongols dominated Russia for two hundred and forty years."

"And Prussia is squeezed between Russia and France." I put my arm around Astiza's waist. "A sausage in a vise."

"I would call us a walnut, because of our discipline."

"Nuts crack."

"Forgive my joke with my arm, Ethan Gage. I lost my hand to the French revolutionary armies at Hohenlinden and have experimented with utensils ever since. Some men are tempted to bully a cripple so I give sting to my stump. It makes a statement, does it not?"

"Was I bullying you, sir?"

"I merely sought your attention. I'd hate for an American innocent to be caught on the wrong side."

"You mean the French and Polish party of Czartoryski, as opposed to the Prussian and English party of Dolgoruki."

"The dowager empress favors Prussia," Von Bonin noted.

"And the tsarina favors France."

"And which, mother or wife, influences Alexander more? It's only in friendship that I warn you not to get over your head in this Russian ocean."

"Unless the tsar looks my way, and not yours." And I gently pulled Astiza to stand where she'd catch the royal eye.

"Ethan," my wife protested quietly.

"Hush and smile, my brilliant beauty."

Alexander was as I remembered him from Austerlitz, a handsome autocrat as stiff as a wedding groom. He wore a snow-white military uniform, boots as glossy as a Chinese lacquer box, his sash blood red, his epaulettes golden, and his collar stiff. Muttonchop whiskers balanced his receding hair. He was by instinct an intellectual who'd translated Smith's *Wealth of Nations* and founded five universities. Alexander's head was usually cocked because he was partially deaf in one ear, and he moved diffidently, looking to the throng for redemption after his defeat at Austerlitz.

Which he got. After the lunacies of his father Paul, this tsar seemed normal. The nobility genuflected and rose as he advanced like the rolling swells of a sea.

Far grimmer and more forbidding was Alexander's mother Maria Feodorovna, the dowager empress. She was not so much plump as hard as a ham, mother of nine, her own hair a jeweled tower, her necklace twice the weight of Alexander's medals, her sash sky blue and her train bigger than a blanket. She steered her son by using his arm as a tiller, and peered shortsightedly but sternly to ensure we displayed respect.

The habit of putting the tsar's mother ahead of Tsarina Elizabeth had shocked the court at first, but was the result of brutal political bargain. After Alexander guiltily acceded to the military murder of his balmy father Paul, his mother had tried to claim succession for herself. She agreed to her son's coronation only if she was retained as the highest-ranking female in Russia.

Nor would Mama forgive. As a reproach for the assassination she granted her son rare audiences with a coffin placed between them, the box containing her husband's bloody shirt. She referred to her son's friend Czartoryski as, "That Pole."

So Tsarina Elizabeth not only followed mother and son, but also was sandwiched behind by Princess Maria Naryshkina of Poland, Alexander's beautiful mistress. This minx leaned on the arm of her openly cuckolded husband, Prince Dmitri, as if he was a convenient mantelpiece. He looked hollowed by humiliation. Maria meanwhile was all smoky eyes and swaying gait, her gown displaying as much of her shoulders and breasts as physically possible without the assemblage plunging to the floor. Male heads pivoted toward her like weathervanes. I confess I took a good long gander myself.

The tsar's wife was as pretty as his mistress but in a very different, doll-like way, with pursed mouth, delicate chin, and downcast eyes. She had a fine figure but a more modest gown, and her pose was demure. The mother commanded attention, the mistress compelled it, while Elizabeth wished to escape it. I felt sympathy, but then her former lover Adam was my friend.

I was waiting to tell Alexander that the weakness of the Russian army was not its generals but its lack of sergeants. Russian soldiers are brave, but without initiative. Their noble officers are eager, but remote. Lacking is a bridge between. So I stood tall, heels lifting, hoping for a glance, but mother and son passed by without acknowledgement. A royal reception has something in common with The Last Judgment.

Alexander's pretty wife, however, let her shy eyes find Astiza. I beamed as the tsarina fell out of line to address my curtseying partner. "You're the Egyptian seer, Madame?"

Astiza's knees went almost to the floor, and she jerked at me so I bent like a marionette.

"A student of the Tarot, tsarina, but far from an oracle."

"Yet you've studied the ancient arts of Egypt and did alchemy in Bohemia, I've heard."

"You are well informed." Astiza slowly straightened.

"St. Petersburg is a very small village." She looked at me. "I've heard of your ingenious husband as well. An electrician and an explorer, no?"

I stood as close to attention as I ever get. "You flatter me, tsarina. I hope to be a friend and consultant to your husband."

"The tsar has more advice than is good for him. And more friends." Her eye strayed a moment to his mistress, and then turned back to Astiza. "I sometimes wonder if Bonaparte discovered secrets in Egypt that would explain the Corsican's rapid rise."

"He—we—did find a book of ancient wisdom, but Napoleon is more a creature of action than learning."

Now Alexander's eye did find us, as he looked back for his wife like a straying dog. It was too late to wait for her, however, because a herd of courtiers swarmed between, Dolgoruki and Von Bonin among them. Czartoryski, meanwhile, hung back to watch Astiza converse with his former lover.

Elizabeth kept her eyes on my wife. "I'd be curious to learn more about what you think of Napoleon and the great events of our time." She gave me a cool glance. "Your husband's views too, of course. But first we ladies, together."

"I'm flattered," Astiza said uncertainly.

"It would amuse me to have you tell my fortune."

"If it's truly for amusement, tsarina. I don't want to

exaggerate my ability. I was recently held prisoner for it by criminals, and barely escaped with my life. Men sometimes use knowledge for evil."

"So true! Which proves you have wisdom. I won't hold you prisoner, priestess, but if you cast my fortune I'll show you a key to your own future." And now her gaze did swing to her old lover Czartoryski, who still looked smitten as a schoolboy. What torture is love! She aggravated his longing with a glance, and then looked once more at us. "I saw you talking to the Prussian," Elizabeth went on. "There's something you should know about his mission here. He's a dangerous man."

"With a wicked arm," my wife said.

"Your husband's resourcefulness might be just the counterweight we need." She turned to me. "Should Monsieur Gage dare?"

"I'm but an amateur savant." Modesty doesn't come naturally, but it's something of a requirement around royals.

The tsarina lowered her voice. "I believe Ethan must commit a daring deed to save Mother Russia. A noble crime."

"Must I?" Blazes, what now? I was just becoming respectable. By thunder, had the girl even winked?

"First let us spend time as spies together," she said brightly to my wife. "Shall we say tomorrow at ten? I'll have an officer call at your apartment. We'll make it a picnic."

"Certainly, tsarina," said Astiza, who was not certain at all.

"Elizabeth!" boomed the cello-deep voice of Alexander's mother. "We're neglecting our other guests!" The royal party pushed deeper into the crowd. Elizabeth's silken gown swirled as she moved to rejoin them, her husband's mistress now closer to the tsar than she was. Nobles parted to let the tsarina through and then closed around her like water.

Prince Dolgoruki and the Prussian Von Bonin, meanwhile, were in deep conversation. Then they fixed their decidedly unfriendly gaze upon me.

CHAPTER 3

I received my own unexpected invitation to rendezvous with Czartoryski that midnight in his study at the Winter Palace. This vast edifice is on the embankment of the Neva River in the middle of St. Petersburg, and, as the name implies, the windows are smaller and the fireplaces more numerous than at Catherine's summer place. It's so vast that different wings are painted rose, green, and pale blue, as if a single color were insufficient to cover it all. The plaza on the palace's landward side is big enough to muster an army, and in all directions in this government town of two hundred thousand are monuments such as the Admiralty, the War Ministry, and bulbous cathedrals as intricately painted as Easter eggs.

I walked in the hushed dark to our meeting, the streets frozen, and presented my written invitation to silver-helmeted dragoons. A chamberlain led me up a cavernous marble staircase and down vast paneled corridors, life-sized paintings of stern ancestors giving me the eye. The magnificence was intimidating, and yet I was also proud to have a foothold in this sumptuous world. Apparently I was important.

Apparently I was necessary. And the foreign minister was a man who trusted me. Did that mean I could finally trust?

Czartoryski's office was an imposing but impractical twenty feet high, its fire giving a cone of heat against relentless cold that frosted the windows. Beyond the glass I could see the lanterns of sledges loaded with firewood that skidded on the frozen Neva. St. Petersburg is an arctic Venice built on forty-five islands with three hundred bridges. I turned back toward the fire and Czartoryski offered me a chair, some port, and conspiratorial intimacy as a clock gonged twelve.

"I've been a soldier," the prince began, "a prisoner, an exile, a public servant to the royal family which confiscated my family estates, an ambassador to a Sardinian king without a kingdom, an antiquarian, an art collector, and now foreign minister for the nation that dismembered my own. Our peripatetic careers have something in common, Ethan Gage."

You've also been the Tsarina's lover, I silently amended, and it was no wonder the empress had succumbed to his charm. Czartoryski's face was chiseled like a classical statue, with strong chin, regal nose, and gently slanted, liquid dark eyes that could seduce a diplomat or woman in turn. His hair curled magnificently to his shoulders and his body was lithe, just the type to scale Vesuvius or the royal bed. "We're both curious, too," I said. "You about America and France, and me about Poland and Russia."

"Our cozy cabal."

I glanced about. Czartoryski's office welcomed visitors like the den of an explorer. There was an enormous globe on which fingers had rubbed Eastern Europe almost bare. More maps were pinned over bookcases, and a long birch table was covered with treaties, reports, newspapers, and pamphlets in several languages. Leather-bound books, wool oriental carpets, and gleaming wood expressed confidence that our planet can be measured and understood.

"Nations are peculiar things," the minister went on. "Each a distinct individual, with not only a language but a culture. No one would mistake a Prussian for a Frenchman, or a Russian for a Roman." He gestured to his maps. "You can draw nations out of existence, like my native Poland, and yet the underlying country is as persistent as bedrock. Do you know that Poland was Europe's largest nation in the 16th Century, when it combined with Lithuania? Tsar Alexander knows how rooted my people are, and yet he needs Prussia against the French, and Prussia will not allow Poland to be reconstituted."

"I thought Alexander dislikes Prussia as much as his mother favors it."

"He fears Napoleon more, and German alliance has a long tradition. Alexander's father Paul was fascinated by Frederick the Great and trained the Russian army like Prussian marionettes. He even put metal braces on soldier's knees so they'd be forced to goosestep. Paul was his wife's creature, and thus quite mad." Such candor was risky, but the foreign minister found release by confiding.

"That's why America and France got rid of our kings," I said. "Although now the French have an emperor, which shows how inconsistent people can be. First they cut off the head of Louis, and then they crown Napoleon."

"He crowned himself, I hear."

I was sensible enough not to mention my own role in that affair.

"But people swing to emotion as much as reason, and no mob is rational. Napoleon promises order. Strength. Pride. Glory. For the mere price of servitude! Here in St. Petersburg, Alexander's dislike of Prussia ended at Austerlitz. He needs the Germans. King Frederick-Wilhelm hesitates, but his wife Louisa badgers him for war. Wags call her 'the only man in Prussia.'"

"But you think resurrecting Poland is a better strategy?"

"With French guarantees. The name of my country is our Slavic word for prairie, and Poland's rich plains always tempt invaders. My country is a beach, awash with barbarians from the east and tyrants from the west. Yet every handicap has its benefit. Poland is the link, and our learning has made us the Greece that informs Russia's Rome. We gave the world the astronomer Copernicus, the mathematician Brozek, and the geologist Staszik. Bonaparte views us as civilizers."

"So Poland is eternally vulnerable, and eternally necessary."

"Well said! Nothing is simple, including my own birth. Poles have complicated identities."

"Yes. You have the name of Prince Adam Czartoryski, but—"

"But Stanislaw Poniatowski was made king of Poland after sleeping with Catherine the Great, and so knew the power of the bed. My mother was a sexually adventurous Polish beauty, and Stanislaw persuaded her to sleep with Russian ambassador Nikolai Repnin as a patriotic act. The side result was me." His expression was wry. "My mother's husband, the man I am named for, was rewarded for her infidelity with command of Poland's military academy. This is how things work. Sometimes we sleep with the Russians. Sometimes we fight them. Those same Russians burned my own home palace of Pulawy during Kosciuszko's Rebellion. So I joined Russian service to recoup our losses."

"And that was Tadeusz Kosciuszko, who fought with George Washington?"

"Exactly. He helped win your Battle of Saratoga and build the fort at West Point. I'm told Washington so struggled with Polish names that he spelled Kosciuszko eleven different ways, but he loved the general's reliability."

"Another Lafayette."

"Kosciuszko also met your mentor Franklin, as did my mother. Circles within circles."

"Old Ben seems to have met half the people on the planet." Which slightly tarnishes my own claim to him.

"And then Kosciuszko," Czartoryski went on, "brought the revolutionary ideas of the New World back to the Old. He led a ragtag army of Jewish cavalry, burgher gunners, and illiterate peasants against battle-hardened Russians."

"The Polish Spartacus."

"But no foreign armies came to his aid. Now Kosciuszko is a crippled old man in Paris, still petitioning Napoleon to liberate Warsaw."

"Do you trust Napoleon?"

"Of course not. Five thousand Poles fought for Napoleon in Italy in hopes he'd become Poland's champion, and instead he shipped them to suppress the slave revolution in Haiti. All died or deserted. Napoleon the liberator has always been Napoleon the oppressor. But who is surprised? I don't trust Napoleon, but Franklin said that if you want to persuade, appeal to interest rather than intellect. Napoleon's interest and mine coincide."

"Do you trust me?"

"No, I just told you—we've the same interests. You want a title. I want a country. Your advice to Alexander might serve to get both. So I conspire to use you and you conspire to use me, and we Poles conspire to use Bonaparte, as he will conspire to use us. Vesuvius, I warned."

I like cynics. It seems honest, somehow. "And I'm an American who knows Napoleon, Jefferson, Red Indians, and Haitian slave generals, and is now working with a Pole."

He smiled. "Exactly."

"Which means I accumulate enemies the way a dog attracts fleas."

"Sometimes enemies testify to character. Your shifting alliances make you judicious. Most men assume, but you consider."

"You want me for my wisdom! I thought it was my looks."

He laughed. "Our friendship does give me a chance to admire your pretty wife and yes, I've seen the ladies give you glances. But no, I'm intrigued first because you're American, and thus have a natural affinity for liberty. Yet that's not your utility either. There are many freethinkers in Alexander's court."

"St. Petersburg has as much heated idealism as the salons of Paris."

"As much hot air, at least." Czartoryski's sense of humor was much like my own. "Russians love to talk of life and death, love and fate. In many ways they're medieval. Their onion domes represent the shape of divine flames. They believe in religious miracles and the devil. Do you believe in evil, Ethan?"

The question surprised me, since Adam Czartoryski didn't seem very religious. I was cautious. "Most men are complicated. Greedy, and even cruel, but they justify it to themselves. What's common is temptation and betrayal. True evil, unfeeling evil, is rare."

"One hopes so. Yet it still exists in the dark places of the world and emerges at times to seize men's minds. It abides in foggy mountains, old castles, and deep caves. The Russian peasant knows this and prays. Russia's mystics and hermits practice self-flagellation, self-castration, and self-burning. Mary is their God-bearer, a goddess herself, and *their* holy trinity isn't Rome's, it's reason, feeling, and revelation. The haughtiest intellectual believes the witch Baba Yaga, Old Mother Boney Shanks, might live in the dell next-door. It's night in Russia for half the year. Morana, the ancient goddess of darkness, reigns here."

I felt a chill. "You don't sound like a man of the Enlightenment."

"I am. But I'm also a man of Eastern Europe, where Chernobog is the god of evil and the dead."

Odd to have this educated minister—a student in inquisitive England, and an ambassador in sunny Italy—talk like this. There was hope in him but sadness too, and his idealism was tempered by disillusion. "Russia is beautiful in its own way," I offered, warding off his somberness as if making the sign of the cross. "All this snow. And endless light in summer, I'm told."

"Have you heard of the *upyr*?"

"The what?"

"A Tartar word for a malevolent spirit—a witch, or a vampire. Even today, graves are opened after seven years to make sure the dead are truly dead."

That sounded ghoulish, but I went along. "In the West, many fear being buried alive because doctors can diagnose death too eagerly. Corpses have woken from a coma and pounded to get out of their coffins. Sometimes the dying insist they be buried with picks so they can dig their way back to the surface."

"That's not what I'm talking about. Here, people sometimes don't die at all. Possessed people. Evil people. Heads are severed from corpses and their mouths stuffed with rocks or garlic to ensure they don't arise. By lore the *upyr* still exist, and retain strange powers and ancient possessions. My Polish mother told me many tales when thunder rolled."

"Which surely you didn't believe."

"You haven't wandered the trackless taiga, Ethan, or the crags of the Carpathian Mountains. The Russian serf believes the forest is both haunted and blessed, and healers are called tree-teachers. Morana is a seductress who captivates men to lead them astray. Wolves are the devil incarnate, and saintly relics are a shield. Do you know the story behind the great church being built near your apartment?"

"The Cathedral of Kazan?"

"Its central icon is a religious painting claimed to have repelled a Mongol army at the city of Kazan in eastern Russia. It hardly mattered if the assertion by a possessed child was true. Russian troops believed it true, and victory resulted, just like Joan of Arc. Franklin sought to link lightning to electricity to explain the world. Russians observe lightning to experience the *next* world, because fire is a window to the divine. And tonight you straddle those worlds, Ethan, the West and East, the rational and the mystical, and in that way too we're alike."

"So that's why we've formed our cozy cabal?"

"Not exactly." He took a heavy book down from a shelf. "Yes. And no. My motive is very practical. I know you're a thief of the sacred, Ethan. Don't deny it, I've heard too many stories of the wayward American prying into tombs and seeking lost oracles. You're the perfect man for Poland, and the perfect man for our times. You'll advise the tsar, who is well meaning but inconsistent. We'll make peace with Napoleon, reconstitute Poland, and I'll persuade Alexander to make you a prince as a reward."

"A prince!" I couldn't help grinning. I'd denigrated Dolgoruki's title to my wife but I too would puff if someone gave me that name. Prince Gage! It was absurd, but then wasn't life? Hadn't I met men and women in ridiculous positions of wealth and power because of wild twists of fate? Why not me?

"Or a count, at least." Everyone hedges.

"But you want me to commit a crime?" I remembered Elizabeth's word.

"Not a crime, but a recovery. Not a theft, but a liberation."

"The rightful owner is you?"

"Poland. When Catherine the Great dismembered my country she tried to take our soul. Prussia and Russia agreed in 1797 to even remove the name 'Poland' from common usage. They also took our symbols of nationhood. Berlin stole our Six Sacred Crowns. Even more precious relics were spirited away to St. Petersburg. Now they're about to be even further lost."

"Destroyed?"

"Given away to German brutes in return for alliance against Napoleon. Lothar Von Bonin was sent from Prussia to bring my Polish heritage back to Berlin as trophies, to seal Prussia's pact with the tsar. The man is a lizard, and you and I must stop him." He gripped my shoulders. "A night of daring can change history, rescue Poland, ensure peace, and make us both rich." He leaned forward as if to share a great confidence. "All you have to do, my American friend, is risk life, freedom, and your eternal soul."

CHAPTER 4

Astiza's Story

My husband apologizes for the dangerous task we've agreed to, but it's rekindled our energy. I've locked away my worry and kept the Tarot cards unturned. I'm wary of ambition, but Ethan says—or hopes, promises, yearns—that our luck has finally changed. We all needed rest after reaching St. Petersburg from the terrors of Bohemia, but now we're enlisted in a gamble that might set us up for life. As a result, Ethan's mood is feverish. Sketches litter our apartment. Our servant Gregor has been sent for odd supplies. My husband has scouted his objective with a telescope, taking Harry to allay suspicion. His enthusiasm infects my own. Men are easiest to live with when employed, brightest when challenged, and bravest when dared. Our mission is quite mad, which means it's exactly the sort of thing that fits our eccentric family. Our child Horus helps.

Czartoryski is inquiring for a suitable corpse. I work with rubber, silk, and thread.

It was my visit to St. Petersburg's island fortress that set our plan in motion. I was surprised by the invitation of the pretty tsarina, but Elizabeth has retained a close relationship with Adam Czartoryski who befriended us. All sense opportunity in our era's tumult. Napoleon's royalist foes call their nemesis "the torrent" because he's flooded the world with change, and everyone hopes to ride the current to their advantage.

I rose early and in the local fashion scrubbed my face with ice, on the Russian theory that this trial makes a woman's cheeks rosy. Honey and ash are used to brush teeth. When a lieutenant of the tsarina's guard called at our apartment at ten, my husband had already left to take Horus to the sled ramps of St. Petersburg. These are elaborately roofed and decorated platforms eighty feet high, with stairs at one end and a long ramp on the other that is sprayed to make ice. Sleds whiz down at terrifying speeds. I won't try it, but Horus isn't afraid to ride in Ethan's lap. Our boy is thrilled that winter is embraced here. The Russians enjoy skating in line, snapping the snake to accelerate the endmost skater. Their winter sleigh rides are swifter than summer carriages, because river ice is smoother than any road. The inhabitants throw snowballs, build snowmen, hunt, fish through the ice, and warm themselves in saunas and steam baths.

Horus also begs to see the pit fights between bears and dogs, but I told my husband to forbid this barbarism and he promised to obey. I never entirely trust those two—what sensible wife and mother would?—but their sledding was a welcome recess from watching my boy.

"This is an unannounced outing," the escorting officer instructed as I put on my coat. "Her majesty's sleigh is waiting nearby in an enclosed courtyard."

Our boots squeaked in the snow as we trudged, St. Petersburg's winter oddly reminding me of the Egyptian desert. The dry powder is like sand. The canals and rivers are frozen as hard as ancient pavers. The cold is sharp as the sun. In both places, breath burns the lungs.

We went through a gate. The door of a covered sleigh opened. Elizabeth lifted a polar bear pelt and beckoned me beside her, a finger to her lips. As I sat, she snugged the fur around our hips. With the crack of a whip and song of sleighbells our team trotted into a street, down a ramp, and onto a frozen canal, our shoulders jostling as the sleigh swerved. Lace on the glass windows worked with frost to hide the tsarina's face from the public. She turned to face me, still pretty as porcelain at twenty-seven years old.

"Priestess! Are you prepared to tell my fortune?"

"If it will truly amuse you, tsarina. The trouble with sharing the future is that many find they would rather not have known it."

"I promise to accept fate bravely if you promise to be honest."

"I'll tell you what I see."

"What method do you prefer?"

"There are a dozen ways to forecast. The physiognomy expert Johann Lavater contends we can tell past and future by simply studying the face. One's character, personality, and destiny are molded into its shape and lines. Your face is angelic, tsarina. That suggests good fortune."

She laughed. "What a flatterer you are!"

"This is not true of all pretty women, whose less symmetrical faces betray worry, jealousy, or greed. Your features are good."

"Only good and not perfect?" She was teasing.

"This world does not permit perfection," I risked.

"Neither does court gossip! You're not just a seer, you're a truth teller. A formidable combination."

"At personal peril, tsarina. Historically, many fortune tellers have found it wisest to bend the truth to prevent execution."

"Don't worry, I only imprison." Her amused tone was much lighter than at the reception.

"I'm relieved." We both smiled.

"Seriously, continue with the truth. A royal has difficulty differentiating between truth and flattery, and between friends and seducers. The fate of the mighty."

"The fate of everyone. All of us want things from each other."

"Especially love. Now. Would you like a teacake?"

"I actually have another means of fortunetelling that uses your cake."

"Oh my. I hope the baker knew."

I reached into my satchel as we glided beneath several bridges and emerged onto the broad white Neva, its ships and boats frozen in place until spring. St. Petersburg is built on an archipelago on the Gulf of Finland and so water serves as the city's highways. Light snow was falling this day, making the city a fairyland. The Winter Palace and Admiralty were foggy bergs, and across the river was the glacier of the new Stock Exchange. The Peter and Paul Fortress was a softened gray mesa punctuated by the steep golden spire of the cathedral in its middle. That bell tower rose four hundred feet, highest in the city. Instead of the usual onion domes, Peter the Great had chosen a Dutch-style steeple as sharp as a needle.

We aimed for the fortress pier, which was somewhat disquieting since the fort also serves as a prison. Was the Tsarina really joking?

"What test?" Elizabeth prompted.

I brought out a goblet and flask and poured water. "This is liquid from the Fountain of Epidaurus in Greece, where people flocked to Asclepius the Healer." The water was actually from our neighborhood well here in St. Petersburg, but truth can be embroidered. "In ancient times, people would come to the fountain pool and cast bread to see if it floated or sank."

"And what did each result portend?"

"Try it first. Toss in a bit of cake."

The fragment bobbed as I expected. Always rehearse your magic.

"It floats. Good fortune, again."

She glowed. "You are the most delightful companion!"

"And I'm thrilled you believe my prophecies. So many doubt these days. My own husband, a Franklin man, likes to tell the story of an ancient army which came upon an augur watching a bird in a tree. The prophet said that birds fly closest to heaven, and thus reflect the gods' will. So the general gave the fortune-teller a coin to tell which way the army should go. The augur explained that if the bird flew onward, the army should advance on the enemy. If the fowl flew the other way, the army should retreat. If it flew toward the other cardinal points, the army should go that way."

"What did the bird do?"

"Nothing. It wouldn't fly. Thousands of men sat to wait. Finally an impatient lieutenant took up his bow and shot the animal dead. 'What are you doing?' the general cried. 'If that bird was so prophetic,' the lieutenant replied, 'why didn't he foresee *that*.'"

Elizabeth smiled. "So you don't really believe our games."

"On the contrary, tsarina. I am *not* a Franklin man and, as much as I love my husband, I don't always agree with his skepticism. Like many men, he's blind to mystery. It seems to me that fortune is determined largely by chance, that the world has an order that implies divine intelligence, and that any sensible person thus recognizes both destiny and free will. I tell this amusing story to be fair, but I tell fortunes because they come true."

"So the signs still seem positive?" I'd made her anxious.

"If I'm reading them correctly."

We sleighed a moment in silence, me gambling that I'd deepened our relationship with honesty. I've encountered enough powerful people to know that they are just that, people. Marriage at fourteen to sixteen-year-old Alexander eventually turned the German princess Louise of Baden to Elizabeth, Tsarina of Russia, but ruling is a heavy fate. Many of the great are melancholic, and Elizabeth is no exception. Her dynastic union with the tsar is, by all reports, joyless, each finding romantic partners elsewhere. Her tyrannical mother-in-law still intimidates the tsar. Alexander's wanton mistress takes pride in Elizabeth's humiliation. So when the tsarina's gaze strayed sideways to look down the river, her pretty lips sagged. She's in a gilded prison.

"I think I trust you," she finally decided. "So this outing is our secret, and we're both tempting fate. Here, hold my hands for warmth and tell me how you met your infamous husband."

"I was a slave in Egypt," I began, knowing the admission jolts the listener. To be born fortunate doesn't interest people, but to rise above low station intrigues them. "But before Ethan freed me I was educated by my Egyptian master."

"Favored for your beauty?"

"Not in the way people assume. My elderly owner showed no romantic or sexual interest. He longed for companionship. He appreciated my looks as a man appreciates a flower, but he courted my mind."

"An unusual master, and a fortunate slave."

"It came to pass that my master was shooting at Bonaparte in Alexandria during the French invasion, and I was reloading his guns. Master was killed by a cannon shot and Ethan found me in the rubble. At first I assumed him a conquering mercenary with a man's idea of repayment, but he, too, actually listened."

"You must be able to seduce with words."

"I recognized Ethan's good character before he recognized it himself. We eventually fell in love along the Nile."

"How romantic!" Elizabeth sounded wistful. "Like Antony and Cleopatra."

"There was no royal barge, I assure you. We eventually had to separate, but I was pregnant with our son. Fate in the form of pirates reunited us, and destiny has driven us since. Just recently he rescued me again, or I rescued him—I suppose it was both. And then the tsar invited us to Russia. Your court has been very kind."

She laughed. "Surely you're the first to ever say that!"

"You listen too, tsarina. I'm flattered."

"What stories swirl around you, Astiza! You've been called a fortune-teller, a priestess, a sorceress, a witch, a philosopher, and a seeker."

"I'm proudest of being a mother."

"Which I envy. My own daughter, Maria Alexandrova, was a child of love." She meant her child by Czartoryski, not the tsar. "But she died at little more than a year old."

"There's no greater tragedy." I squeezed her hands under the fur.

"So now I'm going to tell you a secret." The tsarina squeezed back. "I may be pregnant again. Can you confirm it with your powers?"

"I have no powers. I know only what I've learned from reading. Nor am I a midwife or doctor. But I share your excitement, tsarina. I hope your suspicion is true."

"Women understand, don't we?"

"If we're wise." I wondered who the father was this time. Her captain? "Is this why you've asked me here? I can't cast a fortune for the unborn."

"No, no. I simply trust you with this secret, as one mother to another. A favorable fortune suggests my suspicion is true. Can you look at my palm and see if it says anything about this pregnancy?"

I was again reluctant. I prefer not to deliver bad news, and had promised to tell the truth. But I'd trapped myself in her sleigh. I brought out her right palm and studied its lines. These can be interpreted a hundred different ways, and yet her heart line actually intrigued me. I bent to examine it more closely and then looked into her eyes. "Nothing about a baby, but one pattern is suggestive, tsarina."

She was rapt. "What is it?"

"I'm not sure if you should know, and certainly no one else should."

"Is it bad?"

"I wouldn't say so, but your reaction will be your own."

"Oh, please tell! You've made me so curious."

I took a breath. "Someday you'll be reunited with an old lover." That's what the lines said, and I was certain they meant Czartoryski.

"What? Who?"

"You cannot get names from a palm, tsarina." A small lie.

"Oh my." She sucked in her breath, eyes suddenly far away. Yes, we don't forget love easily. "What a marvelous day this is. I was right to enlist you."

"Enlist me in what, tsarina?"

"You'll see. And I want to show you another mother, the God-bearing mother, so you understand Russia. And then something quite different that could change history. God sent you to us, I think."

The sleigh coasted to the fortress's Nevsky Gate. Elizabeth told her footmen to wait and we climbed snowy steps, sentries peering down from the rampart above. We walked the pier and passed though a tunnel in the thick wall to the grounds inside. Soldiers snapped to attention as rigidly as Horus's lead toys, but otherwise the huge fortress, star-shaped like a snowflake, seemed hushed and deserted this snowy morning. Its stone was frosted, and its parade ground was an unmarked blanket. Built against the far walls were the cells of the empire's most dreaded prison.

I expected a guard of honor for such an esteemed visitor, but we walked across the fortress courtyard alone, two monks swerving as if we were forbidden. "I've given orders to be ignored," the Tsarina explained. This of course was impossible; soldiers gaped and several loped in all directions to warn of our presence. But the absence of the usual phalanx of attendants and guards clearly exhilarated Elizabeth, even as it made me feel more responsible for her. She wore bright blue boots on the slippery cobbles, the fur hem of her coat swishing the snow as we walked. Flakes hemmed it like diamonds. The bottom of her purple dress stained the color of wine from the wet. She held her mouth slightly open, like a little girl wanting to taste the snow.

Government buildings surrounded the courtyard. Russia's tallest church was opposite its newest mint, God and Mammon eyeing each other like duelists. Atop the cathedral's golden spire was an angel that pivoted with the wind. Ethan had told me when we first toured St. Petersburg that the holy sculpture hadn't prevented the tower from being struck by lightning. Any failure of divine protection always amuses him; maybe because it confirms that our family's bizarre luck is as natural as storms.

"I understand this cathedral burned," I said to Elizabeth.

"Yes, and was rebuilt by Catherine. Providence, perhaps, sent a thundercloud to encourage improvements. The new steeple incorporates a lightning rod to prevent another fire."

"Ethan admires Mikhail Lomonosov, the Russian Franklin. Lomonosov experimented with lightning and had a colleague killed by it, we've been told, and independently came up with the idea of the rod like Franklin did. He also managed to put lightning in a bottle, or rather he bottled its charge."

"Every disaster has odd benefit," the tsarina said. "Lomonosov was encouraged to invent. Catherine built a better church and fortified her chance at heaven. The monks got a new carillon from Holland."

The result soars like a hymn, a rich yellow at the base and gold leaf on the spire, like a bridge between sky and earth. The top of the steeple certainly seemed to be poking heaven this day, its angel lost in the flurries. I felt it a conduit for sacred power, grace running down like lightning to cross the snowy plaza and dash against the evil of the prison walls.

"I want to show you the Goddess-mother," Elizabeth said. "This way."

On one side of the rectangular church, sheltered by an alcove, was a picture of Virgin and Child in the flat Byzantine style. In this portrait Jesus was more childlike than the midget man often depicted by Orthodox artists. The baby clutched its mother, cheeks pressed. Mary's face was a serene oval, her pursed mouth much like Elizabeth's, her elegantly long nose ruler-straight, and her eyes deep and farseeing. She looked from this world to the next.

"One of my favorite icons," Elizabeth said. "The word comes from the Greek *eikon,* meaning 'likeness,' and indeed the common Russian regards the tsar as the living icon of God and the Orthodox Church as the icon of heaven." Her voice betrayed a German wife's skepticism. "I show you this to help you understand where you are, priestess. The style of the Russian icon, inspired by Constantinople, is not realism but dematerialization, a window from the physical world into the divine. It's very different from paintings I grew up with on the Rhine, and at first I didn't understand its appeal. But Russia always has one boot in this world and one boot in the next, which makes its soldiers obstinately brave. Russian misery makes Russians pious; the saying is that the less successful God is for you, the more you have to pray to Him. The Orthodox candles are like the flames that came down on the apostles. An icon can have supernatural power."

"They're building a cathedral to the Icon of Kazan near our apartment."

"Yes. A dream led a young girl to that holy painting and it won a war. Russia isn't about the brain, like Germany, or the heart, like France. It's about the soul. Symbols have power here. Faith and superstition are more potent than reason. I'm telling you this because of the other thing I brought you to see."

"I'm mystical too. My husband looks to the future, I to the past. We balance."

"I hope your husband's interests can be applied to the peculiar problem that Minister Czartoryski and I have. Let me show you why we've come." She led me behind the cathedral to a plain brick building with a peculiar roof. The top was a line of squat, sturdy domes, presumably built to resist cannonballs. All were covered with snow. The building's windows had been bricked up so that the entire structure looked like a squat loaf of lumpy bread. Two bundled soldiers miserably filled sentry boxes that flanked the stout door. Two cannon also stood guard, snow frosting each bronze barrel.

"The Royal Treasury," Catherine told me. "A vault surrounded by a fortress with a thousand men."

"It certainly looks impregnable."

"My husband never visits, but I do. As a woman I pretend to be enchanted with the Treasury's jewelry. What really draw me are the stories the objects tell. History is a record of unchecked passion and desire. So I'm no stranger here, but today you must help discourage obnoxious escort. Come."

Our approach from the side startled the nearest sentry.

"Colonel Karlinsky," Elizabeth demanded in the crisp royal voice of habitual command.

"Tsarina!" Eyes like saucers, he bolted to announce us. The second sentry fell to his knees and pressed his forehead to the snow, an act of obeisance that of course made him useless. The first soldier pounded on the thick door, the second trembled as if we might cast him into stone, and the tsarina waited like an impatient Madonna.

Most Russian soldiers, I knew, could neither read nor write.

Karlinsky popped out in seconds to usher us inside, no doubt having been warned to wait in the anteroom until our stroll came his way. He apologized profusely for the moment of delay. "No footmen, your highness?"

"A quiet visit. No fuss."

"We're once again honored by your presence." He looked puzzled by me. "I'm afraid you've taken us by surprise."

"I'm here to get advice from my new companion. This is Astiza of Alexandria, a priestess and savant from Egypt. She's an expert on the artifacts of the East."

"A woman … scholar." He hesitantly bowed. "It's my honor … priestess." Like most men his eyes paused to appreciate my features, his mouth frowned at the idea I might be capable of thought, and he then turned back to the tsarina. "Rarities of the Byzantine church?"

"Of the Turks and Persians, but our business is not yours, colonel. Astiza can establish the provenance of many fabulous things, but which treasures, and why, is my concern alone." She looked as if this were my cue.

"I'm Greek as well as Egyptian," I said. "Of Isis and Thoth, Athena and Odin, Enoch and Buddha. I've studied all creeds and all cultures."

He looked wary. "But you're satisfied, I trust, by the revelations of the One True God?"

"All spiritual paths lead to the same destination, colonel. At least according to Napoleon Bonaparte."

His expression narrowed. "I've lost comrades to the fight against the French usurper. I wouldn't heed anything he says."

"This is a holy woman," the tsarina injected impatiently. "We didn't ask for your views."

He bowed stiffly. "I'm honored to escort you both."

"We'll tour the repository alone."

Now Karlinsky blanched. "That is against procedure."

"It is *my* procedure, colonel. With *my* expert."

"I annoy people with my unorthodox views, and find it simpler to consult with clients alone," I justified. "My scholarship would bore you."

"Apologies at my presumption." He looked unhappy.

"As I've explained before, discretion and privacy remain a necessity," Elizabeth said. "This visit, like my others, will go unrecorded."

"Yes, tsarina."

We passed by an office and then guardroom where the door had been shut on the soldiers inside to keep them from gawking. Next was a massive wooden door leading to the treasury. The colonel unlocked this, handed Elizabeth a ring of heavy keys, gave me a lantern, and hesitated. "May I again offer assistance?"

"Shut the door behind us."

Its boom made us jump.

We were in a barren cell, looking ahead at a succession of grilled iron gates. Each marked a treasure room roofed by one of the brick domes, reminding me of the succession of chambers in Catherine's palace. The storehouses were dark, their windows bricked. I lifted the lantern. The building felt like a tomb.

Elizabeth smiled like a conspirator. "Thanks for helping shed him. It's quite enchanting to see these treasures and much more fun without Karlinsky hovering like a bat. He regards the repository as his." She unlocked the first gate. "It's even more enchanting to be, for one moment, alone."

"I don't count as a companion, tsarina?"

"You don't count because you're tolerable. Despite my commands Karlinsky spies, makes mental notes, and acts as impatient as a man in an embroidery shop. Besides, you were never here. Understood?"

I nodded.

The chambers beyond were like Ali Baba's cave.

Weighty crowns. Jeweled scepters. Ermine robes. Sparkling tiaras. Ornate clocks. Golden swords. Inlaid boxes. Gem-encrusted rings. A mechanical peacock. Any single item would set an ordinary person for life. They gleamed like toys at Christmas, or the sacred candles in the Orthodox cathedrals. Many had been gifts from other monarchs or ambassadors. Some were spoils of war. Precious treasures are captured light, drops of the sun, and these shone with soulful fire. They were usually shut away in the dark unless brought out for a coronation or funeral. I felt privileged, but uncertain why I was here.

We passed through five rooms, unlocking each gate and then relocking it behind us. "The colonel will not come upon us unawares," Elizabeth said.

The sixth room held Persian and Turkish items. I paused to admire their intricate Islamic designs in onyx and alabaster. Fabulous carpets were rolled and stacked like logs. Ancient gold jewelry from long-lost empires, crudely heavy, dated to gods as old as Egypt's. The accumulated wealth throbbed with time. And there the treasury ended, except for a final solid door. I wondered which Zoroastrian prize Elizabeth wanted me to examine.

But she was fitting a key in the last lock. "The treasury stores both items of antiquity and those used for ceremonial occasions," Elizabeth explained. "It has bullion to ballast our currency, valuables to trade for weapons, and jewels to dazzle queens. This is the fruit of conquest, gifts, and taxation from a million estates and businesses."

"A Prussian told us your country is an ocean of soil."

"Von Bonin?"

"Yes."

"Then these are the shells upon that ocean's beach. But that's not what I want to show you. This last room is where objects are taken preparatory for use, so that they can be removed without organizers snooping on the rest of the treasures. Come see what that Prussian, a dog sent to fetch by his masters, most covets." She unlocked the final door, its thick wood banded by iron. The entry squealed as if rarely opened.

The chamber beyond was almost bare.

The exception was an oval stone table that occupied the room's center like an altar. It looked like a mummification slab from Egypt, or a tabernacle for the Grail. On top lay two medieval broad swords, dark and plain except for gilded hilts. There was no cloth, no case, and no decoration. The brick dome was blank overhead. The only light was from my lantern.

"Go ahead, take a look."

I examined the weapons. Their steel was pitted and their edges nicked. They were clearly antique, but not particularly decorative. The swords seemed of little value compared to the hoard we'd just passed through. I glanced around. The gloomy brick walls were plain and impenetrable. The temperature was frigid.

"These look like prisoners in a cell," I said. "Or quarantined, as if diseased. Why are they alone?"

"To await removal," Elizabeth said. "If icons are the window into the soul of Russia, these represent Poland. My friend Adam Czartoryski calls them the most precious relics of his nation. Yet he dare not go near, lest he confirm his sympathies and give ammunition to his enemies. For the same reason I didn't bring your husband here, and instead made up a story about silly women studying ancient jewelry. There's an advantage to being female; Karlinsky has promised to be quiet about my visits because he believes them frivolous. I told him the tsar fears me a profligate spender constantly searching for new inspirations, which merely confirmed prejudices the colonel already had. Such secrecy might last just long enough."

"Long enough for what?" The cell was very oppressive, making me think of the prison nearby.

"For your husband to liberate these."

When you accept charity such as an apartment and servant, payment must always come due. My heart began to thump. "Tsarina?"

"You may call me Elizabeth, Astiza, because we must be the closest of friends. Partners. Sisters. What you see here are the Grunwald Swords, the soul of Poland. In 1410, at Grunwald Field, the grand master of Germany's Teutonic Knights sent these swords as a challenge to King Vladislaus II of Poland. The Poles won the ensuring battle, helped by early artillery serviced by Chinese monks. The Poles kept the swords as spoils of victory, using them in coronation ceremonies ever since. The Germans have smarted from the defeat for the same four centuries. When Poland was partitioned in 1794, Catherine the Great took the swords to Russia. And now Russia, seeking an ally that happens to loathe Poland, has promised the swords to Prussia in return for partnership against Napoleon. Von Bonin is here to collect them."

"He has only one hand and one eye."

"He's deadly with that prosthesis. I've heard that when he duels—which is often—he proposes that his opponent fight with one arm tied and one eye blindfolded, to make it fair. They foolishly agree. But if he begins to lose the battle with his left hand he raises the stump of his right, and shoots and slashes. It's little more than murder."

"The Prussian showed us the blade during the reception at Catherine Palace. It juts out like a snake's tongue."

"Lothar is a boastful lout. I tried to persuade the tsar against granting him these swords, but I've no influence. Alexander is desperate to drag Prussia into war in order to prolong the fight against Napoleon. But Adam thinks that if the swords were to disappear first, the Germans might suspect Russia of going back on its word. The pact might be broken. Czartoryski favors peace with France and so do I. Too many brave Russians were cut down at Austerlitz. And war will be a disaster for my own German homeland, which I predict will be colonized by France. It's women who have the sense to bring peace, Astiza. Peace for your child Horus. Peace for my coming baby. A theft of these swords is best for Russia, best for Germany, and best for us. With peace, Bonaparte might persuade Alexander into reconstituting Poland as a buffer state."

"Adam Czartoryski's dream."

"And Prussia's nightmare. So these swords in Von Bonin's hands mean turmoil, while their disappearance gives a chance for reconciliation and restoration. Besides, they belong to Poland. My Adam's idea is to seize them and secrete them until his nation rises again."

My Adam. One wondered, of course, why this former German princess was prepared to foil her husband to serve the foreign minister. "You still love Czartoryski," I ventured. "Despite Captain Okhotnikov."

"Captain Alexis gives me pleasure. Adam inflames my heart. Isn't it amazing how easy it is to forget debts, and how difficult to forget old lovers? It's awkward now that he's foreign minister, but feelings don't conveniently disappear. So I offered to recruit you. Have I succeeded?"

"Tsarina—Elizabeth—I don't see how Ethan can steal these. They're buried in a treasury in the biggest fortress in St. Petersburg, surrounded by a thousand men, with no way in but a succession of locked doors."

"Yes. And yet your husband has a reputation for finding his way into all kinds of improbable places with the help of his ingenious wife. Perhaps you can work your magic and he his science. Will you at least ask him?"

No good could come of this, yet how could I deny our benefactress? And how I longed for a home! "If you insist."

"You have three days. On the fourth, the Prussians intend to transfer the swords to Berlin."

"Three days!"

"The swords must vanish. No one must attach their disappearance to you or me."

Once more I felt we were in a black underground river, reaching for a last gasp of air. "And if we fail?"

"If by some miracle you aren't killed or arrested, you'll have to flee Russia. So it's high risk, but high reward as well." She took my cold hands in hers again. "If you succeed, I promise that Adam will find a way to persuade the tsar to reward Ethan Gage for his military advice."

"Reward him how?"

"By giving you a palace in which you can finally raise your son in peace and safety."

CHAPTER 5

Harry

I t's too cold where we live now, but I get to play with a
boy named Ivan. And I get to help Papa.

This city is better than the dark place where Mama
and I had to stay in the bad days. We killed the bad people,
and then we came here.

When I play with Ivan I don't think about the smelly
place. We play soldiers or wooden animals, or sometimes we
go outside in the snow. I like snow. Ivan lives in our building
and there is a courtyard where we build forts and snowmen
until the horses trample and poop too much. Sometimes
Papa helps, and then Mama makes hot milk with sugar when
we come inside. Ivan doesn't speak French or English, but
he's taught me Russian words. Snow sounds like sneg.

Sometimes I have bad dreams, so Papa moved my bed next
to theirs. My old room is where I help him with his inventions.

The inventions smell again. Grownups do stinky things.

Papa is very smart. He said he learned everything there is to know from an old man named Ben Franklin, who is dead. But Mama may be even smarter because she reads books all the time. I can already read many words. My parents say that if I keep reading I can learn everything there is to know in the world. And they say that if the inventions work, we might live in a palace.

I wouldn't like to move away from Ivan.

They also say winter will end and it will get warmer, but every day in Russia seems colder to me.

I had to promise not to tell Ivan about our inventions, but here is what we did.

Papa showed me rubber, which is dark and soft. We put this in turpentine, and I liked that smell. The rubber slowly melted and disappeared. Then Mama used the muddy turpentine to paint silk. She said we are making a balloon.

Papa also built a big copper hat with a tube that curled out the top. Then he poured smelly acid over old metal, which made fumes. The hat collected the fumes, but we still had to open the window. Snow blew in while Papa used a pump to fill brown jugs.

Mama said it was that big word she likes, alchemy.

Papa said it was science.

Mama said they were the same.

Papa said they weren't.

Then they kissed.

Then he made a machine he said could produce invisible lightning. I'm scared of storms, but Papa said this is a tame storm, like a pet. I got to crank the handle. Some wires led to a bar of metal.

"Now comes the magic, Harry," Papa said. "We've made a magnet."

He held the metal bar over loose nails and they jumped to it like fleas.

I wanted to show Ivan. Papa said I couldn't.

"Not until summer," Mama said.

Mama and Papa are very smart. But I don't know if summer will ever come.

CHAPTER 6

I hope that Count Stanislaus Podlowski, who fell afoul of mad Tsar Paul and died in the tsar's island prison, is looking down to appreciate his role in the cause of Polish independence. Prison deaths require a steady stream of plain wooden coffins to be shipped to the Peter and Paul Fortress, and Czartoryski and I used the count's demise as a way to transfer our strange supplies. I didn't know the late nobleman, but apparently Podlowski had spoken too openly about Poland and been jailed for his opinion. Cold, disease, and confinement had done the rest.

Now we'd make his sacrifice meaningful.

The patriot's widow was required to pay for her husband's casket, as a tax on treason. So she eagerly gave foreign minister Czartoryski permission to use the box for our secret cause. I disguised myself as a Russian laborer, brought along sullen house-servant Gregor to help lift and interpret, filled the coffin with what I needed for my adventure, and fell in with a sleigh convoy delivering eight of the caskets to the prison. It was foggy and the desultory procession took no particular note of us since everyone was busy using ropes, pulleys, and profane grumbling to slide the sledges down to the Neva and across the river to the brooding fort. Then chanting serfs carried the coffins through the Nevsky Gate. Bored sentries offered no help.

Gregor and I stacked the casket marked for Podlowski near the fortress cathedral, at a spot where brief last rites would be recited for the latest dead criminals. The deliveries created a knot of confusion as peasants, priests, soldiers, and bureaucrats mingled for the delivery. I ducked behind the mint, draped a cassock over my clothes, and came back to pay off my servant. I'd given Gregor one extra ruble to reward this special labor, and now gave him another to ensure his silence. I hardly needed to spend it since the truculent servant rarely spoke, but it was a trivial expense from my newly fat purse. Conspiracy comes cheap in Russia.

He grunted what might have been thanks and trudged away to re-cross the frozen river, glowering at all creation.

Disguised as a priest, I edged the other direction and darted briefly inside the cathedral for some necessary mischief. Then I hid in the privy of the cathedral garden, unused in winter when few worshippers visit. It was a two-hole bench uncomfortably sheened with ice, so I consoled myself with the palace I'd soon win. Count Ethan! I recited as I waited. Prince Gage! Life often pokes me with the little end of the horn, as they say, but from descent in Bohemia I'd ascend in Russia, and at some point take my title back to America.

My countrymen positively fawn over nobility, now that we don't have any. I'd study pretension and dress up my wife.

I listened to the wind blow snow off the Baltic and periodically shifted, so as to not be permanently frozen to my throne. Soon enough it would be dark at this latitude, and I'd set to work.

Mine was a reckless, perilous, intricate, inventive, and risky plan, and thus typical of the ones I come up with. I must not only commit a noble crime, but also prevent any investigation of said crime by vanishing. Success required a conjunction of weather, time, and science worthy of an astronomer, plus no small amount of luck. If I failed I'd probably be imprisoned. Then tortured. And finally either shot, beheaded, or hanged; I wasn't sure of the Russian custom.

All for antique cutlery! And I had to retrieve the swords tonight, because Lothar Von Bonin was scheduled to take them to Prussia in two days. It was word of his planned retrieval and departure that forced our own scheme in hasty motion. The swords must be well away from St. Petersburg before anyone noticed them missing.

"The transfer is a state secret so the loss won't be announced," Czartoryski assured me. "Success will prove God is on Poland's side."

"This is more what the devil would come up with, but I'll take miracles from either party."

Our St. Petersburg apartment had become a makeshift laboratory, my wife the collaborating scientist, and my son a sorcerer's apprentice. The lad is as clever as his mama, and while he's seen more of the world's underbelly than I'd prefer it has made him a precocious adventurer. Like any boy, Harry ordinarily just wants to play and read, but he's proud to help Papa and is cursed with his parents' curiosity. More than once, with some guilt and a great deal of self-justification, I've pressed him into risky tasks. He's big enough to be brave, old enough to follow instructions, and small enough to squirm into tight places. Wretched lad! He'll make a fine treasure hunter one day.

Harry was waiting for me right now. It was imperative he not be jailed, so my strictest instruction was that he stay in his hiding place only until full morning and then, if I didn't appear as promised, sneak back home.

Which meant that my operation had to advance as inexorably as a lighted fuse.

The Peter and Paul Cathedral closed at dusk. I peeked out. Doors were   locked by black-clad Orthodox priests who marched back to their fortress rectory like a procession of bulky crows. I froze in my privy an additional hour, to make sure no one lingered or returned, and then crept to a church window overlooking the marble tombs inside. I hauled up the sash I'd unlatched in my brief visit hours before. I crawled through, locked the window, turned, and confirmed I had the church to myself. Pale light sifted from the snowy gloom outside.

The cathedral was a baroque masterpiece, with enough gold, marble, porphyry, jasper, serpentine, onyx, alabaster, and crystal to make anyone a Christian. A soaring ceiling promised Heaven to the stark royal tombs below, each marble sarcophagus badged with a horizontal bronze Orthodox cross. I shivered at the magnificence, crossed myself just in case, and then lifted a bar on a side door, cracking it to peer for sentries. They were all in shelter. I scampered out, burrowed in the snow to my coffin and its supplies, and left the container empty for poor Count Podlowski. By dawn, wind and fresh flakes would cover my disturbance.

Then I barred myself inside the cathedral again.

The luminescence of foxfire allowed me to check my pocket watch, a necessary gift from Czartoryski. I'd consumed an hour.

More burglary followed. I picked the lock to the bell tower door and began portaging my equipment up steep, ladder-like steps, obsessively keeping track of time. The carillon would ring at 7:30 a.m. to wake the fort and city for prayers, just enough before winter dawn to make my scheme feasible. I counted at least fifty carillon bells, stacked and ranked to churn out coordinated clamor, and was glad I'd thought to bring stuffing for my ears. Then I ascended to a higher chamber that displayed the gearing of four tower clocks that faced the compass points. They were pointed near midnight.

I was now high above the fortress walls, but went still higher. As architectural plans had promised, a ladder led to a platform above the clocks that served as staging area for maintenance of the needle spire. Louvered doors gave access to the outside.

I'd no need to ascend all the way to angel and cross; I was already three hundred feet above the frozen river. I opened the louvers that faced east and peered out. Snow sifted down, so I waited for my eyes to find form in the void. Yes: I could barely make out the rear of the cathedral. Beyond was the squat treasury building with its brick domed roofs like snowy hillocks.

While it seemed like an elaborate detour to break into one building to enter another, I'd given the matter great thought. The treasury was always guarded. The cathedral was not. The treasury's windows were bricked, while the cathedral's glass could be opened. The treasury was impenetrable, while the church invited entry.

I couldn't very well ask for admission to Russia's vault, or storm it, or chip a hole in the side. A thousand Russian soldiers were sure to object. But what if I came silently from the sky? And then didn't enter at all?

I'd purchased in St. Petersburg some spliced Cossack lariat, thin and strong, and a small deck windlass of the kind used on a fishing schooner to crank in an anchor. Clay jugs held hydrogen gas that Astiza and I had liberated by pouring sulfuric acid on iron, as Jacques Charles had done when making the world's first hydrogen balloon in 1783. Peasants attacked that inventor's flying machine with pitchforks when it came down fourteen miles from Paris, but Franklin had concluded that hydrogen was more reliable than heated air.

I later acquired ballooning experience of my own in Egypt and France, making me a reluctant aeronaut. I also needed a reliable wind, a good shot, and some luck with fortress masonry. As my reward, Czartoryski would convince the tsar to give me respectability that I could pass onto my son.

Such was the plan, anyway.

Astiza had sewn two contraptions. I carefully laid and smoothed the first, the skin of a small balloon. We'd neither time nor resources to build one big enough to lift a man, and that would be too conspicuous anyway. The steeple provided an alternate way to climb. I braced the windlass, readied my tools, and settled down to study my watch. Periodically I'd stand to windmill my arms and squat my legs to keep warm, my breath a white cloud. Then I'd sit down to wait yet again.

At seven, the day still dark, I suspended the balloon skin out the louvered opening and began to inflate it with hydrogen, using a copper spigot from the jugs I'd pumped full of gas. It was dark, wet, cold, my fingers were numb, the wind was pesky, and the balloon fidgeted as it swelled. I used a bowline to tie my lariat to a grappling hook, lashed this to the underside of the balloon, and tied the other end of the rope to the windlass, which would serve as reel. I wound the line onto the drum and readied my new Bavarian hunting rifle. It's a pretty piece with a silver patch box, engraved trigger guard, and raised cheek-rest, but the German custom to shorten the barrel for portability crimps its accuracy. I didn't entirely trust it.

Despite the cold, I was sweating. I checked my watch again. Time! The world already had a grayer cast that rumored dawn. Now I could make out the far end of the treasury building, a barren tree, and even the faint line of the fort's snowy parapet. Minutes ticked. There was a creak and thud from the church door below. I crawled across the narrow tower to peek out the other direction. A trail of fresh prints marked where priests had filed to the cathedral for the dawn bells.

Time to stopper my ears with cotton.

I began unreeling the rope. At first the balloon bobbed aimlessly, but then the steady Baltic breeze caught the orb and carried it east toward the treasury as planned. Rubberizing the silk had left the balloon a dull red, which helped as I squinted to follow its progress. Onward it danced, to the treasury and then over it, bucking back and forth. I feared a shout, a bugle, or a thunder of alarm drums, but who looks upward in the snowy dark? Maps had given me the precise distance to the far end of the repository, and mathematics the angle downward to its roof, letting me calculate the necessary reach of rope. Silk ribbons marked every fifty feet of line.

If my geometry was off, I was dead.

As each rope ribbon played out, I made chalk marks on the louver sill. Finally the balloon had sailed the necessary eight hundred and fifty feet. The weight of the unreeling line had dragged the sphere lower, toward the far eave of the treasury.

I picked up my rifle and aimed.

Half past seven. True dawn an hour away.

Time to awaken fort and city. There was a faint cry of priests from below, a jerk of bell rope, and the carillon began to move.

Sound exploded.

Church bells are all very well from a mile away, but in my little echo chamber the music sounded like a broadside at Trafalgar. I winced but the clamor would mask my gunshot, so this moment had dictated everything else.

I aimed at the bobbing orb and fired.

Had the balloon jerked?

I reloaded and watched for long, agonizing seconds, waiting for confirmation I'd punctured the bag. The globe wobbled frustratingly aloft. Could I have missed? Was I that rusty? Damn this German gun, I longed for my old Pennsylvania longrifle. I began to hastily aim again. If the carillon stopped, I couldn't risk shooting in the quiet.

But then the leaking balloon began to sink as planned, until it disappeared beyond the far edge of my target. The rope sagged in a long curve to the brick domes.

On and on the clanging bells pounded, as heavy as a hammer, and then finally stopped. My head throbbed.

With the gong still echoing in my skull, I used the windlass to reel my rope. The slack lariat lifted off the Treasury roof, and I began dragging the emptied balloon back toward me.

Its grappling hook snagged the repository's eave, far away

and far below. I winched tighter. Now a straight line extended from cathedral steeple to treasury roof, like the hypotenuse on a right triangle. I reeled more, stretching the rope until it was taut as a bowstring, and finally hitched it tight. I took out my next invention, a two-foot-long dowel with a metal eye in the middle that I fastened on the line. This would be my trapeze.

When attempting something daring it is advisable to think long and hard when planning, and to stop thinking to do. So I did.

I donned my pack, strapped my rifle, slipped mittens onto my hands, grasped the handle, and rolled out the louvered window to drop, dangle, and gasp. My breath huffed out in a cloud.

Then I began to slide down the rope, snow stinging my face.

Too fast! I wasn't traveling, I was hurtling.

At least the lariat hasn't broken, my brain managed between a mental mix of profanity and prayer. *At least no one is shooting at me yet.*

I swooped like a wounded hawk, aimed to crash into the far end of the treasury. It hadn't occurred to provide a brake.

Can't think of everything.

It was my own weight that saved me. As I descended the line stretched and sagged, lessening the angle of decline and slowing my plunge. In moments I went from fearing a collision to fearing a humiliating halt in midair.

But no, I skipped across one dome, drooped some more, and splatted with a thump onto another, skidding over its swell in a belly flop that jammed my mouth with snow. I spat, let go of my trapeze, and caught my breath while resting between two domes as white as igloos.

By the dueling pistols of Aaron Burr, my scheme had worked.

I waited for cries of alarm.

Nothing. The weather was foul, the morning still dark, and every sensible man, from prisoner to commander, was snugged inside.

I cut the line, letting it fall against the back of the bell tower where it was unlikely to be noticed until full daylight. In the other direction I heard a soft thump as balloon and grappling hook lost tension and fell onto a drift.

My own boot steps were muffled as I scrambled across the roof to the last dome in line, as Astiza had instructed. I scraped the snowy coverlet from the keystone at the dome's peak.

The blocks in a dome get their solidity from falling against each other as gravity squeezes them tight. But should the uppermost keystone be removed, the rigidity begins to weaken.

From my pack I took another flask, this one filled with hydrochloric acid for the mortar joints. I poured and watched them bubble as chemistry went to work, a trick I'd used before. Hammer and chisel cracked the weakened bond and I pried the brick out. There was another layer beneath. I boiled and cracked more joints, prying out bricks to excavate a hasty hole in the dome's peak about a foot in diameter.

A cannonball might bounce off. A patient thief did not. I soon had chipped bricks scattered all around me.

The day kept lightening. Time, time! My burrowing had been as quiet as it had been swift. I dared not pause to look at my watch. Would Harry wait?

The slim hole revealed only blackness in the unlit

chamber below. Out came the magnet, tied to another cord. I lowered it like a fishing line.

There was a metallic clang. I pulled. A sword came up, its point glued to the massive magnet by nature's mysterious force. The weapon was tarnished and looked quite ordinary to me, except for a gilded hilt and a small insignia of the White Eagle of Poland on the blade. I pried it loose and lowered the magnet again. Nothing. The other sword must have slid sideways as I fished out the first. I carefully rotated the line, giving the magnet a slow orbit. Precious seconds ticked by. Finally—clang! I hauled up the second Grunwald trophy, congratulating myself on my genius.

I slid down the dome to rest a moment and then tie the swords to my back. It's hell-fired difficult for the lowborn to become a prince, I reflected, and yet a night's perilous work might just have made me one.

"And if not a noble, at least rich from Polish reward," I reflected. I stood. Dawn was near, but no alarm had been raised. Nobody had looked up. With luck, my theft wouldn't be discovered for hours.

"A pity no one saw my daring."

And then a shot rang out, kicking up a feather of snow. I heard a shout in German, and then in French that Russian officers might understand.

"*C'est l' ingérence américaine. Tuez-le!*"

"It's the meddling American! Kill him!"

CHAPTER 7

I leaped from the roof to a drift and rolled, the sounds of shots, alarm, bells, and bugle momentarily muffled. Then up, white as a snowman, the fortress a disturbed anthill. Soldiers were boiling out of the treasury and nearby barracks, guardhouse, and prison. Priests were running like stampeded cattle. Prussian rogues were in a cluster near the river gate, their muskets smoking. Their guns slammed butt down and ramrods plunged and lifted like Fulton's pistons as the Germans reloaded.

With those shots, my ambitions were dashed. What were the Prussians doing in Peter and Paul Fortress a day earlier than planned? And how did they recognize me as the "meddling American" from one hundred yards through falling snow? I'd been betrayed, and if betrayed then news of my role would reach the tsar. I'd go from *dvorianstuo* to bandit and spy, with no title, no estates, and no friends. I was once again ruined and likely to be executed if my emergency escape didn't work.

Yet what use is frustration? Napoleon taught that no plan survives the first gunshots, and that a good general plans for every eventuality. I'd test his maxim.

Fortunately, the light was still dim and flakes were still

falling, so obscurity was an ally. Guards collided, or slipped on ice. Shots went wild. I gallumped through snow to the perimeter fortress wall and bounded up icy steps, hearing more cries as I was spotted again. Bullets pinged off stonework. Tufts of snow erupted. Then I was up on the parapet and dashing toward the Neva side of the fortress like a shadowy target on a shooting range. The Winter Palace on the far shore was a blur. The frozen ships in the Neva loomed like offshore rocks. Shots whizzed and hummed with hot trajectories that left flakes dancing in their wake.

The outer wall sloped slightly to lend stability against bombardment. Even as a line of Russian soldiers scrambled up the interior fortress stairs to intercept me, I vaulted the parapet lip and skidded down the outside wall to another drift. The tumble at the bottom twisted my ankle, but the pain was clarifying. Harry!

I squatted on the ice of the frozen river edge and unfurled Astiza's other handiwork, a small chute of silk.

"There he is!" Shouts above. The bang of more muskets. A chip flayed my cheek and irritation intruded. Why can't I have a career more suitable to my talents, like paramour to a bored princess, or court jester, or perhaps ambassador to an obscure nation where nothing ever happens?

The wind snapped the silk taut and jerked me forward, my boots skidding across river ice. I sailed out onto the Neva on heels and rump, teeth gritted against the sore ankle and my chute dancing madly in the wind.

Now the Prussians were running back out of the Nevsky gate, leaping onto the river ice to chase me. Several slipped and fell. It would be a comedy if not so perilous.

I clung desperately to my chute, skidding before the wind and kicking up a rooster-tail of snow. As I picked up speed I allowed myself to hope that the most disagreeable part of my mission might be unnecessary. Perhaps I could just slide away into the fog of early morning.

But then I heard the clatter of horseshoes on ice.

I looked back. Several mounted men had bounded from pier onto the frozen river, their horses slipping and then finding purchase on the brittle surface. The animals neighed in consternation and excitement.

Meanwhile the wind began to drag me awry, sending me up the river instead of across to the frozen ships and St. Petersburg. Our invention had gained me precious minutes, but I had to rendezvous with my son.

I let it go.

The chute whirled away like a leaf. I coasted to a regretful halt and stood, wincing. Damnation! I didn't relish the last part of my plan, but choice was shrinking as the horsemen spurred.

I set off at a limping trot, too pained and unsure of my icy footing to run flat out. Behind, the sound of pursuit was like knives rapping on marble.

"There he is! Halt, rogue, or we cut you down!"

I panted, struggling painfully to the place I'd carefully sawn the night before we crossed the river with the casket. Despite recent snow, my disturbance had left a slight depression in the snow.

My pursuers were closing. I had to give the Prussians pause.

I un-shouldered my rifle, turned, took quick aim at the lead horseman, and fired. He jerked and pitched backward, his horse sprawling hard. Other animals swerved and tumbled, skidding across the ice. Germans cursed and howled. Now the empty gun was an anchor, but I *had* gained a few seconds.

Of dread.

If the river ice had refrozen too firmly where I'd sawn before joining Gregor and the coffin, I'd either be sabered or spend my last days in the fortress prison. But if it was still sufficiently fragile …

The remaining cavalry circled, the animals kicking up a surf of snow. Saber blades made a whooshing sound as excited Prussians and Russians slashed back and forth in the air, treating the chase like sport.

A hobbling run. Just yards away.

"Lance him!" A spear point came down and leveled.

"No, I'll finish him." It was Von Bonin's voice and I glanced back to see the Prussian taking aim with the appendage on the stump of his arm. His sleeve was up, exposing the flint mechanism, and the muzzle hole was aimed square at my back.

I grimaced, leaped headfirst for the spot I'd prepared with my rifle as spear, and took a huge breath.

The arm's gun went off.

As I crashed through the ice, a bullet seared my scalp.

The cold water was a shock. First the pain of falling through brittle blocks, and then the bite of the bitter Neva. The river jolted like electricity. I plummeted, the swords on my back another anchor, and for a moment I feared they'd carry me straight to the bottom.

But my clothes had trapped some air, neutralizing my descent. The devil's luck, again. I let go of my pretty rifle, steadied, kicked, and looked up. I could just make out faint cracks of light against the morning sky where I'd sawn to weaken the ice. There was a longer line I'd cut to point out my necessary direction. Swim that way! Doing so in winter clothing with two old swords was as ridiculous as dancing in a grain sack, but terror works miracles. I stroked for my life.

The river's current sucked at me, and I had to take care it didn't pull me too far downstream.

I'd already imagined the scene above. A pathetic fugitive, about to be spitted or sliced, has an even more ignominious end when he falls through a weak spot in the frozen river. Horses skid to a halt, their riders fearful of plunging themselves. The posse gingerly dismounts and surrounds the icy hole, waiting on the unlikely chance that their quarry might resurface through broken floes. And when ten minutes pass with no sign, the obvious is concluded. Ethan Gage's thievery carried him straight to the Neva mud, and he will not surface until the spring thaw, if then. Salvage sailors might eventually drag in hopes of snagging the old swords, but would eventually conclude I'd been washed out to the Baltic, the military relics washed with me.

I would sink out of history and pursuit. Or so was my plan.

It was a lung-busting thirty yards to my goal. The cold clamped like a vise and burned like fire.

The already dim water darkened even further as I passed under the hull of my target ship. I kicked upward, feeling its slippery keel. There was a curve as it arched to the bow, meaning the current had carried me several yards downstream of where I'd aimed. I desperately breasted back toward the stern, just moments from drowning. My lungs clenched in protest. My vision narrowed. The chill was rusting my muscles.

But there, at last, was the black opening in the bottom of the hull.

The ship we'd chosen was a harbor maintenance vessel fitted with what sailors call a moon pool, a wooden well in its hold from which underwater obstacles could be winched, anchored, or driven, out of reach of bad weather and loose ice. The sides of the box were higher than the waterline, and a hatch kept the sloshing waves out when the ship was underway. Being beneath the main deck, the moon pool was shielded from view above.

I burst the thin ice of the river surface inside the dark lidded enclosure, almost shrieking from pain and cold. I was close to passing out.

My survival depended on Harry.

If my young son hadn't become frightened from waiting too long as the day lightened, he should lift the lid we'd kept closed so as not to alert the night watchman.

But my escapade had taken longer than I'd hoped. Had Horus already run home? If I couldn't get out of the moon pool in moments, I'd freeze and sink. Had he heard the shots and waited? Or fled in fear?

So I pounded on the wooden well's sides, the signal to hoist the lid and lower a knotted rope to Papa.

No answer.

Mother Mary, I was frozen. I pounded again. "Harry!"

Nothing.

I was shaking uncontrollably now, teeth chattering, and every second of entrapment seemed a desperate hour. I'd surfaced from the river in the one place no one could see me, but it did little good if I was helpless as a crab in a trap.

I pounded once more, weakly this time. It was Czartoryski

who'd first scouted the ship, using arrogance and a stolen hat to pose as a marine inspector. He reported back on the moon pool, its hatch, its watchman who made predictable rounds, the rope and pulley to raise it, and the feasibility of exiting the river that way. It would be my last resort, if chased.

But when we returned to make preparations, a guard had been posted on the ship's top deck by a captain hostile to any regulation. Only my boy had been small enough to crawl down a mooring line and squeeze through the hawsehole that bound the ship to the pier, invading like an enterprising mouse. He was tiny enough to hide should any watchman come searching. He seemed, if not the best helper, the only one possible.

Unless he'd gone home as I'd told him. "If Papa doesn't come when its full morning, you must crawl out sly as a fox and hurry back to Mama. We cannot have you caught."

"When is it morning, Papa?"

"When the day gets bright."

"But I'll be inside." The lad was as sharp as a tack.

"Watch the light through the hawsehole."

I'd been more worried about him than me. But now I knew I should have entrusted the job to a bribed adult. Corrupt the watchman, say, or hire a desperate rogue who could somehow bully his way aboard. I'd hesitated to spend the money and would die a miser.

A final exhausted rap. My hair was crusted with ice. My boots were lead weights. The swords dragged to drown me. "Harry." It was a croak.

And then, in a miracle equal to that of the light that fell on Saul over the road to Damascus, the hatch opened and a small head peered over.

"You're late, Papa."

"Harry," I chattered, "the rope!"

He pitched it in. My last strength was spent dragging myself out of the pool, my boy helping as best he could. Water poured off, and bits of ice rattled on deck when I collapsed.

Harry pulled the swords free to lighten me. "They're heavy!" The weapons clanked as they fell to the planks.

"Not too loud, son." I gasped like a fish, water draining, my hands plucking chunks from my hair. I was shivering uncontrollably.

My five-year-old regarded me with concern. "Do you want a blanket? I found a sail."

"Yes, thankee." I shook like an epileptic. "I feared you gone."

"No, I found a kitty. Do you want to pet it?"

A ship's cat, for rats.

Fingers numb, I began to unbutton my wet coat, ice water still sluicing out. "The sail first. And then we'll hide under it until any outside search is given up. Hide until nightfall if we have to. The days aren't long."

"You said go home by morning."

"This is a new game."

I could hear shouts outside as soldiers ran along the quay, studying the ice of the Neva on the unlikely chance I'd surface near shore.

I rolled myself in the tarp with the precious swords, wincing as thorns of warmth returned, the pump of blood as painful as shards of glass. Harry sat next to me with his hat and coat, but then took his mittens off and beckoned.

"Here, kitty," he whispered.

CHAPTER 8

We've fallen into the volcano's throat.

Our sleigh runners hiss like snakes as we flee St. Petersburg, dreams dashed, pursuit inevitable. Astiza is silent, clutching Harry to her side, her silence toward me an accusation. No, her quiet is shared guilt, because she brought word of the swords. Foul choice, or foul luck? If Von Bonin hadn't spotted me at the fortress, all would still be well. But he'd inexplicably been there a day ahead of schedule. Now we hurtle into the wilderness of Eastern Europe, rootless and betrayed, our immediate hopes pinned to a fat, middle-aged, would-be-king in exile. We abandoned our apartment so quickly that it might as well have been on fire, ambition dashed, Gregor dead, us fugitives.

Our one mare isn't enough. We need a full team.

When have I last slept? Night and day have merged into nightmare.

When the shouts of soldiers searching the ice for my corpse finally abated, I sent Harry crawling out the ship alone to tell Astiza I'd survived. Since I couldn't fit the hawsehole, I waited until dark before creeping out on deck past the watchman and hurrying home. If Astiza's pale, anxious face hadn't told me what I needed to know, the presence of the Russian foreign minister in our parlor—Czartoryski disguised in the clothes of a workingman!—confirmed our plight. She'd sent word to plead for advice. He'd grimly come in person.

"The authorities have pronounced you dead and the swords lost, but it won't be long before it occurs to the police to search your home," he told us. "Your only hope of survival is to stay drowned by permanently disappearing. All is calamity, bad timing, and confusion, your theft played out in view of half the city. Von Bonin has already come to me in an accusatory panic, fearing that Berlin will blame him for loss of the swords. I told him you were a loose cannon whose shocking thievery I failed to anticipate. I speculated you'd have fled to Sweden had you survived, but that you obviously hadn't. That river would freeze Satan. Don't expect him to rely on my lies. He'll hunt you."

"And how did Von Bonin happen to come to the fortress at precisely the moment I was a target on the treasury roof?" I demanded.

"Someone betrayed us both."

Czartoryski's tone was bitter, but that didn't mean I trusted him. My hours shivering in the ship's hold had given me plenty of time to suspect everyone. Had the foreign minister tipped the Prussians to somehow win favor in his diplomatic games? There was no need to petition the tsar for my title if I was dead or caught. But there'd be no swords, either. I tested him. "At least the Grunwald trophies are recovered. You might as well take them."

Adam's reaction was alarm. "And run the risk of their being discovered in my possession? Tsar Alexander would give them to the Prussians, I'd be implicated in the crime, and Poland's hopes would be ruined. No, no, no, my American friend. You achieved the impossible by liberating the relics, but your task isn't done. Now you must spirit them to my family estate of Pulawy, southeast of Warsaw. There my mother, Izabela, can hide them and you."

"And if we're caught along the way?"

"Elizabeth and I will deny involvement. Not out of betrayal, just commonsense. We can't help you if we're suspected too."

"They'd execute us!" Astiza said.

"I'd ask for clemency, but yes. Or prison, or Siberia. I'd lose both you and the swords." He studied our despair. "Listen, all this may actually work in our favor. You'd have eventually been a suspect since Astiza visited the treasury and suspicion would have dogged the promotion I won for you. I'd have had to entrust smuggling the swords to someone with less of a personal stake than their own lives. Now, Russia thinks you're drowned and the weapons lost. Now, my mother Izabela can hide a man already believed dead. Slip out of the city, make for my estate, and be a hero when Poland rises." He grasped me again. "You're almost at the finish, Gage. Don't give up."

"How many miles?" My voice was hollow.

"A thousand. Perhaps less." He threw the number out as if we were sleighing to the Peterhof, a couple leagues distant.

"You're abandoning us," Astiza accused.

"I'm saving you at Pulawy." His voice was stern. "It's too bad you were spotted but there it is. We've no time for recrimination, only for our next move. It's a long journey, but you can seek help midway from the Bourbon exile at Jelgava. The Count of Provence, who hopes to become King Louis XVIII, has inquired about you."

"Me? How has he heard of Ethan Gage?"

"You conspired against Bonaparte with the royalists in Paris two years ago, correct? And spied for the British?"

"Among others." My resume is complicated.

"So you have natural allies as well as natural enemies. An American who knows Bonaparte intrigues the Count, and he and I keep in touch, just as I keep I touch with the Bonapartists. Napoleon reputedly tried to poison Louis, but failed. The royalists in turn tried to assassinate Napoleon, and failed as well. You've been inside both camps. Use your notoriety, Gage. Trade your insights for resupply. Don't reveal the swords. Use everyone, but trust no one."

I considered. Would-be Louis XVIII is the brother of the king who was beheaded in the French Revolution along with Marie Antoinette. This new Louis is a stateless fugitive, given refuge four hundred miles southwest of St. Petersburg. The French count hates all revolutionaries, I guessed, including American and Polish ones. But I could imply that our escape would aid the royalist cause. It was risky, but maybe we could get fresh horses.

"All can still end well," Czartoryski insisted. "Your family will vanish. Napoleon will smash the Prussians and force Russia into peace, with a resurrected Poland as its guarantee. You'll have helped make it happen! Get to Jelgava, persuade Louis to lend help, and get the Grunwald swords to my mother's estate in Poland."

"No title." I know Americans aren't supposed to hanker for such things, but life is damnably difficult as it is. Any leg up helps mount a horse.

"Not in Russia," the foreign minister replied. "But Poland has an aristocracy as well. You'd be happier there than under the thumb of the tsar." He looked at skeptical Astiza. "We won't forget your courage and ingenuity, my lady—so long as you finish the quest. Here in the Russian capital you face nothing but enemies. At my family's estate at Pulawy, you and your boy will find nothing but friends." And with a quite unconvincing smile of encouragement, he departed as hurriedly as he'd come.

Astiza morosely began assembling traveling clothes. "Adam has put all the risk on us," she said, "and it's my fault. I succumbed to Elizabeth's temptation, and now we've been expelled from paradise."

"Our fault, love. And St. Petersburg is a very chilly Eden." I bundled some food. "Let's look on the bright side. We have the swords. Wretched luck the Prussians were there."

"Not luck, but treachery. Or divine retribution. Now I have to uproot Horus again."

"To a better place, maybe." But we both doubted that.

What came next was bizarre horror. When I descended to the courtyard stable to hitch our mare to our sleigh, all was shadowy in the weak light of my lantern. The horse nickered as I lifted her harness from a peg on the wall, and she shifted uneasily.

"A midnight jaunt, Katrina," I whispered to her.

Her ear twitched and her head jerked, swinging her mane.

Something glinted at the edge of my vision, and hers. A

lifetime of bad experiences gave me just enough instinct to duck away as the air was cut like paper. An ax whooshed by my shoulder and bit into the rim of the open sleigh with a sharp crack, wedging tight. It was my servant, Gregor, grunting as he tried to wrench the weapon free. His eyes were wide with either fear or madness. With no time to figure out what was going on, I punched him in the throat, collapsing his windpipe. Then I kicked his crotch as hard as I could. The peasant sprawled on the icy cobbles, glaring.

I grabbed for the ax and attempted to twist the ax. Gregor seized a hunting knife from his belt and struggled up to stab me.

I couldn't get the ax free.

Just as my servant lunged, however, there was a shot. Gregor jerked, his expression turning to shock, and then he coughed and fell as heavily as a sack of flour. One moment the tip of his blade had been six inches from my belly, and the next he was dead. A bullet had broken his back.

Someone darted out the gate of the courtyard and ran away hard.

Should I follow? I was in shock. First I was about to be assassinated by my own servant and then, even more unexpectedly, I was saved.

Was it Gregor who'd betrayed my timing to the Prussians? Why?

And who fired the fatal shot?

I freed the ax, peering fretfully about. No one else seemed to be lurking.

I'd just dragged the body into the shadows, a bloody stain as wide as a rug, when Astiza and Harry came down. I hurried to block the boy's view. "Get him into the sleigh."

"Ethan?" She spied the assailant's boot tips in the dark, pointing upward and skewed like the hands of a clock. "What have you done?"

"Should have given him another ruble, maybe. But it wasn't me that killed him." I pushed the sleigh into the courtyard, Harry obediently sitting where he was told. "I'll hitch the horse. I lost my rifle in the river, but now we have an ax." I threw it in the sleigh.

Astiza climbed on from one side and I the other, taking the reins. Now we were really afraid. Was this some prelude to a wider attack? Would other bullets come out of the dark? With a crack of the whip we bolted onto Nevsky Prospect, the sleigh swerving as I turned hard to take a lane toward the southern gates. Every lit window seemed like a gigantic eye. Every passerby was a potential Prussian. The mare trotted briskly, a pedestrian shouting angrily when forced to jump aside.

"Where are we going?" Harry asked.

"To a big palace," I evaded.

"Can Ivan come?"

"Maybe later," Astiza lied.

We slipped through the city gates without challenge and accelerated into dark forest. St. Petersburg receded.

"I'd paid the man for silence," I said after a while, as much to me as to her. "He attacked me with hate."

"Von Bonin must have paid him more."

"Who recommended Gregor to us?"

"I can't remember. Czartoryski. Dolgoruki. The landlord. Suddenly he was just there."

"And then someone shot him and ran. Who can we trust, Astiza?"

"Only ourselves. Always."

So we flee the city. The stars are shards of ice, the snow gray in dim light, and the trees a palisade of black trunks and limbs that squeeze the highway like prison walls. No farmhouse lights shine at this late hour. I imagine wolves out there, both the actual animal and the wolf of eternal evil, stalking our happiness—the evil that Czartoryski warned about in his study.

We have a few days food, a leftover length of Cossack lariat, a brutal ax, and the old swords. Astiza is buried to her chin under furs, Harry asleep between us. The swords rest against her other hip. It's too dark to see her expression, and that's a blessing.

The night is vast, as if we've sleighed off the edge of the earth. Our horse's breath is an icy cloud as I push her, and the runners scrape and rasp. The sleigh jolts and pitches from frozen ruts, but I dare not slow until we gain some distance.

"Von Bonin wasn't due to visit the fort for another day," I finally repeat.

"It's possible he changed his plans." Astiza's skepticism undercuts her own sentence.

"He shouted that I was the meddling American."

"That, at least, is true."

"He shot and cried recognition from a hundred yards away, in pre-dawn murk with snow falling. How could he appear just then? Why did he look in my direction, when no one else in the fortress noticed? Gregor told him, Astiza, but Gregor didn't know all my plans. So who else knew I'd be on that roof at dawn?"

"Adam has gotten his swords out of confinement while

shedding his original promises to us and still keeping us in his service. Czartoryski knew he couldn't really deliver a royal title to an American. Nobility is at the whim of a tsar who didn't like you at Austerlitz. Yet Czartoryski needed your help. So he promised what he couldn't give. Nor did Adam want to risk smuggling the swords out of St. Petersburg himself. Now he has no need to go the tsar on our behalf. No need to buy us a big house. Instead we're forced to flee to his estate for refuge, delivering the swords when we do so."

"No. He's my friend."

"A foreign minister is no one's friend. Surely you know that from the Frenchman Talleyrand. He led us on with moonbeams."

"But why tip the Prussians? I could have lost the swords."

She was quiet a moment. "Yes. It makes no sense. We're being manipulated for reasons we can't discern."

We skidded as we descended a bank and skated across a frozen creek. Then a pause as the horse gathered herself to haul us up the far bank. The whip cracked. The sleigh lurched. We swerved and ascended.

"And Jelgava," I said. "Will that be safe?"

"Of course not. But we need more supplies to get to Poland."

"And why Gregor with an ax? Why not expert killers?"

"He didn't know what you stole. Just treasure. Perhaps he hoped to take it for himself. Kill you and rob and rape me."

"Gregor didn't strike me as sly or vicious."

"Yet he surprised you. Or maybe he had some motive we haven't guessed. He thought you an enemy of Russia. Russians are mystic. Superstitious. Patriotic."

"A serf? And then an anonymous savior?"

"It doesn't matter," she said. "He's dead, we're fled. The key now is to finish. Maybe everyone will forget us as Adam hopes."

Neither of us believed that. And as if to betray our forced optimism, a glow appeared on the road ahead. I pulled the reins and our horse slowed.

"A fire?" Astiza said. "This late? It looks built on the highway."

"Roadblock."

"How could the police have gotten ahead of us?"

"Not police. Prussians. Or Russian thieves."

We slid slowly nearer, still hidden by the dark. I saw that a bonfire indeed occupied the middle of the road, effectively plugging it. The blaze was built like a pyramid six feet high, sparks funneling into the night sky. Pools of melt-water reflected light at its base. Its builders were nowhere in sight.

"They've blocked all the roads," I guessed. "Prussians are thorough."

"Can we turn around?"

"We'd risk arrest. We could even be accused of Gregor's murder." I studied the terrain. A slight rise on the left side of the road, a slight dip on the right. "These scoundrels expect us to stop. Which means hang onto Harry."

"Ethan?"

"And if you have to, use the swords."

CHAPTER 9

Our only chance was surprise. I cracked the whip and the sleigh leaped forward, our mare galloping hard toward the flames. My reins were in one hand, the ax in another, and I lifted off the seat in a balanced crouch. I'd spied a keyhole to squeeze through.

The rogues lurked out of sight in ambush, counting on me to be lit and blinded by the fire. I relied on the surprise of charging out of the dark, and the devils didn't start to shout until the final seconds of our dash. I slashed with the reins and yanked the mare toward the rising side of the road. Guns banged, flashes in the dark, but the shots were hasty and badly aimed.

We careened like a toboggan and swept just left of the bonfire, one runner tilted high on the road bank, the other slicing through melt water and coals. A bullet buzzed. I leaned and swatted at the fire pyramid with the ax, clipping a burning log and sending it arcing into the woods like a meteor. More cries of surprise and hasty shots. The fire collapsed in an explosion of embers. A man screamed. The fools were hitting each other! But I also heard lead smack our sleigh.

Past them! I glanced at my family. "All right?"

Astiza nodded.

Then something hurtled down at us from the road bank like a pouncing lion. A man crashed onto the back of our sled and clung tenaciously. I awkwardly swung at him with the ax and the assailant leaned backward out of reach, balancing on the runners as my weapon awkwardly hovered. He used one hand to grab Astiza's hair and she shrieked as he hauled her backward, Harry gallantly pulling the other way. "Mama!"

The bastard let go of the sleigh, hanging onto my wife's scalp, and drew a pistol to aim at me as I drove. I could see the white of his snarl.

There was nothing to shoot him with. "Harry, get down!"

The assailant cocked the pistol. Astiza was bent over backward, mouth open, eyes wide with pain, groping under the furs.

"Where are they, American?"

As if in answer a pitted sword struck from the blankets like an angry snake. Astiza rammed it with all her strength into the assailant's grizzled throat, its point grating on bone. The man's eyes rolled, his pistol went off harmlessly, and then the assassin was gone as abruptly as he'd come, thumping onto the frozen road. The sword had popped clear of his neck. Astiza fell back onto the seat, gasping, the old weapon dripping on her furs. She clutched Harry.

I lashed the reins.

More shots, aimed at nothing. The wrecked bonfire was far behind, the road bent, and finally darkness clamped back down like the lid of a pot.

"That's the way," I exulted. "And I think the fools shot

one of their own men." Then I remembered to ask to ask again. "Are you hurt?"

"Of course it hurts. But quite alive, thank you." The sword lay across her lap and her expression was fierce. "Horus, are you safe?"

"You got rid of the bad man, Mama."

We could still hear distant shouts. They'd probably mount horses.

I used the whip, keeping our exhausted horse at a gallop. The sleigh bounded over dips and rises, the animal's nostrils exhaling big puffs of steam, her flanks heaving. Runners quivered when we glanced off rocks. We needed to hide, but the road trapped us like a tunnel.

"We can't outrun them," Astiza said. "The land is flat, the ferries frozen, the lanes snowbound. And we can't win forever with an ax and antique swords."

"So we have to truly vanish, my sorceress. We've gained precious minutes but they'll run us down like hounds."

"The devil they will." My wife is ruthless when our family is threatened. "Is there a bridge ahead?"

"We'll soon cross the Slavyanka River."

"Let's vanish there. But we need a wider lead to give us the necessary time. Ethan, watch for a tree leaning precariously over the road. We'll set an ambush of our own."

"I love your resourcefulness, my pretty Amazon."

"I believe it's called desperation. And you drive a sleigh like a charioteer, my handsome thief."

"I believe it's called terror."

We halted at an aged birch that tilted as if drunk. "Undercut it," Astiza directed. I swiftly wielded the ax while she tied our remaining lariat between the leaning tree and a stout fir on the other side of the highway. Astiza has taken a keen and necessary interest in sailor and teamster knots in our travels, and now she used a haymaker's hitch to pull the rope as taut as a harpsichord wire. It was the height of a horse's neck but virtually invisible in the dark. Harry used a fir limb to brush out our footsteps.

Then we sleighed on, slower now to rest our panting horse. The mare would be going further than we would.

Minutes later we heard the scream of horses and the crash of the undercut tree as it fell across the road. I could imagine the confused tangle.

"Maybe they'll give up," I said.

"No, but we've gained ten minutes. Horus, do you still have your fir broom?"

"Yes, Mama." He enjoyed responsibility, not to mention the novelty of being up so late. Maybe he thought every family traveled this way.

"Help make us vanish."

"Yes, Mama."

The bridge over the Slavyanka was a hundred meters long, built on two towers of timber cribbing that rose from the frozen river. I reined to a halt at mid-span, we climbed off, and I gave a sharp smack to the rump of our horse. Off she trotted to follow the road, no doubt surprised at the sudden lightening of her burden. The tracks of the sleigh's runners were like an arrow pointing into the dark. It disappeared.

We worked to do the same.

Fifteen minutes later there was a rumble of hoof beats as a dozen anxious riders pounded over the icy bridge to chase our empty sleigh. They never looked or slowed. Our mare must have gone on for some distance, because it was an hour more before our disappointed pursuers returned the way they'd come, after catching an empty conveyance. They rode more slowly this time, peering into woods that were going gauze-gray as morning slowly took form. Flakes drifted down like blossoms. Fog hugged the frozen river. The men halted in the middle of the bridge.

"They ran into the trees," one speculated.

"Without making a track?"

"It's snowing."

"Not much. Not fast."

"Or they climbed a tree," another suggested.

"Or drowned in the river," said a third.

"The trees are bare and the Slavyanka is hard as a rock. I am surrounded by imbeciles." It was Von Bonin.

"Or crawled into a snowdrift."

"If so they're dead," another man said. "It's freezing out here."

"We must have the swords," the one-armed Prussian said. "Without them we dare not go back, not to St. Petersburg and not to Berlin."

"There's no proof that the American even has the swords. I say he lost them in the river, if he's alive at all. Who knows who was on that sleigh?"

"The man who killed Heinrich, you fool."

"Bah. The American is a ghost. He drowns, he lives. He sleighs, he vanishes. His bitch of a wife, too."

"That woman is a witch," another chimed in. "Everyone says so."

"All of you sound like gibbering old maids! No. We don't give up until we find them. Half of you this way, half that. Search the road margins for signs of where they abandoned their sleigh. Give a shot if you spot anything. And you two—down on the ice. See if they fled on the river."

Hooves thumped as our grumbling pursuers moved off on assignment. Two slid on foot down the bank, cursing, and we watched as they walked under the bridge and stumbled away, one upstream and one down.

No signal shot was fired.

Our hiding place was the timber cribbing where it joined the beams of the bridge. I'd used the ax to chop and pry a timber so we could crawl inside to hide, scooping up the chips and swinging the log shut behind us. We lay on a bed of ballast rocks, the bridge deck inches from our noses. Astiza kept her hand close to Harry's mouth, but he was already old enough to know not to cry out. Our boy will worry me someday, when his bravery becomes boldness and boldness makes him reckless. But for now he's exemplary.

We lay and shivered until the Prussians gave up for good and clopped west. "We'll ambush them again," Von Bonin vowed.

And then it was quiet. We'd lost everything except the swords.

"I'll make it up to you," I whispered, as much to keep up my spirits as Astiza's. "Catastrophe now, but soon we'll have royal help, if Czartoryski is right. Then Adam's mother Izabela will welcome us in Poland. A title can still be ours. Then our life will truly begin."

"This is our life, husband." Clinging to the underside

of a bridge, inches from discovery, in a wintry forest, flakes drifting down. "This is our destiny." And sadly, sweetly, with real love and real regret, she kissed me.

CHAPTER 10

We eventually arrived as beggars at Jelgava Palace, trudging on foot while swaddled in enough peasant coats to look like tubs of dirty laundry. Our journey had taken us more than four hundred miles southwest of St. Petersburg and thirty miles inland from the Baltic Sea. Our clothes were wet and dirty, our bellies empty, and my face crusted with stubble that Astiza assured me was entirely unflattering. Just as well not to have a mirror. Ethan Gage, ambassador to the powerful and aspiring prince!

I looked across Latvia's Lielupe River to the island where Jelgava sprawls. Completed in 1772, the edifice is one of those bloated and bland baroque slabs of a mansion that Italian architects churn out for any aristocrat who can afford the vanity. Inherited taste is rare among the rich, so the highborn hire swarms of Romans to choose for them. The result is that one noble's sumptuous pile looks pretty much like another's, with coziness and sense sacrificed to grandeur and debt.

Not that I wouldn't like to have one, if I could afford the wood to heat it.

The island is an easily guarded place where Tsar Alexander

granted refuge to the future Bourbon king of France, would-be Louis XVIII. Louis is impatiently waiting for Bonaparte to fall, while Napoleon has asked Louis to renounce all rights to the French throne in return for being allowed to return home. Neither event—Napoleon's fall or Louis's renunciation—seems likely to happen very soon. So the brother of the beheaded king spends his days warily looking out on a snowy landscape for French spies, while fantasizing about his own crowning. This was the man Czartoryski told us to rely on.

Our escape from Von Bonin's henchmen had been deliberately slow, in hopes that further pursuit would overshoot us. They'd galloped off in the direction of Berlin while we left the main highway and trudged on peasant tracks, winding from cabin to farm in a daze of disappointment. Our cautious route took us east of gigantic Lake Peipus and then southwest into wintry Lithuania and Latvia.

We were a world away from relations or friends. Astiza was a refugee from Egypt, I a pilgrim from America, and Harry had been forced to leave his only childhood companion. We knew we'd been betrayed, but didn't know who, entirely, had done the betraying. We assumed my drowning was likely no longer believed. We had no sleigh, little food, and scant money, and were weary from tension. To be hunted is to never relax. To distrust is to sour every encounter. Hunger initially sharpens the mind with desperation, and then dulls it with exhaustion. The cold bites deeper. Winter nights are endless.

Two things saved us.

The first was rustic Slavic hospitality. We followed snowy tracks through rolling hills and coastal plains to avoid grand estates with their brick-walled gardens. We also cautiously skirted snug villages with their onion dome churches, haze of wood smoke, tantalizing scent of food, and too many people. Instead we called on rural peasants for help, and thankfully Astiza and Harry had the knack of winning over these simple farmers. The men were bearded like shaggy bears, grinning with missing teeth. The bright scarves of the women framed cherry-red cheeks and kindly eyes in chapped faces. I'd no weapon—we kept the swords carefully bundled—and the wary serfs quickly judged us harmless and needy. The poor often show more charity than the rich and so we journeyed from hut to hovel, explaining by signs that we were almost bankrupt and harried. Our hosts nodded in commiseration and shared beet soup, coarse bread, and honey mead without expectation of payment, watching indulgently as Harry gobbled. They even gave us old coats and cloaks.

Our second salvation was the abiding peace of nature. Winter's beauty became our antidote to despair, its blacks and whites starkly scenic. Oddly and unexpectedly, I found our plight lightening my spirit as much as it depressed it. Instead of maneuvering for advantage in cutthroat Russian society, we'd escaped to fundamentals. We gave ourselves over to the rhythm of the earth, its pale dawns and pink sunsets, its bitter freezes and cheerful campfires. The outdoors was pure compared to the hives and muck of cities and castles. I liked the company of my family, which required no posing. I liked that choices became simple. Which lane? When to rest? Where to collect firewood? Which cabin to approach?

It reminded me of my fur trade days. While I didn't confess to Astiza that I'd begun to secretly wonder how happy

I'd really be with noble title and overseer responsibility, I did wonder if Rousseau was right that our natural state is a more primitive one. "He who multiplies riches multiplies cares," Franklin once warned me.

Some nights the aurora borealis was on display. Harry was initially uncertain about its eerie shimmer, but I told him it was a promise of better days to come.

"Is that heaven, Papa?"

"Maybe heaven's door."

The winter days were slowly lengthening and brightening. Snow sparkled by day and glowed by night. The stillness let us listen to the woods slowly drip to life. The forest streams smoked at dawn, their water sharp as champagne. The first birds of the year called and flitted. Moss had the glisten of fine raiment.

Sometimes Astiza and I took turns carrying Harry, but most of the time he marched manfully in the snow, fatigued, hungry, curious, and rarely complaining. He had us all to himself, after all, until he could bask in the attention of the fussy farm matrons who spoiled him.

The peasant huts were low, snug, and colorless, given that paint is one of the boundaries between city and country. On the outside the logs were weathered as gray as the periodic overcast, and inside they were stained almost black by hearth fires and rush lights. Yes, the habitation was rude. But there was a Red Corner for guests beneath an icon of Mary, shelves for precious cups and pots, and pegs for guests' fur coats and woolen mittens. The wealthiest peasants had a prized ancestral samovar from which they would serve tea in tiny cups, guests taking ten servings each during the long winter evenings. The blackened ceilings were lightened by burning eggshells in the hearth, the heat carrying the white bits aloft to stick overhead and sparkle like little stars.

The rudest huts had no chimney or windows and an open hearth, which meant the door had to be cracked for ventilation when the owners lit a fire. We learned to wait to enter until heat carried the worst of the smoke to the ceiling, and then not to stand lest we spend our visit coughing.

Prouder cabins had a real oven, chimney, and even glass windows. Farm animals would be housed in stables either below or above the human quarters, lending heat, and we learned a cow was worth seventy iron nails. Chickens were kept in cages in the living rooms each winter. Dogs sprawled, and cats patrolled against mice. The men fished and hunted while the women weaved, everyone waiting for spring.

In sum it was rustic but surprisingly comfortable. Above and behind each hearth was a brick and clay platform warmed by the constant fire. Here was the master bed, our hosts always surrendering this prized perch to visitors while they took the cold floor. Richer peasants fed us potatoes, pork, peas, sauerkraut, and once some kielbasa sausage. When I gave them a coin or two, their eyes widened as if it were a fortune.

My reflexive greed shamed me.

"Our dreams are so foolish, Ethan," Astiza murmured one night as we lay under their blankets, our hosts snoring on the other side of the oven. "These people seem more content than all the nobles in Russia. We contend for palaces and they abide with the seasons."

"I've had the same thought. But we also know their lives are brutal much of the year, and that we'd never be content with a life like this. We've seen too much. Experience has doomed us to be strivers."

"Which will be the death of us someday." She tried it as a joke, and yet we both knew it wasn't one.

"But what a life we'll have led!" I rolled atop her, Harry sound asleep beside us. I was restless with desire.

Astiza shifted her hips away. "Easy for you to say," she said as she pushed me off. "Horus hasn't had a life yet."

"He's had the life of a dozen boys his age. I vow that someday he'll live the life we dream of. He'll be a great man."

"And what makes a man great?" And then she did hug, but only that. By the curse of Casanova, we spend entirely too much time in awkward situations. That's what striving does to you.

The Baltic clouds were like clammy canvas when we traveled that last day from forest farmstead to Louis' refuge, and it was early dusk when we reached the still-frozen Lielupe. Like wary animals, we peered from the trees. The palace across the ice seemed as big as a mountain range, lights and lamps glowing in half the hundred windows we could count. "We couldn't even afford the candles," I remarked. The snowy lawn was an unmarked white sheet, and on the roof flew both the Russian flag and the fleur-de-lis of the displaced Bourbons. Maybe I could persuade Louis we were fellow exiles.

First I took precautions. We backed into the forest and found a hollow log to hide the swords, Harry cheerfully crawling far inside to secrete them securely. Then we took bearings to mark the spot and returned to the riverbank. Now we'd nothing to tempt our new host with, or arouse suspicion, or rashly trade away.

"Ready for a royal audience?" I asked my family.

"If he consorts with paupers."

"What's a pauper, Mama?"

"Us, Horus. People like us."

We walked cautiously across the frozen river, in full view of the house, and then up the meadow toward the main entry. Armed guards with lanterns came out to challenge us, gigantic in their greatcoats and towering bearskin hats. They had muskets, pikes, swords, and pistols.

"*Nous sommes amis!* We are friends!" I called out in French.

"Friends are recognized," their leader replied in heavily accented French of his own. "Who are you, and why do you trespass?" A woolen scarf around his mouth and nose muffled his voice, his eyes sharp and quick as an falcon's. His companions reinforced his stare.

"We're ambassadors, come to pay respects from the United States of America to the Bourbon heir to the throne of France," I said, bowing slightly. Yes, our appearance made this absurd, but best to make an entrance. The art of the bow is to adjust the amount of incline to the station of the person being addressed. Sentries deserve a swift bob, beauties a slow tilt that hovers at their décolletage, and kings a full duck and flourish, fingers out and one boot extended. "I know we look hard traveled, but we've been hard used."

"United States?" He made it sound like the Moon.

"Americans by way of France, Bohemia, and Russia," I said. "A confidant of President Jefferson and a protégé of Benjamin Franklin. Something of an authority on Bonaparte, as well."

One of the soldiers snickered at my name-dropping.

Astiza stood taller. "And the Tsarina Elizabeth."

Their leader looked at her with interest, as men tend to do, and squinted dubiously down at Harry, an unexpected dwarf. What sort of diplomat materializes with a child? "You conduct your embassy in rags?"

"We were ambushed by bandits," I replied. "We look molested because we were. But I truly do represent my country—or at least I have, occasionally—and it is in all sincerity that I've come to the future King Louis for sanctuary while offering insight into his usurper, the dictator Napoleon. Please, sergeant—if that's what you are—send word that the American diplomat Ethan Gage and family are calling to bring reports from Trafalgar and Austerlitz." I'd had the bad luck to participate in both battles, and have since tried to turn misfortune to profit by describing them. People love horror.

"Ethan Gage, is it?" Our interrogator actually sounded as if he'd heard of me, but then I do have dubious renown. "Lean closer." He raised a lantern.

I tried to look dignified while unshaven, rank, and damp.

"You are he? The infamous gambler and spy?"

"None other. Though I would better describe myself as the exemplary sharpshooter and celebrated antiquarian. An electrician. A savant. A consultant on grand strategy." I attempted the assured tone of the celebrated. Part of notoriety is playing the part.

"You have diplomatic credentials?"

"My knowledge of Napoleon and his schemes is my passport. This is my wife, Astiza, and my son, Harry."

"Your wife." His tone was oddly flat. His gaze flickered from Astiza to me in a way I didn't care for.

"Sergeant, these may be French assassins," one of the soldiers said.

"Of course they are," his leader slowly replied. "With woman and child, weaponless in the snow, looking more like scarecrows than human beings." He turned to his men. "I've heard of the rascal Gage. An adventurer with allegiance to none but himself, or so it's said." He looked back at Astiza and Harry. "No mention of family, though. Something of a scamp is what I heard."

"We were married, sir, on an American ship."

"An *American* ship? What name?"

"Off Barbary, the *Enterprise*. During Jefferson's war with the pirates." It's a long story, as all of mine are, but another trick is arousing curiosity.

The man considered still longer, me noticing that it was damnably cold while he did so. Astiza shifted from foot to foot. Harry shivered and barked a cough. Finally the bastard relented.

"Corporal, take this lot inside and get the fleas off them. I'll consult with his majesty's advisor, the Count of Avaray."

"But sir, if these are imposters …"

"Impersonating a rascal? A poor choice. Beggars, yes. Assassins? No. Quickly now!"

So we were marched into the palace, through a high chilly foyer to an anteroom warmed by a ceramic stove and several candles. After being relieved of coats and cloaks and carefully checked for hidden weapons, we were given soup, bread and watered wine while baths were poured by plump Latvian maids. Harry slurped. I spewed breadcrumbs like an exploding bomb. Only my wife ate with restraint, proving again that women are very much a mystery.

"Is this our new house, Papa?"

"We're just visiting. There's a better place down the road."

A mirror confirmed our disarray. We smelled like a stable and I wouldn't have blamed fat Louis for heaving us out. What I was counting on was curiosity. It's dull to wait in exile and we'd prove diverting. Or so I bet.

CHAPTER 11

The maids brought screens to allow us to strip and scrub, and Astiza supervised Harry. Our clothes were taken for washing and we got presentable substitutes: mine a white guards' uniform and my wife's the dress of a lady-in-waiting. For Harry they fetched a sailor suit, which thrilled him. Then a chevalier came to escort us to an audience with Louis.

I complimented the nobleman on his lord's charity.

"The king has sympathy for all refugees because of his own misfortune at the hands of the execrable Bonaparte," the chevalier replied. "The king is interested to hear your insights on the usurper and the United States. Royalist France was the father of your country's independence."

Interesting that they pretended Louis already had the crown, and gave their aid so much credit, but I figured it was smart to agree. "I hope its not too late to say thank you. We revere Lafayette."

"An idealist who proved foolishly liberal in our own revolution. I, for one, regret ever helping America. It was the start of all our troubles."

Like all palaces, this one was a dozen times larger than it needed to be and less comfortable because of it, with drafty corners, echoing hallways, and clattery stairs. The pomposity was made worse by the structure's emptiness. I knew that erratic Tsar Paul ordered Louis out of Jelgava five years ago when he abruptly tired of his royal guest. The French refugees were already so bankrupt that they'd had to auction off most of their remaining furniture simply to move away. Now Tsar Alexander, who judged Louis a potential pawn, had invited the French royalists back without providing money to buy new belongings. Louis might wish to restore the rituals of Versailles, but he lacked the tables, chairs, knickknacks, or courtiers to pull off such pretense. The palace did shine from French scrubbing, and boasted that upper-class smell of candlewax, floor polish, tobacco, chamber pots, and mildew. By Russian custom, the servant who led our little procession swung a charcoal censor that burned perfume.

A wide corridor absent of carpet, its decorative niches barren, led to a broad double door. Two grenadiers flanked this entry, stiff as statues and wearing antique royal uniforms with tricorne hats. Both had muskets. The exile was taking no chances.

At the chevalier's nod the soldiers swung the doors to reveal an inviting library with ample furniture and crackling fire. Harry bolted so quickly to the heat that an embarrassed Astiza had to rush to corral him.

"Monsieur Ethan Gage," the chevalier announced. "And family." This last was said with disapproval. Then he shut the doors behind us.

The king-in-waiting sat in a shadowy corner on a stuffed

leather chair, its arms spotted with crumbs. Did he eat in this hideaway? The library was walled with books, tapestries, maps, and heavy oil portraits of Louis's royal ancestors. Two of those pictured—Louis XVI and Marie Antoinette—were now headless, but here they gazed with neck firmly attached. The picture frames were scuffed from frequent traveling, I noted, and the chairs looked nicked and stained. Louis had fled for refuge to Holland, Italy, the Duchy of Brunswick, Prussia, Warsaw, and twice to Jelgava, begging for subsidy from other rulers. So long as they pretended he might some-day be king, he could pretend to be one.

Astiza and I bowed deeply, Louis regally nodding in reply. "Harry, take a bow," I ordered, and my son bobbed as told.

"Are you a real king?" he piped.

Louis was taken aback. "Indeed I am," he said. "Or will be." The "king" had none of Napoleon's magnetism. His lower lip was plump as a pouting girl's, jowls hung around his chin, and his complexion was pasty. He was an over-weight, sedentary, fifty-year-old conservative still favoring the court dress of the 18th Century, meaning an evening robe atop waistcoat, tight knee-breeches, silk stockings, silver slippers, and a high collar to warm his own neck. His legs looked swollen and his hands putty soft. His gaze was shy yet curious, like my child's.

Since he didn't invite us to sit we stood like petitioners. "Monsieur Gage," he prompted.

"Your… majesty." Always err on the side of flattery. "Ethan Gage, diplomat and military attaché, at your service. I bring you greetings from America and the best wishes of our presi-dent." I brought no such thing but I could put into Jefferson's mouth any words that came into my head, since the Virginian was a safe six thousand miles away.

"A diplomat who comes as a ragged refugee, my sergeant-of-arms informs me."

"We were beset by thieves while on the way to Poland."

"Poland no longer exists."

"Unless you ask a Pole." Since no royal will tolerate boredom, a diplomat needs just enough cheek to remain interesting. Louis chuckled.

"Indeed, indeed. Persistent as lice! And you beset by thieves. The scum of the earth prowls like wolves since the wars of Bonaparte. Renegades, deserters, tramps, camp followers, gypsies, Cossacks, Jews, pirates, peddlers, and mercenaries. Should be hanged, the lot of them. Will be, when order is restored." He gazed into this elusive future. "Well. I seldom get a diplomat at nighttime in winter, accompanied by wife and child, in garments suited to a Huron or Ojibway." He smiled thinly. "We are amused."

"Determination, combined with your reputation for wisdom and charity, brings us here, my lord …"

"I'm not a lord, I'm heir to a king, displaced by a tyrant, and slandered by traitors." He glanced at my boy. "*Oui*, the rightful king."

"Yes, your majesty," I said again. "The Russian foreign minister suggested you might find me informative. I've worked for and against Bonaparte … "

"The usurper."

"The usurper, your majesty. I know his strengths and weaknesses."

"You witnessed Austerlitz?"

"Fought in it, on the French side. And at Trafalgar as well."

"You contrived to be at both battles?" They'd been six weeks apart.

"I'm an energetic traveler." This, at least, was true. "Terrible struggles, the havoc of hell. I also helped the United States purchase Louisiana after exploring there. Now we're on a mission for Prince Czartoryski, but barely escaped the criminals who plague the roads."

"What times we live in." Louis shook his head. "Me, an exile. You, a diplomat. Baffling, no?"

"We need refuge and supply before resuming our journey. As a protégé of Benjamin Franklin and confidant of President Jefferson ..."

"Won't you introduce your wife?" He peered at her as intently as the sergeant outside had done.

"Her name is ..."

"Astiza, your majesty." She used her serene tone that can be as arresting as her beauty. "A priestess, student, and philosopher of the East, as well as a seer and alchemist." She smiled, which she can do very well, and performed a curtsey with a grace that emphasized her charms as a woman. Frankly, Astiza is better at this game than I am.

"Alchemy? The art of transformation?"

"Indeed, your majesty."

"Did you know that the Italian sorcerer Cagliostro once stayed at this palace and astounded the aristocracy of Latvia with his prophecies?"

"I sensed his lingering spirit."

"Some thought him immortal."

"Cagliostro?" My heart quickened. I'd run afoul of his sect and put an end to a lieutenant or two of the famed Egyptian Rite. Was Louis tangled up in their intrigues? That would be the worst luck.

"I'd be interested if he left any writings or experiments, your majesty," Astiza said smoothly. "I'm anxious to learn from remarkable men in our remarkable times."

"Ghastly times. And you a woman! Astounding, astounding. Well." He sipped from a goblet. "There were witty women at Versailles, you know."

"There are witty women everywhere, majesty."

"I suppose. Can't include my wife, homely as a hound and mindless as a squirrel, bless her troubled heart. Now the Countess of Balbi, *she* could carry a conversation." This was Louis's mistress, as all the world knew. "And are you aware I wrote a biography of Marie Antoinette? Lost times, lost times." He peered at us in turn. "Well. A most peculiar family."

"Even Horus here contributes to our search for wisdom."

"Does he now? And have you met a king before, my boy?"

An ordinary child might be too shy to answer, but mine gabbed as rashly as his Papa. "I saw Napoleon. He's an emperor!"

"Hmph," Louis said. "So he claims. But not a king."

"He's a bad man," Harry went on blithely. "I hope you're a good king."

In a year of diplomacy I couldn't have thought of anything to better break the ice with our host. Louis beamed. "Actually, I'm presently the Count of Provence and heir to the French throne. My brother was king of France, and someday I shall be too."

"I think I shall be President," Harry said solemnly. And with that the two of them, one five and the other fifty, bonded.

"I approve of your family, American. But mother and son are no doubt exhausted and in need of rest. It is bedtime, is it not, young Horus?"

"I suppose so, king."

"Your family will be shown to a bedchamber while you and I talk, Gage." Louis reached to a side table to ring a silver bell and summon back the chevalier, who in turn fetched other servants. In short order Astiza and Harry were escorted to a bedroom. I was finally offered a chair and a glass of wine, although a bowl of raisins Louis plucked at was kept well out of my reach. I was exhausted too, but worked to stay alert during an extended interrogation about America, Czartoryski, the mood of Tsar Alexander, and the terrible battles. The exile's questions were surprisingly sharp.

The one subject Louis avoided was Napoleon himself, the Colossus astride Europe. Bonaparte's success, and Bourbon impotence, must gnaw at him like a cancer. The exile had no army, no revenue, and a hollowed court. His sole remaining asset was his ancestry. Louis was the most pitiful of men, a king without a throne, a ruler with no idea how he might rule, claiming leadership of a country that had no use for him. And so I answered as patiently as I could while waiting for his real inquiry, the vulnerabilities of the "usurper" he must in turn usurp. It was when the clock chimed eleven that Louis got to the point of our meeting.

"I invited you into my presence, Monsieur Gage, because I'd already received correspondence about you."

I smiled as much as I dared. "From Minister Czartoryski?"

"Not the first time I've heard mention of your adventures."

I was puzzled. How else would Louis have heard of me? "I hope it was flattering. I try my best."

"A treasure hunter, I was told." He picked up a raisin. "With a treasure, perhaps?"

Here was danger. "I'm afraid not, your majesty. All I've possessed has been lost." I was glad we'd hid the swords. "I'm simply a diplomat on a mission of peace, robbed of horse and sleigh. Thank goodness you're Adam's friend. Minister Czartoryski sends his goodwill."

"Yes. Well. But I was told you might be bringing some artifacts. Patriotic relics. Old things." It was almost a whine of disappointment.

Odd. Czartoryski had said to keep the swords a secret. "I carry only ministerial messages, I'm afraid."

He was dissatisfied. "Messages to who, about what?"

"The foreign minister bound me to secrecy. He said you, the target of poisoners, would understand. It concerns the ambitions of the tyrant Napoleon."

Now the heir held my eye for a long time, judging both my truth and my resolve. I put on a gamblers face, which is to say no face at all. Finally he looked away. "You said you were both for and against Bonaparte?"

"I served with him in Egypt, but barely escaped a massacre he organized in Jaffa. Accordingly, I wound up on the Turkish side in the Holy Land. Since then the two of us have circled like boxers." Best to be honest about my allegiances, since Louis seemed to know more than I'd expected.

"You've no moral compass?"

"My lode star is my family."

"And yet the usurper still trusts you?" He ate the raisins one at a time, using his fat fingers as a forceps.

"Hardly. Napoleon uses me. Bonaparte prides himself on finding the utility in every man, even me, and thinks he can seduce anyone on earth, man or woman. He trusts no one, but we're both gamblers. Napoleon believes in boldness because aggression has served him well. Someday he'll gamble too much, and reach too far."

"And meanwhile he dictates to Europe while I stew in Jelgava." It was said with grave dissatisfaction at the unfairness of life. "No monarch will give me men, and each fights him their own stupid, stubborn way. Prussia shrank from last year's campaign so they'll stand alone this year. Then Russia the next. Fools! But no one listens to fat forgotten Louis." In popped another raisin.

"Waiting may not be unwise, your majesty. Napoleon is too proud, too impatient, and too reckless. He unsettles everyone. You, sire, could be the stalwart around whom Europe rallies. I want to carry word of your readiness to Poland." My mission was to reestablish Poland as a buffer state, not to make Louis a standard, but vagueness, delay, strategic silences, and answering questions with more questions are all tools of the statesman. "Our goal is a peace that gives time for Bonaparte to fall."

"Or to consolidate his empire. I want war and his overthrow."

"You have royal legitimacy he can never obtain," I insisted. "No self-crowned emperor can match you. Meanwhile, I ask only for a horse team, sleigh, and supplies in order to complete my mission."

"For a Russian government that starves me of support."

"Perhaps Minister Czartoryski can persuade the tsar to grant more, now that the two of you are cooperating. Don't give up hope. Fortune turns swiftly."

"Does it? How the hours crawl." He paused, lost in thought. A clock chimed midnight. Other timepieces in distant rooms repeated the announcement, bong answering bong through the half-empty palace. "Does Napoleon stay up late?"

"He sleeps very little."

"I, neither. Well." He stood up. "I'm keeping you from your family. Let my servants show you to your chamber and we'll talk more tomorrow. When fortune, perhaps, has turned." He gave a wan smile. "Goodnight sir."

I bowed. "I'm honored by your patronage." Doesn't hurt to inject a note of expectation.

"Patronage is a reward for loyalty and service." He picked up some papers for nighttime reading and I backed from the library.

Our bedroom was ornate in the 17th Century baroque style, but again under-furnished. Its soaring ceiling only emphasized the chill, and the Gage family shared the single bed for warmth, since the chamber's ceramic stove seemed under-fueled. Louis couldn't afford the firewood either.

Harry nonetheless slept with the rhythmic, reassuring breath of childhood. How we envy their oblivion! Astiza woke and asked in a whisper about my interview. I quietly told her what I remembered. "It went rather well."

She frowned. "Ethan, I don't trust Czartoryski's strategy to send us here. Once more we're dependent on ambitious ministers and scheming monarchs. We need to get away and rely on ourselves."

"How? We're penniless. And go where?"

"Egypt. America."

"And do what? What do I know beyond being a spy and envoy? Now we've this chance to deliver a Polish relic and be rewarded. Some flattery of Louis, his loan of a sleigh, and we get to Czartoryski's mother and refuge. Finally we have powerful patrons."

"Who always keep us in their debt."

"At Pulawy all this will be finished. I might even have a title."

"Oh, my hopeful, naïve husband."

We eventually slept, sleet rattling the great window, the grand home creaking in the night. I awoke with the ambition of securing breakfast.

Instead there was pounding as morning dawned gray. When I opened our door a half-dozen guards pushed into the chamber with fixed bayonets. Harry and Astiza watched from the bed covers, his eyes wide with surprise, hers with resignation.

"What's this?" I blustered. "I'm under the protection of Louis."

"You mean the prosecution of Louis. Ethan Gage, the king has received information that suggests you may be guilty of murder, theft, conspiracy, and high treason."

"Not treason. I'm an American."

"What you are, American, is under arrest."

CHAPTER 12

I demanded explanation and got none. I pleaded that they not imprison my family and was ignored. I suggested there was a monstrous misunderstanding and that a second audience with Louis would clear up all confusion. No one would even reply. We were given our laundered traveling clothes and marched down a servant's stairway and deep, deep, into the bowels of Jelgava Palace. At a windowless cellar where the only illumination was from candles, we were pushed into a barren room.

A heavy wooden door with small grilled window slammed behind us.

"So much for royal patrons," my wife said.

"Well, he's not a king yet."

"Be patient," our jailer said through the grill, and I thought he meant Louis's ascension. But then he said, "The Prussians will be here soon."

So we were boxed for delivery to Von Bonin. What foul luck. Lothar must have told Louis about the swords.

The three of us stood dispiritedly. From the smell of it the cell had once stored food and wine, but now was empty and damp. I was proud of Harry for not crying. Still, he looked understandably depressed. He'd been underground before. Eventually Astiza and I sat on dirty straw, the stone of the floor like ice. Our captors hadn't let us bring our coats. Harry prowled the small perimeter like a caged cub. He rapped on the door as if gauging its thickness, and fingered the rough wood.

"We need Mama's magic, Papa."

"Indeed we do."

"Will the king bring us breakfast?"

"Probably not."

"I thought he was a good king."

"I thought so too. People are peculiar, Harry."

"I'll be glad when we get to the better palace."

I remained bewildered by this reversal. Hadn't my audience with Louis gone well? Hadn't my son amused him? But I hadn't offered the swords, had I?

"Hug us, Ethan," Astiza said. "It's cold." It was the most useful thing I could do.

Bread and water didn't come until midday, and we got no more than that as the hours on my pocket-watch stretched to night again. Neglect and hunger are crushing, and I felt increasingly morose as we waited for fate. Nothing is crueler than helplessness.

Finally a lantern lifted on the other side of the little grill, providing a flare of illumination so its holder could inspect us. Prussians? I shuffled to the door.

"Are you ready to tell the truth?" The voice was gruff. "It will go better for your family if you do."

I tried to look out but the lantern was held to the window, blocking my view of our interrogator. The voice didn't sound like Von Bonin or any other Prussian, but the man's French did have an accent.

"I always tell the truth, unless matching wits with liars. I'm the most honest of men, which gets me in constant trouble. Come in or let me out, and ask anything you want. The price is a blanket for my wife and child."

There was a long pause. Then, "Don't bargain for a mere blanket, Ethan Gage. No man who settles for such low stakes will ever rise."

What game was this? "What would you suggest, then?"

"Your lives and your freedom."

I could hear the intake of Astiza's breath.

"You're in graver danger than you know," the voice went on.

"Who are you? What do you know of our enemies?"

He ignored my question. "Prove yourself. What talents do you have?"

This took me aback. "What kind of interview is this? Move the lantern. Show your face."

"Answer, if you wish to survive."

"Are you a friend?"

"Answer!"

"By the ashes of Vulcan..."

"Quickly now!"

What did we have to lose? "I'm an electrician. I told your sergeant."

"I'm that sergeant, fool. And how did you learn God's fearful lightning?"

"From the savant Franklin. One of many learned men I've partnered with. Cuvier. Monge. Jomard. Fulton."

"Yes, yes, we've heard your boasting. What else?"

"What else what?"

"Talents, I said."

This was very odd. "I'm a good shot."

"From a man with no rifle."

"Give me one and I'll prove it."

"What else?"

"A good card player."

"With no cards."

"A treasure hunter."

"With no treasure."

"A diplomat. A spy. A go-between. An ambassador."

"With no patron and no portfolio."

"A husband and a father."

Another long pause. "Yes. Surprising. Who was *your* father?"

"*My* father? Why does that matter?"

"Perhaps you've forgotten him? Perhaps you never knew him? Are you a bastard or an orphan?"

"Certainly not. Josiah Gage of Philadelphia. A gentleman and a patriot, sir, wounded fighting with Washington at the Battle of Princeton. A respected businessman whom I suppose I disappointed." How distant my American childhood seemed.

"Your siblings?"

I was becoming exasperated. "It's you who are wasting time! What's the point of this?"

"The point is your life, I said, and perhaps the future of Europe, should you be believed." His tone was impatient, but not hostile. What was going on?

"Erasmus. He was the responsible one, I suppose. Susan. She married well. Caleb, who disappeared on a privateer in the American Revolution. He was the oldest. The unhappiest. The bravest."

"Is it brave to disappear?"

"I can't judge him. No word ever came."

There was a long silence. A click as the lantern was set down on the floor outside. I heard nothing, and then a sigh.

"That's all my family," I finally said. "Are you still there?"

"Don't you recognize me, Ethan?" The question was sad.

I started. A flood of memories, and yes, there was *something* familiar in his voice, faintly remembered from a quarter century ago. I had a jolt of embarrassment and astonishment. Could it possibly be?

My older brother Caleb! My closest sibling, and my first real enemy. Suddenly I felt soaring hope. And forbidding fear.

Yet surely I'd have recognized Caleb had I seen him. And how had he seen me? But a muffler had masked the sergeant-at-arms, and how could a long-lost teenaged brother be a royalist guard at Jelgava? Impossible! "Caleb? I assumed you dead." And now felt guilt, relief, and confusion, all at once. "How in the world?"

"Listen, Ethan. Louis hopes to sell you to the Prussians. He's desperate for money and they're negotiating right now. It was I who warned that the notorious Gage family might slip away if left unconfined, in order to get you locked in a place where I could speak to you alone. But you must trust me and flee tonight, before you're handed over to a one-armed scoundrel."

"Von Bonin."

"I don't know what trouble you're up to this time, little brother, but I've spent the day preparing. Do you know that you're famous in the taverns and whorehouses of Europe as the worst spy and antiquarian on the Continent?"

"I'm famous?"

"These royalists know me as Caleb Ruston. Like you, I hire on where I can. It's a wicked world we navigate."

"It *is*, brother! With rare angels! We're of the same heart!"

"We shared a heart."

I winced. "Yes."

"You made me grow up, Ethan, and bitterness tempered me. Since then I've been a privateer, mercenary, smuggler, swordsman, and soldier. I was hired on at Jelgava to help keep French spies at bay. Louis had been informed of your coming but didn't believe in you for a minute. He fears anyone close to Bonaparte, and resents that you wouldn't trust him with your secrets. If the Prussians don't buy you, he intends torture to ferret out your treasure."

"Not treasure. Antique junk."

"I'd heard rumor of a Gage in St. Petersburg, but it's a common name. The last I heard, you were lost in a hurricane. Or was it a sea battle?"

"I've made a specialty of being dead. You're willing to help after all these years?"

"I'm willing to use you after all these years."

"For what?"

"Half of what you gain. As fair payment."

I hesitated only a moment. If offered a miracle, don't quibble until it's occurred. "Agreed. Let us out."

"We'd be instantly discovered if I did so."

"Then how are we to escape?"

"Like all palaces, Jelgava is riddled with secret staircases and passageways. The wall at the end of your storeroom separates you from a tunnel leading to the kitchens. Built to aid a secret rendezvous for lovers, perhaps, or to transfer food, or as an escape route during war. From the kitchens at midnight you can slip outside unseen."

"But the cell wall is solid."

"Near the bottom you'll find a stone with loose mortar. Pry it out and make your way to the trees at the far end of the garden. I'll meet you there. If you're caught, swear that you discovered the escape hatch by yourself."

"Of course. Such a claim enhances the reputation."

The grill opened. "Use this spike to pry the stone, and if discovered before escaping, say you smuggled it down. Don't implicate me! Feel your way through the passageway and don't hesitate. Now, before the Prussians come for you."

"Wait! Are there sentries outside?"

But Caleb was already trotting up the stairs.

There was no choice but to trust. I hastily went to work, using the small spike to attack the broken mortar and lever the massive stone.

"That was your brother?" Astiza asked. "How is that possible? Can good fortune be that coincidental?"

"I doubt it." I was sweating despite the cold. The leverage was awkward, and we needed to hurry. "If it's even good fortune."

"What does that mean?"

"Only that more is afoot than we know. But let's get away from Jelgava first. We don't want to be sold to One-Arm."

The stone shifted a millimeter at a time. Slowly I wiggled it just free enough to seize the edges and pull, dragging the rock into our cell. A puff of air chilled us.

"You made a hole, Papa," Harry said.

"Me and your uncle." How odd to say that.

I peered through the opening. Pitch black. I tucked the spike in my waist just as we heard the tread of footsteps. Men were descending. Astiza went to the grill and listened.

"Von Bonin," she whispered.

CHAPTER 13

"Quickly!" I pushed Harry. "We're right behind."

Astiza tore her skirt while squeezing through, and getting my shoulders into the secret passageway was like stuffing and pulling a cork. I wriggled just as the Prussians were unlocking our prison door. The tunnel was bigger once I got through the wall. I wormed around and pulled the stone to stopper our escape hole.

The cell door squealed as it opened, threads of light piercing the stone's edges. I pressed my face to the crevices to hear.

"Have they been moved?" Von Bonin asked.

"They're gone!" said a guard who was not my brother, announcing the obvious. "But it's impossible!"

"Is this some joke? Is Louis cheating me?"

"Go, go," I hissed to wife and son. "Feel your way!"

"It looks as if they've escaped," the guard said.

"Would you be so kind as to tell me how, imbecile? And where?"

"Perhaps someone let them go."

"Perhaps that someone was you, muttonhead?"

"No, no, I locked them in. No one has seen them leave.

They couldn't get through the palace." There was a puzzled silence. Then, "Look, mortar. They moved a stone! Maybe you can follow."

Von Bonin took a step, studied the wall, and hesitated. "Crawl in the dark with one hand and one eye, offering myself for ambush? This is your plan?"

"To follow ..."

"Where does the passageway go?"

"The storerooms? The kitchens? Who knows?"

"*Gott im Himmel,* you're a dumbkin. We're in a race." And I heard the door bang and boots thump as Von Bonin dashed back up the stairs.

I scrambled after my family on hands and knees. "We have to get out ahead of the German. Harry, go as fast as you can!"

"Something ran across my hands, Papa."

"Then crawl back over it. Go, go!"

We scrambled forward, the passageway turning once, and then turning again. "Stairs," Harry finally reported. "It's bigger here."

"Let me go first." I squeezed by and felt my way up spiral stone steps. There was a door, bolted on our side and not the other. I slid the bolt free and peeked out. A single candle cast wavering light in a deserted pantry. We crept into a storeroom with a brick barrel roof. Shadowy hanks of meat hung from ceiling hooks. Wine and beer barrels were stacked horizontally. Flour and pickle barrels sat upright and jugs crowded crude shelves. The cooks and bakers were asleep. Caleb had timed our reunion to avoid them.

"Just minutes to sneak clear," I warned.

We ventured into the main kitchen. The stove fires were banked and the copper pans hung neatly. The floor was still damp from the day's final mopping. Somewhere would be an outside door. The finger to my lips was unnecessary. Astiza and Harry crept like cats.

"A door might be guarded," Astiza whispered. "Look: A chute for wood and coal." She pointed towards the shadowy far end of the kitchen, where a ramp led to a hatch that must give access to a supply courtyard. Yet even as she gestured there was a crash of a door flung violently open on a landing above, and the slap of boots as someone hurriedly descended. Von Bonin! We had to hide until he gave up and looked elsewhere. Interestingly, we'd not heard a general alarm. He wanted to hunt us down alone.

Had he not paid Louis? Who was cheating whom?

There were several hutches holding food, china, and tablecloths. The last, the size of an armoire, was empty enough to barely fit the Gage family. We crammed inside and I squeezed the doors shut with my fingers, peeking through the joint.

Steps cautiously approached. Yes, it was the accursed Prussian. Von Bonin was breathing hard, his one good eye peering like a telescope, trying to guess which way we might have gone while being alert to ambush. He aimed his prosthetic arm as he rotated his body, as if pointing to a distant horizon.

"Gage? I've run you to earth, haven't I?" The words echoed in the empty kitchen. He hesitated, not at all certain we were really there.

We held our breath.

"I sense you, American. I can smell you, I think."

He turned a full circle, examining the room.

I could burst out to try to tackle him, but had nothing but the crude spike.

"Come, save your family. Let's talk."

I risked a shallow breath, but felt he could hear the pounding of my blood. A few more seconds silence …

Then—thump.

Harry's foot bumped the side of our cubby.

Von Bonin cocked his head like a bird. Astiza put her hand over our son's mouth and I gripped his ankles.

It was too late.

"Ah, the mouse." The Prussian slowly advanced on our cabinet as his scowl began giving way to a grin. "Gage? I expected your Judas servant would dispatch you, since Gregor took his thirty pieces of silver. But someone murdered him instead and blamed it on you. Well, no matter. Have you packed yourself for delivery?"

He reached with his good arm to open the hutch and then thought better of it. What if I sprang?

He aimed with his stump, the muzzle hole looking like a cannon, but didn't fire. A shot would bring others running and he wanted the Grunwald swords for himself. Instead, the wicked blade snapped out.

"But we should shake hands first, I think. Unless you surrender."

We said nothing.

The hutch was cheaply made, its door thin birch. Von Bonin paused just a moment, savoring our suspected helplessness, and then lunged. With a grunt he rammed the blade into the cabinet, shoving through the joint where the doors met. I pushed Astiza and Harry to one side and I leaned to the other, so the short sword squealed between us. We all tried not to gasp. A thread of light picked out the sharp edge.

Von Bonin paused just a moment and then wrenched his blade back out and checked for blood. Nothing.

"This is a game, yes?"

He stabbed again, harder this time, smashing the wood in the middle of the door on my side of our hiding place. I twisted just enough. The steel sliced my shirt, licking my skin and drawing blood. The blade was thin enough to quiver from the impact. "Yes, I will whittle."

The English have phrases for men like the Prussian: Mad as a March hare and savage as a meat ax.

He yanked his prosthesis back and inspected it. "I felt something, American. Do you wish to come out, or will you have your family oil my appendage first? A little lubrication from your flesh?"

Von Bonin slammed the blade in a third time, this time piercing the other door. It came within a whisker of my wife's breast, and a hand's width of my son's eye.

That was enough.

I kicked hard as a mule behind me, splintering the cabinet's back. Astiza squeezed Harry, who had begun bawling.

"Ho! Yes, you finally say hello? So I say hello back." And he pulled and rammed again, through the thicker wood at the door's edge, the board splintering and Harry yelling from behind Astiza's hand.

"No, still shy?"

Von Bonin leaned backward to pull the blade out, but the thicker wood clung. He pulled to unstick it, slightly tipping the hutch toward him. So I kicked again, roared "Forward!" and pushed the cabinet away from the stone behind us with all the force I could muster. In throwing my weight at Von Bonin, Astiza and Harry were toppled to do the same. The hutch leaned, the Prussian roared a curse as his trapped prosthesis twisted, and then the armoire crashed on top of him. There was a twang as his sword snapped and Von Bonin screamed as the device ground against his amputation. Now its gun did go off, the report dampened as he shot into the wood, narrowly missing us. I bucked up and down to slam the doors on him, listening to him groan in pain, and then thrust upward with my torso, breaking the back of the cabinet to smithereens. It was like bursting the ice in a river, or lurching out of a casket. Astiza came up too, pulling Harry with her, all of us balanced on the ruins of the hutch and the prone Prussian. Von Bonin had gone quiet. Was he dead?

I snatched the spike from my waist to make sure.

Astiza grabbed my arm. "If you kill him, the pursuit from the other Prussians will be relentless. He's finished, and his failure will ruin him in Berlin. Let's get the swords to Poland."

Shouts from above. Guards had heard the shot. I hesitated.

"Ethan, we've no time! He's more crippled than ever. We have to get out of here."

We heard a stampede above, pounding feet and clanging weapons. People were coming down the kitchen stairs.

"Damnation," I muttered.

"No profanity in front of our son. No murder, either."

So we kicked free of the broken hutch and dashed for the chute. Up we climbed, dirty in moments, and threw back its outside door to crawl into snow. I jammed the spike beneath the hatch handles to lock it shut.

It was freezing outside and we had no coats. I glanced for sentries but saw none. The soldiers were rushing to the clamor in the kitchen, I guessed.

We crept along a wall. Behind, a bullet punched through the hatch to no effect. New movement caught my eye and I watched a sleigh at the other end of the estate race for a bridge that led from the island toward the main highway, soldiers running after it, its driver lashing the reins. Who the devil was that?

Ahead were the trees. I was about to sprint when Astiza stopped me with her hand, her voice insistent.

"You and your brother collide?" she whispered. "It's either magic or conspiracy. Can we trust him?"

"Everyone tells me not to trust. Remember?" I kissed her. "But now we have no choice." Then we rushed across the gardens, feeling hideously exposed. No one shouted.

I looked back just once. The palace loomed cold and seemingly watchful. There were muffled shouts. Candles and lamps passed by windows. Doors opened and slammed. But the activity was concentrated on the far side of the palace where I'd seen the sleigh. For a moment, at least, we'd escaped notice. I looked at our tracks and gave a silent prayer for more snow.

The grove of pines we ran to was dark as tar. We stopped, uncertain what to do next.

A voice hissed. "Here, brother! You look underdressed!" Caleb met us with coats, hats, and mittens, which helped overcome our doubts. "Did you have any trouble?"

"Von Bonin discovered we were missing and tried to stop us in the kitchens. Something fell on him."

My brother gave just the faintest of smiles. "Will he be getting up?"

"Not for a while. He was disarmed. Literally."

"Ah. A Gage handshake."

Caleb had brought knapsacks with food and a device I'd never tried—skis. These were skinny wooden boards nearly nine feet in length, upturned and pointed at the front, and cambered so that they arched where one put the foot. A leather strap held the toe of a boot. I'd seen a few of these odd devices when crossing the Alps, but never had used one.

"The Swedish army can cross a snowy forest in winter faster than a grenadier can march it in summer," Caleb said. "Here, wooden poles to help balance."

"We don't know how to ski."

"If you can walk, you'll learn. I brought short ones for your son. It's hard work at first, but with practice you'll glide."

"You can teach us in ten minutes?"

"Or ten days."

"You're coming with us? What about King Louis?"

"I suspect I've ended my employment at Jelgava. And I've always envied the stories of my adventurous brother and his fabulous treasures. Though why you haven't retired to a castle, I don't understand."

"It's Greek tragedy. I keep trying to rectify our fortunes."

"And your plan to do so now, Ethan?"

"By completing a mission to Poland and gaining a title."

"A noble Gage?" He laughed. "A contradiction, I suspect. But, let's see how far we can get you toward your goal. We've a head start. I recruited a disgruntled servant who was planning to quit anyway, and helped him steal a sleigh to drive west toward his Dutch homeland. Any pursuit should follow. The man's a gambler, like you, and betting he can outrun royalist pursuit long enough to sell the vehicle, pocket the proceeds, and start anew."

"Caleb, you've already risked too much," Astiza warned. "It's extraordinary that you and Ethan have had this rendezvous. But you face ever-greater danger if you come with us. We're fugitives, with contraband that powerful people desire."

"Which means, Madame Gage, that you have no chance without my expert help." He broadly bowed, the gesture waist deep. "I think your family's problem is that you always find yourselves alone. Well, now you have a brother, considerably more handsome and wise than wretched Ethan." He grinned at her for a fraction more than necessary, and I noted that fraction. My wife is very pretty, and Caleb and I have had a difficult history. What was it that he really wanted?

"You're not very wise if you accompany my wretched husband," she quipped in return.

"Brave, then. Desperate. Greedy. I'm betting he'll lead me to riches."

"And lose them when found." Her laugh caught because we were so weary and frightened. The banter was release.

"Your demand for half our reward is certainly bold," I said, reminding them how fraught this partnership was.

Caleb clapped me on the shoulder. "All right, I'm neither handsome, wise, nor brave. Just curious, little brother. I've been a drifter my entire life and now fate has given me purpose. What's this contraband Astiza speaks of?"

"Relics I've hidden across the river. We need to get them to Poland. They aren't precious themselves, but apparently they have symbolic value to certain rich people."

"God bless the eccentricity of the wealthy! There's no time to waste; shoulder your gear. Harry can ride on my back for now while you two learn the skis. When we get some distance I'll teach him, too."

Caleb had a musket slung on his back. "Is there another gun?"

"Didn't think to bring one, brother."

The hell he didn't.

"You don't care where we're going?" my wife asked him.

"I care that it prove interesting. I care that I do something good for once in my vagabond life. I care that I, a man without a family, has by miracle found one." He knelt in the snow. "So let me strap you in, Astiza. We'll ski to this secret cache of yours and into the forest beyond. I smell more snow and by dawn it will cover our tracks. We'll have all of Latvia and Poland to hide in."

"You leave Louis so readily?" I asked. "Without your pay?"

"Well, payday was two days ago. I borrowed a little more from a guard strongbox, and have another patron in France who promises to pay still more. I'm as mercenary as you, brother, and keep track of accounts. The real reason I'm volunteering is that I was never really employed by Louis XVIII."

"What do you mean? You were his sergeant-of-arms."

"While working, in secret, for Napoleon Bonaparte."

CHAPTER 14

Astiza

I'd married a man, not his family. Ethan had spoken very little about his relations. Now his brother had materialized in the unlikeliest of places and saved us in the timeliest of ways. I was intrigued. I was charmed. I was wary.

Caleb had been a sailor, and like a ship navigating at sea he used a compass to steer us a southern course from Jelgava toward Czartoryski's ancestral home at Pulawy, between Warsaw and Lublin. This was a journey of nearly four hundred miles as the crow flies, crossing several rivers. It seemed immensely longer as we wound through woods, wintry fields, and frozen lakes. A modern coach or sleigh can race as fast as nine miles each hour. We were lucky at first to manage one.

Fearful of pursuit, we didn't seek a cabin the first few evenings lest a peasant betray us to Louis or Von Bonin. The initial night we napped briefly in a shallow cave, and the next

I lay with Harry in a hollow log. The men took turns standing sentry. It was too cold to sleep soundly and our rest was ragged.

During the day we struggled to ski. Initially Caleb tied Horus onto his back alongside his musket, but this was exhausting and our son was eager to learn. In short order he was skiing better than his parents. Caleb betrayed the impatience of the amateur teacher as Ethan and I labored to master the unwieldy planks of wood, but he won me over by being encouraging to Horus. "Right, lad, we won't leave you behind. Here, a slope to slip down! That's my boy! The grace of a Gage, eh, Ethan?"

Yet the harder Caleb worked to win our trust, the more cautious Ethan seemed. We still weren't certain who our friends and enemies were. All we could do was run.

The first week of travel took us less than a sixth of the way to Pulawy. Yet we slowly gained skill, and exertion shoved aside worry. In time, skiing was fun. Any dip let us glide as if getting a push from angels. We ascended hills by crisscrossing their slope. The quiet of our swish through barren woods made us as furtive as deer. There was peace in schussing far away from schemers. Each mile away from Russians and Prussians lifted my heart. Each evening campfire promised hope.

Winter was also slowly loosening its grip, the sun climbing noticeably higher and the snow softening. We complained good-naturedly about its increasing stickiness.

So why did I feel so apprehensive? The long nights still squeezed. More importantly my foresight came unbidden, a premonition that our trials were just beginning. The brothers had some kind of history. We'd once more escaped, but to what?

"Did Napoleon order you to adopt us, Caleb?" I asked.

"He predicted that you'd adopt me, Madame."

"But how did he know we'd meet?"

"Because the French work with Czartoryski."

"Who is on who's side?"

"It is a contra dance, with multiple partners."

Caleb is nearly as tall as Ethan and thicker, with broad shoulders and sturdy arms, his torso hard as a saddle and his hands callused. He moves without wasted motion, and seems as inexhaustible as a dray horse. Pirates would pick him as captain. Women would be intrigued. Ethan had more drawing room charm, but Caleb has the rugged cheer of a mercenary. He skied off periodically to hunt game and "liberate" provisions from rich manor houses, his cocky manner that of a merry robber. In fact, my new brother-in-law was so hearty that he left us wondering how much of his manner was natural and how much was acted.

By the time we consumed the week's provisions that Caleb had brought, our guide judged us far enough from Jelgava for him to risk buying provisions from strangers. He also used his money to pay for us to stay in cabins. The peasants were wary of his musket but accepted vague explanations that we were peddlers returning from a trade mission to Riga. They prudently bit our French coins before accepting them.

After two weeks with no sign of pursuit we purchased a farmer's mule and wood sledge, the four of us barely squeezing onto the small sleigh. We paid for the vehicle with all but one pair of our skis, Caleb keeping his pair for hunting or emergencies. When even these proved awkward, he left them propped in the crook of a tree "for whoever can use them."

It would only be much later that I realized the ski tips came together to form an arrow, in the direction we were taking.

With the sledge we made better time, traveling south along the eastern bank of the Nieman before finally crossing the river into Podlesia. Then the spring thaw truly hit and the sleigh grounded like a ship on a lowering tide. The world became a pinto pattern of white and brown, the mud as wet as a mouth. Brush swelled so red that it looked as if blood beat within every twig. We traded the sledge for more food and trudged by foot, Harry riding the mule. I joined him at times, taking a break from muck that added a pound to each of our ankles. Then I'd slide down and slog with the men to give the beast a rest.

As the world continued to warm, the soil dried and hardened. We crossed the Narew and then came to the Bug River, and there sold the mule and took a proper stagecoach into what had once been Poland. The vehicle still bogged down a dozen times, requiring the passengers to help push, but we felt we were flying.

"We've escaped our enemies," Caleb announced.

"And are nearing friends," Ethan promised.

Poland is mostly flat, each log village an island in a lake of fields. The crops in turn are surrounded by forest. Suddenly every field was being plowed, and every tree was gauzy green. Spring had come in a moment.

Wealth was the neighbor to poverty in this landscape. The grand estates were archipelagos of self-contained prosperity, each with barns, orchards, grain silos, cattle, bakeries, breweries, pigsties, and chicken coops. The peasant towns next door had rude cabins along a single muddy street, a wooden church or synagogue anchoring each hamlet.

"I learned in Jelgava that most of Europe's Jews live in Poland," Caleb informed us as we rode along. "King Casimir granted the Golden Freedoms in return for Jews taking the most despised work, which was banking and tax collection. They make up a tenth of the population, and pay double taxes for their faith."

"Some freedom," I said. "Golden fetters, it sounds like to me."

"Aristocrats and burghers are another tenth. The Christian peasants who make up the remainder are a mix from a hundred invasions: Avars, Bulgars, Huns. You'll still find Tartars from the Mongol empire. Poland is a crossroads of the world, like Constantinople."

Ethan nodded. "Yet it has identity and soul, Czartoryski said. Roots. Being."

"Yes. Stubborn as Scots, proud as Gascons, persistent as the Irish, and as independent as the Swiss. Each conquest and partition simply makes Poles long all the more for their own country. Which is why Napoleon sent me here. Sent *you* here, Ethan. We're part of his plan."

"Not me, brother. I've escaped the Corsican's clutches and am working for Czartoryski now. Or rather, *with* Czartoryski. I'm my own man."

"And who is Czartoryski working for? Tsar Alexander, yes, but he also has feelers to Napoleon, to Kosciusko in Paris, to Jefferson, to Talleyrand, and to the Pope in Rome. We're ants on their maps."

"I want to get off their maps entirely," I told the men. "Deliver the swords, accept whatever fee Czartoryski's mother deigns to grant, and leave the continent. To Egypt. America. The South Sea isles."

"And give up our title?" Ethan quipped, but the question was not really a light one.

"Yes," I said firmly. "It would come with a catch like those Golden Freedoms."

"We have to satisfy Napoleon to get off his map," Caleb said. "Once we do that, we don't have to go far. Spain, perhaps. Good wine. Better women."

"Neither of which entice this female, brother-in-law. And doesn't Bonaparte have his fingers into Spain, as well?"

"We'll follow opportunity, then. Circumstance. Serendipity, Astiza. Wherever the wind blows, or your fortune-telling takes us."

"Does serendipity explain the remarkable coincidence that brought two long-lost brothers together?"

"That wasn't coincidence at all. I was smuggling from Sweden to Britain and caught by a French frigate. After two months in prison I was brought to a minister named Dacre who said the emperor, who notices everything, had taken note of my last name. The French determined that I was related to a rather more infamous brother who'd disappeared in Bohemia and resurfaced in St. Petersburg. A mischief-maker but useful, they said of Ethan Gage, with a lovely wife and a precocious child. I was offered my freedom in exchange for arranging to meet this gypsy family in Jelgava and offering them help. To do so, I posed as Caleb Ruston and hired on with the exiled Louis."

"Quite a gamble," Ethan said. "Jelgava is four hundred miles from St. Petersburg. How could you or Napoleon know we'd fetch up there?"

"Because you'd be sent by Adam Czartoryski, who bets on

France to reconstitute Poland. Bonaparte knows all about the swords. So Napoleon allied with the Russian foreign minister to enlist wayward treasure hunter Ethan Gage to retrieve patriotic relics and take them to Czartoryski's ancestral home. With my help, of course, for the mere price of half of any reward you receive."

"That suggests he knew my theft would be discovered."

"Ask your foreign minister friend about that."

"And why would the infamous Ethan Gage need his long-lost brother's help?" I asked Caleb. "Adam told us we'd get Louis's help at Jelgava."

"Czartoryski misled you."

"Lied, you mean," I said, glancing at Ethan.

"Perhaps I should say that Czartoryski actually led you," Caleb corrected. "He always planned that you would go to Pulawy, knew Jelgava was halfway to that goal, and knew that Louis trusts no one, and has no interest in Poland or any cause but his own. So Czartoryski sent you to meet me."

"Couldn't he have said so? Couldn't you, when we met on the palace lawn?"

"Of course not. First, my men would recognize me as a fraud and traitor, a Bonapartist in the home of the royalist heir. Second, Ethan wouldn't necessarily trust my help, given past estrangement. Third, I wasn't certain that Ethan was truly Ethan, not after nearly a quarter century. You could have been a trap. When Lothar Von Bonin alerted Louis that refugee Americans might have valuable relics, it was I who suggested your imprisonment, giving me the opportunity to make sure your husband was really Ethan Gage. Now, if I help deliver your contraband to Pulawy and report to Paris on the weaknesses of Louis, I confirm my freedom and win reward. Instead of French prison, I make my fortune!"

"You're as ludicrously optimistic as I am," Ethan said.

"Both of us have half-luck, brother. Combined, we might become fully lucky. Fortune will finally shine on the Gage brothers!" He grinned, as raffish and handsome as my husband.

Caleb's rationale didn't fully convince me. Czartoryski's scheme had worked, but just barely. There was another move in this chess game, a hidden strategy, and it might put us in peril. Why had Caleb vanished from Ethan's life? What did he really want now?

So I waited until Ethan and I were alone, Caleb playing with Horus, and broached the past that my husband was so reluctant to talk about.

"First we find your brother in the unlikeliest of places and then he performs like our protector," I said. "A man who announces he's also Napoleon's spy, secretly allied with your mentor Czartoryski. A minister who neglected to mention Caleb at all."

"Convenient on all counts," Ethan agreed.

"You share my misgivings, husband?"

"Only that we're guided, lovely wife, by a privateer who demands half our reward. Which means he's as mercenary as I am."

"Neither of you is really a mercenary. Opportunists, perhaps."

"Yes. Independent contractors."

"After a palace that recedes like a rainbow."

"I'm sorry, Astiza. I thought us so close to triumph in St. Petersburg and here we are on the road again, risking all, with a brother who indeed seems suspiciously convenient. It's Caleb all right, but I hope this ends at Pulawy."

"He's gotten us this far. He's good with Harry."

"Yes, the favorite uncle." We could see that Caleb had picked out stones for a little game of marbles with our son. "I'll admit he's more competent than I remember, but then he was just nineteen when he ran away to join a privateer during the American Revolution. We all grow up, even me, and Caleb is a man's man. Perhaps blood truly is thicker than water."

"Perhaps?"

He sighed. "A brother whom I thought would never tolerate me again, let alone rescue."

"Never?"

"Caleb and I have a history, Astiza. My fault, not his."

"You didn't get along?"

"We got along very well, until we didn't. That made the falling out more painful. Then he disappeared before I could apologize and he could forgive. And now he's back but not talking about it. Which is why I feel as uneasy as you do."

"Gracious, Ethan, what did you do?"

"Broke his heart. You'll note he has no wife, and no home."

"His life is tumultuous."

"My doing."

Clearly there was more going on here than treasure hunting. "I think you'd better confide in me, husband. What's our new fellowship really about?"

My husband looked at Caleb chasing Horus with a hearty laugh, pretending to be a bull. "Many years ago Caleb fell in love with a beautiful Philadelphia girl a few years younger than him, and thus very close to my own age. Everyone noticed her joyous personality. Every lad was smitten. And when our father came back wounded from the Battle of Princeton and announced it was time to put his affairs in order, he decreed that Caleb would inherit the business, thus giving the eldest son the means to ask for Lizzie Gaswick's hand. Papa's condition was that Caleb not join the revolutionary army, lest he be killed. The implication to me was that I and my younger brother, Erasmus, were more acceptable cannon fodder."

"Ethan, no. Your father was simply being prudent."

"Of course he was. I took offense where none was intended. The truth is that my brother was for the most part smarter, stronger, more agile, and better liked than I was. My father's sensible plan made me insensibly jealous. I was no stranger to trouble, or women. I'd been sent to a college called Harvard but studied gambling and drinking more than the classics. So I inexplicably took it into my adolescent head to seduce Caleb's fiancé. Lizzie turned out to be easily tempted, and easily made pregnant. Her family was infuriated. Mine was embarrassed. Gaswick fury could hurt the family business. So money was paid and I was hurriedly shipped to Paris to be an intern to the aging Benjamin Franklin, whom my father knew from Philadelphia business circles. Lizzie brought the baby to term with distant relatives. And my anguished brother defied my father and went to sea as a privateer. We heard nothing of his fate. As a result, my father lost two sons, me to Europe and Caleb to the sea."

I knew Ethan was by nature an exile and outsider, but this gave me new insight as to why. He carried more guilt than I'd known. "So you have another child?" He'd never confided this.

"I suppose. An adult by now."

"You don't know?"

"I was in Paris, trying to forget the entire catastrophe. I reasoned years later that plunging back into Lizzie's life would be no favor. Nor was I ready to be a good father. I'm not proud of any of this."

"You don't know if it was a boy or a girl?"

"No. I never inquired, and no one ever wrote. You're my family now."

"You didn't write Caleb?"

"I didn't know where he was. I finally assumed him dead. I suspected that I'd hurt him more deeply than I'd initially imagined. He's tender beneath the bluster. I had thought love an infatuation that passed like the weather, and that satisfying lust was as necessary as breathing. I thought my sin was small. The girl was willing, and my brother would still inherit her and the business. Such cynicism! But Caleb truly loved her. And fled in humiliation. Now he's saved us without uttering a single bitter word. So yes, I wonder."

"Perhaps he's long since forgiven you. Perhaps this is your opportunity to do penance with partnership."

"Perhaps. And perhaps he has in mind a second price."

"What would he demand?"

His intense look surprised me. "What prize indeed? Be careful, Astiza."

So now our fellowship seemed dangerous.

At the same time, I wondered if old guilt was exaggerating Ethan's fear. Caleb was careful not to be flirtatious. He showed no sign of animosity toward my husband or son. Ethan might have balked at the Jelgava rendezvous if told of Caleb's presence there, so Czartoryski's secrecy seemed understandable to me. Caleb's motives seemed plausible.

But it didn't help that the men wouldn't talk it out, which I'm convinced is the cause of half the troubles in the world. They joked, jostled, and competed. Caleb challenged my husband to a shooting match with his musket, which might have been an opportunity to do accidental mischief. But he was genuinely congratulatory when Ethan won.

"I thought your reputation was inflated, brother. It's not."

Ethan had been the first to shatter a jug. "I need a rifle to hit from a real distance. But your musket shoots fairer than most."

"Fairer for you than for me."

"Aye. We should have bet."

"The gun is a pretty piece I stole from the household of fat King Louis, who will howl when he finds it missing. So now let me get even with swords. I've fenced with the cutlass." He indicated the wrapped Grunwald weapons, demonstrating that neither Gage boy had an ounce of sense.

"Fools!" I intervened. "If you don't kill each other by accident or design, you'll break the weapons that are the entire point of our journey. Or draw attention to them if anyone comes upon your mock duel. Why are men such idiots? Who knows what examples you are putting into Horus's head?"

They pretended chagrin. "At least concede I'd have won," Caleb said to Ethan.

"You're the better man," Ethan replied. "We both know that."

Which was a step toward an apology, I thought, and Caleb gave a mock bow, adding a wink for me. "The better swordsman, and you the better shot with a remarkable wife. I envy you, brother."

Which was just the kind of compliment that could cause trouble. "I'm flattered, Caleb, but your envy is misplaced," I said. "Ethan is cursed by my female caution and sense. You're a bachelor, able to come and go as you please. I'm sure it's Ethan who envies you."

"Do you, brother?"

"A wise husband knows when to affirm and when to keep silent," my husband replied. "I'll concede only that I'll win at shooting, Caleb at fencing, and you at prudence, Astiza. And someday I hope to win a treasure worthy of my bride!" He solemnly addressed his brother. "The way to husbandly happiness, Caleb, is a happy wife."

"Yours is the voice of experience?"

"Experience hard won."

I snorted at both of them. "In that case," I announced, "you fetch the firewood, Caleb the water, and I'll be happy enough. As for treasure, I believe Franklin said that the great part of mankind's misery comes from falsely estimating the value of things. Being poor is no shame, he said, but being ashamed of it is."

"She's Athena, goddess of wisdom!" Caleb cried. "But being rich is no shame either, I suspect. Or at least I'd enjoy finding out."

And on we traveled, but my restless mind couldn't let the situation rest. As we rolled and jounced in our coach, I again aired the past. "Did you ever go from privateer to pirate, Caleb? Not that I'd condemn you for it."

"Explain to me the difference beyond a piece of paper supplied by a warring government," he replied. "But the answer is no, since I don't care for the hangman's noose. I smuggled,

I helped ships fend off pirates, and I served as a mercenary sailor in foreign navies. But most of the time I delivered fat, dull cargoes on fat, dull boats, to fat merchants in dull ports."

"You learned the cutlass?"

"I learned to use whatever comes to hand. It's a brutal world."

"Yet you don't seem gloomy."

"A waste of time. As is hate, envy, resentment, and revenge."

I looked at Ethan, since this seemed as good a closure as we could hope for. "You sound like a good Christian."

"I sound like a man from any good religion, and I've encountered a score of them. I learned the value of forgiveness the hard way, just as I sailed around the world to make sure it is truly round." He winked at Harry. "I'm not necessarily a good man, nephew. But I'm a practical one."

"Did you see any monsters?" my boy asked.

"Only the kind that wear skirts."

"I hope you weren't too badly wounded," I said drily.

"I was, Madame, but wounds scab over: There's not a girl yet who kept me from sailing, or who saved me from my own mistakes. So under French arrest I was told my only salvation was to seek my wayward brother." He laughed. "Or was that my punishment?"

"We often don't know until long after the fact," I told him. "Fate has a sense of humor. But I for one am glad we reunited. Aren't you, Ethan?"

"I'd better be. It's costing me fifty percent."

Caleb leaned forward with the grin of a horse trader. "Well put, brother. Aye, I'm sensible enough to know that no member of the Gage family tromps through a snowy wilderness without chance of reward."

"And danger," Ethan said. "I had to break into an island fortress and pretend to drown to get those swords, Caleb. Other men are willing to do just as much to get them back, I suspect."

"But now you have an ally!" He tousled the head of Horus. "And an uncle! Together we'll prevail." And then he snuck a glance at me.

There was nothing untoward in his look and yet it reinforced my unease. I've learned to trust my instincts, and instinct warned that Caleb still hadn't told us everything. Yet didn't everyone have secrets?

So why did I have trouble falling asleep that night as I picked at our conversations with my mind?

At length, however, in the alternately bright and dreary weeks in which winter gives way to spring, we finally came to Pulawy. From its village square we could see the Czartoryski palace roof, a sturdy reef amid waves of greening trees, the silver Wisla River just beyond.

Ethan sent a message. The courier returned with a carriage and orders to drive us the last mile. It was a scrubbed and breezy afternoon, birds singing, the warming sun casting lovely shadows, and at last I allowed myself hope again. Izabela Czartoryski had sent a letter.

"Come to a place of rest and safety," she wrote.

CHAPTER 15

I decided Astiza's worry about Caleb could be made irrelevant by simply arriving at our destination and delivering our cargo. Pulawy was approached on a gravel avenue through a forested park, and had the same monumentally broad shoulders as Catherine's palace outside St. Petersburg or Louis's refuge in Jelgava. The palace was in the shape of a U, its center three stories high and painted a cheery yellow. There were the usual sprawling wings, high windows, and the obligatory decorative pillars, urns, cornices, escutcheons, and statues. In front was a rectangular reflecting pool big enough to fish in. Shrubbery was cut as upright as soldiers, cobbles were swept clean, and the pruned limbs of the nearest linden trees bent as artfully as the arms of Oriental dancers. Outbuildings included a stable, theater, barns, storehouses, servant's quarters, and an infirmary.

We descended in the arched carriageway like frontier refugees, in stained clothing and weathered hats. The swords slung in a bedroll on my back. Caleb shouldered his musket. Astiza held Harry's hand.

"Is this where we're going to live, Papa?"

"Looks like it has room."

A footman announced our arrival and after a wait of several minutes a dubious butler led us into a grand foyer and relieved us of coats, hats, and gun. Ahead was a marble staircase, the room smelling of new paint. Descending regally to greet us were two women. The elder must be Adam Czartoryski's mother Izabela, as elegant as we were begrimed. She was a slim, handsome woman of sixty with silk dress, topaz pendant, and hair pinned as erect as her torso. Accompanying was a spectacularly gorgeous young woman with eyes as vivid as the topaz and thick dark hair that fell to bare shoulders. A daughter? The two didn't resemble each other. Izabela had the same strong face as her son, her nose long and straight, her smile firm, her chin firmer, and her eyes shrewd. She embodied authority and sophistication. The younger woman had a rounder face, delicate nose, and the voluptuous body that men conjure in fantasies. Caleb stiffened like a hunting dog. I tried not to.

Izabela paused three steps high until we remembered to bow. Then she addressed us in French with fluency honed by what Adam had told me had been several years in Paris. "*Bonjour*, Ethan Gage! My son told me to be on the lookout for a band of determined wanderers."

"Princess Czartoryski," I replied. Again, 'princess' did not mean daughter of a king, but was rather an honorific for a powerful noblewoman. "Thank you for receiving us. I bring you greetings from your son Adam in St. Petersburg, as well as a package he entrusted us to deliver."

"At great peril to you and your family, I understand. Adam wrote me about your mission and we've been anxious about your fate. And here you are, by the grace of God whom still blesses Poland. I'll try to make your relics as useful to my country as they were troublesome to you. You've the character of Washington, Monsieur Gage, to have returned our heritage so gallantly."

Well, I liked that. Izabela had rare good judgment, I decided, and probably *had* been quite the beauty in her day. "Adam befriended my family. We've tried to return the favor. And we hope to continue our partnership." Couldn't hurt to hint at the expectation of reward. Napoleon had cynically said to promise everything and deliver nothing, so I was gambling such advice hadn't infected the Czartoryskis.

"You've assembled a curious fellowship."

"My family, princess. This is my wife Astiza, my son, and my brother Caleb."

"I understand that you're the guiding angel, Caleb, guarding the Gage family with gun and skill."

"No one has mistaken me for an angel before, princess. And I ask your pardon for arriving armed. All our possessions are in our hands or on our back."

"Because you're Spartans! And please, call me Izabela. What's the name of our littlest soldier?"

"This is my son Horus," Astiza said. "Ethan calls him Harry."

"Named for the falcon god?"

My wife was pleased at the recognition. "Yes. I'm from Egypt."

"That's a pretty lady," my son said, pointing past Izabela.

Izabela glanced at her companion. "Indeed she is: Almost as pretty as your mother, young Horus. This is Countess

Marie Walewska, married to Count Colonna-Walewska. She's visiting for a few weeks and seems to find this old woman's company tolerable."

"I find you inspirational, Izabela," Marie said in a pleasantly melodious voice. "And instructive." Her buoyant gaze was intoxicating, and I felt Astiza imperceptibly stir at my equally imperceptible appreciation, demonstrating just how married we were. But Marie was very young and very married and, like a new flower, was something to admire, not pick. Besides, this girl was still a promise; my wife is beauty realized. Which was such a good line that I thought I'd try it that night.

Izabela smiled indulgently at her guest. "Marie is only nineteen, appreciates the flattery of children, and is not yet entirely skeptical of her elders. Still, it's good to have admirers, is it not, Monsieur Gage?"

"I'd assume so. My own family knows me far too well to play that role. I get the flattery I deserve, which means it's heavily rationed."

"You simply don't look like Marie, Izabela, or Astiza, little brother," Caleb said cheerfully.

"Adam wrote that you two brothers were reunited after long separation," Izabela said.

"Yes. And your son apparently had a role in our reunion. Caleb rescued us from imprisonment by Louis, the French king-in-waiting."

"Such adventure! Life is full of coincidence, is it not?"

"And coincidence is sometimes a sign of fate," Astiza said.

"Do you think so?" Izabela looked keenly at my wife.

"Or necessity," Caleb said. "My brother is in need of frequent rescue."

"But only because he undertakes astounding missions," Izabela said. "And you, Caleb, have the look of an able rescuer. A hunter, perhaps. A soldier. A sea captain. And Ethan is a protégé of Franklin. Did you know that I met the American philosopher in Paris in 1772? Rousseau and Voltaire as well. So long ago, and yet I remember them as if it were yesterday. That's a prerogative of age, I'm afraid."

"I was Franklin's apprentice late in his life," I said. "And I've been a friend of Jefferson, and a friend and enemy of Napoleon, depending on your preference."

"I haven't decided whether to admire that man or fear him."

"It's reasonable to do both."

"You know the French emperor, Monsieur?" Marie asked me. Like everyone in Europe, she was curious about Bonaparte. And he, rogue that he was, would almost certainly be interested in her.

"Better than I might wish, Lady Walewska."

"As you know," Izabela told her, "We hope Bonaparte can be persuaded to reconstitute Poland, should his victories continue."

"Perhaps I'll have a chance to ask him," Marie said boldly.

Izabela nodded sagely, probably remembering her own diplomacy in bed. "Perhaps you shall. We see Polish resurrection as the key to peace in Europe. Isn't this so, Ethan?"

"So Adam explained. Then we're all a fellowship, princess—Izabela—with you and Marie our newest members."

"Very good! Now: My membership dues will be to give you a roof over your heads tonight. Marie's will be to charm you, which is her habit. In return, where is your contribution to the cause of Polish independence?"

"Here." I unslung the bedroll containing the old swords, rested the hilts on the floor, and began to untie them.

"Not yet, my new American friend, not yet. Anticipation is as delicious as consummation, and revelation must be precisely timed. The antiquities will be unveiled tomorrow. Right now, let's have you bathe, rest, and dine this evening. Would you like supper, Harry?"

"Yes, Princess," he said gravely. "You have a big house."

She laughed. "I had to rebuild it after a fire, so you'll find everything very new. Can you smell the paint?"

"It smells like Mama's workshop."

"And what would you like to see in my big house?"

"Supper."

She clapped in delight. "I love the honesty and wisdom of children! And so you shall, sensible boy. In the meantime, I think my footman can find you a candy." As if by magic, a servant came forward with a sweet on a silver platter. This won instant loyalty from my son, who chewed like a beaver.

"Ethan, we'll wait until morning to inspect what you've brought, when I'll show off a surprise of my own. Tonight we can gossip and plot. We follow the norms here. Coffee at nine in the morning, dinner at 1:30, tea at six and supper at 9:30. Oskar and Lena will find you some clothes."

"Plot what?" I've had enough of those for a lifetime.

"The uses of Napoleon." Her look was as conspiratorial as her son's.

Marie spoke up. "Is he as handsome as we've heard?"

"He has the dash and vigor of a thirty-six-year-old soldier," I said.

"My husband is almost eighty." She said this blithely, as

if it was the most common thing in the world. Four times her age!

"Marie made a political union," Izabela explained.

"We're fond of each other," the girl added.

No wonder this Walewska was interested in the virile new master of Europe. "Bonaparte's power gives him allure," I said. "He has magnetism, which made me think of using that electrical phenomena to fetch what I've brought. But Napoleon's looks are something for women to judge. What do you think, Astiza?"

"Handsome, but beginning to put on weight. Intense. As frightening as he is fascinating. Quite brilliant. He's really extraordinary in so many ways, and because of his role he's always on stage, delivering like a performer. I urge you to meet him should he ever march to Poland, Lady Walewska, but beware. He'll use you at least as much as you try to use him."

She nodded. "Intriguing. And how extraordinary his victories!"

"On the battlefield and in the bed," I noted drily.

Marie wasn't insulted. She was an opportunist like the rest of us.

With Harry listening, my wife changed the subject. "What's this surprise you promise to show us tomorrow?" she asked Izabela.

"If I tell you it spoils the surprise, does it not?" She winked at Harry.

"I like surprises," he said. "Like candy."

"We'll get you more, with Mama's permission. But my surprise for tomorrow, Horus, is a grown-up secret, and grown-ups are poor at keeping them, so I might as well tell your mother right now. Don't you think?"

"Are you really a princess?"

"Yes, but I'm more of a scholar and a patriot. I've built a Temple of Sibyl, named for the prophetic women of the past. I'm quite proud of it. I understand you're something of a sibyl yourself, Astiza."

"I've read The Tarot and once encountered a mechanical oracle," my wife said. "I don't claim to be a true seer. If I were, my family could avoid our troubles. But sometimes fate whispers in my ear."

"My temple is dedicated to the sibyls but its design is based on the Temple of Vesta in Italy's Tivoli, built for the Roman goddess of the hearth. Ovid equated Vesta to the Earth itself. But I also like to think my temple represents Minerva, the goddess of wisdom, art, and magic. She's closest to the building's purpose."

"Minerva goes by many names," my wife said. "Athena. Isis. Freya. Sophia. All represent the insight of women."

"Best combined with the energy of men. Minerva had an owl. Do you speak to animals?"

"The trick is listening to nature, not lecturing it."

"Well said! My, what an intriguing quartet you are. I can see why Adam befriended you. Now, let my servants show you to your rooms. A hot bath first, and then supper. Caleb, we'll return your musket in the morning, but tonight you're perfectly safe at Pulawy. I've two hundred servants, adopting more than I need to give them homes after the recent wars. *Noblesse oblige*, no?"

Obligation that bought protection. Adam's mother was clearly shrewd. I bowed, Astiza curtsied, and Caleb gave a salute. "I suspect they are loyal," he said.

"You've no gun, Ethan?"

"Lost in the Neva River, I'm afraid, which is my habit. I've had guns broken, stolen, chewed, and dunked, and yet always feel naked without a rifle. I was accustomed to one in my early days on the American frontier."

"Adam reported that you're a good shot," Izabela said. "Not a hunter, he said, but a marksman."

"I don't like to shoot at animals that can't shoot back. Doesn't seem fair."

"And I don't like to shoot at men that *can* shoot back," Caleb said. "Doesn't seem safe."

"Heart and head in two brothers! Come; let me show you my house. Ignore the hods of plaster and pails of paint. Our family roots go back one hundred and fifty years and we've rebuilt this residence many times. Repairing the fire is only the latest."

The restoration was sumptuous. A game room held a billiards table. The library had bright new books, their titles gilded. A study table supported a mechanical model of the circling planets. A music room had violins, a harp, and a harpsichord. Izabela pointed to a timepiece. "That clock plays eight tunes."

"You said this was burned by the Russians?" Caleb asked.

"They accused us of supporting the Kosciuszko uprising twelve years ago, when our country was partitioned and devoured. The vengeful Russian soldiers swarmed through like maggots, taking furniture, china, silver, paintings, bronze statues, and curtains. They set fire to the rest. Adam had to swear obedience to Tsar Paul, but then found greater favor with Paul's son. Thanks to Alexander's generosity, we've repaired the damage."

"You don't hate the Russians?" Astiza asked.

"I don't hate the ignorant soldiers who burned Pulawy, but I hate their leaders for burning the idea of Poland. I'm an old woman who can't take up arms, but my revenge will be to make Pulawy a repository for the dream of Polish independence. My temple is a national museum in disguise."

"But you've gone from being looted by the Russians to having your son work for them?" Caleb clarified.

Her smile was grim. "Only so they don't come again. Haven't we all made compromises? Hope for the best and prepare for the worst. Which is why I want to show you my trophy room."

Servants swung wide a pair of heavy wooden doors and we entered what looked like an elegant armory. Oak-paneled walls were decorated with all manner of muskets and rifles, from earliest times to the present. Racked swords and pikes glinted in the angled light of a setting sun. An oriental carpet covered almost the entire floor. A banquet table occupied the room's center. On it was a blue felt cloth felt that held a breathtaking display of pistols, knives, bayonets, powder horns, and bullet molds.

"For a woman who can't take up arms, this is quite a collection," I said.

"Make your choice, Monsieur Gage. I fortify my champions."

I rotated. "Some of these are priceless."

"Oh, I hope you choose a pretty one!" Marie exclaimed. "With gold filigree and mother-of-pearl!"

I shook my head. "I understand your preference, Countess, but better to have a weapon that draws less attention. The last thing you want when stalking an enemy is to throw off light. A plain and sturdy gun is less tempting to steal and less liable to break." I studied the array. "That one, for example, looks like a frontier rifle from America."

"You've a good eye," Izabela said. "My late husband acquired it from Virginia."

"I used to have one much like it," I said, stepping close. "Often called a Pennsylvania longrifle, although they're made in other states as well. A hunting gun, but one that stood my nation in good stead during our Revolution."

"Not as elegant as some of the others," Marie objected.

"And considerably more accurate than most," I replied. "Here's the mark of the gunsmith who made it, a man called Stanwick. I've heard of him, I think. Izabela, can you spare this one?"

"I'd be devastated if you didn't take it. Your brother is welcome to choose as well."

"I'll stick with my standard infantry musket," Caleb said. "Not as good a target shooter, but quicker to load and stout enough to drive tent stakes."

Another oddity caught my eye. "Speaking of tent stakes," I said, "I yearn for another tomahawk. Something to chop and pound that doesn't misfire."

"The medieval weapon you're looking at is called a horse pick. It's a Saracen weapon the Crusaders brought back to Europe."

I picked up a slim hammer with a long curved spike behind the head, instead of a claw. The leather-wrapped handle was two feet long. About four or five pounds, I judged, and nicely balanced. "Wicked. Either end would crack a skull like an egg."

"The point pierced armor and dragged a knight from his horse," said Izabela, "The blunt head could stave in a helmet."

"It's so ugly!" objected Marie.

"And a pistol can kill at ten or twenty paces," Caleb advised.

"But this is a stake pounder." I balanced the pick in one hand and the rifle with the other. "Not a tomahawk, but close enough. You've reunited me with my country, Izabela."

She nodded. "And tomorrow you'll unveil the Grunwald Swords and reunite me with mine. Now, to your rooms."

The bedroom wing was big as an inn, She even offered Astiza and me separate rooms, which we declined. Harry's room opened off our own, and I relished the luxury of marital privacy.

Caleb was down the hall. "I trust you'll be comfortable," Izabela said to him. "And after cleaning up, may I invite you to tea in our orangery alone? I have some questions about the Baltic trade that would bore your family."

His eyes flickered from us to her. "Of course you do." Caleb bowed. "I am at your command."

CHAPTER 16

The next morning Harry was shown a playroom complete with toy wagons, balls, soldiers, dollhouses, and favored children of the staff, all of it overseen by the watchful eye of a French governess. "Horus can enjoy himself here while we visit my museum," Izabela said. "Anna reads them stories."

My son readily agreed. "I like this house!"

The rest of us set out in late morning for the newly constructed Temple of Sibyl, built a quarter-mile southeast of the palace. I once more carried the wrapped swords on my back and, at Izabela's suggestion, my new rifle. "We might spot some game." With the medieval horse pick dangling from my belt as if I was marching to a mine, I felt equipped for the apocalypse.

Caleb's musket was returned and he carried it as well. "I'll do my best to provide dinner," he said, "but it would be quite the stag to repay last night's feast."

Indeed, Czartoryski generosity had been disorienting after our recent hardships. Astiza was almost embarrassed by the evening clothes provided. "Ethan, the dress is silk and the chemise Egyptian linen. The shoes are from Paris."

"So are you, in a roundabout way. Apparently they like us."

And then long conversation over a meal that included goose, slices of tongue, beef in gravy, spring greens, winter cabbage, and maize mush. Izabela was anxious to hear all we could tell about Adam, the tsar, and Louis. Marie returned obsessively to Bonaparte, who presumably had more firepower than her eighty-year-old husband. "He seems triumphant in everything he grasps," she said.

"Certainly he's grasping," Caleb said. "But yes, he plays the game better than anyone."

"War is no game," Astiza interjected.

"Some men think it is."

"And what kind of Europe does he want to create?" Izabela asked.

"An organized one," I said.

"Meaning him in charge," Astiza elaborated.

"With the result that everyone has a claim on him," Caleb put in. "I've been a captain, and no one is more ceaselessly tormented than a commander."

"But everyone *talks* about Napoleon," said Marie.

"What good is that?"

"He's not invisible like ordinary men. He has glory."

"We all decay in the grave."

"Ideas and nations don't," said Izabela.

And so we philosophized. Then a good night's sleep, a pleasant breakfast of coffee and rolls, and now a fine spring stroll through woods and lawns to the Roman temple. Caleb and I strode in the lead while Izabela, Marie and Astiza followed a few paces behind, laughing and singing. The princess looked as intently into the woods as Caleb did, but we saw no animals besides a few flitting birds. It was a brilliant morning, the sun playing peek-a-boo with puffy clouds and the soil smelling damp and fecund. A prettier place could scarcely be imagined. The woods had been cut, pruned, and planted in the English style to create a pocket Eden.

Yet Izabela boxed our fellowship with two of her armed groundsmen in front, two more behind, and one to either side on the fringe of the lane. No wonder we saw no game. I turned to ask her about such careful escort.

"Since the Russians burned Pulawy I've made my servants into a private army," she explained. "Perhaps my caution is excessive, but does a bodyguard in these tumultuous times really surprise you, Ethan?"

"I suppose it's prudent for a lord, and brave for a princess."

"The safety of guests and their treasures is my responsibility."

"Safety from what, though?"

"Desire. Ambition. Greed."

The round Roman temple came into view, its white stone a classical poem among the trees. The structure was an elegantly simple cylinder about forty feet in diameter topped with a green copper dome. A portico of Corinthian columns surrounded this core. Broad stone steps led from the gravel lane up to double iron doors twice the height of a man. One could imagine a goddess gliding toward the place, harps singing in the mist.

"Construction began five years ago with restoration of our palace," Izabela said. "This temple is for sundered Poland, and what you've brought is key. Come, I'll show you."

The building was perched on the brow of a small hill. We

first strolled to the temple's rear and looked down the slope to the brick wall of the temple's understory. A sturdy oak door gave access to a small lawn below. "Workers and caretakers can go in and out that through that cellar," our hostess said.

"A storage room?"

"A depository for Polish memory."

The forest was thick beyond, and I appreciated its serenity. And yet even as I savored its peace I sensed movement, flickering at the periphery of my vision. I peered and saw nothing. The woods were still. Even the birds had quieted.

I put my thumb on the hammer of my rifle.

"Did you see some game?" my brother asked.

"None, which is why I'm looking." It was so hushed that I could hear the murmur of the distant river. "The birds are silent."

"Is your alertness a habit from the American frontier?" Izabela asked.

"If so, an impolite one." I released my thumb. "Don't let me break our mood. Shall we go inside? I'm ready to shed the relics on my back."

"And I'm anxious to receive them."

Back at the main entrance, two reclining lions flanked the stairs. "A gift from the tsar as reparation for the burning," said Izabela. "He intended them for the main palace but I prefer they guard my Polish museum. One tries to take every advantage, but then you already know that, don't you Ethan?"

"Franklin preached it, Napoleon practices it, but riches still slip from my grasp. Maybe that's why I'm so watchful."

"I suspect you're richer than any of us. What is life but rich experiences, and what is money but a means to live them?

If half the stories about you and your family are true, you've seen things most men can never hope to behold. Now you'll see another, as reward for your courage in St. Petersburg." She led me up the porch and took out a heavy key.

The lock was oiled and turned easily, but the double doors were massive. Her men helped push them open. We stepped into a circular room under a coffered ceiling. Light shone down from the dome's bright oculus, glazed with glass against Poland's harsh weather. The floor was marble. A frieze of bas-relief winged horses flew around the lip of the dome. Against one wall was a cavity where stairs led to the cellar below.

"This is my secret, until Napoleon liberates my country."

The rotunda's white walls held another armory, or rather a museum of Polish pride. Displayed were spears, swords, shields, armor, iron crowns, faded flags, and antique muskets. There were the famed winged breastplates of the Hussar Knights. Trophies included captured standards, pikes, bloodstained Turkish uniforms, scimitars, turbans, and spurs. Hanging like tapestries were Oriental rugs and the pelts of leopard, tiger, bear, and wolf. Drums, horns, and bugles dangled. There were royal robes, suspended gowns, and massive crucifixes. Here a bishop's miter, there a knight's war mace.

"Extraordinary," I said. "Surely you don't need two more swords."

"On the contrary. The Grunwald trophies are the most important symbols of Polish triumph that we have. What you brought back will be my museum's centerpiece. But everything else you see inspires us as well. The Turkish items date from the Polish rescue of Vienna in 1683. That sculpture of a white eagle is carved from dragon bone. This spear of Saint Maurice is claimed to be the one that finished Jesus at the Crucifixion."

There were plenty of less martial objects as well: paintings, furniture, sacramental treasures from old cathedrals, and books. Izabela pointed proudly from item to item. "That is Shakespeare's chair. The painting of the lady holding an ermine is a Da Vinci. That urn contains the ashes of El Cid. I've jewelry alleged to have been worn by Romeo's Juliet, and a crucifix tied to Abelard and Heloise."

Romeo and Juliet? Better not to question the provenance of a patron's prizes. I've followed fables myself.

"These are the memories nations are constructed from, my new friends. Leaders come and go, and laws are abstractions to most people for most of their lives. But history beats in our blood, and past battles inspire future resolve. Adam and I have collected memorabilia from Stockholm to Pompeii."

"Yes, Adam mentioned Vesuvius. Do you know that the husband of Nelson's mistress pottered about in Pompeii? I met the lady once."

"We all still long for the unity of Rome."

"Napoleon certainly does," Caleb put in. "He fancies himself Julius bloody Caesar, without the assassination."

Izabela smiled. "And we Poles need our Cleopatra." She eyed Marie. Oh yes, Mrs. Walewska would meet Napoleon.

"Bonaparte will find himself in Berlin this year, I wager," Izabela went on. "Warsaw soon after. We'll welcome the emperor with the swords captured from the Teutonic Knights. That is, if you have them, American?"

"Let the trophies make their entrance." I slung off my burden and let its fabric unroll on the floor, the swords tumbling out like Cleopatra tumbled from her carpet into the presence of Caesar. Unlike the Egyptian queen, the two blackened hackers didn't look like much.

Yet Izabela drew in her breath.

"It's truly them," whispered Marie.

"This is what all the fuss is about?" asked Caleb. "Couldn't cut a ham."

Izabela picked one up. "They're heavy." She thumbed the edge. "And still a little sharp. I think they'll cut ham better than you think, Caleb. As symbols they have enormous power."

"I'll bet they clean up well enough," I said, rather proud of my delivery. "Ready for a coronation in no time."

"Yes, we'll polish them. The vault below this rotunda holds jewels, gold, the bones of saints, and books of ancient law. The Grunwald Swords will join them until time is ripe for their unveiling. Your doughty little fellowship has nourished hope, Ethan Gage, and possibly changed history."

"All in a night's work. Although I did nearly freeze to death."

"The retrieval made you desperate fugitives." She was sympathetic.

"Even your little boy," Marie chimed in. "What a brave lad!"

"Perhaps Poland will show some gratitude," I speculated. "Nothing extravagant. A title, perhaps, if there's one to spare."

"Adam told me you should be rewarded."

"A modest castle, a summer's rest, some recompense for my brother here—I'm just thinking aloud. Whatever the local habit."

"Patience, Ethan, patience. Poland's time is near."

She reminded me of Ben Franklin's quip that every fault will be mended tomorrow, and tomorrow never comes.

"And who knows how events will turn?" she added.

Just then there was a shout from one of Izabela's groundsmen standing watch on the portico outside. He fired a musket and we heard a cry from the woods. A moment's silence and then came a blast of answering gunfire, the quiet morning suddenly exploding. Bullets rattled like hail against the stonework.

"What the devil?"

"Get inside!" Izabela shouted to her men.

Her guards sprang from their cover behind the Corinthian columns and tumbled into the rotunda as the enemy reloaded. The servants swung the great iron doors.

"Not all the way," Caleb ordered. "We'll be blind."

I peered through the slit. Soldiers in green uniforms were slipping from tree to tree, moving to surround the temple. Guns flashed, more bullets pinging and ricocheting. Gunsmoke hung like haze. One of Izabela's groundsmen came up behind me and shoved his musket out past my ear to fire blindly through the gap in the door. The report stunned me.

"Who's attacking?" Izabela demanded.

"Russians," her man answered. "They've come back."

CHAPTER 17

"Surrender what you stole!" a voice demanded in accented French.

By the hounds of hell, who was chasing us now? I lifted my own rifle through the crack in the doors, aimed at a spot between the trees where I calculated a Russian would try to dash, and fired just as he was filling my sights, dropping him. Another blaze of gunfire barked back, and I dodged behind the iron to reload. "I'm guessing at least thirty men," I said. Now I knew why the birds had gone silent. They'd spied the creeping assailants.

Caleb and Izabela's servants also got off shots, but the furious firefight was somewhat ineffectual. We were firing almost completely blind through a narrow slit, while the Russians were hitting nothing but stone and iron. The temple was stout as a bank, bullets bouncing off like raindrops.

"It's a standoff," Caleb said. "But we're trapped."

"How did they even know we were here?"

"They must have been watching for your arrival," said Izabela. "Or tracking you."

"We'd have spotted them," my brother insisted.

"Sent from St. Petersburg to intercept us," suggested Astiza. "While the Prussians chased west, Russians deduced our true destination and came here."

"Have they arrested Adam?"

"My son would never betray Poland," Izabela said.

"Well, someone did," Caleb replied.

I stepped up to shoot again. The enemy was circling toward the temple's rear where the cellar opened to that lawn. "They're making for our backdoor," I reported. "I hope it's impregnable."

"The iron sheathing has yet to arrive," Izabela said.

"Then they'll soon cut a battering ram."

"Perhaps our attacker is a rival to Adam who guessed his strategy and seeks to undermine him," Astiza speculated. "The Russians will seize the swords, denounce the Czartoryskis, and force Adam's fall from the foreign ministry. With Izabela complicit, they may burn Pulawy again."

"Perhaps Louis told the tsar we were making for Poland," Caleb said. "As a way to get his revenge for our escape."

I reloaded, requiring almost a minute to push the stubborn ball down the tight spiraling. Rifle shots can't be wasted. "And perhaps all this perhapsing is academic if we don't find a way to turn the tables."

As if to confirm, an ominous thud came from the door below. Another, and another. Boom, boom, boom. Two of the groundsmen descended to see if the wood could be reinforced.

"We can't let them pound away unmolested," Caleb said. "I'll circle outside, using the pillars as cover."

"And be killed. They'll have fine sport as you dance from column to column."

"They'll have fine sport if they get inside."

Too late. The wood began to crack and the Russians began firing blindly into the cellar. One of Izabela's men was wounded and they were forced to retreat up the stairs. Then there was a crash as the door finally burst open. We heard cries of triumph as the enemy occupied the room below.

"All right, I'll get the first one as they come up the stairs," Caleb said. "You the second, Ethan. Izabela's men next." He sounded almost cheerful at the prospect, as if enjoying the fight. "A Polish welcome."

"While they tighten their trap," I said grimly.

"We'll sell the temple dearly."

"Just fight for time and rescue," Izabela said. "They've stumbled into a trap themselves." She'd grabbed an old war horn from her trophy wall, put it to the gap in the iron doors, and blew like a Viking queen. I jumped. The blare was tremendous. The temple itself seemed to shake. "Help is coming."

Gunfire slackened in surprise. The sound from the cellar briefly stopped. Russians shouted to each other in consternation.

She blew again. And then again, like the French hero Roland at the Pass of Roncevaux. The sound echoed across her estate as a call to arms. Hearteningly, I heard hunting horns call in response.

"The entire countryside will rise," she promised, her chest heaving.

"I love your music."

"We practiced after the last invasion."

The Russian shooting began again, becoming more urgent.

"We may be the best shots," I said, "Caleb and I can man the upper door while your men defend the cellar stairs. A volley when they charge upward. Pikes for Astiza and Marie."

"I don't know how to use a pike!" Countess Walewska protested.

"You stab," Astiza instructed. "With the pointed end."

The Russian commander called out again, his voice betraying anxiety. "Give up what you've stolen, Ethan Gage! Surrender it and we'll leave you alone!" By Satan's luck, the voice was wretchedly familiar. Was it possible?

The princess sucked in breath, puffed her cheeks, and blared. The temple reverberated like a bell. She gasped for breath, face red, eyes bright, tendrils of hair plastered to her cheeks. "My estate and village can muster hundreds with guns, scythes, and pitchforks," she wheezed. "More, if the women join. The Russians have stumbled into a hornet's nest, Monsieur Gage." Sixty years old, a princess without a principality, and she could shriek like a Valkyrie. I am forever attracted to strong women. This one could spit brimstone.

Caleb and I took turns firing out the slit in the front, a game of marksmanship in which it was damnably difficult to keep score. The tree cover was thick and the Russian soldiers had gone to ground.

"I can get off two shots for every one of yours, brother," Caleb said.

"And I can hit a target twice as far."

Shots were fired from down below up the stairway, pinging into the dome. Outside, hunting horns echoed from every direction, a Polish rally that unnerved even me. The Russians were sounding desperate as they, who'd surrounded us, were being surrounded. Yet just as the tide was turning in our favor the men in the cellar stormed the stairs.

"Fire!" Izabela's groundsmen volleyed and Russians cried

and tumbled. Answering bullets came from below. One of our men fell, writhing from a leg wound. Marie yelled and hurled her pike, leaving herself empty-handed but eliciting a howl from one of our enemies. A Russian head appeared, Astiza viciously jabbed, and the man fled downstairs again. There were calls of frustration as the attackers regrouped. Then they surged once more, before the Czartoryski servants were done reloading, so some groundsmen hurled down suits of armor on top of them. "We need more guns!"

Outside, Polish reinforcements were beginning to shoot into the Russian attackers from the rear.

"This is madness!" Astiza called. "Can't we talk?"

I looked outside for the man demanding the swords. A miasma hung in the air, punctuated by muzzle flashes and the whiz and whap of bullets. How serene the pagan temple had seemed an hour ago, and how quickly it had been yanked into modern barbarity! I shouted out my suspicion.

"Dolgoruki, is that you?"

The gunfire slackened again. "A prince of Russia," came a reply from behind a tree, "reclaiming what you stole."

"You're going to be massacred, idiot!"

"Not before we kill you first."

"You'll die uselessly for antique iron?"

"For honor and restoration!" His men banged away.

"What lunatic are we dealing with?" Izabela asked me.

"Prince Peter Petrovich Dolgoruki," I said, the name sour on my tongue. "He combines blustering arrogance with courageous stupidity, and was a fool at Austerlitz. He no doubt thinks seizing the swords will get him back in favor with the tsar."

"Is he amenable to reason?"

"Barely."

"Can he set aside his passion?"

"Barely. Better to get a clean shot."

"No, your wife is right. Let's parley. A determined assault will absorb all our bullets. They'll use the captured temple to bargain for their lives, threatening to destroy our heritage. Talking will buy time to make their position hopeless. What can we use for a flag of truce?"

"Let me at least contribute something," said Marie. "I, too, believe in negotiation." She reached under her dress and ripped off a piece of white chemise, giving us a glimpse of leg and ankle. It's odd what a man will notice.

Izabela used an old spear to thrust a white flag through the doorway. "Parley, Dolgoruki! Parley! Cease fire before more are needlessly killed!"

"You surrender?" His voice was shaky.

"I've a proposition to save both our lives."

"The only proposition is to give up the swords!" The imbecile had spark, I'll give him that.

"The only proposition besides compromise is death, my bold prince." Izabela's voice was cold with warning. "Your men are surrounded. By dusk there will be a thousand Poles here. Each one remembers Russian savagery. They'll hunt you to the last man."

There was a long silence.

"At least hear what I have to say," she persisted.

"The rogues below have dragged off their wounded and backed into the cellar," Caleb reported. "They're waiting for orders."

"Use the respite to barricade," I said. "Take the sturdiest museum pieces and choke the stairs."

Servants began to comply.

"I'm low on powder, brother."

"Me too. I may have use for my medieval horse pick."

But finally Dolgoruki stood away from his sheltering tree and stood defiantly, holding a useless cavalry saber. "I'll listen."

"Sheath your silly sword," Izabela commanded. "And approach on foot, alone." She shouted into the forest. "No shooting, by order of Princess Czartoryski! Hold your fire as long as the Russians do! If they break the truce, kill them all!"

Horns tooted to signal understanding.

The prince was in a general's uniform, somewhat pretentious for the leader of a few dozen men. I guessed he didn't want the other commanders of the Russian army to know this side errand and had marched off with a modest company of volunteers, assuring them quick victory and easy loot.

Instead, Izabela had given him a real fight. Dolgoruki came to the foot of the stairs and stood as truculent as a school bully. The princess stepped out the iron doors and studied him with distaste, her war horn at her side.

"Get Ethan out where I can see him," the Russian demanded. "I don't want a rifle in his hands."

So I made sure I *did* keep my rifle in hand as I stepped onto the portico. I stayed close to a pillar, grounding the loaded weapon by its butt. "Indeed you don't, Dolgoruki."

"You're a thief and murderer, Gage. The report is that you killed your own manservant. And you, Princess Czartoryski, are jeopardizing the fortunes of your entire family by sheltering a criminal."

"Which Gage are you referring to?" said my brother, stepping out to a pillar on the other side of the door and grounding his musket as well.

His appearance made Dolgoruki gawk. He looked from one to the other of us as if we were a magic trick. "The snake has molted."

"For a blundering soldier surrounded and outnumbered, you have a risky instinct for insult, lieutenant," Caleb said, deliberately misstating the uniform rank. "Strong words and weak position gets a man killed."

"I am a prince of Russia."

"With a lieutenant's command."

My brother had his own knack for insult. Must run in the family.

Dolgoruki flushed. "How are you two related?"

"Brother and guardian," Caleb said. "I'm the responsible one."

"You've joined an odious conspiracy, guardian."

"It's called return of confiscated treasure to its rightful owners," I said. "Princess Czartoryski is assembling a museum of national heritage to celebrate her nation's rebirth."

"When Bonaparte reestablishes our country," Izabela put in. She had her own skill at getting under Dolgoruki's skin.

The prince did his best to draw himself up with haughty scorn, but he couldn't very well look down his nose at us since we were up on the temple portico and he was at ground level. "You can defeat me with your village militia," he tried, "but unless you want war with the tsar you'll give the swords back now."

"It seems to me we're already at war, thanks to your bumbling ambush, and that you're losing it," Izabela replied. "I have an offer. If you accept, we become allies. But if you don't, by nightfall you'll be my prisoner and your men will be dead. I'm not exaggerating about a thousand followers."

He glanced behind, as if to count. "You'll die too," he said stubbornly.

"Possibly. This war is as stupid as any other. So we can fight it out to the end or you can accept my proposal."

"Which is?" He sounded like Harry when contemplating vegetables.

"That you partner with the Gage brothers here."

That struck a blow not only to him, but us as well. What in Hades?

"Are you joking?" the Russian said. "For what possible reason?"

"To retrieve a relic even more valuable than the Grunwald swords, an artifact that will restore your career and save Russia."

Dolgoruki looked suspicious. "What relic is this?"

"Something that again and again has changed the history of the world. Something that could insure Russia's survival in the coming wars."

"What coming wars?"

"Come, prince, you've met Napoleon. Don't be naïve. The Gage brothers can help you as they've helped me."

"We can?" I asked.

"But it will require enormous valor on your part, Prince Dolgoruki, and enormous sacrifice on mine, since I'd dreamed of retrieving this icon for myself. It's my compromise for peace. In return, the Grunwald swords must be guaranteed to Poland and the Gage family gets to live in peace and safety when they complete the quest. Russia must grant them amnesty."

"That's unacceptable. Besides, I've no amnesty to grant."

"You'll be in a position to seek any favor you wish from the tsar, once you retrieve what I'm offering. So I demand your word of honor that you'll guarantee Gage family safety. Otherwise you surrender, or die, and the swords still stay here, and Russia gets nothing. Your choice is a futile death, or a chance at heroic immortality."

"Why me?" he asked suspiciously.

She let the question hang in the air a moment. "Because you're expendable. No man who has sought this prize has ever returned."

Incredibly, this seemed to intrigue Dolgoruki as much as it alarmed me. "If we stop this battle, you'll reveal this prize?"

"I'll tell you where it is, and how to get it." She was cool as an estate agent striking a bargain.

"I must go with the execrable Americans?"

"They're all quite necessary to success."

"Princess, what is this place?" Astiza whispered anxiously.

Izabela ignored her. "Do you agree?"

I wanted to interrupt too, asking just what it was we were necessary for, but it did seem expedient to end this battle—even if it meant partnering with the annoying Russian. So I waited.

"Agreed," he finally said.

"Agreed to what?" Izabela pressed.

He hung his head and muttered. "I agree to give up the swords in return for a better trophy. If you convince me it exists."

"No." Her voice was clear, carrying to the Russian soldiers and the Poles beyond. "You agree to stop this ridiculous attempt to steal back swords that have been the rightful property of

Poland for four hundred years, in return for my revealing an alternative. Otherwise, all of you perish. Your men must lay down their arms and return to their army. You must proceed by yourself, alone, with the Gage family."

He shook his head in frustration, but what choice did he have? "My men will not surrender their arms," he stubbornly tried.

"They will or die. And if Russia dares comes again, they'll find my servants armed with captured Russian guns."

Dolgoruki hesitated.

"Sire, do not humiliate us!" one of his men pleaded.

"I'm offering you redemption and your men life," Izabela insisted.

Dolgoruki fumed, but the hopelessness of his position was clear even to him. It looked like half of Poland had filled in behind him. His depleted command was surrounded by an armed mob. He turned to another officer. "Take the men back across the river. If I don't return in four hours, return to our regiment and explain that I'm on a mission for Mother Russia."

"But prince, I don't trust these Poles!"

"Neither do I, but neither do I fear them. Nor will I throw away your lives for nothing. Today, do as I command. We'll find better fortune tomorrow."

The man reluctantly saluted, and the Russian soldiers slowly began to stand up and reveal themselves. The agreement was whispered from man to man, and conveyed to the troops in the basement. After a low debate, the cellar soldiers filed out its broken door, carrying their wounded.

"Leave your weapons," Dolgoruki commanded. His men reluctantly stacked muskets and slowly backed through the

Polish ranks, hundreds of Izabela's fighters watching them go with ominous silence.

Soon the prince was completely alone.

"Done," he said, as if the retreat had been his idea. "Where and what is this prize?"

"It's not to be shouted," Izabela said. "Step up here." Dolgoruki mounted the steps between the lions in his high cavalry boots, spurs jangling, sheathed saber swaying like a tiger's tail, brave and humiliated. He scowled at me.

"The icon is in another castle," she said, "at the edge of the Ottoman Empire in the high Carpathian Mountains. All of you must work together in order to get it."

"Why?" I asked.

"That will become clear in due time. You'll agree to help the prince, Ethan, in return for amnesty from Tsar Alexander and reward from Poland. Success will give the prince new renown, you forgiveness, us the swords, and laurels for all involved. A title, I think you said."

So one difficult task by my confidant Adam Czartoryski had turned my family into fugitives, and now I had a new one from Adam's mother. Did Czartoryski let slip to the Russians that the swords were coming to Pulawy, only to turn the tables on Dolgoruki? Izabela had made sure Caleb and I came armed. What had she told my brother last night? How much of this had been planned, how much accident, and how much fate?

Once more we were in bondage to someone else's ambition, and in partnership with a man I despised. Prince Ethan was apparently pawn Ethan, and my greed in St. Petersburg had ensnared me in webs I still didn't fully understand. I looked at Caleb. Was my brother a part of this manipulation as well? He neutral look revealed nothing. "And why haven't you already fetched this prize yourself?" I asked our hostess.

"Yes. If this icon is real, why don't you already have it?" Dolgoruki seconded.

Izabela lowered her voice. "Because the Trojan palladium, prince, is possessed by Cezar Dalca."

And at that, both Dolgoruki and Caleb sucked in their breath.

PART TWO

CHAPTER 18

The Carpathian Mountains are a thousand-mile-long crescent of rugged peaks that wrap around a land apart. All of the range is wild and cloud-cloaked, but its southeastern quarter soars eight thousand feet to cup a rugged frontier region called Transylvania, Latin for "beyond the forest." This windy tumble of cliff and pine is the reputed refuge of a renegade duke and bandit chief named Cezar Dalca, a reclusive warlord whom our expanded fellowship pledged to find. In his stronghold we hoped to seize an icon as old as history itself, and finally redeem our ambitions.

Our goal, I was told, was the Trojan palladium—an old Greek statue with powers I'd yet to fully understand. Caleb and Dolgoruki were apparently aware of its reputation and owner but declined explanation until we neared Dalca's stronghold.

"Best not to worry until you have to," Dolgoruki said.

"Don't put stock in tavern stories," Caleb added.

Which made us worry all the more.

The Romanians call Transylvania Ardeal. The Saxon settlers who dominate the valley towns prefer Siebenburgen, or "the seven fortresses." Here the proud Dacians made a final stand against the conquering Roman emperor Trajan, who lusted for their gold and silver mines. Later invaders included Hun and Magyar, Avar and Turk, soaking the land in blood. Today the Carpathians are a rampart of the Austrian Empire. The Ottoman provinces of Moldavia and Wallachia lie just beyond, their captive Christians oppressed and restive. Even as we traveled, Russian armies were marching to brew another war.

Transylvania seemed detached from such events, gripped in its own universe. By legend this is where the world's darker creatures stalk, crawl, and fly. Its treasures are supernatural, guarded by gypsies, thieves, vagabonds, witches, werewolves, vampires, sorcerers, wizards, necromancers, and hermits—or so claim the mystic texts. If our sojourn in Prague last year brought us to the European capital of mystery, this is mystery's hinterland. Magic resides like mist in Transylvania's hollows, and wolves still prowl its forests. Two bears once rose on their hind legs to inspect us as we passed. Astiza told us that Transylvanians believe bears are trapped, enchanted men.

More ordinary inhabitants are a mongrel mix of races. The Szeklers are descendants of the Huns, paid by Vienna to guard the frontier. The valley dwellers are German immigrants and Slav peasants, sturdy and secretive. Their name for their limestone peaks is *Lumea pierduta*, or "the lost world." There resides Cezar Dalca: A ghost, guarding a legend, in a ruin, from a fog of time.

Izabela had generously equipped us with horses and supplies. Even Harry rode proudly on his own little pony, clopping obediently behind our bigger steeds. We regretted having to leave the luxuries of Pulawy, but once we set out we traveled impatiently. Astiza, Caleb, Dolgoruki and I may have been forced into expedient alliance, but we knew we were an ill-matched group: A brother I'd once betrayed, who always seemed to know more than he revealed. A proud Russian recruited because his alternative was death or humiliation. My eccentric, rootless family. Dolgoruki sulked, Caleb brooded, and Astiza fretted. Harry was simply confused that we were on the road again.

"I liked that house, Papa."

"Maybe we'll find a better one."

We were also a fellowship of greed, as all treasure hunters must be. Redemption for Dolgoruki, a possible title for me, a home for Astiza and Harry, and reward from France for Caleb. All we needed was to obtain an antique wooden statute that may or may not exist, held by a reclusive madman, fortified amid the wildest peaks of Europe. "We have a plan," Caleb promised.

I'd debated trying to persuade Astiza to stay at Pulawy. But no one thought this a good idea, least of all my wife. She refused because too much misfortune befalls us when we're apart. Izabela also insisted that Astiza was uniquely equipped to evaluate Dalca's powers. "It's women who have insight," the princess told her. "You may be the only person who can really understand him." And Astiza wouldn't hear of leaving Harry. So we once more rode into adventure as a family, hoping this 'palladium' would finally be the end of our rainbow.

We departed in lush spring. The brooks were a torrent, the trees bursting, and birds were mad with breeding frenzy. Showers scrubbed the sky so clean that rocks sparkled as we rode south. Wildflowers erupted, and the green cheered our spirits. Saxon steeples began to supplant the bulbous church towers of the Orthodox faith as we approached the

Carpathians. Sheep with new lambs surged across meadows like waves of foam. Pastures sang with the clank of cowbells as cattle were herded to higher pastures. The bucolic setting seemed reassuringly normal.

But as we mounted the foothills the season began to reverse, as if time was running backward. The land became colder and more rugged, the peaks ahead still snowcapped. Trees shrank and went back to bare winter. The ground reverted to mud, stone, and dead grass. Villages became smaller and poorer, and finally disappeared almost entirely. Lonely cabins clutched ridge-tops to overlook precipitous fields. The inhabitants became furtive, watching us from cover like wild animals. The men wore sheepskin jackets, astrakhan hats, and hide moccasins not that different from Dacian barbarians. The women wore leather corsets, heavy woolen skirts, and wide embroidered aprons faded from time and hard use. Some families had the red complexions of northern Europe, others the swarthy cast of Cossack and Mongol.

Empires collide here. Northwest was Austria, east was Russia, and southeast the vast Ottoman realm ruled by Sultan Selim III in far-off Constantinople. We came across the bones of old battlefields. Combs of ribs jutted from dry grass. Skulls had eye sockets plugged with dirt. Rusting metal and tattered cloth decorated some remains.

"Who are the dead people, Papa?"

"Soldiers from long ago."

"Turks, Szeklers, and Cossacks," Dolgoruki surmised. "See the scimitars? A border skirmish, boy. Now the Serbs are revolting against the Ottomans, and Russian regiments are threatening Moldavia in support."

"The Turks once ruled this area, did they not?" asked Astiza.

"Until defeated more than a hundred years ago."

"But the Ottomans and Russia still quarrel?"

"War never ends."

Harry was shivering when we stopped at a hut to chew bread and sausage and interrogate a squat, ugly shepherd about Dalca. The man's initial response was simply to make the sign of the cross. Then Caleb bribed him with a coin and we learned we were almost to a crossroads village called Szejmal where we could seek directions to Dalca's stronghold. The reclusive duke was reputed to live in a remote fortress high above the town.

The shepherd annoyingly stared while we ate our lunch, so I turned my back on him. Then Caleb asked to speak privately with Astiza and me. "It's time to say a little more." Leaving Harry with the Russian prince, we walked to the brow of a ridge that looked across a labyrinth of hill and canyon. Everything had gone gray. The trees were crabbed. Grass was beaten down from the snows of last winter. Eroded gullies cut across a road that was little more than a trail. The land looked cursed.

"I've not been entirely honest with you, brother," Caleb began.

"Something of an understatement, isn't it?"

"No one confides everything," allowed Astiza.

Caleb looked at her then with a curious expression of appreciation and guilt to which I should have paid more attention. "And because we don't confide, all men are fundamentally alone," he went on. "Isn't that so, Ethan?"

"It is for some. Family helps."

"Yes. Now I've reunited with yours. It's curious how fate swings in great circles, isn't it?"

"Perhaps time is a circle," Astiza said. "Or perhaps time

doesn't exist at all, and we're trapped in a life in which everything that ever happened and ever will happen is right now."

"And death the key which frees that trap," Caleb amended.

"I'd no idea privateers were so philosophical," I said drily to my brother. "Or could try so hard to impress my wife."

"There's a lot of time to think on a quarterdeck, the ocean hissing tediously by. You remember everything, and thus remember it a hundred different ways. Sometimes the more you remember the less it stings, like massaging a wound. Sometimes you get confused about what really happened. And sometimes remembering makes wounds worse. Brooding isn't productive, but it swallows time." He glanced at my wife. "If time exists."

"So what have you been dishonest about?" I asked impatiently.

"Yes. Well. I didn't fully explain that Napoleon believes you remain in his debt. The emperor says you were sent in search of a mechanical man that served as an oracle, and that you're rumored to have found it."

"That was our project, not his," I said.

"Bonaparte disagrees. He said he's saved you many times but that you never repay his charity. So he offered a bargain. If I could deliver to him what you wouldn't, I'd be saved and you'd be forgiven. He gave me the devil's mission of finding you and using you."

"The mechanical man was a fool's errand. The automaton is wrecked forever." I actually wasn't sure if that were true but I'd no interest in ever going near the infernal machine again.

"He said you'd inevitably pursue some new relic. Perhaps he even recommended you to Czartoryski as a man who could retrieve the swords. Did you ever wonder why the foreign minister was so friendly to a vagabond American family?"

"I assumed it was our charm." I considered my brother. "So Bonaparte has a hand in our manipulation as well. And you're his tool?"

"I've been looking after you longer than you know. Did you ever wonder who saved you from your manservant?"

"*You* shot Gregor?"

"No, but I warned Czartoryski to be ready for betrayal. The foreign minister took the unusual step of coming to your apartment, did he not? So I suppose it was he or one of his men. We're in a bear pit of competing Russians, Prussians, French, and Poles. But now we're at the end of Europe, beyond reach of our masters. We can decide our own route and destiny."

"You've shared this revelation with our Russian partner?"

"Of course not. We need Dolgoruki until we don't."

"Hard sentiment, brother."

"Realism, little brother, from a lifetime of survival. I only mention this because I want us to see things clearly. To win your trust I'm confiding that Napoleon feels you're in his debt. There it is."

"Which is scarcely news. I wish you'd be as candid about this mysterious Cezar Dalca and this so-called palladium."

"Prince Dolgoruki can help with that as we ride to Szejmal. He knows more than I do, and we need to reach the village before nightfall."

"To the horses, then."

Dolgoruki and Harry were already saddled, my boy wearily still beneath a broad-brimmed hat, his cloak's hood pulled up against the cold. We swung onto our own steeds and kicked into a trot, the track winding ever higher. Streamers of cloud blew off the highest peaks. Eagles orbited like sentries.

"So, Caleb and Peter," I prompted, "is our quest finally to be explained? When Izabela mentioned Cezar Dalca your eyes filled with dread."

"And desire," said Astiza.

"Some of this comes from tavern tales," Caleb said. "Whispers. Legend. But it's consistent enough to convince me Dalca is real, not a myth." We could see the village of Szejmal high up ahead, its rambling lanes and huts dangling like spider legs from a razorback ridge. "A recluse, in a wreck of a castle, with a smattering of henchmen, so removed from most of civilization that no one bothers with him anymore."

"Yet he still inspires fear?" Astiza asked.

"Yes. I was told in Paris that even the Turks avoid him. The rumor is that those who visit never return. Some claim he's some kind of robber baron. Other that he's mad aristocrat. Some say he's a malevolent spirit, some contend he's immortal, and some that he's a sorcerer."

"Conjuring what?" I asked.

"Collecting," contributed Dolgoruki. "The legend in St. Petersburg is that he's an obsessed antiquarian. Old books. Old manuscripts. Old relics, talismans, icons, potions, and spells. And where does he get his gold to do this collecting? Some claim he makes it by alchemy. That would be a pretty trick to know."

"We tried that in Bohemia," I said. "Or rather, Astiza did."

"I made an explosive, not gold," she said. "An explosion *from* gold."

"I suspect transformation is a fraud," I added. "It's difficult to change anything, least of all ourselves. People claim more powers than they have. Dalca too, maybe."

"Yet others have more power than we can explain," Astiza added. "Cagliostro. The Comte Saint-Germaine. Alessandro Silano. Wolfgang Richter sought such powers. We've had glimpses of the shadow world behind the veil, husband. Mysteries have their magic."

"I'll admit the world is an odd place."

"The tsar would like such magic," Dolgoruki said. "Useful against Napoleon."

"So would Napoleon," said Caleb. "Useful against the tsar."

"So would Ethan Gage," I said, "but this relic we're after seems unlikely to be all that magical, since I've never heard of it."

"Haven't you?" Dolgoruki replied. "I know Americans ignore the classics, Gage, but surely even you have know the *Iliad, Odyssey,* and Virgil's *Aeneid.*" His tone was condescending toward the ignorant colonial.

"I intend to get around to all three, once I retire."

"The Trojan War lasted ten years," my brother informed me.

"Yes," I said, although in truth I hadn't kept track. "So?"

"Something prevented a Greek victory year after year," Dolgoruki said. "Yet in the end Troy fell rather suddenly."

"The Trojan Horse," I said, able to show I wasn't completely at a loss. "The Greeks built a gigantic hollow horse, the Trojans dragged it inside their city, and Odysseus slipped out to open the gates. A rousing tale, up there with Hercules and the golden fleeces in the labyrinth." There's nothing like a good story, though my mind did tend to wander at Harvard. It's possible I mixed one myth up with another.

"The real key, brother, was the Trojan palladium," Caleb said.

"Which is what, exactly?"

"Just as icon comes from a word meaning likeness, a palladium has come to mean protection," Dolgoruki explained. "The goddess Athena was called Pallas Athena because she'd defeated the titan Pallas and wore his skin as armor."

"Wore his skin?"

"It was a primitive time."

"Long before she was the patron of Athens," Caleb contributed, "Athena was a protector of far more ancient Troy. That city was rich and powerful because it controlled the mouth of the Dardanelles and thus the straits between the Mediterranean and the Black Sea. Ilus, who founded the city, prayed to the gods for favor. In response, a wooden statue of Pallas Athena fell from the sky."

"The gods were much more addressable in those days."

"Troy kept the statue as a protective icon with supernatural powers. When a temple fire threatened the statue and Ilus saved it, he was blinded for having the temerity to touch the divine."

"That's the trouble with old stories. Every time someone begins to get ahead, something goes horribly wrong. Reminds me of me, actually."

"Admit you don't know the story of the Trojan War, brother."

"I've forgotten a detail or two."

Dolgoruki resumed as pompous lecturer. "Because Troy was so rich it was envied, and the abduction of Helen gave the Greeks a convenient excuse to try to sack the place. One of the Greek heroes of the war was Diomedes, King of Argos.

He captured and interrogated a Trojan noble who revealed the palladium's existence and its role in protecting the city. So Odysseus disguised himself as a beggar to gain access to Troy, and lowered a rope to the stronger Diomedes. The two Greeks stole the wooden statue."

"Why weren't *they* blinded?"

"Because this allowed prophecies of Trojan doom to be fulfilled. The Greek gods could be capricious and inconsistent."

"Or the storytellers didn't fill all the plot holes. In any event, go on."

"The stage was set for the Trojan horse, and Troy fell and was burned."

"But it wasn't the hollow horse trick, it was this wooden statue that was key to the Greek victory?"

"Correct. The *Odyssey* and the *Aeneid* made the horse better known, but the palladium had to be captured first."

"Isn't that the truth of it? Ben Franklin liked to say applause waits on success, but the truth of the matter is one needs the right biographer. Pity that this palladium lacked a better poet. That's my problem too, I suppose."

"Diomedes supposedly made off with the palladium after the sack of Troy, and there the myth gets muddy," Caleb said.

"Putting the emphasis on the word 'myth.'"

"Actually, brother, the most interesting thing is that this palladium is said to have worked its charm again and again Some say it was present at the founding of Athens, making that city great. Then to Sparta, which prevailed over Athens in the Peloponnesian War. Then to Italy and Rome's Temple of Vesta."

"Vesta? Izabela based her design on one of that goddess's temples."

"She, too, has heard these legends. In any event, Rome prevailed against Hannibal when the palladium was in Roman hands. Another Roman, Marcellus, is said to have been blinded when he again rescued the icon from fire."

"A devil of a way for Athena to reward her rescuers, but then I've had my own problems with women."

Astiza poked me.

"The statue protected Rome for nearly a thousand years. And then Constantine the Great brought the statue with him when he founded his new city of Constantinople on the Bosporus Strait between Europe and Asia. He secreted the relic under the Column of Constantine. The Eastern Roman Empire and Byzantium ruled supreme for another thousand years."

"Until the Turks came along," I objected. "They conquered the place a few centuries ago, as you'll recall, and Europe's been fighting them ever since. I believe you were on the way to join in, Prince Dolgoruki, when you diverted to attack us at Pulawy."

"These relics have the potential of being a thousand times more important than another Turkish skirmish," Dolgoruki said.

"My point is that this wooden statue—which should have decayed away a couple thousand years ago, by the way—didn't save Constantinople. And that it should be in Turkish hands."

"Yes, except they've never claimed so," Dolgoruki said. "Some speculate the palladium was displaced by rampaging Crusaders who sacked Constantinople on their way to the Holy Land in 1204. Byzantium dramatically declined after that, and the city fell to the Turks two and a half centuries later. Some believe the statue is still in the Ottoman capital, but forgotten. Some believe new adventurers stole it. What if Izabela, who scoured Europe for relics to buttress Polish pride, learned that Dalca has it? What if it can be found and seized? What if it could make invulnerable whichever nation possessed it?"

"That's a lot of ifs, my Russian treasure hunter. Why would this Carpathian hermit have it?"

"It's only a rumor that he does. Or that he knows where it is. Or that he can confirm its existence. Dalca has sent emissaries on secret searches around the world. We captured and tortured one at the Peter and Paul prison. Hard man to break. Descended from the Huns."

"So you knew of this palladium before coming south? And the tsar knew as well? Did Czartoryski know too?"

"Yes."

"Now we have our answer, husband," Astiza said. "We've been manipulated not just to deliver the Grunwald swords but to search for this second prize as well. Your friend Adam was sending us not on one mission, but two. It's all been a trick from the beginning."

"For fabulous reward," Dolgoruki justified.

"Can we clarify just what this reward might be?" I asked. "I've been promised titles and palaces and all I have is saddle sores."

"Any reward is ultimately up to He Who Gives," the prince said, meaning Tsar Alexander.

"So we're dependent on royal whim."

"It's not even that simple, brother," Caleb said. "Another ruler has also heard of this palladium and is pressing his own claim and offering his own reward. We might as well share that truth with our Russian partner here."

"What claim?" Dolgoruki demanded. "What ruler?"

"Napoleon Bonaparte," I said. "My brother Caleb secretly works for him, and Caleb rescued me and my family for that emperor, not yours."

The Russian was horrified. "You're an agent of the tyrant?"

"Which means, my friends," I blithely continued, "that we're a fellowship riding into the Carpathian wilderness with two of its fellows diametrically opposed to each other. Caleb is working for France and the prince for Russia. I'm still pursued by Prussia, for all I know. While the woman who gave us this mission is a Polish patriot. Which leaves us with an awkward question: Which monarch gets this palladium?"

There was a moment's silence, Caleb and the prince eyeing each other.

"First we have to find it, which means finding Cezar Dalca," Dolgoruki finally said. "Let's see which of us survives the encounter before deciding whose master gets the spoils."

"A cheerful solution," I said. "And it's just possible that the Gage family will wait in the village while you, Caleb, risk your life for Napoleon, and you, prince, risk your life for Alexander. We'll watch you climb Dalca's mountain and toast your health on the way up."

"I'm afraid that won't work, Ethan," Caleb said.

"You're always the fool," Dolgoruki added. "It amazes me that you've survived this long, Gage, given your naiveté."

"I'm naïve? You're the one who bungled an ambush and blundered into a battle at Pulawy you couldn't win."

"A blunder contrived to bring your wife here, American

imbecile. The outcome of the fight was decided before it ever started. It was staged for Astiza. Izabela was expecting us. We had to have Astiza propose the parley and accede to the bargain to ensure she'd come along."

"Me? What have you been keeping from us?" Astiza asked.

"I'm afraid you're the key to Dalca," Caleb told her. "You're the only way we can get to him."

"My wife? I'm the one Czartoryski and Napoleon recruited."

"As useful as you occasionally are, Gage, you were never the reason our elaborate scheme was put in motion," Dolgoruki said. "By all reports, the only person who can actually penetrate Dalca's stronghold is Astiza. The monster is obsessed with beautiful women with witchly powers. You were allowed into the Russian court by the foreign minister so we could use her."

Vesuvius, Czartoryski had warned me. "Are you mad? Why would I allow my wife to go to the castle of a monster?'

"To get back your son."

"Harry?" I twisted in my saddle to look back at the pony, even as Astiza moaned. But there was my boy, riding on his fine pony, quiet and erect as—

A palladium. His hood fell back to reveal a small figure made of straw.

Horus was gone.

And then a blow hit my head and all went black.

CHAPTER 19

Harry

The Pig Man told me that if I went high up in his castle, I could watch for Mama. So I do. The bad soldier squats next to me, a chain from my neck to his belt. He has bowlegs, a scraggly beard, dark skin, and puffs a pipe like a dragon. He smells bad because I don't think he washes. He has a knife as long as my arm, and his boots ring from hobnails.

I don't know what happened. I fell asleep with the Russian prince and woke up tied to the saddle of the bad soldier's horse. My head hurt. The bad soldier talked ugly words I couldn't understand. We climbed and climbed and climbed until it got so cold that I shook. He finally tied a dirty sheepskin on me. When I cried he hit me, so I made myself stop crying.

The clouds were dark and thundery. When we got to the castle I didn't think anyone would live here because half of it has fallen down. The windows are like dead eyes. A creaky bridge leads across a deep canyon to a castle gate made of rusty bars. The gate squeals. All the bad soldiers are short and thick, with tight caps on greasy hair.

I heard an animal howl when we arrived, but there was no animal. Instead there was a tube flag like a filthy sock. It is sewn to look like a wolf's head with a body as long as a snake. When the wind blows it fills and a wolf call comes out.

I hate this place. It smells dead. All the carvings are of dragons and bears and demons. Every corner is dark and dirty. The soldier who chained me won't say why he's mean, so I asked him why he lives here.

For a long time he didn't answer. Then he said, "It's home."

We still don't have a home. I don't understand why we had to leave Russia, or Izabela's palace, or why Mama and Papa left me alone. I'm glad Mama is finally coming.

We went downstairs to where it was dark except for torches. There sat the ugliest man I've ever seen. I thought of him as Pig Man.

"I will beat you if you're bad," the Pig Man said. He's fat, with shaggy hair and squinty pig eyes so sunken that I can hardly see them. His teeth are pointy, and his voice sounds like a big drum. "I, Cezar, am your master until your mother comes to my banquet."

"I'm hungry," I said.

"Maybe we will fatten you." But all I got was potato and lard.

The bad soldier is named Decebal. He put me on his chain and yanked me like a dog. He always seems mad.

I started to cry again. They said Mama is coming.

We wait. The wolf flag howls and howls.

CHAPTER 20

"It was the only way, brother," Caleb said.

"You'd never agree to let Astiza go alone," Dolgoruki added.

"We have a plan," Caleb repeated.

"That requires all of us," the Russian assured.

I was dazed and bleeding, a bandage wrapped around my head and a rope tying me to a chair. We were in a rude hovel in the village of Szejmal, somewhere below Dalca's lair in the mountains above. It was a vile hamlet, or at least I was in a vile mood. The villagers I spied out a tiny window seemed to scuttle rather than walk. All the men were bearded as bears, their hands tough as roots, their squint suspicious. All the women were stolid and homely, scarves wrapped like a wimple around faces as wrinkled as old vegetables. Our room was dim as a cave, and there was this odd distant howling which didn't sound real. "What happened?" My tongue was as thick as my mind.

"A strategic decision," said Dolgoruki.

"You couldn't be reasoned with," Caleb added. "Astiza will distract the enemy."

My head pounded where they'd clubbed me. "Where's my wife? Where's my son?"

"Conferring with Cezar Dalca."

"Conferring? I thought he was a madman."

"He'll listen to women," Dolgoruki said. "He's fascinated by them."

"And women always go to their children," Caleb added.

"We hated our choice, but it's carefully calculated."

"Astiza will keep him occupied while we sneak up from behind."

As realization rose, so did my fury. This was the worst treachery I'd ever encountered, engineered by my own brother! I wrestled my bonds, the chair banging up and down. "You sent my wife *alone?*"

"As soon as you agree we'll go get her," Caleb said. "We'll take Dalca by surprise, grab the palladium, and vanish. Much better than fighting our way."

"It was all planned from the beginning, Gage," the prince said. "I know we haven't shared everything, but discretion was necessary. The castle is too strong for the three of us to assault directly. There's also no way for we men to win Dalca's trust. He'll only admit women who intrigue him. We sent word of Astiza's learning and powers, and it turned out he'd heard of her. Your wife has her own fame. She agreed to rescue Harry."

"And what in Hades did you do to my son?"

"Drugged and sold to a Szekler guard, who you thought was a shepherd. Dalca has to believe we've turned on you."

"Believe? Betrayal is exactly what you've done!"

"I know this looks callous," Caleb said. "But without Harry held captive, Astiza might never have agreed to meet

Dalca alone. And even if she had, you might have forbidden it."

"So we relieved you from having to choose," said Dolgoruki. "She's to help let us in the back way. We have another informant."

I roared and rocked furiously, the chair crab walking across the dirt floor. "By all that is holy and profane, I'll kill you both!"

"You *need* us both," Dolgoruki said.

"We're the only hope of getting your family back," Caleb added.

I toppled over, gasping. The ropes cut my flesh. My head pounded, and my hands were numb. I was sick at my own stupidity.

I saw it now. My jealous brother told by the French of long-lost Ethan and his fabled wife—a brother still grasping at revenge for a wrong I'd committed decades before. If Caleb couldn't have his life's love, I wouldn't have mine. The jailing at Jelgava and the skirmish at the Sibyl Temple had all been part of an elaborate ploy to get us within range of Cezar Dalca and risk Astiza in the brigand's clutches. All for a preposterous legend.

Did Czartoryski know of this monstrous plan? Parts of it, perhaps. Izabela had heard of this Trojan icon, and suddenly men at odds with each other politically were united by greed to seek the palladium. My boy kidnapped, my wife sent to hideous peril, and myself knocked unconscious. What bitter irony that in escaping villains in St. Petersburg and Jelgava, we'd traveled with even worse ones to the Carpathian Mountains. And now I couldn't stop any of it.

I looked at them balefully. Their return stare was cool and firm.

"There's no other way into his castle, Ethan," Caleb said. "Its drawbridge is guarded by a hundred henchmen."

They knew how badly they'd crossed me, and must be calculating how many hours I'd be incapacitated by rage before I'd relent and help them rescue my family. But my memory was long, too. Yes, I'd wronged Caleb many years ago. But that was a stupid tryst, and this calculated plot put my wife and son in mortal danger. Could I kill my own brother? It had now become a possibility. Cain and Abel had turned from fable to instructive history.

Yet I was trussed and helpless.

"I know you hate me right now, brother, but work with us for the next perilous hours. All can triumph if each does his part. Work with us to rescue Astiza and Horus and fetch the palladium, and we can live happily afterward, rich and satisfied."

"You can't even agree which nation gets it."

"The highest paying one," Caleb said.

"Russia will show the most gratitude," the prince added. "You'll get your title and I'll be first among equals to the tsar."

Dolgoruki I could kill without pity. Caleb with fury.

But suddenly a new realization flooded in and I looked at the two of them in horror and amazement. I'd been used, all right, but far more diabolically than I'd thought.

"Wait. Dolgoruki, it wasn't the tsar who told you to fetch the notorious Ethan Gage and his family to Russia after we fled Bohemia, was it? The tsar would scarcely have remembered me after the disaster of Austerlitz. But you rode back to Napoleon's lines with me, and you remembered being played the fool by the French emperor and the renegade American.

And as revenge, it was *your* idea to bring me to Russia. You, Dolgoruki, the royal Russian fool. The man I dismissed as an arrogant idiot. You plotted this for months. Plotted with Czartoryski. Steps ahead of us all."

"Finally you begin to see, Gage. Having wrecked my reputation, you're going to help me restore it. After the battle I was wracked with despair. How to redeem myself? And then I heard a legend of an ancient relic that conveyed invincibility, and remembered your devious greed, and heard of your reputation as a treasure hunter with a remarkable wife. I knew you'd trust Czartoryski in a way you'd never trust me. And then the minister secretly contacted the French, and the French your brother. So yes, everyone has manipulated you from the beginning. I thought a hundred times it could all go wrong. I thought you'd drown in the Neva, or be captured by the Prussians. But no, your reputation for dumb luck is well deserved. Perhaps you're invincible yourself."

"This is a sin, using us. You're tempting Satan."

"All sides worked to bring you here, Ethan," Caleb said. "You know that Astiza believes in fortune and destiny. This was destiny tripled. It's good luck what's happened, not bad."

My mind whirled, trying to piece back just how I'd been directed. "You left the skis to point our course to Russian pursuit," I said to Caleb. "Izabela knew the Russians would come to the Temple."

"I needed a battle so I could desert my command with a good excuse," Dolgoruki said. "My men will report I was forced into a temporary truce to save their lives. I'll return a hero."

"Some of those men dead or wounded."

"Destiny has its casualties." He looked impatient at my

reluctance to forgive all and merrily press on. My wife and son in danger, treasure waiting, companions primed for action. Fait accompli.

"This Dalca and his women," I finally said. "Why? Is he some kind of lovelorn obsessive? A wicked de Sade? I thought you said people who went there never came back. Do only women go there? Do they never return?"

"Men have tried to gain admission without success," the prince said. "It's only pretty young women he'll entertain. But not, we think, for sex."

"You think? My God, you're the most scabrous scoundrel, a pit of iniquity, a moral monster! Both of you! Why would any woman go near that place if not coerced by the abduction of her child?"

Caleb picked up a knife and eyed its point, and at first I was afraid of what he might do. But he was eyeing my bonds. "Your indignation is understandable, Ethan. But we're wasting time now that you're awake. It hardly matters why they go there. The point is that they never come back. So Astiza has entered his lair and we must rescue her."

"But they must always come of their own free will," added Dolgoruki. "It has to be, or he won't accept them. He invites them to his banquet."

"He promises them immortality."

CHAPTER 21

Astiza

I was invited to a women's banquet in what, from a distance, appeared to be a ruin. Balbec Castle is a fossil that must date from medieval times, since the centuries have pitted its walls and its windows are dark arrow slits. Some of the parapets have collapsed into rubble from age and neglect. The fortress overlooks a narrow shepherd's pass in the Carpathians once used by barbarian raiders, but this threat is as anachronistic as the castle itself. Yet while the aerie is too high and remote for ordinary life or commerce, it is useful as a remote hideaway.

A sinuous ridge wound ten miles upward from village to castle, the world brown and gray as I rode my horse up the rocky path. Lingering snow patches were old and dirty. In the last mile the vegetation disappeared entirely except for lichens on wind-scoured stone. Taller peaks cast Balbec into gloom, and swirling cloud gave it a malevolent air. Thunder rumbled constantly, as if lightning was curiously attracted to its towers. A mournful keening rose and fell with the wind and, as I drew nearer, I saw that the cry's source was a curious flag. It was a tubular wolf's-head standard that inflated like a Chinese banner and howled with every breeze.

I trembled with anger that our 'fellowship' had gambled my son's life in this foul place. Yes, I will lead my family out of Balbec Castle. But not necessarily Caleb and Dolgoruki.

My journey began with an invitation. In the deepest dark of the previous night, a leather binder had been slipped under our crude door in the village of Szejmal. Inside was a parchment invitation inked in red from a careful hand.

If you seek unity, come to my castle before sundown tomorrow. Instead of a signature, there was the outline of a wolf.

And under that, *Alone, to my Banquet of Immortality.*

Or he dies.

I left while my husband was still unconscious, reluctantly admitting to Caleb that yes, Ethan might not let me go if awakened. Our resulting plan is quite mad, but Caleb and Dolgoruki have essentially burned our ships and bet all on desperation. Somehow I must distract and bargain with Cezar Dalca. Somehow I must employ my son.

Caleb promised the men will follow but he wasn't brave enough to even face my gaze. I'd thought his odd glances had been from male desire, but now I know better. He'd planned my sacrifice from the beginning. "Soon, all debts will be balanced," he promised.

"The woman in Philadelphia? Is that was this is about?"

"It's about putting things right."

"You preached reconciliation."

"I strive for it, but also for justice."

"Only forgiveness frees the heart. So I forgive you, Caleb."
He winced as if I'd slapped him.

"But I can never respect you. All you've accomplished is
to prove you're a small man, much smaller than my husband
or son."

"Astiza—"

"No antique icon is worth eternal damnation."

"Can't you see? This is for all of us."

But I'd already swung up onto my mare and started her
on the road to Balbec. There's nothing bitterer than revul-
sion toward one I'd hoped to love as a brother. Nothing more
dispiriting than being the pawn of cynical calculation.

I was shadowed. Dalca's henchmen followed my horse as
we climbed, the soldiers flitting from tree to rock on either
side. His minions are short and swarthy men, goat-quick,
with spears and bows but no firearms. They reinforced my
suspicion that I was ascending into the past. The dim history
into which I rode was not Egypt's time of august pharaohs
and animal-headed deities. Dalca's gods are far older, the
cruel pagan idols that were once placated by Dacian blood
sacrifice and druid incantation. Their god Perun controlled
thunder, and Chernobog the underworld.

Would their darkness swallow us now?

The road ended at the lip of a sheer ravine, so deep that
I couldn't see its bottom. A decrepit drawbridge led to a
gatehouse and portcullis on the other side. Helmeted sentries
watched from a broken rampart, and the entire castle looked
gnawed by a dragon. No one challenged, no one beckoned.

My horse snorted and shied, as if sensing something wicked in the castle beyond. When I dismounted, she bolted.

I hesitated, my heart beating. But beyond the gate was the higher keep, and two figures peered from there as well. One of them waved. Horus! My heart soared and then settled into resolve. Now I was a lioness, come to recover her cub. I had a mother's power.

I strode across the drawbridge, boots thumping. At mid-span a board broke from my weight and fell away like a broken bird, hitting the ravine side and dislodging pebbles. I listened to them rattle into the crevasse, making tiny echoes. Then I gathered breath and went on.

The bars of the castle gate had been lifted into the portcullis, bottom spikes pointing downward like daggers. In the gatehouse passageway beyond were dark chutes through which boiling oil could be poured onto invaders. I felt eyes up there, watching me.

The castle courtyard was small, enclosed by walls on three sides and by the castle keep on the fourth. Balbec is not big, and formidable chiefly because it perches on an impregnable pinnacle of rock. Thousand-foot cliffs fell away from its stonework on all sides, gusts buffeting the spire. I wondered if any army had ever successfully stormed it.

Now the Gage family would try.

"Mama!" Harry's faint cry floated away on the wind to join the mournful howling. I looked up. His head suddenly jerked back as if yanked.

"Horus!" A murder of crows burst from crevices, the birds shrieking abuse before wheeling away. Gargoyles leered from the lip of the battlements.

The keep's massive wooden door, bound with iron, was firmly shut. No escort had appeared, and no challenge was made. I'd no idea how to enter. I stood for a moment, looking upward for another sign of my son. He'd disappeared. There was a ponderous squeal from the portcullis behind me and I turned to watch the iron grill of the main gate descend until its points ground onto the paving stones, locking me in. So I turned back. Carved over the archway, I noted, was the bas-relief of a swollen spider.

Dalca's web had trapped me.

It was only when I was safely sealed that there was a clank of machinery behind the keep door. With a slow grind, the entrance cracked open. Then the machinery stopped. There was just room enough to squeeze through, and beyond was dark silence.

I reminded myself of lioness courage and pushed inside.

Two bars of gray light fell from arrow-slit windows to faintly illuminate the reception room. The stone heads of demons peered down, as well as the stuffed heads of bear, wolf, and stag. I seemed alone with this menagerie and wondered who'd opened the door until a voice came out of the shadows.

"He's waiting."

A servant materialized, so tall and thin as to be cadaverous. The room was barren of furniture. "Cezar Dalca's quarters are below. You're a sorceress of Egypt?"

"Scholar. Priestess."

"Magician."

"Where's Horus?"

"Come and see."

A spiral stair was hewn into stone. Torches gave undulating

light. We descended into bedrock and I surmised that the castle's foundation was a hive of excavated tunnels where the dark duke could lead a troglodyte existence away from the sun. The rock gleamed where it sweated. At the base of the stairs, two stone dragons stood guard like the two lions at the Temple of Sibyl.

Dalca's reception hall was a windowless cave with a vaulted ceiling reinforced by stout stone pillars, like the chamber of a mine. It was warmer than the chilly anteroom above, almost uncomfortably so. His refuge had a cellar smell. Thick woolen Turkish carpets covered the floor, their patterns long-faded. Ragged tapestries decorated the walls, eaten by moths or vermin. Between the hangings were the antlers and horns of a dozen species, along with battered shields and antique weapons. There were runes incised near the ceiling, and an un-lidded stone sarcophagus to the left. A bed?

A fireplace and hewn chimney explained the heat. Three lanterns cast pools of illumination. The eye skipped from one light to the next until finally settling on a candelabrum thick with old wax that burned at the far end of the hall. It lit a raised wooden platform that bore my host on a lazy throne. Dalca reclined on a gilded Roman-style settee with Egyptian decoration. Servants squatted in the shadows nearby. Also standing sentry were two human skulls on pedestals, one of each end of the platform.

My host liked theater, I decided. He relied on fear.

"So you've come for immortality," he greeted in a guttural voice.

Dalca was corpulent almost beyond belief, his face bloated, his arms and legs swollen, his belly round as a balloon, and the mass of him compressing the couch like the weight of a planet. He seemed not just fat but swollen, like a tick, head sunken toward his shoulders, neck lost behind jowls, fat and immobile. Was he carried from place to place?

My host's hands, in contrast, were thin, with long, skeletal fingers, and his feet seemed tiny. A smaller man had once inhabited his bones. Dalca's bulk was exaggerated even more by his sumptuous costume of rich brocades, velvets, and a collar of wolf fur, a layered ménage of clothes that seemed cobbled together from several centuries. The heavy gold chain of office that hung from his shoulders seemed inspired by portraits of ministers from three centuries before. He had round gold earrings in each ear, pit-like eyes, and a thick beard that meshed with the tangled hair that fell to his shoulders like a mad monk. His chest visibly rose and fell as he sat, as if breathing took conscious effort, and his thick lips were the color of liver. His nose was as rumpled as the country we had ridden through, perhaps broken in old battles. His face was creased and pocked.

In sum he was the most hideous man I'd ever seen, as forbidding as a leper. No wonder he lived a recluse. This beast desired beauties?

"I've come for my son." My voice quavered slightly as I said it, making me furious at my own tremble. Courage! My weapon must be my wits.

"And the whelp has been waiting." Shadows shifted and one of Dalca's soldiers dragged something into the light. To my fury I saw it was Horus in an iron slave collar, chained to his captor's belt like a dog. He was squirming under his keeper's grip.

"Mama!" He twisted enough to break free. But when he ran toward me he was snapped short by the chain and fell on his rump. Servants laughed.

I, in turn, was blocked from rushing to embrace him. The sallow escort who'd led me downward spread his arms to prevent me from advancing, and I stopped short lest I wind up in his foul embrace.

"Let me hug my son!"

"It's enough that he's here," Dalca replied.

"It's not enough for a mother, kidnapper. It's not enough when my heart has been torn from my breast. Horus!"

My son half-choked as his captor leaned back against the throat chain, his sneer casual and cruel.

"If you don't let me touch him, I'll not attend your banquet."

Dalca frowned. "Then you'll abandon your boy."

"Until I come back with an army." I turned. Squat sentries moved to prevent any retreat. They were not just Tartar in stature but almost dwarfish, as if malformed in some troubled experiment. This was a truly evil place. I whirled to face Dalca again. "Or until I summon my own magic. I warn all of you, I've plumbed the ancient texts. I've memorized the incantations."

The imps actually stepped back.

Dalca's reply was mild. "Such threats from a companion mind! I'm disappointed, sorceress."

Now I was filled with lioness spirit, and addressed him with fury. "I'm disappointed how a duke of Transylvania treats a pilgrim family and blackmails a mother into accepting his invitation. Disappointed that Dalca's soldiers show their strength by bullying a little boy. Disappointed that their ruler fears a mother's love. Disappointed that the great Cezar Dalca hides in the bowels of the earth behind demon carvings and deer antlers."

At last I elicited a scowl. "Your own fellowship sold your boy into my service. You came here of your own free will, as required. Do you always insult your host?"

"Only when he foully kidnaps."

"Purchased, I said."

"Enslaved. If you want my attendance at this banquet of yours, you must let me comfort my son."

The room went quiet, his power and my will gripped like wrestlers. I was outmatched, and yet I also sensed the faintest thread of fear in the chamber. This castle was under Dalca's spell, but I'd brought in memory of the righteous outside world. Finally the duke gave a dismissive grunt and limply waved his hand, as if it were effort to raise his wrist. "Let them touch."

The leash-man led my son forward, unnecessarily jerking the collar, but my dour escort stood aside and at last I embraced my weeping boy. I hugged Horus fiercely, my mouth to his ear, whispering courage. My son looked up at me with wide eyes, full of fear and hope at what I murmured. I gave him a solemn nod even though I'd no faith that what I promised was true. Yet it was our only chance. Then I turned to Dalca. "For that small mercy to a devoted mother, I thank you."

"You have the temper of a she-bear," he grumbled. Then he looked at his servants and barked a laugh. "My other women are quieter."

They cackled as if this were the height of wit.

"I'm not your woman. And I am a lioness, not a bear."

"But you've acceded to my banquet?" He nodded to himself. "Come, I tire of the same faces. First we'll have an exchange of philosophies. Yes, step under that lamp where I can best see you. Your boy is only here to prevent you from being rash. I've lived a long time, and learned to take precautions."

Even from ten feet away I could smell his odor, a stink like bad cheese. Dalca was sick, I guessed, gripped by some corruption that bloated him. "You struggle to breathe?"

"Heavy from a recent meal." He shrugged, as if his sluggishness was normal, or even necessary. "You think me grotesque. Don't deny it, all do, so I've removed myself like a dutiful outcast so as not to offend precious sensibilities. Oh yes, I make sacrifices. I observe propriety. I leave this place only for the most urgent necessities. But I'm also an intellectual, a scholar of mystery, and a collector of antiquities. I was informed of your coming, and told of your past, and I understand you're a student as well. We aren't meant to quarrel, you and I. We're similar beings."

"I worship the light."

"Don't be sure the light is all that different from the dark. All men are dual, good and evil, high and low. Come, sit beside me on the platform here and tell me of your journey. I'm a lonely man, despite my servants. I enjoy hearing about the world."

With no weapons and nothing to bargain with, I had little choice but to comply. The unspoken assumption was that I was negotiating for the life of my son. Caleb and Dolgoruki had made me their decoy, and made my son a piece of bait. But while buying time for our desperate scheme I'd also try to learn if this precious palladium even existed. So I sat on the edge of the platform with my feet on the carpeted floor, a careful four feet from the reclining ogre.

"I'm a student of the past seeking antiquities of rare power," I began. "I come from Egypt where knowledge began, and have studied in a dozen great libraries. My goal is to obtain wisdom."

"You mean power," Dalca said.

"Wisdom is power."

"Nonsense, sorceress. A man can be stuffed with knowledge and be both a fool and a weakling. Science is powerful, but no individual can own it. Scientific discoveries are shared, or stolen, or copied. Bah! What use is knowledge that anyone can know? I seek *objects* of power, and their magic. The ancients knew how to call on the underworld in ways we've forgotten. I don't pretend that I only want to learn. I want to control. To dominate. To rule. Any sensible man is selfish."

"No parent would say that."

"Children are the most selfish of all, making their parents into slaves. Look at you, required to come here and submit to me."

I wouldn't dignify his absurdity with argument. "Children give us immortality," I said instead. "They carry on what we give them."

"I want *real* immortality, not brats as my surrogate. Sons disappoint. Longevity is a triumph."

"You've defeated death?"

"I've lived a very long time. Do you know I was once a great warrior? No, you don't believe, I can see it in your eyes. No matter. I persist, and my wisdom is that while all people desire, few obtain. Frustration is the fundamental condition of mankind. So I refuse to be human; I strive to be superhuman. I don't merely yearn. I possess. I feast. I live."

What strange image did he have of his own bag of a body? What triumph did he think he'd achieved in this wormhole? What satisfaction did he live for? But I saw opportunity. "Then we can work together. Find together. Treasure hunt together." I'd rehearsed this bargain to buy time.

The greed of his grin was ghastly. "Offer me something I don't have."

Here I had to invent. "There's an elixir of eternal youth held by the defiant Maharaja Yashwant Rao Holkar of Indore." I'd read in the newspapers about this Indian prince who doggedly resisted the British. "A sip makes you a god. That's what our fellowship is after, my duke, eternal youth. But Yashwant has an army of a hundred thousand men. We can't take his potion from him. We need something to tempt him to share it, and something to allay his greatest fear."

"Which is?"

"Defeat and subjugation by the English. All India is falling under their control. Another war is sure to come. But my family heard of an ancient artifact, a wooden statue of Athena, that makes a nation unconquerable. Yashwant would desire such a relic. He's fascinated by Greek myths. If we could locate this statue we could be partners." I tried to watch Dalca's eyes, to see if they'd give away his secret of possession, but I couldn't even see the orbs. It was as if someone had driven fingers into the dough of his face.

"You want to trade this statue away?"

"For an elixir of youth. The Trojan Palladium is an old icon, all but forgotten, possibly impotent. Men assume it lost.

But it's said that the pagan world lives on in Balbec. Rumor says you may possess it, and together we could tempt this Moghul prince. Antique rubbish from your cellar exchanged for the vigor of a twenty-year-old."

"You mean the ancient image that protected Troy. Older than the Egyptian pyramids. Fallen from the sky. Wood that never decays."

"So you do have it. Fate has indeed brought us together."

"This palladium is what brought you to the Carpathians?"

"We'd make the dangerous journey to India for you."

Dalca laughed without mirth, and his thick lips parted to reveal pointed teeth, so sharp that I suspected they'd ben filed. It was a guffaw without joy, and an expression of slyness deteriorating into madness. "How bold you are! I'm to give you a relic of impregnable power and send you thousands of miles away to pursue another rumor? Surrender invulnerability? Give up what has controlled the fate of the world?" He shook his head. "It would be absurd even if it was possible. But it isn't. You offer what I don't need in return for what I don't have."

"You don't have the palladium?" My heart sank. All this risk for nothing.

"I know the legend, and I know where the statue might be—in a palace a hundred times as impregnable as this one. And I don't believe in your elixir, priestess. Eternal youth? Alchemists sought immortality from the philosopher's stone. Ponce de Leon sought the fountain of youth. Faust bargained with the devil. Cagliostro and the Comte St. Germain boasted they lived for centuries. Religious prophets promise eternity in the afterlife. It's all a rainbow. What paradise won't become tedious after a thousand years, let alone a trillion?

What hellish torture won't become boring as it extends to forever? Endings are what makes existence meaningful."

So he wasn't tempted. "You accept death."

Dalca shook his massive, shaggy head. "I fear it with all my heart. I dare not join it, for dread of my soul. So I don't embrace eternity, sorceress, I endure it, outliving everyone and everything I cherish. Except for my immortal companions."

"Your female banquet guests."

"My harem." His tongue protruded for an instant, brushing his lips. "Are you curious, Astiza of Alexandria? The Egyptians prepared for the eternal journey. Greek heroes sought elevation to the ranks of the gods. Jesus was resurrected. Mohammed ascended into heaven. You can't have the palladium, and you can't have Indian elixirs, but you can have my own formula for eternal preservation."

My task was only to buy time. "You've used this secret on yourself?"

"How old do you think I am?"

"Old enough to be rooted to that settee."

"Old enough to learn what can be done and not done. Old enough for genius the outside world is not yet ready for. Come!" He pointed to the man chained to Horus. "Decebal, bring the boy, too."

He clapped his hands, servants rose from the shadows, and the couch became a litter. Dalca's slaves carried it to a doorway where a ramp curved deeper into the earth, torches flaring on the walls. The duke went first with a coterie of guards, then Horus and his warden, and then I followed with more guards behind, snickering at me as they waddled and leered. Sulfur scented the air. This place was already hell,

I suspected, hell on earth, and the last thing a guest would want is to stay here forever.

Its bloated overseer disappeared into a wider chamber ahead and stopped. Wicks were lit. Horus entered and gave a cry and whimper. And then I stepped inside, to survey a macabre scene lit by a table of candles.

"I've reserved a seat for you," Dalca said.

Two-dozen young women with waxen skin sat around a long banquet table set with plates of gold and tableware of tarnished silver. All were erect, hands artfully placed near a crystal goblet as if dining. Heaped in the middle was wax fruit and meat. The women spoke not a word, every mouth set in a warped imitation of a laugh, molded from a grimace of final horror. They saw nothing because their eyes were milky agates. Cobwebs draped from cheek and elbow. Dust was on their shoulders and brittle hair.

They were the opposite of what Dalca promised.

"What a gift I can give you, Astiza!" the mad duke exclaimed. "Instead of the certainty of rot, the eternity of preservation. I've far surpassed the priests of Egypt with my taxidermy and wax. Here sit the most beautiful Romanian women I could lure, promising them eternal youth as you've promised me, and here they enjoy each other's company for all time. There's no need for your elixir. Look how they chortle! Look how full their breasts remain, how blushed their cheeks, how delicate their painted nails. A special bath of my own for-mulation will allow you to join them, while your son joins me. I know I seem a solemn man, a dour duke, a reclusive tyrant, but here I sing and joke with my ladies as we share an endless last supper. Like these others, you'll give your essence to me and we'll both keep living in very different ways." Now his look was one of raw hunger, monstrous and insatiable.

Upyr was the Tartar word that Czartoryski had given Ethan. Evil spirits. Witches, warlocks, and vampires.

The women's skin was curiously preserved like veined marble. Their gaiety was a failed façade, gums receding from yellowed teeth, clothes rotting, and makeup thick in a vain effort to give them color. They were mummies without wrapping. "My essence?"

"Your life-force. Your blood. I'll take it in return for your immortal preservation and adoption of your boy into our fraternity. You'll become my twenty-fifth wife. I'll drink you dry, and maybe then I'll whisper the real secret of the palladium into your preserved ear." He laughed, jowls and belly shaking, as his servants grinned in a scene from an asylum. Reason had fled this castle long ago. "After my soldiers have had you first, of course."

No one would ever hear my screams.

"Don't hope for rescue. Your husband and his foolish friends have been watched for hours, and the bear's jaws just snapped shut on them. Ethan Gage will see you after your chemical bath, I think. I'll let him kiss your eternal corpse before I put him out of his misery. It will be touching, yes?"

"You're insane."

"I'm a creator."

As I'd warned my son I pretended to faint, drawing everyone's attention to my collapse on the floor.

Horus bit the man who chained him, the one named Decebal.

The warden howled. The collar came free.

CHAPTER 22

B albec Castle perched atop a rock tower, sheer cliffs descending to a canyon on all sides. Its gate was connected to the ridge road by a spindly drawbridge. The only other possible approach was to descend to the canyon bottom, swim a mountain torrent, and climb the other side. There's no trail. We picked our way down into the chasm on icy rocks, clinging where we could to saplings and tree roots. Caleb, Dolgoruki, and I each fell several times, bouncing and skidding until a tree or rock stopped our fall. By the time we reached the floor of the ravine and crossed its icy river, it was dark. We were shaking from wet, cold, exertion, and the dispiriting drag of fear.

"You're certain there's a tunnel entrance somewhere up that cliff?" I asked for the hundredth time. We could see little except that frost rimed the ledges and overhangs challenged every feasible route.

"So I was told after a mixture of threats and bribes to the village smith," Caleb said. "He could have been lying, but then I'd kill him."

I studied the sheer face. "On the contrary, I think he was

fairly certain we'd plunge to our deaths. He could tell you whatever you wanted to hear."

"Most fortresses have some kind of sally port and escape gate," Dolgoruki insisted. "Look. There's a dark hole up there. And there."

"Or shadows. Or discolored rock. You're both mad." Even as I said so there was a rumble of warning thunder from a cap of cloud.

"Madness is opportunity," Dolgoruki said impatiently. "It's not whether this is the best plan, Gage, it's the only plan. It's as difficult to go backward as forward and your family awaits rescue."

I despised the man but I respect bitter logic. "Well said."

The prince swung his arm to the cliff face. "After you."

We started up. It didn't help that we each had a shouldered gun, Dolgoruki a sword, Caleb a coiled rope, and me the medieval horse pick. There was nothing to tie the rope to so we climbed without its aid, each of us taking a turn leading. We were climbing blind, unable to see the castle, a best route, or any enemies. I waited for a shot, arrow, hurled spear, or dropped stone, but none came. Had Astiza succeeded in preoccupying Dalca? We'd timed our attempt before moonrise, and climbed in a cocoon of darkness.

The plan forced upon me by my two conspirators was to make Astiza our Trojan horse. Her job was first to get through the gate, distract the wicked duke, and with Harry's help somehow find this rumored back tunnel and lead us to the castle's core. We'd seize Dalca as a hostage, grab the palladium, and bluster our way out by using the duke as our shield. I calculated there were only half a hundred things that could go wrong with this scheme, but my son had been sold as bait, my wife had been sent as trophy, and I still needed the scoundrels I was partnered with. Only the very real chance of falling a thousand feet kept my resentment at bay. Fear is wonderfully distracting.

The rock was rough and fissured, and in a couple hours we made slow but commendable progress. Yet finally we came to what appeared to be an insurmountable pitch. The cliff blistered, its face angling outward like a sloped ceiling. There was a small ledge beneath where we paused to reconnoiter, but when we crept left or right we couldn't find a way around the overhang. We were stuck.

"This wasn't obvious from the bottom," Dolgoruki said. "No wonder they don't post sentries."

"Yes, how lucky," I said sourly.

"We can retreat and search for a different seam," Caleb said.

"That could mean all the way down to the river," the Russian calculated.

"We've already gained a thousand feet," I said. "Now you want to go back?"

"Not back," Caleb said. "Around."

"That will take hours."

"It will take a day if we have to go all the way to the bottom," Dolgoruki warned, "because the moon will rise and reveal us."

"You didn't consider this possibility before sending my wife and son into the lair of a reputed monster?"

The other two were silent.

"Give me the rope."

"Ethan, it's impossible."

"It's impossible not to try. Give me the rope. If I make it, I'll tie it off and you can pull yourselves over the overhang. If I don't, my death will relieve me of the regret of ever having met either of you."

"Your grumpiness is unfair," Dolgoruki said. "We're just as determined."

"Except for Caleb's preference for going backward."

"I'm only thinking aloud, little brother. I salute your courage."

"Hold the salute and take my rifle. I'll haul the firearms up with the rope before you follow." I paused. "When you're clinging to the line for dear life, hauling yourself over the bulge, nothing but air beneath you for a thousand feet, pray that I don't take it into my head to let go as payback."

That silenced them.

I put the horse pick shaft in my teeth and flexed my fingers. At least there were cracks in the sloping overhang in which to jam my hands. I reached up, seized one, and stepped up off the ledge, my toes still finding purchase. The other hand advanced and clutched. I climbed a few feet until my head was pressed sideways against the rock, my body tilted outward, my torso trembling from the strain.

"Ethan, by the holy Mother …"

I released my lower hand, groped upward, and slapped rock blindly, feeling for a hold. There, a ledge an inch wide! I seized it with my fingertips and my feet lost their grip. My legs swung out into empty space, the river a gray line far below. I gasped. My other hand fell away so I was dangling by one arm.

"Gage!"

Lightning flickered, dazzling my vision. The boom shook but it illuminated another fissure in the rock.

I seized the pick from my jaws with my free hand and swung upward at the crevice. The point penetrated and stuck. For a moment I simply hung, swaying like a pendulum as my muscles squirmed. Then I leaned my head out, sucked air, and pulled with all my might, chinning myself upward. Now my belly was against the pregnant rock, giving me slight friction. I shifted some of my weight onto the hammer of the pick. My fingers were screaming, arms throbbing, I let go my free hand and slapped again.

Another handhold! I rammed my fingers in so tight that my knuckles bled, but for the first time I had the leverage I needed. I kicked, pumped, and squirmed, my knee against the bulge. I wrenched out the pick, swung it hard into a new crevice, clawed, and suddenly I was past the overhang and atop its inward slope, charging like a spider. My bleeding palms found a flat spot and I hauled myself onto it and collapsed, shuddering with relief. So my medieval tomahawk was proving useful! I twisted my head around to see where I was and grunted with satisfaction.

I'd climbed to the mouth of a cave.

Rusty eyebolts showed where a chain or rope might once have hung into the chasm below. Could Astiza and Harry really be near? I turned back toward my companions.

"Ethan?" The quiet call came from below.

"Let me tie off."

The cave opening was just roughly my height, the roof slanting down as its throat penetrated the castle mountain. Protuberances of rock provided a kind of fence on its sides.

More extrusions jutted from the lip of the cave roof. Not trusting the old iron rings, I tied the rope around a lower rocky fang and let it fall to Caleb and Dolgoruki.

"Got it," they hissed.

First I hauled up our guns. Then the two conspirators climbed after and collapsed with me at the entrance.

"You didn't cut the line," my brother said.

"I thought the weight of your lies might break it."

We recovered breath, looking out at the dark basin of mountains that surrounded Balbec Castle. The strange, cold, rainless lightning storm continued to rumble. A lurid flash briefly lit us.

"*Dalca* means 'lightning'," Dolgoruki said.

"Now you tell us."

The cave safely sheltered us from watchers above. I examined the rock protrusions and felt their sculpted smoothness. "These aren't natural," I said. "They're carved."

Dolgoruki inspected them. "Like teeth. Pointed teeth. Animal teeth."

Caleb leaned out, studying the cliff above, and then pulled himself in. "Bear teeth. Our cave, gentlemen, has been shaped into the mouth of a bear."

The Russian grimaced. "I ran from the wolf and encountered the bear. It's an old proverb."

"Meant to swallow?" I wondered.

"Meant to frighten," Caleb said. "Like that damned howling from the castle. This Dalca warlord tries to scare everyone away."

"Maybe he's all bluff." But I doubted it.

I used a tinderbox to light a candle, took my rifle, and led the way. We bent as we penetrated the bear's throat, the cave ceiling lowering until we were bent almost double.

"Defenders could pick off attackers one by one," Dolgoruki said. "Be ready for ambush."

"It's worse than that." I saw a dreaded pattern ahead. "Iron bars." I crawled forward to inspect. A grill blocked the passage. "Did your informant mention this?"

"I believe he didn't," Caleb replied. "Again why they post no guards."

We inspected the barrier. The grill was a door with a heavy lock. I grasped the barrier and shook. The bars were set solid.

"We have to retreat," the Russian mourned.

"They hell we will."

Then there was a snap and sharp squeal.

With a resounding crash, a second iron gate fell from a fissure in the cave ceiling behind us and slammed into the floor.

We'd climbed our way into a cage.

CHAPTER 23

Harry

I bit the mean soldier's fingers as hard as I could and came free as Mama promised. I had to get away from the dead ladies! Mama had whispered as she hugged me, and slipped a pin from her mouth into the lock on my neck. She told me to do three things. Bite the man when she fainted. Pull hard on the chain to make the lock open. And run very fast to find Papa. She told me he'd be in one of the tunnels under the castle.

Now I'm lost and scared. Decebal came after me with his iron collar, snarling very bad words. I hid in a chest while he rushed by. Then I climbed out to search. Tunnels led everywhere like an ant's nest. Somewhere I heard Mama scream. The Pig Man was shouting.

I finally thought I heard Papa's call and ran that way. I saw a lamp ahead but the tunnel floor was very dark. Then I heard Papa again and ran as fast as I could. I was running too fast in the dark and I tripped.

It hurt! I scraped my hands and knees, and started crying. But I realized there was a big hole where I'd been rushing. I felt with my arm. The tunnel floor disappeared.

If I hadn't stumbled I would have fallen into a pit. "Papa?"

Maybe the pit was a well. I smelled dirty water. I felt with my hands. The reason I tripped was a curb of stone near the edge of the hole, maybe to warn people in the dark. But I couldn't go any further.

"Witch's spawn! Now I'll flay you!" Decebal was coming, yelling bad words. I could see the flare of his torch and hear the drag and bounce of the chain.

A single oil lamp gave tiny light. Otherwise it was all black and scary. I sobbed and wet my pants. I hated this place. Where was Papa? I felt frozen and there was nowhere to go.

The bad soldier called Decebal came around a tunnel twist, saw me lying in the shadows, and charged, swinging the chain. I wanted to be brave and stand tall, but when he reached for me with his wild eyes I curled into a ball at the edge of the pit. I was so afraid!

Then a strange thing happened. Decebal tripped on the same stone bump I had, but he was taller and fell further.

He fell into the hole.

I turned to see. His torch fell too. Decebal screamed and screamed but he disappeared into darkness. The torch went out. There was a huge splash, and a wait, and then I heard him, very deep and far away, call me more bad names.

Then there was a bigger splash. Was something else down there? Decebal went very quiet. He was afraid too.

I was glad the bad soldier fell. But I also remembered how he seemed sad and angry. Unhappy people do mean things.

I stood, shivering. I tried to stop crying but shook all over and smelled from wetting myself. I was so ashamed. But then I heard Papa call again, and suddenly I didn't care.

"Harry! Astiza!"

"Papa!" I don't know if he heard me. But I heard him. There was a tunnel on the other side of the pit where the voice was coming from.

But if I tried to go there, I'd fall like Decebal.

I listened. No one else was coming so I tried to calm down. Papa told me the most important thing in fighting is thinking. So I tried to think.

Why would grownups put a pit in the middle of the tunnel if you couldn't get to the other side? That's silly. I looked around.

There was a chain near the pit that came out of a hole in the wall. I pulled it. It was heavy and at first nothing happened. So I pulled as hard as I could and with a thunk the chain began to come. It made a rumble sound.

I crawled to the edge of the pit. Just below its rim, a log had started to poke out of the pit wall.

I pulled the chain some more.

The log came out more.

When I pulled the chain as far as I could, the log slid all the way across the pit and into a hole on the other side. The log's top was flat, but the flat part was hardly wider than my foot. There was nothing to hang onto, and it was really dark.

I looked down into the dark and wondered what made the big splash at the bottom of the pit. Decebal was quiet. Was he dead?

I heard Papa shout again. "Harry!"

It's very hard to decide to be brave, but I decided. I was brave to bite the bad man who came after me, but then he fell! So I'd be brave again. I need Papa to rescue Mama.

I pretended the log was just a line on my bedroom floor, if I had a bedroom. This helped me balance when I walked across. When I got to the other side, I saw another dim light down the tunnel, very far away.

"Papa?"

"Harry! Here!" And then: "Be careful."

I crawled on my hands and knees, feeling for holes. It was a long way, but I didn't want to fall like Decebal. Finally I came to iron bars. On the other side were Papa and Uncle Caleb and the prince.

"Harry, thank God! You're bleeding. Damnation—no, don't listen to that word, but by Jupiter—Harry, we can't open this gate. Is your mother alive?"

"She fainted. On purpose."

"Do you see any tools on your side to break down the bars?"

I looked. "No, Papa. Maybe you can go another way."

"A gate closed in back of us. We're trapped."

"The Pig Man said it's a bear's mouth."

"Can you fetch Mama?"

"She told me to bite a bad soldier. He fell in a hole. The Pig Man wants to make her join the dead ladies. He was yelling. I ran away."

Papa picked up his gun. "Are there other bad men?"

"Not yet."

"Harry, look carefully. Is there a pry bar, or a pick, or

a shovel, or a saw?" Papa had his funny hammer out but it didn't seem to help.

I looked and felt in the dark. "No."

"Harry, we need something to get us out." Papa's voice was tight.

"I'm sorry." I began to cry again.

"Don't cry. It's not your fault, son."

"We'll get to you somehow, lad," Uncle Caleb promised.

Now I bawled. I was so tired and afraid. I felt bad because I couldn't find the tools Papa wanted. I tried to talk but it was hard because I choked and hiccupped. I just wanted him to hug me.

"I'm so sorry, Papa!" I hiccupped and hiccupped. "All there is are rusty old keys!"

CHAPTER 24

So my son was once again a hero. The fact that he was wet and sniveling didn't concern me, given that I've been that way myself more than once. Besides, there's no courage is being too dense to understand danger. My boy is smart enough to know he has to be brave, and resourceful as a mouse in a beggar's bowl. "There's a big hole," he warned after freeing us. So I snuffed out my candle and we crept instead of charged, and thus heard a snarl of voices ahead before they heard us. We made ready.

Sure enough there was a flare of torchlight on the further side of a pit that seemed to plummet to Hades. The illumination silhouetted Dalca Cezar's henchmen as they crowded the far side of the cavity. A narrow log crossed the void and my amazement at my son's grit grew. I swear my boy would dance across the yard of a topgallant to fetch his wayward Papa.

I crawled to the edge of the well. The chasm was absolutely black and seemingly bottomless. Then I heard a groan of despair from its depths. I backed up to the others.

"Someone's down there," I murmured.

"The bad soldier," Harry said. "He made a big splash."

I remembered my own desperation in the moon well of the Russian ship in St. Petersburg. "He's got a long climb or a slow death." And then a thump echoed up to us, followed by a splash and scream. Then silence.

"Not so slow," Caleb whispered. "There is some *thing* as well as some *one* in that perfidious hole. Suddenly that log looks skinny as a wire."

Dalca's men looked nervously down into the chasm, arguing nervously in a guttural language and pointing at the narrow log. Dark still hid us.

"The beam is our only path to Astiza, and my child has already crossed it." I turned to my imperfect partners. "A volley and we'll dash across. Sword and pick to finish off any survivors." My patience was gone and I felt cruel as a Turk. "Harry, get behind. You two, ready?"

Caleb and Dolgoruki leveled their muskets.

"Ready. Aim. Fire!"

Our shots flashed like a lightning bolt. Three of Dalca's bastards dropped, one toppling with a howl of despair into the cavity. I rose, gunsmoke in my nostrils, in order to press our attack.

"Look out!" Caleb jerked me down, slamming my son to the cave floor as well. An answering volley punched through our smoke and bullets combed our hair. There was a bigger company of louts across the chasm than I thought. My brother had saved my life.

"See? I'm not entirely bad, Ethan."

"Let's reload. Stay prone."

Guessing that we were momentarily without powder, some of Dalca's brutes risked rushing to the lip of the pit and inserting an iron bar in a fitting on the far side of the cavity. As they levered back and forth, the log bridge popped from its socket on our side of the chasm and began to recede like a worm into its burrow. A chain rattled as it wound back into the earth.

"We'll be trapped again," Caleb hissed, scraping his ramrod out of his musket barrel and priming his pan.

"By the Icon of Kazan, we most certainly will not," growled Dolgoruki. Without asking he crawled over and past us, snatched my horse pick, rose up, brandished his sword with his other hand, gave a mighty Russian oath, and sprang into the void.

It was an impossible jump toward the receding log, the well far wider than he could ever cross. Yet the prince flew just far enough to swing my pick like a grapnel. It bit the logwood as he fell so he swung, clinging like a monkey while still clutching the golden sword awarded by Tsar Alexander. Then with a kick and heave, he boosted himself by the pick handle and got an arm around the log.

Russians don't lack courage.

Dalca's preoccupied henchmen were still frantically hauling the log in, inadvertently drawing Dolgoruki to their side of the pit. Perhaps he'd take them unawares. But no, another Szekler, this one taller and thick as a bull, had seen the daring leap and ran up with a pike to stab. The prince peered up, helpless where he hung. The scoundrel lifted his weapon, ready to impale.

Caleb fired. The warrior gave a great cry and pitched over the prince's head and down into the pit, his pike clanging against the well's sides as he plunged. A distant splash was followed almost immediately by a bigger one, and another terrified scream.

"What in hell is down there?" my brother asked.

"Hell indeed. Don't slip."

Our Russian used the reprieve to clamber over the lip of the pit to attack with saber, pick, and hammer. One man cranking the lever took the blade through his heart, and another staggered away with my pick impaled in his back. A third pulled his own scimitar to foolishly fence. It was no contest for a noble taught swordplay since infancy. The ruffian quickly fell. Their blood looked black in the dimness.

That would have ended it except that a fourth charged Dolgoruki from his blind side, hurtling out of the dark. I killed that one with my own rifle, and then the Russian chased down the wounded man and thrust deep to finish him. He jerked out my horse pick and tossed it back where I'd retrieve it, once across. We'd now accounted for eight or nine of the demons, a satisfying slaughter on the pit's far side. Other shadows ran away to get reinforcements.

Dolgoruki came back and hauled on the chain as hard as a sailor, the log bridge surging back across the well to slam into its socket again. Emboldened by the Russian's example we danced across, Caleb carrying Dolgoruki's musket and me carrying Harry. Then everyone reloaded.

"Bold work, my Russian friend," I congratulated.

"Ha. I'm your friend now?"

"I don't want you as my enemy." His beautiful inlaid sword was slick with gore. "Let's go get my wife."

We proceeded cautiously, wary of ambush. Our opponents were noisy so twice we did the ambushing ourselves, seeing torchlight approaching and lying prone until we had a clear shot at their silhouettes. Both times we killed three. No general alarm had been raised, meaning the deep tunnels must be swallowing the sound of gunfire. We probed through a labyrinth. Harry, who'd seen enough mayhem in his young life to be untroubled by the dispatch of "bad men," was an able guide. He pointed to this stair and that corridor as the way he'd come, content that I'd finally arrived and perfectly confident we'd rescue his mother. He hesitated only at one door.

"We have to go past the dead ladies."

Beyond was the most bizarre and hideous tableaux I'd ever seen. In the bowels of the castle was a banquet room filled with the desiccated corpses of two-dozen young women around a long heavy table. Their features were waxen, their color false, and I sensed they'd somehow been drained dry and re-stuffed. Yet there was no rot, only some gruesome kind of pickling.

"What in God's name would draw a woman to a place like this?" Dolgoruki wondered.

"Not God. The devil. So where's Mama, Harry?"

"That door wasn't open before." He pointed.

At the far end of the room a tapestry had been pulled aside to reveal another exit from the banquet room. Stairs led down toward an odd chemical smell.

"Some kind of laboratory," I guessed. "Harry, stay here to stand watch. Yell if anyone comes."

"I'm afraid of the dead ladies."

"They're just dead, like the bad men. I'm going to bring Mama to you here." If she hasn't already been transformed into a mummified trophy, I thought. If she wasn't already a wax corpse. "These ladies don't like the bad men. They'll help you keep watch."

"Hurry."

I began to creep down the stairs, rifle primed and ready. Caleb excitedly caught my arm.

"Now comes reward, Ethan!"

"If your palladium exists."

We advanced. Two sentries jumped in surprise, drew scimitars, and were killed. We reloaded and kept going.

And found something even more bizarre than the banquet room.

We entered a barrel-roofed chamber lit by a hundred candles. In the center was a bubbling pool of mud-thick liquid, fumes wafting, that producing a noxious and cloying haze that stung. Shelves held vats, vials, and bones—lots of bones. Skulls were lined like apothecary jars. Leg and arm bones were stacked like firewood. Tendrils of leathery flesh still clung, and some of the skulls had wisps of hair and scraps of scalp. There were rust-colored stains on floor and walls, and brown spots spattered the ceiling. Was Dalca a cannibal?

"This is an evil place," Dolgoruki muttered, crossing himself.

"So you've come to watch," a deep voice rumbled.

The monster was at the far end of the pool. He was a sickeningly obese creature in dressing gown, leather apron, and leather boots that reached to fat thighs, his body slumped in a wicker wheelchair. He had the bushy beard and wild hair of a Russian hermit, and sunken, nearly hidden eyes that nonetheless seemed to probe with pitiless scrutiny. Pig Man, Harry had called him.

"Or we can bargain," he continued in a voice as heavy as a millstone.

No more servants were present, but Dalca wasn't alone.

We froze at the sight of Astiza. My wife was embarrassingly nude and strapped to a table that tilted over the foul pool, her feet aimed at its contents. Next to her was a second table, horizontal and sturdy, that held a demon's collection of surgical instruments. There were scalpels, glass suction cups, coiled tubes, needles, and clamps. Her mouth was gagged, and her eyes wide with fear and fury that seemed even more naked than her body, a look as wrenching as that of the insane. Astiza, usually so serene, so philosophic, had been stripped bare in more ways than one. There was nothing erotic about her humiliation, and nothing beautiful in her exposure. It was a betrayal of all that was decent and proper.

"That's my wife." My voice rasped like a bayonet lifted from its scabbard, and the muzzle of my rifle pointed at Cezar Dalca.

He lifted one lazy hand in his defense. His fist held a rope, leading through a pulley in the ceiling down to the tilted table. The meaning was clear enough. If he yanked, or I shot, Astiza would slide into his tank.

"Sorcery," Dolgoruki said with the gagged contempt only the noble can fully express. "Witchcraft. This man is an *upyr.*"

"Utter blasphemy," agreed Caleb, his voice breaking. "Ethan, I never suspected, never dreamed. Astiza, I thought him only a crank—"

"What your wife is, my new friends, is my contribution for admission to your fellowship," Dalca rumbled. Even as he spoke I began to mentally measure distances. "I'd dearly love to add Astiza to my immortal banquet but she informs me you're after a higher prize. Is that not true, my dear?"

A leather strap on her forehead prevented her from nodding or shaking her head.

"You're an instant from death, Dalca." I was squinting down my barrel.

"My hand can twitch as fast as your finger can pull, Monsieur Gage, and then your wife *will* join my banquet. I prefer to empty my guests first, eliminating any pain from the bathing, but your intrusion has robbed me of time to drink. If you prefer to make a fight of it you can watch her boil alive. Her screams would be one of the last things you hear, because there are a hundred Szeklers between you and any exit from Balbec Castle. But why dwell on such terrible contingencies? I want to be your partner, not your executioner."

"Partner in *what?*"

"The Trojan Icon." He nodded. "Yes, Astiza and I have discussed your quest at some length. Unfortunately I don't have it. You can search my home but you'll find that I keep my belongings in more secret places than this, and don't have the palladium of Pallas Athena at all. Your entire quest, and all the risk to wife and son, was in vain." He coughed what might have been a laugh. "But I think I could lead you *to* the palladium, *if* you could contrive to carry me there."

"Where?"

"Constantinople. The Ottomans call it Istanbul, I believe."

Their capital was hundreds of miles away. "Where in Constantinople?"

"That's part of our bargain, is it not? Your derring-do, my research. I'm a rather conspicuous treasure hunter, unable to travel unnoticed, but you have a knack for worming where you don't belong. We'd be superb collaborators."

"Would we?" I began to move toward him.

"Ah! Not with your rifle, please. Firearms disturb me. But yes, a brilliant fellowship. None of us are hobbled by morals, are we? A society of thieves."

Another step. "Release my wife first."

"Now the prince's sword, *that* I can appreciate. Russian, I assume? A pretty prick. Is that sweet blood on the blade?"

Another step.

"Gage! Lower the guns while we come to understanding."

"Not before you get your hand off that rope."

He considered, eyeing us, and then slowly released his grip and dropped his hand to his fat belly. "Done. See? I'm a man of compromise. Like you. Now. Lower your gun."

I did so.

"All the way, where it can't harm me."

Reluctantly, I laid my rifle on the floor.

"Ethan!" Caleb protested.

"He's insane. Don't startle him." Then I spoke to Dalca. "Move away from the rope." I slowly edged closer.

"Alas, that defeats my bargaining position, which is this. I'll trade Astiza to you for a half-share of the palladium. We'll find it together, sell it together, and split the profits. Half for me, and half for the rest of you."

Another step. "Shares equally."

"No. Your beauty of a wife is worth a full half-share. It's true you've penetrated my castle and fought past my sentries. But it's equally true that I could add Astiza to my banquet and swarm you with the remainder of my garrison. I'd rather given up on the palladium, but your arrival reassures me of its existence. So exciting to imagine possessing it."

So Dalca's interest was our proof, while our interest was his. Rumor feeding rumor. "Harm her and you get nothing." Another step.

"Harm me and all of you die as well."

"What chance do we have of finding the palladium and stealing it from the Turks?" Closer.

"I'm a scholar, much like your wife. I know things. You're a thief, much like your brother. A partnership, I said." His fingers were still clasped, his gaze fixed on me instead of Astiza. My wife was squirming in her bonds, her eyes pleading. Were they warning?

"You bully a woman?"

"To persuade her man."

I was close. I lunged.

"Misjudged, Ethan Gage." His hands remained clasped, but one booted foot shot up and out. Attached was a cord tied to a support under the tilted table. In an instant of horrified regret I realized that the rope to the ceiling had been a ruse, and it was this other prop that had kept my wife from the boiling mud and wax. The tilted table began to slide toward the pool.

"And you, Dalca." Because the monster had also miscalculated: I wasn't diving for him but for Astiza. The horse pick came out from its loop at my back and its point punctured Astiza's table, braking its slide. I kicked the surgical instrument table into the bubbling pool, its instruments flying, and its edged jammed the lower edge of my wife's platform.

Ooze lapped inches from Astiza's toes. Our eyes locked

for the briefest of moments, mine sympathetic, hers despairing and half-mad.

Dalca howled in frustration and fury.

Caleb fired. My brother was a crack shot but the duke didn't even twitch. How could my brother miss? Was Cezar truly immortal?

I hauled at Astiza's bizarre bed with my pick. Caleb moved toward my rifle. And Dolgoruki charged with his golden sword, crying to the saints.

Dalca snarled, and I got a glimpse of teeth more animal than human. The creature's instincts were lightning fast despite his bulk, and somehow he caught the edge of the prince's sword with a hand even as the saber cut toward the villain's head. The blade stopped as if it had hit stone. Dalca bent, and bit.

Dolgoruki shrieked.

The prince's sword fell with a clang and a sizzle, as if suddenly hot, and I saw to my amazement that its fine steel had bent. I heaved again and managed to twist Astiza's table off its precarious balancing point, toppling her away from the pool. Now she was face down, still strapped, but the table was a crude shield between her and Dalca.

"Ethan, I've got your rifle!"

Dalca cast Dolgoruki aside like a toy and the creature turned to us, his eyes like sunken musket balls in suet, his mouth blood red and snarling like a rabid dog.

Caleb pulled the trigger. The gun clicked impotently. What the devil? But perhaps this *was* the devil, the real devil, bending swords, deadening rifles, and fending off death by consuming other life.

I tried to remember legends. "Ram the barrel into him

like a bayonet!" I'd no idea what effect such desperation might have, but Caleb was immensely strong. This fight would be won at the most primitive level.

So now my brother charged, my gun a blunt stake. Dalca's face bulged in fear.

I wrenched the horse pick free, its point bright.

And then there was an explosion, a great flash of light, and a blow like a thunderbolt. I was kicked back across the rim of the pool, almost falling in, and Caleb flew as if cuffed by a giant's blow. Smoke billowed, and most of the candles snuffed out. There was a whirl of wind.

For long seconds we were lay stunned, uncertain what had happened. I coughed for breath. "Astiza?" Aching, I finally sat up and stared.

My wife was still bound and helpless.

And Cezar Dalca, immortal lord of Balbec, had vanished.

CHAPTER 25

"It was a magician's trick."

The flash and smoke had seemed supernatural, and for a moment we thought it had been. But Dalca's chair was gone, too, and eventually we found the outline of a trap door now locked from below. He'd escaped down some kind of diabolical chute. We'd search, but my bet was we wouldn't find him.

"He's no upyr, vampire, witch, warlock, sorcerer, werewolf, or wizard," I insisted, as much to myself as the others. "He's a fat lunatic who murders and mummifies and who fled like a coward."

But even as I said it, I wasn't sure. *True evil, base evil, unfeeling and implacable evil, is rare,* Czartoryski had said.

But it exists.

I unstrapped my wife and ripped down a tapestry to cover her nakedness. Caleb and Dolgoruki averted their gaze but poor Astiza squeezed her eyes shut in shame and shock. Harry came down the stairs, reporting that no bad men had appeared, and then he ran to his mother. The two fiercely clutched next to the steaming chemical bath like one fragile organism. Both were stunned from accumulated horror, staring out at nothing and seeing far too much. My wife had come within a moment and inches of horrible mummification. My son had been chased by a demon. And now that Dalca had disappeared, my fury at Dolgoruki and Caleb truly boiled. Resentment hung in the room as thick as its foul fog.

All this tragedy for a trophy that wasn't here. Madness!

Yet my anger was kept bottled by one troubling fact.

Something was terribly wrong with the Russian prince.

Caleb had wrapped the hand where Peter Petrovich was bitten. But Dolgoruki was alarmingly pale and copiously sweating, his breathing labored. Dalca's bite had some kind of poison.

Even more disturbing was the bent remnant of the prince's beautiful sword. It was as if the twisted weapon had served as some kind of lightning rod for a surge of malevolent power. Its gold and silver had dulled to iron gray. The blade looked enfeebled. And Dalca had caught its edge in his own hand without apparent effect.

What *was* he?

I shuddered. There was something deeply wrong with Balbec, so steeped in evil that the stone itself seemed corrupt. Dalca's vanishing was a mortal magician's trick, but with a true necromancer behind it.

"He threw my clothes in the banquet room." Astiza weakly gestured. I brought them down and held up the tapestry as a shield while she shakily dressed.

"How could you miss?" I asked Caleb.

"I didn't, little brother."

I test-fired my rifle into the pool and it functioned perfectly. Why had it misfired at Dalca? We reloaded in case soldiers came to avenge their lord, but we sensed that Balbec had emptied. The castle was eerily quiet.

We did methodically search the tunnels for the palladium, since we couldn't trust Dalca's claim about Constantinople. We found a library stuffed with medieval volumes, an alchemical laboratory, and storerooms that at one time or another might have held artifacts and treasure. If so, all such prizes had disappeared. It was as if that puff of smoke had not just removed Cezar Dalca, but all his minions, all his belongings, and all his power. What remained was an infected shell, as derelict as an abandoned beehive.

The grisly banquet was still there. The women sat frozen in hideous eternity, their souls as imprisoned as their bodies.

"These girls deserve burial," Caleb said.

"We don't have the time or place for that," I said. "The pinnacle is solid rock. Dolgoruki is sick, and Astiza and Harry are half-mad." I didn't add, but could have, 'Thanks to you.' Caleb looked away but his expression was not just guilty, I thought, but guilt tainted with awful redemption. He'd disrupted my life and woman as I'd disrupted his, and achieved a wretched parity.

We're even.

So I hated my brother. And yet if I were to confess completely, I was also liberated by his treachery. He'd erased decades of debt by abusing my family; he'd absorbed my sin with sin of his own. We *were* sadly square. His plot to use my wife and child was a perversion of sacrifice, the exact kind of thing a dark creature in a grim place like Balbec would encourage. So our brotherhood was befouled. Yet at the same time, Caleb and I were bonded more tightly than ever by mutual resentment and need. Ours was a partnership of pirates, a communion of scoundrels. I felt contaminated. I felt reunited. I resented. But I also wearily accepted.

"A cremation, then," he said.

That felt right. The wicked pool had an oily smell, and when I threw a torch into the brew it caught and flared. Fire and smoke roiled and rolled, and we hurriedly retreated as it flamed its way up the corridor into the Immortal Banquet. The mummified supper began to burn, the captive women igniting like torches. Their frozen faces melted, in tragic liberation.

We backed up winding stairs with torches, igniting an intricate network of supporting beams, wooden floors, carpets, hangings—anything that would burn with cleansing fire. The blaze made a greedy crackle. Fire ascended into the ruined towers, flames climbing like vines. The drumming heat pushed us out into the castle courtyard, where we watched smoke pour out of the slit windows of the keep. We winched up the portcullis gate and retreated across the drawbridge, setting it afire too. Dalca's followers could have cut us off by destroying this span, but the survivors had vanished as suddenly as he had, like a nightmare erased by morning.

We looked back, Dolgoruki swaying from fever. Balbec had become a gigantic funeral pyre. As the flames ate wooden bracing, the castle walls began to lean and tremble, wavering in the heat like a horrific mirage. Black smoke swirled skyward. The wolf banner caught and burned to nothing, silencing its eerie howl. Yet even as the column of smoke boiled, a curious reversal happened. The overcast that had hung over Balbec Castle so persistently began to dissipate, shreds of sunlight poking through. It was dawn. The thunder grumbled and died.

Sparks showered us as portions of the battlements began

to collapse. Finally, with a great roar, the entire castle dissolved and its stones avalanched in every direction, cascading down the pinnacle to crash into the dark canyons below. The drawbridge went with it. The sound of the landslide bounced back and forth in the chasm like a drum, the river steaming. I looked at its thin gray thread, far below. Was that debris floating downstream? Or boats with fleeing Szekler soldiers, slipping round a bend in the gorge?

What was finally left was a blackened pillar of rock, pierced by the black cavities of winding tunnels and orbited by a halo of agitated, displaced crows. The wintry sky continued to lighten. Balbec's spell had been broken.

We wearily made our way down the mountains to grubby Szejmal, Dolgoruki balancing dizzily on our shoulders. His face was colorless, his eyes vacant. "It wasn't there?" he kept asking. Caleb and I glanced at each other. The wounded Russian was in no condition to go on, wherever "on" might be.

"Now what?" I wondered aloud. "Do we just go back?" My wife and son were haggard, our hopes in ruins, and the world was literally cold and bleak.

"To what?" Caleb said. "We've given up the swords, for no reward. The prince has nothing to placate his Russian masters. I'm still in hock to Napoleon. And we're already three-quarters of the way from St. Petersburg to Constantinople, where Dalca said the palladium still hides."

"What is this 'we', Caleb? Our partnership is over. And my family, doughty though it is, can hardly waltz into an audience with the Grand Turk and ask for directions to a Trojan trinket. The Ottomans would laugh first, and impale us second."

"That's true. Unless circumstances change." And at that

enigmatic remark Caleb fell silent as we came into the village, the inhabitants cowering as if we'd risen from the dead. Tendrils of smoke still rose from the direction of Balbec. For the first time, I noticed green buds on nearby branches.

Our fearsomeness won us no favors. We were forced to pay triple for lodging in case we might be upyrs. Then we erased any remaining awe by quite humanly sleeping the sleep of the exhausted for the next twenty hours. Apparently we were mortal after all, the villagers decided. They whispered when we woke, gesturing toward the destroyed castle and arguing what to do. Instead of gratitude, they eyed us with resentment and calculation.

So we prudently retreated to the more normal Undarhely, in a broad valley twenty miles distant. There we rested at a farmstead for the next several weeks. Spring continued to advance toward summer. At length Dolgoruki roused himself from sick stupor. He still seemed ill, but now had the feverish determination of a man desperate to die in his own bed. He told us he was returning north.

"You still have an infection," Astiza objected. "Your hand is swollen and your forehead is hot. You need a long recuperation."

"I need a Russian healer. I might journey all the way to St. Petersburg to recuperate at home. This was a grave mistake pursuing pagan icons, and I apologize for ever bringing you here."

"Can you even travel?" I asked.

"I've bargained for a nag that will carry me in slow stages until I get to where I can hire a coach."

"What about Constantinople?" Caleb asked.

"I leave it to you. It's been an adventure, my companions, but I'm in no condition to go further. I suspect this statue of

Athena was a ruse, a myth, and a goose hunt to get all of us out of Pulawy and let Izabela Czartoryski hide her old swords. I was manipulated as much as you. The perfidious Poles are probably laughing right now."

"Dalca did know of the palladium," Astiza said.

"So what? It's a common tale. We've rid the country of him, sacrificed our sanity to do so, and are left with disease as payment. So be it! I'm a soldier, and a soldier I should have remained. God has punished me for deserting my post. So, I accept pain until I find redemption on the battlefield. Triumph or death! That at least gives clarity." He focused blearily on me. "Gage, I never liked you. But I pity your family and respect your courage."

"As I respect yours."

"I ask you to forgive and forget. Perhaps we can savor this adventure in the dusk of life, when memories soften. Or perhaps time will let us forget. Goodbye, Astiza. May fate give you an easier path."

"I fear for you, prince."

"We all die. But I want to die with my family."

Dolgoruki was gravely ill. His skin had parchment-like translucence as if he had been dipped in Dalca's pool. I sensed a man who was already half a ghost. But we were in no condition or mood to escort him and so he rode north alone, taking the road to Bistritz and from there back toward Russia.

That night we ate a subdued supper and retired to bed. Caleb had taken to sleeping in the barn.

The next morning we found he'd disappeared as well. He left behind a purse of coins, and no explanation.

Just a bag of round stones to serve as marbles.

For Harry.

CHAPTER 26

S o we were back to our tight cluster of three, a family trying to heal.

The first to recover was my son. Children are as resilient as rubber and tend to regard whatever condition they are born into as normal. While adults struggle against circumstance, the young adapt. He caught up on his sleep, recovered his strength, found some Undarhely boys to play with, and soon looked ready to travel to wherever Papa and Mama decided. I kept telling him how brave he'd been, and he accepted these compliments as his due.

Caleb's disappearance let me stop stewing about brotherly betrayals and regain some equanimity. Perhaps I was reading too much history into his motives, and his real goal had simply been to make money. He'd thrown his fortunes in with ours in hopes Gage luck would turn, and it hadn't. But neither were we dead. We'd survived the worst, destroyed an evil castle, and come out unwounded, if not unchanged. And didn't I share blame for greed? "He who believes money will do everything will be suspected of doing everything for money," Benjamin Franklin had warned me. The old man was annoyingly right.

At first I preferred to do nothing, but soon grew restless. I began target shooting, giving Harry a sixth birthday present by instructing him to handle a gun. Given our history, such skill was prudent. I bought him the smallest fowling piece I could find and we hunted birds under my cautious supervision.

"Can I shoot bad people?"

"It's not very pleasant. But you have to protect yourself."

"I want to protect Mama."

"So do I."

I also made him a sailboat for the village duck pond. I repaired and purchased our travel gear, since we couldn't stay in Undarhely forever. I began to ask questions about the Turks and their vast capitol of Constantinople. The city straddled the Bosporus Straits more than four hundred miles southeast of where we were recuperating. Could this palladium really be there? Was it all a hoax? Alternately, could we make our way to Bucharest and down the Danube to the Black Sea, and from there take ship to Egypt or America? How would we pay for passage? What would we do when we got there?

Astiza was the last to regain her spirit. Her son had almost been lost, her foray had failed to find the palladium, and she'd been stripped of dignity and almost mummified. She refused to tell me all that had happened in her brief captivity, but it had eroded her confidence.

"I need time, Ethan."

Compared to the dreams of titles and palaces we'd allowed ourselves a few short months before, our situation was pitiful. For several painful days she was remote, talking little and staying indoors. She almost shrank from my touch, not trusting anything or anybody. Only after a week did she relax enough to be briefly embraced. It was a month before we made tentative, gentle, love, which she consented to with trepidation. It wasn't great pleasure for either of us, but the act was a hurdle to get over. It did seem to help restore her composure in that it promised that normalcy was possible someday. But she often woke with nightmares.

So we tentatively healed. It was now late spring, Transylvania a gorgeous green, and Astiza eventually ventured outside to sit against the wall of our farmstead, soaking in the sun. After two weeks she began to take short walks. The sun lifted her spirits as the nights kept getting shorter.

We talked little of where to go next, so perhaps instinctually knew we were waiting for direction. Nothing had been resolved. To pass the time Astiza continued teaching Harry to read, bringing out of a book of fanciful tales she'd been hoarding. He listened, entranced, and then read the stories back with a serious determination that pleased both him and us.

We hung suspended. Perhaps it was as Astiza had said, that time was an illusion occupying an endless now.

And then Caleb came back.

He galloped up to the tiny house we'd rented on a spirited black stallion, dressed in fine new clothes, his musket in a saddle scabbard and a new French cavalry sword swinging on his waist. He reined up with a great shout, swept off a bicorn hat to salute his delighted nephew, grinned like a bridegroom, and grandly announced, "I have redeemed myself!"

I caught his bridle with consternation. "You dare return?"

He bowed from the saddle. "Astiza, I was a beast and poltroon, but fortune has a way of turning for those who dare.

I declare our problems solved and our fortunes made, with or without this Trojan treasure."

"What are you talking about?" she asked. "Where did you go?"

"South to the Ottoman Empire to learn the news. Once more, the battle of Austerlitz has changed everything. The sultan has swung from the Russians and English to the French, and Napoleon's newest ambassador to the Ottoman court wants to meet you, dear sister."

"Meet me?" My wife was bewildered.

"You. Us. Our fellowship. Emperor Napoleon remembers all, and he remembers the brothers Gage. Ambassador Sebastiani is intrigued by our knowledge of the tsar, Louis, the Czartoryskis, and Polish plans, and believes our interests can intersect. Bonaparte has forgiven you!"

"Forgiven?" I said. "As if we'd forgive him, after all the trouble he's caused."

"Ancient history, brother, as forgotten as last year's treaty. In today's tumultuous world alliances are made from yesterday's leftovers and unmade by tomorrow's appetite. The Russians are marching. The Serbs remain in revolt. The Ottomans are at each other's throats. From chaos comes opportunity. Come meet Horace Sebastiani, who has paused in Adrianople on his way to present his credentials to Sultan Selim III."

"Sebastiani fought at Austerlitz."

"Yes, and was promoted to general there. The sultan sees Napoleon as his new best hope, and Sebastiani has Bonaparte's ear. Did you want to teach the tsar what you've learned of the art of war? Teach the sultan's New Army instead. Trade a Russian palace for a Turkish one."

"Caleb, have you been drinking?" Astiza asked.

He winked at her. "No liquor in the land of Islam, Madame Gage, unless you know where to go, which is to every second house in Constantinople." He laughed. "But no, I'm perfectly sober, and simply intoxicated by the new opportunities life has given us. Turkey and Russia are drifting toward war, France is provoking Prussia, Adriatic islands are being traded back and forth like coins in a gambling salon, and bold people are seizing control of fate. I met with Sebastiani and he's intrigued by what we offer. Does he want to meet the notorious Ethan Gage? Of course he does. But he suspects another is even more important, as she has been from the beginning. It turns out that one of the most powerful and unseen people in the Ottoman Empire has a special interest in *you*, Astiza."

The prospect appeared to horrify her. "No. Not again."

"This invitation is as sweet as the other was sour."

"The Muslims won't listen to a woman."

"But the women of their harems might. There's a blond beauty from the island of Martinique, enslaved in Topkapi Palace for almost two decades, who wields more power behind the throne than most viziers do in front of it. She's mightily interested in a woman of your learning and experience."

"A blond from the Caribbean?" I asked.

"A French creole seized by the Barbary pirates, prized for her looks, and offered to the prior sultan as a present, from the pasha of Tripoli. The sultan cannot stock his harem with Turkish women, which offends Islamic law, so he seeks infidel slave beauties from all over the world. This one has captured the Turks as thoroughly as she's been captured. She's persuading them to ally with Napoleon."

"Why would she do that?" Astiza asked.

"Because her cousin, dear family, is none other than that other creole from Martinique, one Josephine Bonaparte." He nodded at our astonishment. "Yes, Empress Josephine. The two played together as children. As a result, we have a key to the Topkapi Palace overlooking the Bosporus and all the riches within it. Our key's name is Aimée Dubucq de Rivéry, now known as Nakshedil, 'the beautiful one.' Sebastiani sent word to her of what I told him about our family, and I've brought back a reply." He handed a note. "Our luck has finally turned."

I opened it. Written in French were just five words: *Venez, Astiza. Bienvenue à Pelée.* 'Come. Welcome to Pelée.'

"And what is Pelée?" I asked, while knowing all too well. We had, after all, spent a difficult time on the woman's home island.

"I had to ask the same thing," Caleb said cheerfully. "It's a code to convince us of her authenticity. Apparently a peak on Aimée's Martinique erupted when she left as a child to study in a French convent. It dusted her ship with ash." He got down off his horse, nodding.

"Yes," Astiza said. "We're being welcomed to a volcano."

PART THREE

CHAPTER 27

The palace of the Grand Turk, sultan of the Ottoman Empire, occupies a point at the edge of Europe with a splendid view of Asia across the Bosporus Straits. A more beautiful and strategic site can scarcely be imagined. North is the Black Sea, south the Dardanelles and Mediterranean, and all the shipping of the world, with all its flags, crowds the Golden Horn. One of the finest views in Constantinople is from the wooden balcony of the French Embassy in the Italian trade neighborhood of Galata, which lies across the watery Horn from Topkapi Palace. Walls, towers, kiosks, gardens, flowering trees, fountains, minarets, and chimneys mark the sprawling seraglio, while the domes of the great mosques of storied Constantinople rise like swollen moons beyond. The fabled city is called Istanbul by the Muslims, Tsarigrad by the Russians, New Rome by the Italians, New Jerusalem by the Jews, the City of Pilgrimage, the City of Saints, the House of the Caliphate, the Gate of Happiness, the Eye of the World, and the Refuge of the Universe.

My new goal was to call it home.

This former capital of the Byzantine Empire, conquered

by the Turks in 1453, fills a triangular peninsula. For one thousand years a four-mile-long triple wall on its landward side resisted attacks by Goths, Huns, Slavs, Avars, Persians, Arabs, Bulgarians, and Russians. Huge Turkish cannon finally made the wall obsolete. Now its moat is given over to gardens, graveyards, and garbage dumps, in that mix of preservation and practicality that marks all places with long history. The wall and its 192 towers still demarcate the city limit, while lower walls hem the city's shores. The vast Top-kapi, meaning 'Cannon Gate' in English, occupies the tip of the peninsula. The palace is made up of four courtyards, each more sacrosanct and mysterious in turn. Europeans are referring to the sultan's last and most ultimate gate when they call the Turkish government the Sublime Porte. The palace is home to up to five thousand ministers, servants, soldiers, and harem women. From this stronghold the Ottomans rule a loosely confederated empire that stretches from the Danube to the Euphrates, and from Arabia to Tripoli.

Its power has eroded. As recently as 1683, the Turks threatened to conquer Vienna. But revolt, war, corruption, and treachery have left the 1806 empire a wormy hulk, half glory and half ruin. Constantinople is regularly ravaged by plague and fire.

Accordingly, European embassies line the brow of the hills of Galata like patient vultures, surveying what might be a useful ally one day and a particularly rich carcass the next. France, which alienated the sultan when Napoleon invaded Egypt in 1798, now saw a chance to be the sultan's savior just eight years later.

I absorbed this summary from the briefings of Horace

Sebastiani, the new French ambassador whom we'd met in Adrianople. Astiza added more history, and crafty Caleb weighed in on the politics. "You've got a weak sultan trying to reform a military that fears improvement will end its privileges," my brother said. "Ambassadors from Russia, England and France all trying to win the Turks to their side in Europe's quarrels. The sultan's women scheme, his advisors change sides like we change clothes, and his pashas starve him of taxes. Everyone fears the sultan, but few revere or trust him. Ottoman ministers can become fabulously rich one day and brutally strangled the next, depending on palace intrigue."

Sebastiani put it another way. "The neck of a servant of the Sultan is thinner than a hair's breadth, goes the proverb. Some thirty Grand Viziers have been beheaded, drowned, poisoned, or throttled."

"Another volcano," I said, thinking of Aimée's summons. Our strategy, if one could call it that, was to become one of these perilous "servants of the sultan." Advisor. Confidant. Vizier. Potentially strangled with a bowstring if of modest rank, or by a silken cord if particularly favored. "Another St. Petersburg. Another Pelée."

"Another city of gold," Caleb said.

Yes, risk can bring reward. And few great cities were so lovely, or offered the ambitious so much opportunity. With half a million inhabitants, Constantinople was smaller than London, about the size of Paris, bigger than Vienna, Rome, or St. Petersburg, and more cosmopolitan than any. Only half its inhabitants were Muslim, and it had distinct neighborhoods for Italians, Greeks, Kurds, Serbs, Arabs, Jews, Armenians, Circassians, Albanians, Bosnians, Croats, Bulgarians, Romanians, and Hungarians. All were scramblers, drawn by a crossroads of wealth where every home and palace vied for a view. Gardens tumbled down hillsides, their owners competing to grow the best daffodils, tulips, and roses. Minarets jutted like spears. Linden and cypress trees gave shade. The harbor was typically crammed with a thousand sea-going ships and fifteen thousand boats plying between them. These included the elegant *kayiks*, narrow oar-and-sail-driven longboats that spirited the rich from picnic to soiree to supper, darting like water bugs and racing each other. When all were moving, the sea was a hive.

Like all cities Constantinople was noisy, from beckoning merchants, clopping cavalry, groaning ox carts, lowing cattle being driven to slaughter, and the wailing muezzins sounding the call to prayer. And yet the place was curiously hushed, too, the women spending much of their time locked away, the arrogant Janissary soldiers erratically enforcing draconian laws, and the Muslims exhibiting a subdued decorum that would baffle Londoners or New Yorkers. The city seemed half market, half monastery.

Across the Bosporus on the Asia shore were the wealthy estates and vineyards of Uskadar. On the Golden Horn's Galata side were the navy dockyards, the arsenal, the powder works, and the slave prison. The merchant ships docked primarily on the Constantinople side of the bay, their wares carried uphill to the Spice Market, Fish Market, and Grand Bazaar.

"France has long been the Ottomans' biggest European trading partner," Sebastiani explained. "We imported their wool, hides, silk, and spices, and sent back cloth, paper, leather, and glass. Their goat hair made our wigs, and their dyed sharkskin made sword handles and bookbindings. We were allied with the Turks for a century. But the Revolution upended traditional partnerships, Napoleon invaded the Ottoman provinces of Egypt and Syria, England and Russia rushed to exploit the breach, and now Bonaparte has sent me—nay, you and me, Ethan—to repair the damage. The other powers are bullying Selim to let their navies use the Bosporus, even as French victories suggest Paris will control the world. Napoleon is a great believer in luck, and was it not extraordinary luck that brought us all together?"

"I'm beginning to be suspicious of luck, actually."

"I know I jeopardized your family," Caleb put in, "but the ambassador is right. All our fortunes are converging. Dalca said the Trojan Palladium is hidden somewhere in Constantinople, and if that's true, what other treasures await? The sultan is turning to the French. You were planning to be a military adviser anyway. Here at last the Gage brothers will make our fortune, I'm sure of it!"

I remained wary. By now I considered this Trojan icon a myth, Napoleon a plague, and saw no reason for Sebastiani to pay attention to my exhausted clan. Yet he welcomed me like a prodigal son, said he knew of my adventures in Egypt, introduced Astiza to his pretty wife Fanny, tousled the hair of my son, and acted as if it was the most natural thing in the world to invite my family into his entourage.

Which meant he, and Caleb, wanted something: Astiza's help.

The new French ambassador certainly exuded charm. At age thirty-five he was handsome as a stage actor, with shoulder-length curly hair, the erect carriage of a soldier, and a voice as melodious as a harp. He was a Corsican native like

Bonaparte, and as a colonel he'd supported Napoleon's seizure of power in Paris in 1799. He was later wounded and promoted at Austerlitz. Gifted with a smile as bright as a banner, Sebastiani was out to change the world's balance of power.

I'd have been envious, if I didn't like him so much.

Thanks to the ambassador, we'd once more gone from penury to astonishing respectability in a moment, our luck reversing just as things seemed bleakest. Caleb had guided us from the mountains girdling Transylvania to Wallachia, Bucharest, and across the Danube to Bulgaria. We finally met the French diplomat in Adrianople, about a hundred miles west of Constantinople. For weeks Sebastiani had been making his stately way across Europe in a gleaming coach pulled by four horses in silver harness. He delivered tidings from a triumphant Napoleon to this prince and that duke, while his lovely wife exhibited the latest Paris fashions. One reason I liked the ambassador was that he had an expense account, and we were immediately given new clothing and a hired coach of our own.

Our fortune improved even more at Constantinople. The Ottomans play European powers against each other by welcoming favored new diplomats as if they were celebrities. Sebastiani's entourage of twenty soldiers, aides, and hangers-on was met with Janissary guards, a Turkish band of cymbal, trumpet, and drum, and a swarm of officials in beehive turbans. The ones in purple were the *ulema,* or learned men; the green were the *viziers,* or advisors, and the scarlet were the chamberlains. All were topped with ostrich or peacock feathers that rocked in the breeze like plumed grass. We entered the city through the massive old walls and paraded down winding streets lined with mansions, tenements, mosques, minarets, and markets, people rushing to view us as if we were a circus.

The usual civic mix of sewage, perfume, spice, smoke, sweat, tobacco, and hashish assaulted our noses, but in main the city was remarkably clean. There were marble fountains by every mosque so that worshipers could wash before entering, and the city is dotted with Turkish baths called *hammans*.

Parts of Constantinople reminded me of Cairo. Old men squatted on steps to smoke the hookah water pipe. A gate to the Grand Bazaar gave a glimpse of four thousand merchant stalls. Sheep spilled down a side lane to briefly block us; the city devours a thousand a day. Packhorses jostled with camels bearing sugar sacks. Veiled women peeked from wooden grills and high balconies, crows cawing on the eaves above. Craftsmen hammered copper, shaved wood, threw pots, and forged swords. There were schools, barracks, and convents for Sufi dervishes. Pigeons erupted from the paving of every square.

We flew the tricolor while a piper tootled *The Marseillaise*.

"No theaters and no gambling salons," Sebastiani said as we crept towards the Golden Horn. "Parades are one of the few permitted distractions."

"And no alcohol," I said. "No wonder they overran half the world. Had a clear head."

"None in principle, but they were stopped at half because they're as human as the rest of us," Caleb corrected. "'Men desire what is forbidden,' goes the Ottoman proverb. There are fifteen hundred taverns here, and the sultans drink as much in private as they deplore it in public. You can't find a prostitute in the mosques as you can in the alcoves of Notre Dame, but they seem to do business from every other house in the city, and cater to every sailor, Janissary, and gawking farmer who comes to town. The Ottomans still have brutal sports in the old Roman Hippodrome, and to a man they're as greedy as Dutchmen. There is the public face and the private, same as anywhere."

"Napoleon says to never forbid what you lack the power to prevent."

"A lesson he probably learned in Egypt."

We passed chicken and duck coops, pyramids of vividly colored spices, and quayside fish stalls that glittered like silver. Then we boarded *kayiks* and were ferried across to Galata and Sebastiani's diplomatic mansion, called the *Palais de France*. Unlike the stone and brick buildings of Europe, all the *yalis* of the foreigners and rich Ottomans are built of wood to stand up to frequent earthquakes, even though this makes them vulnerable to fire. The European enclaves are painted rust-red, with overhanging second stories to steal airspace from the streets below. In theory the Christian houses must be at least two feet lower than their Muslim neighbors, but this rule is ignored as often as it is observed. Harry has already learned the difference between rules—which his mother imposes—and enforcement, which his father is sometimes slow to perform.

The French embassy had a huge upper-story reception room with Turkish carpets, Ottoman arabesques, European paintings, niches that held flower vases, incense burners of perfume, and gilded trellises. The furniture was a mix of Versailles ornate and severe Ottoman divans placed like benches along the walls. In the Eastern fashion, stools supported the metal trays carried in for meals. A sea breeze usually blew, and after the hell of Balbec, it felt as if we'd ascended to paradise.

Fanny showed Astiza to a bedroom. Harry asked if there were any toys.

Sebastiani seated the men to plot diplomatic strategy. "I hope you like our surroundings," he began. "But our purpose is to serve France, not live off her. You are her instruments."

"I'm unfamiliar with the ritual of the Sublime Porte," I warned.

"I don't need help with ritual. I need to offer the sultan immediate military and political advice. We've little time because Sultan Selim is embroiled in many crises. But that also gives us opportunity."

"The sultan needs new friends," Caleb surmised.

"He does indeed. The Serbs are in revolt and Russia is marching to their aid. An independent Serbia would break the Ottoman hold on the Balkans, and outflank the Turks in Bessarabia, Moldavia, and Wallachia."

"Franklin said a great empire, like a great cake, is most easily diminished at the edges," I contributed. Ben's quips can be applied in almost any situation, and are usually wittier than my own.

"Yet even as the Ottomans are scrambling to prevent this, they quarrel amongst themselves," Sebastiani said.

"You're hoping Selim will be dependent on France."

"The Treaty of Pressburg awarded Dalmatia and Istria to France, putting our forces closer to Serbia," the ambassador said. "In February, Selim finally recognized Bonaparte as a legitimate emperor and dispatched an ambassador to Paris. Now the sultan's own forces are being mustered in Macedonia to march on the Serbs. Muslims in Bosnia will attack from the west. The Ottoman fortresses on the Danube are being strengthened against Russian invasion, while Russian Admiral Dmitri Senyavin has sailed to the Mediterranean to counter we French."

"I knew the admiral in St. Petersburg," I said.

"That could prove useful. The naval and army maneuvers have put Montenegro and Albania into play, the English are supporting Russian demands for free passage through the Dardanelles, and the Austrians fear an independent Serbia will encourage rebels in Hungary."

"I hope everyone has an atlas, just to keep track."

"Napoleon's strategy is to fight Tsar Alexander in the north while the Turks and Persians attack Russia from the south. We'll first crush Prussia, then Russia, and then march through Russia and Persia to India, stripping England of its richest colony. Then Bonaparte can reorganize the world. This great work starts with us, here in Constantinople."

"I'm always happy to give advice," I said. "Rarely taken, though."

Sebastiani pointed across the water to Topkapi Palace. "Selim is beset by his own governors. Some are defecting to the Russian side in hopes of becoming more independent. Other pashas refuse to send troops or taxes. The sultan has tried military reform by creating a New Army, but this is bitterly resented by the Janissaries, who view modernization as a threat to their haughty privileges. It would require them to fight foreigners instead of preying on their own people. The sultan desperately needs to modernize, but every attempt is opposed by reactionaries."

"The Turks seem blind to their own interests," Caleb said.

"This is an empire that banned printing when it appeared

in 1515, and a city where a mob destroyed an astronomical observatory in 1586. The best artists are believed to be those who slavishly copy works hundreds of years old. The Muslims, once the world's leaders in learning, now fear that knowledge blocks the path to God. The result is ignorance, weakness, and frustration. Who knows when the Janissary guard will beat its cauldrons with its spoons?"

"Cauldrons and spoons?"

"The traditional call for revolt. The Janissaries were originally recruited from Christian slaves boys who were forcibly converted to Islam. The idea was that a slave army, indoctrinated from youth, would be more loyal to the sultan than the feuding Turks themselves. Food was critical to the morale of the slave army, and so their symbols became the soup kettle and the wooden spoon. The latter is carried by officers as a badge of rank."

"A spoon is more practical than a scepter."

"But the Janissaries have deteriorated from invincible infantry to an obsolete gang of extortionists. Selim struggles. He's a mild man of the harem, a musician instead of a warrior."

"We're here to train his New Army?" I clarified.

"If we can win the sultan's trust. Historically, one of the ways to get his ear is through his women. The most powerful person in Topkapi Palace is usually the sultan's mother, called the valide or 'mother' sultan, but she's died. We need new allies in the harem."

"I'd volunteer to go recruiting, having a certain knack with the ladies. But I assume you mean this Aimée du Buc de Rivéry."

"The only harem guests are women, which makes your

wife key to our diplomatic scheme. Astiza is the one person in our delegation who Nakshedil can talk to, and thus Astiza is the one who can best press French interests. First we will present our own diplomatic credentials. Then Astiza will continue our efforts behind the secret screens of the harem."

"As a guest and not a slave."

"Yes. Who, in advising one side, will undoubtedly gain the enmity of rivals in the palace."

CHAPTER 28

The key to influencing human behavior is to understand it, and the key to understanding Constantinople was remembering that the Ottomans thrived on their inconsistency between what was said and what was done.

I quickly observed that the citizenry flouted the Muslim prohibition against alcohol with a fondness for arak, a colorless, aniseed-flavored spirit called lion's milk. The imams frowned on coffee, but their followers flocked to coffee houses for cups as thick as syrup. There they took turns at rows of water pipes to smoke banned tobacco, hashish, and opium, the latter as commonly grown as wine in nearby Anatolia. As Franklin warned, many a man thinks he is buying pleasure when he is really selling himself to it.

Sex was no different. The religion forbade prostitution, but rural village men—denied what Europeans would consider ordinary female company before marriage—routinely came to the city's strumpets to slate desire and gain experience. The Turks condemned homosexuality, but attractive young soldiers and slaves were routinely seduced or raped. The society prized masculinity, yet Selim spent nearly all his time with five hundred harem women and their eunuchs. Sultans no longer rode to war.

Selim's servants were infidel slaves, since Muslims were forbidden to enslave each other, and yet any sultan was in essence a captive of these same servants. He depended on domineering Janissaries for defense and domestic slaves for protection, food, comfort, advice, and love. The sultan was perhaps the richest man on earth, but spent almost his entire life in a harem and gardens no bigger, and little brighter, than a prison.

We Europeans were infidels too, and yet increasingly employed for military and scientific advice. The sultan insisted we adhere to Oriental pomp, and yet he secretly wore Western clothes, hired Italian artists to paint landscape frescos in his palace, and sat on European furniture.

In sum, there was enough hypocrisy to make me feel right at home. The gap between ideal and practice yawned as wide in Constantinople as in Washington, Paris, London, or St. Petersburg. By forbidding everything, the Muslims had to allow everything. By expecting piety, they turned a blind eye to vice. By shutting away women, a man could defer to them without public embarrassment.

Winning the whispers of women was key. The ambassador explained that the Ottoman Empire had sidestepped the typical wars of royal succession by insisting that the sultan's heirs come from the closed world of the harem, removing false claims of paternity and the temptation of outside pashas to vie for the throne. The competition was instead extremely intimate, as the sultan's sexual favorites conspired to elevate their sons. The mother of a new sultan achieved enormous influence, while the offspring of losing harem women were often executed. This 'valide sultan' was almost a monarch in her own right. What man doesn't listen to his mother, even when she began as a concubine?

Now harem politics was shifting. Selim's mother was dead and Selim's closest female friend—and his father's sexual favorite—had taken Mama's place in the harem hierarchy. This was the Martinique beauty Aimée, captured by pirates nineteen years ago, cousin to the Empress Josephine, and the same age as Selim. The two had been companions since their teen years. She had her own son, Mahmud, fathered by Selim's father, and thus Selim was Mahmud's half-brother. Aimée's son was a possible heir to the throne, but only if her pro-French policy proved successful.

My brother had left us in Transylvania to glean this gossip and plot how to use it to our advantage. Caleb used his Napoleonic connections to get word to Sebastiani of our talents, and used Sebastiani to alert the Ottoman court to my wife's interesting background. Aimée, who avidly devoured news of the outside world, had immediately invited Astiza.

"But first I must present my ambassadorial credentials," Sebastiani told Caleb and me. "You'll accompany my entourage and serve as an example of the military expertise Constantinople can expect from a French alliance."

"Caleb has commanded ships," I said, "but I'm more of a consultant than a professional soldier. Go-between. Hanger-on. Skirmisher."

"As well as gambler, thief, rogue, and dilettante, yes, yes, I know. But the Turks need not know. You worked with Gaspard Monge in Egypt, who has reformed French artillery. You're known the inventors and savants Fulton, Berthollet, and Cuvier. You can shoot, and have mastered Franklin's electricity. I've told the Turks you throw thunderbolts! Accordingly, you're going to be our artillery expert until a real one gets here. We'll give you a colonel's uniform while Caleb, in captain's garb, advises the navy."

"We've been promoted, brother!"

"I do have a knack for pretending to be knowledgeable," I admitted.

"A man can rise," the ambassador agreed, "by being a parrot."

I'd also keep eyes and ears open for this long-lost Trojan palladium or any other precious gewgaw or knickknack that might be lying about. If I couldn't be a Russian noble I'd be a French colonel and Turkish general. I still didn't trust Caleb, but had to admit he'd given my family another chance. My brother seemed to want to make amends.

Selim's chief astrologer had to be the one to choose the date of Sebastiani's audience with the sultan, but brewing war meant the stars didn't wait long to align. A summons was tendered and we rehearsed the pomp as if practicing for a wedding. We woke on the appointed day to the usual muezzin cries calling the faithful to dawn prayers, sleepily assembled in the embassy, and marched for the harbor. We had servants to lug the obligatory presents, an escort of smug Janissary guards, a priest and imam to guide us spiritually, and a secretary to take notes. Critical though she might be, Astiza was not invited. Muslim ceremonies were a boys' affair.

We marched past the Arsenal where the raw ribs of half-completed warships of French design jutted from a dry dock. "Fastest and most agile in the world," Caleb noted. "But will they be ready in time?" Then we were ferried across the Golden Horn to the vizier's dock below the palace walls. On shore we waited in a large gazebo that the Turks call a kiosk, imbibing morning sweets and coffee. A horse was brought round from the royal stables so that Sebastiani could follow the diplomatic custom of riding up the palace hill and the rest of us trailed on foot to the procession kiosk, where we were met by Grand Vizier Ibrahim Hilmi Pasha, the tenth grand vizier of Selim III's turbulent reign. This pompous character was attired in a scarlet and gold robe, silver slippers, and a white turban fronted by a spray of peacock feathers. Slaves held large umbrellas with golden ribs and sapphire-studded handles to shade him and a dozen other splendiferous ministers.

Sebastiani had his own brass and braid, I posed in my colonel's uniform, and Caleb was costumed like a French navy captain. Taken together, our assembly was bright enough for an Italian opera or a Mummer's parade.

The palace is a quadrangle nearly half a mile long, narrowing as it extends from the city to Seraglio Point. This city in miniature includes kitchens, stables, a mint, a treasury, a hospital, the offices of government, reception rooms, barracks, page schools, gardens, and the harem. Topkapi was additionally crowded this particular day with three thousand Janissaries who'd come for their quarterly pay, which was an excuse to show us Ottoman military might.

We were ushered through the Imperial Gate to the first courtyard, a thousand feet long and five hundred feet wide. Soldiers were squeezed with horses, mules, supply carts, and even a forlorn elephant in one dusty corner. A French-speaking Muslim guide appeared to point out a former Christian church turned armory and the fountain used to clean the blades of the Palace Executioner.

"These are the pedestals for severed heads," he said without emotion, as if every respectable palace had some. A couple long-rotting examples were on display, presumably to keep us on best behavior. "Beyond we have the dormitory for Carriers of Silver Water Vessels, and next to it the house of The Straw Weavers. Here, the mint, there the gate to the water stables."

"Yes, yes," the grand vizier said impatiently. "On to the divan."

Our entourage proceeded through the Middle Gate, which was flanked by two octagonal towers with steeple roofs. The second courtyard was less than half the length of the first. It, too, was jammed, this time by Janissary soldiers in still formation, both the men and the courtyard's cypress trees in trim angular ranks. The slave warriors were beardless, unlike most Muslim men, but sported great drooping mustaches that fell as far as their chests. Their sashes held pistols and knives, their colorful jackets reached to the knees of their bloused pants, and their mitered felt hats, called *börks* in Turkish, were topped with intricate embroidery that flopped over in back to shade their neck. Some had pikes, some swords, and others muskets inlaid with mother-of-pearl. They stood so quiet that we could hear the insects in the trees.

In the far corner was the Hall of the Divan, a single-story domed building with colonnaded porch and a backing steeple called the Tower of Justice. Inside was a cool and pleasing chamber for the Ottoman cabinet, with tiled walls, plentiful windows, and gentle breeze. I noticed one peculiar grilled window up high on a wall. "The sultan sometimes observes from behind that screen," the interpreter whispered. "Always remember, he may judge you."

I resolved not to scratch or yawn.

Much protocol ensued that was designed to both flatter the new diplomat and yet make clear that he ranked well below the sultan and his ministers. We bowed and stood at attention while Sebastiani kissed the hem of the vizier's robe and perched on a low stool, as was custom. The ambassador had warned us that one arrogant French predecessor had refused to unbuckle his sword in the sultan's presence and been ignored for the next decade, so we were under strict instructions not to turn our back, make hand gestures, address Selim's ministers, or speak above a whisper to each other.

Now came payday. Sacks of piasters, florins, ducats, and francs were brought to the room and given to gruff Janissary officers, who in turn went outside and distributed them to their waiting soldiers in what seemed to be an interminable ceremony. The lesson to the Janissaries was plain: This is where your pay comes from, so defend your sultan with your life. The lesson to us was that the Ottomans had sufficient coin to support formidable armies.

Next, Sebastiani formally asked to be presented to the sultan that afternoon, the ambassador and the vizier traded empty compliments, and we sat cross-legged on the floor while huge silver trays were carried in with lunch. There were so many delicious dishes that I was reminded of Franklin's quip, "I saw few die of hunger, of eating a hundred thousand." We ate in dead silence. After an hour slaves removed the food, we were dressed in ceremonial robes called kaftans, and we paraded to the domed Gate of Felicity.

Unlike the first two military gates, this one had architectural grace. Two fountains flanked it, and its guards were white eunuch slaves with silver spears, ivory-butted pistols, and hippopotamus hide whips. "After a long-ago power struggle, the white eunuchs were confined to the gate and the black eunuchs gained the privilege of serving inside the harem," Sebastiani murmured. "The blacks, with the ear of the women, have far more power."

The third courtyard seemed almost deserted compared to the first two, its periphery a shady colonnade and its middle occupied by the throne room. Gates led to the palace gardens and harem and so I glanced around for a girl or two, but so far hadn't seen a single female. The guide did point out the treasury.

"Lots of gold and jewels?"

"Fabulous books, precious carpets, and bolts of silk."

Too heavy to make off with.

The throne room had the same grace as the divan, its interior swirling with arabesques and carved flowers. The Islamic décor had been supplemented with Italian landscapes. Water tinkled in small fountains, and thick carpets of wool and silk were cast across the marble floor. The air was heady with incense. Latticed windows cast spears of dramatic light through its smoke. The Grand Turk sat on a raised platform that looked like a four-poster bed without a canopy, his golden perch draped with jeweled cloth.

While character might improve a face, and dissolution ruin it, we mostly abide with the looks we're born with. Selim was a pleasant-enough fellow, but not one to inspire awe. His skin seemed delicate, his features soft, his eyes large and trusting, and his mouth mild. Like all sultans he had a long beard dyed fiercely black, and his robes shimmered with precious threads and stones. Atop his head was an enormous jeweled turban with an aigrette of heron feathers. It looked heavy.

His courtiers were stiff as statues. There was a gigantic negro called the Chief Black Eunuch who ran the harem, and other servants with titles like The Sword-Bearer, The Master of the Wardrobe, The Chief Stirrup-Holder, The Head of the Privy Chamber, and so on. The general, or Aga, who headed the Janissaries and the Admiral of the Navy stood shoulder to shoulder with The Chief Turban Winder, The Keeper of Nightingales, and The Chief Tent Pitcher, who probably hadn't had much to do for several centuries.

All were solemn as stone.

Somewhat peculiar were a line of dwarves and a rank of meek-looking servants behind them. Caleb noticed my look. "I read that the dwarves are considered amusing slaves," he murmured, "and the mutes and blinded carry messages with the assurance they won't whisper what they can't say, or read what they can't see."

Two black doorkeepers led Sebastiani forward, holding him under his arms as both a sign of respect and as a precaution against any visitor who might be a secret assassin. The ambassador was led about like a marionette to three different places, bowed three times at each, kissed the hem of the sultan's cloak, and finally stood back while his official deposition and credentials were read aloud in Turkish. These were passed to the admiral, who passed them to the grand vizier, who passed them to the throne. The grand vizier then spoke for Selim, welcoming us through the translator.

The sultan gravely nodded.

That signal meant it was present time. Sebastiani's gifts were unpacked and paraded like the haul from an upscale wedding. Included were gold trays, silver flatware, China plates, silver candlesticks, a chafing dish, a jeweled clock in the shape of a rooster, and a jeweled cavalry saber. The sultan was studiously impassive, receiving it all as his due.

And that was usually the end, the ambassador receding until called upon for specific negotiations. This time, however, Selim startled his entire court by limply raising a hand and asking a question. Ministers jerked as if jolted.

"Is your emperor going to fight Russia?" Sebastiani was asked.

The envoy carefully phrased his answer, knowing that Selim would be well informed and mustn't be lied to. "We've recently signed a treaty of friendship with St. Petersburg after our victory at Austerlitz," he said, "but the tsar is courting Prussia, which angers France. The situation is very fluid, which is why Napoleon seeks friendship. Your enemies may become ours."

Selim was silent for a moment, and again I thought the audience was over. But then he spoke again.

"Will Napoleon take the field himself?"

Sebastiani nodded. "Yes. He's our finest general."

"He modernized your army." The aga of the Janissaries stiffened at this comment.

"Yes. It's why we won at Austerlitz."

"Who's the Janissary general?" I whispered to Caleb.

"Abdulla Gelib, the worst of the reactionaries. Don't cross him."

"Did you bring experts for my New Army?" Selim asked.

"Certainly. May I present Colonel Ethan Gage, an authority on artillery," Sebastiani said smoothly, "and his brother Captain Caleb Gage, a naval officer of great experience and valor. These are only the first of many whom our emperor will lend, should you permit."

"The first." He looked at us. "Come forward, colonel."

Sebastiani gestured to me. Nervously, worried that a misstep would send me back to the Executioner's Fountain, I stepped forward.

Selim assessed me with a surprisingly shrewd gaze. "You are American." He had his own spies.

I swallowed. "In French service."

"You're the man who also worked with the English and Russians?"

"I've had a peculiar career."

"I hope it's given you wisdom."

"More than I wish, your highness."

The sultan studied me for a long moment before something seemed to satisfy him. "I want you to improve my forts, colonel. I want your brother to inspect my ships. The Russian and English ambassadors boast about their weapons. I want to boast about mine."

"We are impressed by word of your New Army." I glanced at Caleb, who was watching Gelib. The Janissary aga was tight-lipped.

"I'll require a visit from your wife, as well," Selim went on. "The sultana invites her. I'm told she is an educated woman."

"Self-educated, I'd say, but better-read than almost any man." I was sweating. Selim's courtiers stirred some more.

"We'll talk, perhaps, of reform." He looked directly at his ministers when he said this. They were struggling not to show expression, but their eyes had widened into something between shock, dismay, and mutiny. The French! Americans! A woman!

And then with a wave the audience was abruptly over, we Westerners backing as instructed, me praying that I wouldn't trip over the hem of my kaftan.

Apparently I had Selim's favor.

I glanced at Aga Abdulla Gelib, now glowering.

And another enemy, as well.

CHAPTER 29

Astiza

Despite Ethan's colorful description of Topkapi Palace, I wasn't prepared for the intricacy of its architecture or the quiet within its walls. The center of power is hushed, as if every servant and minister is holding breath. One hears the splashing of the fountains, the tread of sentry boots, and the song of nightingales.

The rambling complex was not so much designed as assembled over three centuries, and the harem where the Sultan and his women live has grown to nearly four hundred rooms. Even at that size a private chamber is prized because Selim's harem numbers five hundred, of which only the most favored are ever invited to his bed. Add to that hundreds of eunuchs, dwarves, and mutes who serve as guards, entertainers, and messengers, and it's a cramped warren with little privacy and many rules, as intricate as a monastery. Whispers are the norm. A quarrel or a laugh echoes so unexpectedly that the inhabitants react like startled animals.

I visited dressed from crown to toe, my face concealed by a dark scarf that covered all but my eyes. Yet never had I felt so conspicuously a woman. Everyone whom a female visitor first sees at Topkapi is a man, and the heads of Janissaries and halberd-armed guards swung toward my shapeless form as if on the same swivel. With women shut away, even the most shrouded become the subject of male curiosity. The halberdiers at the Middle Gate have sidelocks like a woman's tresses that fall across each cheek, grown like horse blinders to supposedly keep these servants from peeking when they deliver firewood or food to the harem. This precaution is no doubt about as effective as a shield made of paper. You could cover my husband with a potato sack and he'd still manage to get a glimpse of forbidden beauty.

The sidelock fashion sustains the fiction that the harem is completely inviolable, but it isn't. Women such as myself have been invited for decades, and the harem is of necessity repaired, supplied, and serviced by outsiders who are often men. A European organ maker spent two weeks installing an instrument and left an enthusiastic account of spying on the harem pool through a peephole. Still, enough mystery remains to make the seraglio far more alluring in the imagination than any possible reality.

A six-foot white eunuch with beardless face and fleshy features named Sunflower was my escort to the harem door. He was a colorful creature, wearing a red turban, a bright blue robe that fell to his ankles despite the heat, and a broad black sash with jewel-hilted dagger. A gold earring decorated one ear, and a tight gold chain wrapped his neck. He met me with reluctance, as if any outsider was an affront, and imperiously led me to an unremarkable arched wooden door called the Carriage Gate in the second courtyard, where favored harem women board carriages for their infrequent visits to the outside world. Sunflower pounded, we waited a long minute, and finally the door opened to darkness within. The eunuch pushed me inside and shut the door behind me.

It took a moment for my eyes to adjust. The room was domed but windowless, lit by a single lamp. For a disquieting moment I felt once again at Balbec. Then bronze doors on the opposite wall swung open and another eunuch, this one black and even more gigantic, stepped inside to give me a friendlier greeting. His smile was bright as a torch.

"Egyptian priestess! I am Kizlar Aga, the chief black eunuch. My mistress Nakshedil, The Beautiful One, is anxious for your company." This specimen was an imposing six and a half feet high, his arms as thick as thighs.

I bowed. "Astiza of Alexandria. I'm honored by your mistress's invitation."

"She's intrigued by your mystical reputation, and believes it destiny that you've come at this most perilous and propitious of times. The Beautiful One is a believer in fortune-tellers and astrologers. Do you believe in ghosts and jinns, lady scholar?"

"Jinns?"

"Genies, the Franks sometime say."

"I believe there are more mysteries in this world than we can explain."

"Indeed! Do you see the closets on each side of this room?

Magical things happened there. One day a novice eunuch so annoyed a sultan with his clumsiness that he was chased with a knife to this very room. The boy hid in that closet, the furious sultan yanked open the door—and the eunuch had completely disappeared! No one ever saw him again. The same happened to a naughty harem girl who tried to hide in the closet opposite. Poof! She vanished." He waited for skepticism, and looked disappointed that I accepted this story so calmly. "This isn't surprising," he insisted, as if I'd said it was. "We know jinns dance, gamble, and argue in our courtyards at midnight, and we believe the harem is haunted by the murdered and executed, of which our sad history has many. So don't be surprised if your senses reveal extraordinary things. You've come to the navel of the world."

"A magical closet? Can I look?"

He solemnly shook his head. "I would not be responsible for your disappearance."

He led me through the bronze doors to a high, dimly lit guardroom where four eunuchs stood sentry with pikes and swords. Then another door and we were in a narrow courtyard open to a slit of sky, with a pillared portico and upper barred windows. "This is the Courtyard of the Black Eunuchs," my escort said. "Our living quarters are in the two stories above."

I thought the place felt more like a jail than a paradise.

"I command the two hundred of us from Africa, castrated at youth after our capture by Arab slave traders," the Kizlar Aga said matter-of-factly. "We serve the harem without temptation. No virile men pass through here except by extraordinary need. You've already seen more than most ordinary mortals can ever hope to glimpse. Should anyone try to penetrate this domain—or misbehave with it—there are dungeons below."

"The women can never leave?"

"Why would they want to? Here they live in luxury, far from the toil of the world. But favored ones go on outings, and the elderly are retired to apartments in the city."

The harem beyond was a decorous refuge. A dwarf whispered to a eunuch in the shadows. People walked on slippered feet. Somewhere I heard the song of caged birds, and the lilt of stringed baglama, a Turkish instrument, but the music was a murmur. We wound through a confusion of corridors and courtyards. What did it do to the mind of a sultan to grow up and live here, so far from ordinary life?

"Were you a Christian you might not be invited," the eunuch said as we proceeded, "but the sultana has heard you're Greek-Egyptian and respectful of all faiths. Is this true?"

"Many paths lead to the One Truth."

"But only Islam leads to Paradise." We passed another guarded door. "This is the Golden Way, the corridor that leads to the sultan. Many harem women are never invited to traverse it, despite their beauty. But Nakshedil was chosen almost at once. Come. We ascend to her salon."

Furtive women scurried as we advanced down a hallway, eunuchs snapped to attention as we climbed stairs, and a mute pressed his forehead to the floor in front of a door inlaid with mother-of-pearl. I was ushered into a room as ornate as a jewel box.

"The quarters of the Mother Sultan, tragically passed, are now occupied by the sultana." The Kizler Aga bowed and left.

The reception room had beautiful Turkish tile on its lower half, a fountain in an alcove, and a fireplace topped by a conical copper hearth. A brass chandelier was suspended from the domed ceiling, and grilled windows lent pale light from secret courtyards. The furniture was an east-west mix of Turkish cushions and French high-backed chairs.

"You can choose to sit high or low," a pleasant voice said from behind.

I turned. A stunning woman with a spectacular mane of golden hair, woven with silver thread and dotted by tiny diamonds, came into the room. She was indeed Nakshedil, still breathtaking at thirty-eight. Her Turkish dress was a modest but shimmering costume of bloused pants tight to the ankles and a silken robe over a gauze chemise. A golden necklace with emeralds was on her breast, and bracelets decorated her wrists and ankles. Her jewels could have purchased a plantation in her native Martinique.

"Your highness." I curtsied.

"I am not royalty, Astiza of Alexandria. I'm a slave, captured by Barbary corsairs almost twenty years ago and sent to this gilded prison. I lamented my fate at first, and screamed and sobbed when summoned to the bed of the sultan. I was a terrified virgin and vowed never to go. But the sultan's mother made me see reason, the sultan Hamid initiated me kindly, and in time I became a kadin, or favored one."

"Understandably. You are very beautiful."

"Appearance is only the beginning. When I was instructed in the arts of love before meeting the sultan I was taught not just the sultan's desires but my own, so that I could perform with enthusiasm."

"Still, it must have taken courage."

"A summoned concubine is bathed in rosewater, scented with the finest Arabian and French perfumes, decorated with gold and jewels, and dressed in multi-colored veils. But yes, it does take courage. My most important lesson was that this physicality is merely the first step toward becoming a kadin. A sultan is the loneliest of men, who can never entirely trust the motives of even his closest advisors. He is never praised for who he is but rather what he is, and every flatterer seeks reward. Only we harem women can offer true companionship. The most successful are not necessarily the most beautiful. They're the ones who can talk, sympathize, tell stories, sing songs, confer, commiserate, and advise. I became Hamid's companion and confidant."

"And Selim's too, I understand."

"Yes, we were like brother and sister. I eventually bore Selim's father Hamid a son, Mahmud, for whom I thank God. And while I was concubine to Hamid I was friend to his son, the sultan of today, since we were the same age and locked in the same harem. Now he reigns, I've taken the apartments of his mother, and my own son, his half-brother, may ascend to the throne someday—if half-brother Mustafa, who also covets the throne, does not murder him! Which means that God moves in mysterious ways, does he not?" Her smile was wry, and she gave a slight curtsey to me. "Aimée du Buc de Rivéry I was in another universe, and Nakshedil I am in this one. And you, I understand, travel like the wind. Which of us is the luckier, I wonder?"

"I, too, have a beloved son," I replied, "so perhaps we're equal."

"Well said. And is it to be chair or cushion? Selim imported the French furniture to satisfy my whim."

"I'm a guest in his home and so we should sit in the Turkish manner," I suggested.

"Very good. We'll have refreshments brought on trays." She clapped her hands and another harem girl appeared. This one was a dark-haired teen, lovely but no match for Aimée in presence. She was, however, dressed more as I'd imagined, with a cap of gold cloth and a translucent chemise. Her short red jacket only partly covered her breasts, and her cotton harem pants were so fine that I could clearly see the shape of her legs. Loops of pearls hung from her neck, and she too had earrings and bracelets.

"Some tea and fruit," the Sultana ordered. "And some pastry with honey." The girl bowed and went to fetch it.

"Some harem women serve others?"

"Hierarchies prevail in all parts of the empire," Aimée explained. "There is rank in the army, in the government, in the villages, and among the slaves. It's no different here. We're all slaves, but the junior serve the senior while they wait for the sultan's favor."

"Are the eunuchs your servants or your masters?"

"Our keepers. It's a curious system. They're castrated when enslaved to discourage desire and prevent temptation, and thus are weakened as men. The white eunuchs have only their testicles removed, but the blacks in the harem lose their cocks as well, since that tool has proven a distraction in the past." She said this matter-of-factly, as if discussing farm animals. "So our protectors make poor warriors, and jealous escorts, and piss like women. Yet their leaders often wield more power than Janissary generals, because they have constant access to the sultan."

"And five hundred women wait like prostitutes?"

"More like nuns. There's only one sultan, and they're not necessarily lustful men. But we are ribald nuns. Human nature doesn't disappear in the harem anymore than it does in a prison, monastery, or convent, and women will find ways to satisfy each other or pleasure themselves. None of this can be openly recognized, of course, and thus we live lives of pretense, whisper, and avoidance. But who doesn't?"

"I appreciate your candor, sultana. You invited us to what you compared to Pelée, a volcano on your native island. Ethan and I once visited Martinique."

"Did you! And how is my home?"

"Beautiful, but for us it was very dangerous. There was much intrigue."

"Like Pelée. I'm candid about my life because we're all in peril, and before you can help us you must understand us. Constantinople can erupt at any time. The empire is troubled, Selim is struggling, and Mahmud and Mustafa are unspoken rivals to succeed him. The choice is important. My son would reform the empire, taking inspiration from France. Mustafa would move it backward, trying to regain the medieval glory of the Janissaries."

"Two different mothers?"

"Yes. The sultans typically confine their attentions primarily to four favorites, of which I was one and Mustafa's mother was another. This selection avoids a proliferation of princes who must eventually compete and conspire. There's also a Court Abortionist, to narrow rivalries even more.

Women particularly favored by the sultan are said to be "in the eye" and may be allowed to bear his children. Others are not. All this causes jealousy and intrigue. I'm favored, and envied for my success."

"We're told you encouraged Selim to study French reform and modernization," I said.

"Which causes even more resentment. Many Turks believe their defeats are caused by too many European ways, not too few. They think modernizers are turning their backs on Allah. So they resent the French sultana who pushes science on a sultan she has supposedly bewitched. Yet without a better army, Selim and my son will ultimately be at the mercy of European monarchs with superior artillery and faster ships. So I seek allies from all reaches of our empire, and word came to me of you and your journey. I was told you came out of the Transylvanian wilderness. What brings a wife and mother so far from home?"

"I have no home, sultana, and keep trying to find one. I'm originally from Egypt where I met Ethan, but fate has made us gypsies."

"Wanderers like Odysseus."

"We tempted fate by pirating a Polish prize away from St. Petersburg and were punished for it. Desperation led us to fall into the clutches of an evil duke named Cezar Dalca. Ethan thinks Dalca may have been what the Slavs and Tartars call an *upyr*, a witch or vampire, or a *koldun*, a male sorcerer. Greed found our fellowship members betraying each other, because in desire the devil finds opportunity. We were lucky to escape at all. One of our fellows was sickened by the bite of this monster." I saw her wonder. "Do you believe my stories?"

"Not in my French convent school, Astiza. But here in Topkapi? Ghosts haunt the harem; everyone has seen them. Servants have mysteriously vanished. Jinns dance away the darkest nights, and anyone who dares peek soon dies of terrible illness or accident." She shivered. "The world is a battleground between darkness and light."

"All things are dual."

"Then we must be friends. You must carry my regards to Ambassador Sebastiani and bring back news that I can use to reinforce Selim and Mahmud. There's no time to waste. Since the death of Selim's mother the Janissaries sense weakness and are plotting to roll back reform. The English and Russians encourage our backwardness. Only France promises progress."

"I'm instructed to tell you that the English and Russian ships are assembling in the Aegean Sea," I said. "They may try to force the Dardanelles and Bosporus. Russian armies are marching on your borders. Some trained artillerymen are being assembled in France to advise you, but until they arrive we have only two emergency experts to improve Ottoman defenses."

"And who would they be?"

"My husband and his brother. Ethan fought against Bonaparte at Acre with Pasha Djezzar, and has also fought alongside Napoleon. He's learned from many masters. It gives him an inventive frame of mind."

"And do you bring new powers from the past to help us, Astiza?"

"Sometimes the key is recognizing the powers you already have."

CHAPTER 30

"Y ou're a lunatic, Gage. A medieval madman."

"Necessity requires invention," I argued to Sebastiani. "It took Napoleon three years to build his Grand Armée that crushed the Coalition at Austerlitz. We'll be lucky to have three weeks before the English navy comes."

"It's an antique! Hours to load. Almost impossible to move."

"A single hit could turn a battle."

My debate with the French ambassador was good-natured. Sebastiani had fought in Italy and Austerlitz and had far more military training than me, but he respected practical experience from my own nasty scrapes. We both knew the forts at the Dardanelles Strait that protected the Ottoman capital were woefully weak, despite Sultan Selim's fledgling New Army. Our puzzle was how to strengthen them.

The iron artifact we were debating was one of the Great Turkish Bombards, iron cannon more than three hundred and fifty years old. They were antique, but bigger than anything in current use. This particular one had a barrel seventeen feet long and weighed seventeen tons. Its granite cannonballs were two-and-a-half-feet in diameter and weighed seven hundred pounds. Simply shaping such spheres was the work of Sisyphus, or rather of Turkish slaves. There were several of these monster gun-barrels left in the Ottoman forts, none of them mounted on the ramparts or a wheeled carriage. To a modern artilleryman, these relics of Ottoman greatness should have been melted down eons ago. But since they hadn't, I thought they were the best hope we had. "The predecessor to this gun was the one that the Turks used to breach the walls of Constantinople in 1453," I reasoned.

"Yes," said Sebastiani, "but it was so slow to load and cool that the Ottomans got off only three shots a day. The Turkish commander tells me that a single shot from these antiques consumes nine hundred pounds of gunpowder. None have been fired for decades, and then only for ceremony."

"I'm sure I could get the rate up to four a day, with a little practice and a lot of powder. Selim has a modern gunpowder works."

"The biggest French field piece fires a twenty-four-pound ball, weighs less than a sixth of this behemoth, and can get off a shot every three minutes."

"But the bombard has two dozen times the punch."

"Moving and firing these guns took sixty oxen and four hundred men."

"And conquered the world's most storied city. Besides, all we have to do is mount them, not move them. It's the ships that come sailing by."

"The powder required would supply an entire battery of guns!"

"A battery that Selim doesn't have, and won't until more French metallurgists, chemists, and gunners arrive." I'm not always so determined, but I had a hunch the coming show-down would turn on morale as much as might. These noisy monsters might bolster the Turks and confound the British. "Ambassador, I'm a Franklin man, an electrician, and a confidant of the American inventor Robert Fulton. I'd much prefer something new-fangled. If Fulton were here he'd make us a steamboat or a submarine, and Franklin would conjure balloons. But there's only me. I can't employ an electric fence as I did at Acre, since the Dardanelles is two miles wide. I can't redeploy the death-ray mirror of Archimedes, since we had to destroy it in Tripoli. Which means that this relic is our only chance. The English fleet is gathering at Tenedos Island, just miles from here. Should Britain finally dare try to force the straits, we need a gantlet of fire to discourage them."

"True." Sebastiani looked across the Dardanelles to the Asian shore, lowered his voice, and leaned close so Ottoman officers couldn't hear. "These Turks have the loudest bands and most colorful uniforms on earth, but I'm not sure they can wield these guns as their ancestors did."

"On the contrary, they're the very devils in a fight—I saw them in Egypt and the Holy Land. They have too much reckless courage, not too little."

"And do you, American? This antique might blow up."

"Then I'll let the reckless Turks light the vent."

He shook his head. We'd won Selim to our side, thanks to Aimée's help, but we'd been struggling for the past half-year to help our new allies. Summer had become fall and then winter, and Selim's strategic position had grown steadily worse. His generals seemed hapless. His soldiers milled like a herd.

"These Ottomans have the worst discipline of any army on

earth," Sebastiani said. "Each commander goes his own way, soldiers dash about on the battlefield like Pamplona bulls, half disappear in winter, and most of the rest were absent during Ramadan. I know they can fight. Can they work?"

"Ramadan ended in December and the English threat has not. I agree, the Janissaries refuse to adopt disciplined firepower. But like the Russians, the Turks don't like subtlety. This is just the kind of weapon to inspire them."

Sebastiani contemplated the bombard and finally shrugged. "You're right, what alternative do we have? We've persuaded them to resist the bullying English and Russians. Now we have to help them any way we can. Any way *they* can."

We were talking strategy in one of the world's most strategic places, the Hellespont of the Dardanelles. Here Persian tyrant Xerxes crossed on a bridge of boats to assault the ancient Greeks, and lashed the waves with whips when the wind kicked too high. Here Leander swam nightly to lie with Princess Hero. On the Asian shore nearby was Çanakkale, reputed to be the site of legendary Troy. And here was the southern chokepoint of the straits between Europe and Asia, the Black Sea to the north and the Mediterranean to the south.

We were standing on a rampart in the Turkish fort of Sestos. Two miles across the channel was its companion fort, Abydos. Both were out of date, ill repaired, and undermanned.

I shivered, from both the cold and the odds. It was February of 1807, and almost a year had passed since that reception at Catherine's cavernous palace outside St. Petersburg. It was winter again, the straits swept by chill steppe winds, the water gray and the hills brown. Despite the seasonal temperature, power politics in Constantinople was coming to a boil.

Napoleon had once more triumphed in Europe. His brother Louis had become King of Holland, and brother Joseph the King of Naples. The Holy Roman Empire had been officially declared dead and Napoleon had created a new Confederation of the Rhine to reorganize his German allies. Most importantly, he'd marched on Prussia as Lothar Von Bonin had feared and within a month had smashed the Prussian army and occupied Berlin. Nor had Bonaparte stopped there. As Czartoryski had hoped, the French emperor had advanced to Warsaw and revived Polish hopes of independence at the urging of a certain Polish beauty named Marie Walewska. By all reports, she was serving her country in bed just as Izabela Czartoryski once had. The newly recovered Grunwald swords had inflamed Polish patriotism.

Meanwhile the Russians had threatened Turkey's Ottoman provinces to support rebellious Serbia. This had pushed Selim into declaring war on Russia at the end of December, and breaking relations with Russia's English ally when he did so. British ambassador Charles Arbuthnot, once the sultan's favorite diplomat, had fled the city to the safety of the English fleet.

Now the ill-prepared Turks were desperately preparing to stave off two enemies at once, Russia and England. Selim was relying on Sebastiani's experts, including me.

There had also been a whirlwind of personal news. I'd wondered if I might once more meet Prince Peter Dolgoruki across a battlefield, me on the Turkish side and he on the Russian. But word had come that his illness had persisted after our encounter with Cezar Dalca and that Dolgoruki had died in St. Petersburg while raving about dark subterranean chambers and implacable evil. He'd been buried, Adam Czartoryski had written, with "appropriate precautions," meaning stakes, garlic, and a stone in the mouth.

Czartoryski had also noted with some satisfaction that Alexis Okhotnikov, his successor as the Tsarina Elizabeth's lover, had met an "accident" and was dead.

"I wish I'd bet on that one," Caleb had remarked.

Meanwhile, the Russian Admiral Dmitry Senyavin, whom I'd encountered at that winter reception at St. Petersburg, was patrolling the Adriatic and might add his ships to those of the British.

Newspapers also reported the assassination of Jean-Jacques Dessalines, the slave general in St. Domingue who'd pressed me into service years before. The Haitian slaves had won both independence and chaos.

I'm ever reminded that life is sweet because it's so precarious.

Despite our own military peril, the grand strategic scheme of Napoleon was within reach. Bonaparte would march on Russia from Poland in the spring, while the Ottomans would strike from the south.

"Persia is also being courted," Sebastiani told me. "A diplomat named Pierre-Amédée Jaubert negotiated with the Persians in Tehran last year. No doubt he could have used the savant Ethan Gage and his bewitching wife Astiza for his embassy."

"Persia sounds very far away."

"Not to a new diplomat named Claude-Mathieu de Gardane, who volunteered to replace Jaubert when the latter fell ill. At first men wondered at Gardane's eagerness for such a far-flung assignment, but then came rumors that this eager aide-de-camp had a grandfather, Ange de Gardane, who was a representative to the Persian court during the reign of Louis the XIV."

"He wanted to continue the family service?"

"In the crassest way. The elder Gardane reportedly assembled a treasure during his years in Persia, and then hurriedly buried it during an uprising. His grandson wants to find it and dig it up."

"A treasure?" I react to the word as I do to a pretty woman or a gambling den. "Of what kind?"

"Old, the story goes. Speculation ranges from the hoard of Genghis Kahn to the lost loot of Nadir Shah, who sacked the Mughal treasuries of Delhi."

"Intriguing." It was more than that, and I filed the rumor away. "I'd still like to tour the treasury in *this* country. Yet to get an invitation."

"Do you need one? Rumor holds that you somehow penetrated the Peter and Paul Fortress and its royal vault."

"I'm behaving myself here." Astiza and I had uncovered not a hint of the Trojan palladium and were relieved not to worry about it. My job as military advisor had given me regular work, predictable hours, and no need to trapeze from towers. "I'm the most trustworthy of men."

"Perhaps. But even Selim has the sense not to let Ethan Gage anywhere near his Ottoman treasury."

Nor would his Janissary generals let me near their proud but ineffectual troops. The Aga Abdulla Gelib and Vizier Hilmi were so opposed to military reform in the capital that I'd come here to Sestos and Abydos in hopes of accomplishing something with its New Army garrison. Meanwhile, Astiza worked as harem go-between.

Our job was made more difficult because Ottoman disunity was leaving defenses undermanned as the Turks waited to see whether it would be the reformers or the reactionaries who triumphed.

Nor was manpower our only problem. The Turkish forts were built to withstand arrows and catapults, not modern naval artillery. Ferns, vines, and small trees grew in the cracks of walls that would topple at the first broadside. Needed was an earth embankment to deflect cannon fire, a moat to discourage British or Russian marines, an abatis of pointed logs to slow an infantry attack, supporting batteries, trenches, and observation towers.

This would take money, men, and time. We had little of any.

"World events conspire in our favor, while local jealousies intrigue against us," Sebastiani summed up. Out on the water, a Turkish frigate tacked back and forth in symbolic patrol, but the Ottoman fleet Caleb was advising was like the Ottoman army, awkwardly suspended between antique pride and clumsy reform, and wracked with internal rivalry. Caleb was as consumed at sea as I was on land, and we'd seen little of each other.

"So we must turn to the tools we have," I persisted. "If we can send just one of these half-ton granite marbles rattling around the decks of the British flagship, it will give the English pause. So I have a simple idea for mounting these great guns."

"Which is?"

"That we don't. We elevate the barrels on earth ramps just enough to lob the cannonballs to mid-channel, secure them to rope and pulley like carronades on a warship, and use the time needed to cool these massive barrels to winch them back into position. They'll lie so low on the rampart that enemy cannonballs will fly overhead. The granite projectiles can be pushed to the muzzle from a ramp on one side. Water to swab and powder to fill won't have to be lifted so far. Our manpower will be just enough."

"And the British will linger while we reload?"

"One good hit is all we need. The English are brave, but they don't want to lose ships to a strategic sideshow. Napoleon told me once that the goal in war is to frighten the enemy more than you are frightened. These bombards would frighten the devil himself."

Sebastiani shook his head. "Well, their age frightens me. But have at it, Monsieur Gage. The tools at hand, as you say."

My scheme was easier said than done. It took four days to organize skeptical soldiers, drag and prop a gun to an optimum position, build a ramp to load it, and get the Turks started on reinforcing the walls. Then a day to assemble the powder and roll a cannonball into readiness, and then two more days for officers and potentates to arrive from Constantinople to witness the test-fire. One was Aga Gelib, who clearly hoped the gun would burst in my face.

Even after I drilled the artillerymen it took two hours to load and tamp the powder. The rock ball rumbled down the barrel with a growl. Despite my quip to let the Turks fire it, the Turkish aga refused to allow any of his soldiers near the bombard, meaning I had to light my own eccentric idea.

Well, the gun *looked* sturdy enough. So I fit a match into the touchhole, lit it, hurriedly backed away, squatted, and covered my ears. Spectators took my cue and crouched, turned, or winced.

The blast was like the bugle of Armageddon. The old gun gave a tremendous roar, bucking so hard against its lines that the ground quaked. Flame flashed, smoke billowed like a thunderhead, we followed a gray streak against the sky, and then the granite struck the middle of the Dardanelles channel with a tremendous splash. It was as if a meteor had fallen from heaven.

There was a long, uncertain silence. Then the garrison began to whoop with excitement. The bombard had worked, and Gelib's dark scowl at my success couldn't change that. The general stalked away as spent smoke streamed from the cannon mouth and the old iron threw off heat like a stove. To avoid cracking the barrel we waited half an hour before swabbing the bore with water, and then followed that with olive oil to protect the metal and lubricate the next shot.

"That frightened even me," admitted Sebastiani, who'd accompanied the aga for the demonstration. "And it may hearten the soldiers enough to bring some back into service. Congratulations, Gage. You've given Selim and his reformers military hope."

"Now all I have to do is ready the rest of the guns."

"Exactly. Except a Turkish officer must complete that task, I'm afraid."

"You mean I get to return to my family in Constantinople?" Astiza, Harry, and I found this new city even more agreeable than St. Petersburg. The weather was better, the people warmer, and the sights varied. We roamed the Grand Bazaar, attended receptions at different embassies, boated on the Bosporus, shopped at the Spice Market, and made excursions to the surrounding farmlands. The heat of summer had given way to the delicious warmth of a long, calm autumn, and even in winter snow was rare. Spring would come early.

"No, you can't have a reunion yet. Word has come that British Admiral John Duckworth's squadron has been reinforced at Tenedos Island by rear admiral Sir Sidney Smith, a combination which gives the English enough firepower to risk fighting their way to the capital."

"Smith! We've known each other for years. Not the easiest man to work for, but then I'm not the easiest employee. We've had a tumultuous relationship but I respect his energy and ability."

"Good, because you may shortly find yourself either fighting him or negotiating with him. You've done wonders with this antique bombard, but before we risk using it I want you to go talk to Smith and Duckworth."

"Talk?"

"Parley. Negotiate. Delay. Your brother Caleb suggested the idea to give us more time to ready the Turkish fleet. It will also give us more time on land. We need to mount more guns and assemble more men, and you've pointed the way. Now you have another task. Given your command of English and your background dealing with the British, the sultan has ordered you to sail a ship of truce to the anchored British flotilla, meet with Duckworth and Smith, and persuade them not to attack Constantinople at all."

"How am I to do that? Redcoats are as obstinate as mules."

"Point out what they already know. The Russians are going to be beaten by Napoleon this spring. Turkish defenses are strengthening. Constantinople is a strategic sideshow. To attack would be pointless and risky."

"The English aren't easily cowed. Once the British navy gets its anchor up and sails billowing, it's the devil's job to stop them."

"Agreed. They're the bullies of the sea; even your United States knows this. So if you can't persuade, delay until the wind blows foul. Delay until they need resupply. Delay, delay, delay, because every day gives us a chance to mount more cannon and gets Napoleon nearer to final victory. Keep the English off balance, Ethan, so I can keep your family safe."

"What does that mean?"

"If Selim is defeated in a naval attack, the credibility of military reform collapses. And should he lose his credibility, the sultan could lose his throne."

"The unrest has gotten that bad?"

"The Janissaries hate him and are waiting for an excuse. His closest confidant is our French harem ally, Aimée, and if Selim goes she may as well. And any of their friends— including Astiza—may find themselves on the wrong side of history and in a Topkapi dungeon or worse."

"Worse?"

"You saw the pedestals for heads by the Executioner's Fountain. The Turks also have a habit of sewing miscreant women into sacks and dropping them live into the depths of the Bosporus."

"Sewn into sacks?"

He nodded. "It would be most unfortunate if that happened to your family or mine." He put his hand on my shoulder. "Keep the English at bay for as long as you can. Because the war, and our wives, may depend on it."

CHAPTER 31

Astiza has convinced me that destiny is dogged by a past that foreshadows our future. It was with an odd sense of having already lived the moment that I was ferried under flag of truce to *HMS Canopus* off Tenedos Island, several miles southwest of the mouth of the Dardanelles. *Canopus* was the flagship of a fleet that included eight ships-of-the-line, two frigates, and two bomb vessels.

The English flagship had a curious history linked to my own. This 84-gun vessel had actually been built by the French in 1798 and named for my late mentor, Benjamin Franklin, who had been ambassador to France during the American Revolution. The *Franklin* was one of the newest and proudest ships of the French navy when Horatio Nelson captured it at the Battle of the Nile, just six months after its launch.

Given that the English still regarded Franklin as a traitor, the battleship was renamed *Canopus*, after a Greek navigator in the Trojan War. I'd barely escaped that same Nile battle by fleeing the burning French flagship *L'Orient*, and afterward I met Nelson for the first time by clambering up the hull of his flagship, beginning a relationship that gave no end of trouble. So it was with mixed emotion that I climbed the tumblehome of this renamed vessel and, upon reaching the deck, encountered yet another figure from my past.

"Good God, it *is* Gage. The man is persistent as a bloody mole."

"Hello, Sir Sidney. Flattered that you remember."

Yes, it was dashing Sir Sidney Smith, the British sailor, soldier, and spymaster who'd periodically employed me in my peripatetic career. We'd been comrades in arms at the defense of Acre against Napoleon back in 1799, and I'd been his agent since. Now circumstance had once more put me on the French side, which is always challenging to explain. My goal was to persuade Smith not to get his head blown off by forcing his way up the Dardanelles, but he rarely took advice. "And now you're working for Boney and the bloody Turk, Ethan? Never let honor get in the way of expediency, do you?"

"Just trying to save lives, admiral. Congratulations on your flag rank, by the way." Flattery, optimism, and persistence are the tools of the diplomat.

"Won not just against the enemy, but against the usual envy, backbiting, and procrastination of the Admiralty. But yes, thank you."

I received the typical piping and saluting accorded to diplomatic personnel, as well as the habitual scowls of distrust I always seem to elicit. Then the two of us were escorted to the cabin of the fleet commander, Sir John Duckworth. The date, February 9, 1807, happened to be that admiral's fifty-ninth birthday. I'd timed my arrival in hopes he'd be in a good mood.

It was not to be. Duckworth was a beefy officer with double

chin, fleshy lips, and a curving Roman nose that gave him the massive features that fit senior command. The admiral was also gloomy. He'd been in the Royal Navy for nearly a half-century, fighting in every conflict since the French and Indian War, and time had given him a combination of sober realism and habitual skepticism I'd have to overcome.

Smith, meanwhile, was vulpine and animated, a restless officer with more ideas than were good for him. And now a rear admiral! Once again an old comrade had risen in rank while I seemed mired in permanent peril—but then he'd done a better job than me of staying on the same side. To answer the pair's dubious appraisal of my shifting alliances, I thought I'd try the, 'one thing led to another' excuse.

English ambassador Charles Arbuthnot was also present. He eyed me like the devil's disciple, no doubt because Sebastiani had completely outflanked him in Constantinople, thanks to Aimée and Astiza's help.

"It's so good to speak English!" I tried.

They scowled. "Damnation, Gage," Smith replied, "it's bad enough to find you back in the clutches of the frogs, who more than once threatened to shoot you. Now you've allied with the heathen Musselman, too?"

"Merely to seek reconciliation in my role as neutral American, diplomat, negotiator, and go-between." I nodded as if they agreed. "Common sense seems to have disappeared from our violent world, gentlemen, but we in this cabin can restore it, given reason and good judgment. England, France, Prussia, and Russia have dragged the Ottomans into their global quarrel. Sultan Selim seeks peace by asking an end to your blockade."

"That's nonsense, not sense," said Arbuthnot. "The sultan pivots like a weathervane and went to Sebastiani's side as soon as word arrived of Bonaparte's victories. Now he's closed the straits to us. The Grand Turk is a schemer, just like his new French master."

"Perhaps such a cynical attitude explains why your diplomatic mission so abjectly failed." I couldn't resist the jab. "Selim is a reformer who is trying to remain neutral. Russia has invaded him; he hasn't invaded Russia. He's closed the Bosporus to all foreign navies, not just England's. It is Britain that decided to ally with Selim's archenemy Russia, which has schemed to seize Constantinople for a hundred years. And Ambassador Sebastiani has simply offered aid and advice when two powerful fleets, yours and that of Admiral Senyavin of Russia, threaten the Dardanelles. I'm here to urge you to serve your own national interest by withdrawing."

No need to mention Napoleon's scheme to employ Ottoman and Persian armies to outflank Russia from the south. Truth works best when edited.

"But the Turks have declared war against Russia, and Russia is our most important ally against Napoleon," Admiral Duckworth pointed out.

"And the Ottomans have blocked one of the world's great strategic waterways," said Smith. "The British navy can no more tolerate this than a manor lord can allow robbers to close his lane to Saturday market."

"Peace is the way to open that lane," I insisted. "Sir Sidney, you and I have a long history and while one thing has led to another, my heart has always appreciated our shared British heritage. This is not England's fight."

"Come now, Gage, I know you too well. All you ever wanted was ancient treasure, wanton women, and dupes for your clever card games."

It was an apt summary, but I pretended to be offended. "I will remind you that I am happily married and much reformed."

"And where is your wife, Gage?" asked Arbuthnot.

"In Constantinople, with my child."

"With the enemy. Whereas my wife is a refugee from that city because of the calumny of the Great Turk."

"Gentlemen." I gave a theatric sigh. "Insults and grievances are not going to open the Dardanelles or change political reality. Let me make my case without resentment or emotion."

"Very well, sir," said Duckworth. "Do so."

There was a European map unrolled on his cabin table, so I pointed to Poland, where Napoleon was presumably either bedding Marie Walewska or outflanking the Russians. "First, St. Petersburg is losing in the most important theater," I said. "The Prussians are smashed, Berlin occupied, Warsaw liberated, and the Russian commander is a frail sixty-eight-year-old who was recently beaten at Czarnomo, Pultusk, and Golymin." I'd memorized these names from the latest dispatches. "It's only a matter of time before Russia is forced from the war." This would prove true, although it would take longer than I expected. "Second, I see no Russian ships here to support England. Admiral Senyavin must be holding his fleet back in the Adriatic."

"To harass the French there," Smith said.

"While allowing us to challenge the Turk alone," Duckworth allowed. "My birthday present."

"Third," I said, "the Dardanelles and Bosporus are plagued

by swift currents and ill winds, especially in winter when weather comes from the north. Even if you sail past the Turkish forts at the Hellespont, the Sea of Marmara is a sack to seal you in. Why risk a dozen ships for no real strategic advantage?"

I saw from their glances that this same argument had occurred to them. This was not an attack they relished.

"And fourth, Sultan Selim is within his rights. These straits are as important to Constantinople as the English Channel is to London, and by keeping them free of foreign fleets he's doing no more than your own country does at home. Let me make a simple proposal. The sultan is always open to reasonable overtures. Don't sail on Constantinople just yet. Exchange notes of grievances and wait for word from the Poland campaign. Should Russia be knocked out of the war, I predict Selim's fear of England will evaporate and free passage will be restored."

"Can you guarantee that?" asked Arbuthnot.

"No, but I can guarantee the Sublime Porte will consider carefully any peaceful exit from this impasse. Remember that not long ago, England was Selim's friend."

Everything I'd argued was true. I could see them weighing my arguments and, more importantly, weighing how persuasive they'd be to the British Admiralty when they had to explain why they'd not attacked as ordered. The English were wavering, ready to buy the nag I was selling. Time to close the deal. "And fifth," I went on, trying to think of another argument, "England's real interests lie—"

"'Lie' is certainly the appropriate term," a new voice interrupted from a dark corner, speaking heavily accented English. "Because lying is what Ethan Gage does so well." I turned in disbelief. Lurking in the admiral's cabin, a thousand miles from where we'd last fought, was none other than that Prussian plague named Lothar Von Bonin, still creeping about like the spider he was. What monstrous coincidence was this? It was as bizarre as my rendezvous with my brother. Von Bonin seemed none the worse for wear for being crushed by a cabinet, and in fact looked annoyingly dapper and self-satisfied. By the Column of Constantine, where had the villain come from?

"And fifth, my esteemed allies," the Prussian went on, "the Turks are feverishly improving their defenses at every moment we waste listening to the American's nonsense. Cannon are being mounted. Walls are being strengthened. I wouldn't be surprised if Gage himself is giving them military advice, even as he preaches peace. Surely we know that Sebastiani is helping the heathens. This so-called envoy, admirals, is a thief who broke into the Russian treasury, and a murderer who has left a trail of blood across Eastern Europe. So fifth, my good friends, his mission here is to delay, obfuscate, and demoralize. To listen to him is to miss our opportunity to force the Ottomans to terms and win eternal glory."

"What is this German lunatic doing here?" I demanded. "This is an ambush, not a negotiation." I glanced at his prosthetic arm. There was a new appendage on his stump to replace the one I'd broken. Instead of blade slot and muzzle hole, a bright silver tube protruded. What now?

He followed my eye. "Yes, American, I've had some improvements made." Then he addressed the others. "This scoundrel took it upon himself to attack a one-armed man and break a bone in my amputated limb. The pain, I can assure you, was excruciating. I passed out."

"Good God, Gage, attacking a cripple?" Smith frowned. "That's low even for you."

"He was thrusting his arm—"

"Gage pinned me beneath an armoire."

Admiral Duckworth looked at me with distaste. "I was unaware our Prussian ally had encountered you. For God's sake, man, fight fair."

"He's the liar," I protested. "He attacked me, my wife, and child while we were hiding."

"Hiding in a cabinet? Are you a coward, too?"

"No! Von Bonin had poisoned the mind of the king-in-exile, Louis, and when we escaped from a prison cell the Prussian hunted us like a wolf."

"You can see how his mind is consumed by fantasy," Lothar said, "including fantastical predictions of French victory and empty promises of Turkish reason. Ambassador, you know how the Ottomans have humiliated you and your family. This conference is more of the same. Sebastiani schemes, Gage misleads, and England suffers. Strike now!"

"A few days," I urged. "Offer a compromise, give the Imperial divan time to debate and consider it, and avoid risking your ships."

"Our wind is fair *today*," insisted Von Bonin. "We should never have hesitated while waiting for this scoundrel to board."

"What are you even doing here, Prussian plotter? Why aren't you in Berlin?"

"I'm trying to liberate my country by helping our ally Britain."

"How? Napoleon has smashed Prussia's armies and occupied your capital." I turned to the others. "*He's* the coward, running from his own country. He's powerless. He has nothing to offer you."

Instead of being persuaded, they seemed embarrassed by my protest. Von Bonin looked at me sadly, as if all his predictions about my sorry character had been confirmed. "Ask Admiral Smith, who knows Gage as well as anyone," the Prussian suggested. "Is he to be trusted?"

"Ethan's only loyalty is to himself," Sir Sidney said. "He's a force to be harnessed if interests align, and to be feared if they don't."

"This same fair wind will blow a messenger to Constantinople," I urged. "Send me to carry your terms and demands. Don't start a war prematurely, Admiral Duckworth. The Dardanelles will be a death trap!"

Their commander's unhappiness with his choices was plain. Birthday indeed! He didn't appear to like any alternative, or appreciate Von Bonin much more than me. He looked from me to the Prussian and back again like guests overstaying their welcome. "How appropriate that you two rascals know each other. From St. Petersburg?"

"An earlier diplomatic mission sabotaged by Ethan Gage," Von Bonin said. "He stole relics solemnly promised by the Russian Court to Berlin and carried his contraband to the Poles. Prussia's interests will be England's interests when we step ashore in Constantinople to dictate peace, admiral. Let's do so under the persuasion of your guns."

"You'll only push the Turks closer into Napoleon's embrace," I warned.

The admiral stewed. No seaman likes venturing into narrow and hostile waters. "Let me ponder this. We don't have enough marines to seize the land forts, and I'm frustrated that Senyavin is hanging back, expecting England to do Russia's fighting. But this American sounds like a complete knave as well. Hiding in a cabinet from a one-armed man! Pathetic." He addressed his colleagues. "I'll announce my decision tomorrow."

Smith and Arbuthnot bowed.

"May I await your decision and carry word back?" I asked.

"Wait, yes," Smith said. "Carry, no. Admiral, this man has worked as both my spy and Napoleon's. His release will eliminate any chance of surprising the Turkish forts."

"May I respectfully suggest that Gage be confined?" Von Bonin said. "At least until you arrive at Constantinople, Admiral Duckworth."

"That violates all the rules of diplomacy," I protested. Not to mention keeping me on board while we ran past the very bombards I'd just help mount and load. By all Creation, instead of stopping a war I'd be putting myself into the receiving end of it.

"Ethan isn't a real diplomat," countered Smith, "and has an extraordinary history of mischief. He thinks for himself too much."

"Aye, let's not tip our hand," said Arbuthnot. "I agree with Von Bonin. Maybe a midshipman's cabin for him until we decide a course of action. We can deliver our own messages to the Turk."

"I'd suggest a place where he cannot see," Von Bonin said. "Leg irons in the orlop might be safest."

"Near our other passenger?" Smith asked.

Von Bonin shrugged.

"What other passenger?" I asked.

The Englishmen looked at each other uneasily.

"Another treasure hunter," the Prussian said smoothly.

"I came under flag of truce," I complained. "You can't lock me in the hold. For pity's sake, my wife and child are expecting my return. Selim will regard my imprisonment as an act of war."

"Yes," said Duckworth slowly. "This scoundrel is an ambassador of sorts, whether we like it or not. But I'll not let him scamper off to give warning either, since our only hope is to slip through the Dardanelles unexpected. Lock Gage in the purser's cabin until we decide whether to proceed. Tell Marine Lieutenant Greeley that it's his head if the American escapes. And if you make any trouble, Mr. Gage, I'll hang you myself." He rubbed his eyes. "Gentlemen, I'll decide this headache in the morning."

I hoped Duckworth might see reason once he was away from the accursed Von Bonin, but fortune continued to twist. First, I awoke to the grind of chains and creak of rope as the ship swung on her anchor. When I was allowed a half hour's exercise on deck, I saw that the wind had shifted during the night to blow down the Dardanelles. The English fleet couldn't sail into the teeth of the wind, and neither could I. We had to wait until the wind blew fair. That meant my palavering had bought Sebastiani and the Ottomans precious time to make the Dardanelles a fearsome gantlet, but it also meant the foul weather was blamed on me.

The shift made Duckworth's immediate decision for him. Since he couldn't sail anyway, he felt safe to announce that the time for negotiation had passed and that he'd follow the Admiralty's orders to force the straits. This decisiveness managed to satisfy his restless captains while the admiral knew they'd remain at anchor for at least another week, given February's prevailing weather. By that time circumstances might change.

The weather also meant I wasn't set free, even though the British could have rowed me to the mainland. While the English were stalled, I'd wait on board in order to preserve surprise and extend Turkish uncertainty. I paced the maindeck impatiently, even as Duckworth stalked back and forth on the quarterdeck above, eye first to the obstinate breeze and then balefully at me. "If I have to wait for the damned wind to swing, then so do you, Gage." After each day's exercise I was locked back in the purser's cabin.

Von Bonin, meanwhile, had the run of the ship. When I persisted in asking what the Prussian was doing on board, I was told only that he had "a critical diplomatic mission" in Constantinople. This likely meant either thievery or assassination, I assumed.

Then bad luck worsened my predicament even more.

Five nights after my arrival, the squadron battleship *Ajax* accidentally caught fire. Flames are a constant hazard on naval ships since they are basically a tinderbox of wood, tar, and gunpowder. The crew's valiant attempt to battle the blaze turned tragic. The northern gale fanned the flames like a bellows, the captain delayed launching his boats lest he be judged a coward for abandoning ship, and with terrifying rapidity the entire vessel became an inferno. Sailors began leaping to get clear, but since most seamen famously refuse to learn how to swim—the tars regard the skill as merely extending the agony of drowning if they fall overboard in the open ocean—the result was disaster. While three hundred were eventually saved with the assistance of other fleet longboats, two hundred and fifty burned or drowned. *Ajax* was abandoned, and in early morning blew up with a roar.

This calamity should've been taken as a sign to quit the campaign. Instead, it too was unfairly blamed on me.

"A Jonah below and this one up on deck," Duckworth's sailors muttered. "Had we sailed with the good wind, *Ajax* would still be floating. We'd be at the bloody harem by now if not for Gage's snake-like tongue."

This was monumentally unfair since I didn't control wind, accidental fire, or the swimming skills of British personnel. But Duckworth found me a convenient scapegoat for his frustrations. I was blamed for delay, delay was blamed for fire, sailors became menacing, and Von Bonin smirked as I was finally dragged and chained below, "for your own safety." The orlop deck is the ship's lowest where the cables are stowed, and it boasts the worst stink of bilge water and dry rot.

There was another odd, disquieting odor as well.

It was only after long hours in the dark, cursing Von Bonin and his bewildering reappearance, that I remembered that some other mysterious passenger was supposedly living here below the waterline—and that he was a treasure hunter too. Had some other unfortunate run afoul of the Prussian madman? There was no one confined to the bulkhead where I was, and I could see only a short way. There was only a single lantern. Listening to sounds forward, I occasionally heard the shift of ponderous weight and the drag and ring of metal as if from a caged beast. Was that my neighbor?

"Hello? Anyone there?'

There was no answer, my greeting faltering in the dark. Yet I had the curious sensation that this mysterious passenger had heard me and was listening. Warily. Malevolently. Like a wild animal with instincts more acute than my own.

"Hello?" I said it quietly this time.

No reply.

So I asked the seaman who descended to give me a dinner of hardtack and stale water. He glanced toward the bow with a nervous grimace and confided in low tones.

"Some Romanian nobleman, we're told, who don't like the sea and don't like the light, so they put 'im down here where he can't scare the crew or be scared by them. Caged up, he is, like an ugly beast. I'd put you both overboard, were it up to me."

"Scare the crew?"

"Lug of a man, with pointed teeth."

My heart began to hammer.

"Aye," he nodded to himself. "Big as a bloody bear."

Was it even possible? With Von Bonin, too?

The sailor leaned close to whisper. "Hardly seems human and the men think it bad luck to carry him, but the officers have told us to hush."

"His name?"

"Caesar, I think, like the name you'd give a big mastiff. Yeah, odd name for an odd fellow. Caesar something, like an old mutt. Don't look like no Roman to me."

What insane conspiracy was this? Had England gathered all my enemies on this ship in case I, by chance, wandered on board? Were the gods laughing at my noble pretensions? I yanked on my chains in frustration. Then I lay back against the planking to think things through with racing heart.

Cezar Dalca was apparently still alive, I was tethered like a sacrificial goat only paces from him, and I'd no way to get warning to my wife and son.

The monster had somehow found Von Bonin, the two had partnered, and they'd tempted the British navy with the best prize of all.

The pair had come after us, and after this Trojan icon.

CHAPTER 32

On February 19 the wind turned favorable for the British and *Canopus* raised anchor to lead Duckworth's flotilla to Constantinople. Our course would take us between the fortresses of Sestos and Abydos, and thus past the enormous Turkish guns I'd so glibly suggested be put to use. I'd have warned the admirals if anyone had bothered to ask, but I'd gone from negotiator to distrusted prisoner, locked near a muttering monster for reasons I couldn't fathom. The more I hollered to be heard, the more I was ignored.

I yanked furiously to somehow stretch my chains and confirm that my neighbor was indeed the Transylvanian villain and, if possible, to finish him off. But the manacles were far too short to give me a view and I was left baffled by how both Von Bonin and Cezar Dalca could contrive to be on the same British flagship. It was evil squared.

The familiar sounds of sea came down: the groan of windlass as the anchor hawser came in, the pounding of feet as men ran to unfurl sail and pull lines, the creak of rigging as the wind pushed, the accelerating splash of waves against the hull, and then the disciplined quiet as ensigns relayed the calm commands of their superiors.

"Let me talk to the Turks!" I shouted. "No need for mayhem!"

"Silence, or you'll get no tack!"

After a couple hours I began to hear the thud of Ottoman guns on shore and, at length, the answering crash of British artillery from the decks above, the long toms leaping and slamming as men cheered and swore. My dread competed with hope. From the lean of the hull I judged the wind was blowing brisk, so maybe we'd clear the fortress gantlet in a few terrible minutes. Yet this optimistic thought was subsumed by the foul stench of Dalca in the orlop, and my fear that he'd get loose. What if one of my granite cannonballs hit home?

Painfully, I counted the seconds as the guns roared, listening to the battle and praying we'd slip by. And then the flagship was slammed by something as big as the fist of God. The vessel heeled like a toy, I heard a spray of lethal splinters as big as arrows, and men screamed.

It's one of the peculiarities of nature that the granite cannonball smashed into us before its sound did. The titanic blow of its impact was followed a full ten seconds later by the gun's deep and ominous boom. Smoke drifted down into our wooden dungeon. "We're ablaze!" I heard the hiss of water and thrown sand. Dismounted gun barrels clanked and rolled. I tensed for the gush of incoming water, but the strike must have been above the waterline. Duckworth's artillery momentarily fell silent at the shock. Dalca made no sound.

I listened to the groan of the ship's timbers. Would we

sink? Would an *upyr* break loose? Would we burn? A long minute ticked away.

At length, a couple guns started up again, boots thumped down a companionway, and two marines unchained and grabbed me. "So you led us into a trap, American."

"On the contrary, I tried to warn you of it."

"Of what? Come explain the havoc!" And before I could fully get blood into my numb limbs, they dragged me to the deck above.

I gaped. Naval round shot typically makes a modest hole as it peppers a ship. It is the explosion of iron and splinters inside the hull that causes the real damage. But what I saw in the hull of *Canopus* was a gaping cavity big enough to walk through, the shoreline of the Dardanelles clearly visible a mile away. Two naval guns were overturned, blood was splashed like pots of paint, and jagged wood hung like stalactites. I shrugged free of the marines and leaned out through the wreckage. The fortress of Sestos was wreathed in smoke as its cannons fired, and a similar cloud fogged Duckworth's flotilla as it thundered in reply. Waterspouts sprang up as ordinary Turkish cannonballs narrowly missed, but periodically there was a crash as shot slammed home. It was a hot fight.

I turned back inside. The light pouring through the gap in the ship's side illuminated an enormous granite cannonball and the broken cannon barrel it had carried with it. The ball had cracked in two.

Duckworth descended. "What did the Ottomans shoot at us, Gage?"

"Granite." I pointed. "It weighs as much all by itself as a full deck broadside. The enemy has cannon as big as houses."

My use of the word 'enemy,' was deliberate, since I didn't want to be associated with this destruction. I guessed a dozen men had been killed or wounded.

"They have a muzzle that can handle that? And they're shooting rocks?"

"Many muzzles. It's the same kind of cannon the Turks used to conquer Constantinople more than three hundred years ago. Not very nimble, but enormously powerful. Can't imagine who could have suggested dragging them out of retirement, but maybe this is why the Russians are hanging back. Somehow Senyavin heard of the old bombards and decided to let the English risk their fire."

There was another enormous boom off our port stern quarter. Another huge gun had fired, and while it missed we gaped at its towering splash.

"My entire flotilla is in peril. Why didn't you warn me?"

"No one has been willing to talk with me for a week."

He scowled. "You're going to help navigate for me now. Get him up on the quarterdeck." He looked at the marines. "If the American does the least bit of villainy, shoot him."

They looked as if they'd relish the idea.

By the time we emerged from the companionway into the breeze of the uppermost deck, our own ship had run past the forts. The wind had blown our own smoke clear so that I could see several Turkish naval ships anchored in a bay past Abydos. I wondered if Caleb was there.

"Signal Smith to destroy those vessels," Duckworth ordered.

Flags began to run up halyards to convey the command.

Repairs began immediately on *Canopus*. It took six men to heave the broken cannons and granite cannonball halves overboard. The wounded were carried below, their terror rising as the doctor went to work on them. The ship's carpenter began sawing away the ends of splintered boards and measuring for new timbers that could be brought up from storage.

Meanwhile, I took in the battle. Sidney Smith began hammering the haplessly anchored Turkish ships, and several were soon either sinking, aground, or on fire. A column of Turkish cavalry galloped on the European shore, tracking our sail northeast toward Constantinople. Merchant vessels in the Sea of Marmara scattered like ducks before our pugnacious advance. Behind, Duckworth's ships were battered but floating. As we escaped the gantlet the firing from the forts growled away.

"A bit of roughhouse, but we're done with those big guns," the admiral said, as much to himself as to me.

"Unless you have to fight your way back out."

His glance was meant as a rebuke, but he couldn't hide his continued doubt about this naval sally. He'd sailed into the sack, and retreat would be as dangerous as advance. "Not enough ships, not enough men," he muttered.

The fleet advanced up the small Sea of Marmara to the Bosporus Straits, the second narrow passage between the Mediterranean and Black Seas. As the day waned, Duckworth took my suggestion and the bloodied ships anchored off the Prince Islands, a small archipelago at the entrance to this second strait. Constantinople was visible in the distance but the British didn't want to risk a blind attack in the dark. After my bombard surprise, they were wary.

"There's still opportunity to negotiate," I urged.

The admiral ordered Captain Capel in the frigate *Endymion* to anchor closer to Constantinople to convey demands to the sultan. But by now the southerly wind had exhausted itself and a cold current swirled down the Bosporus from the Black Sea. Capel made little progress, stopping at midnight just four miles ahead.

All but the night watch turned in, the men exhausted from the day's sailing and fighting. Stern lanterns marked the line of British ships where they anchored. Longboats ferried between vessels, bearing casualty reports and conveying orders. Turkish bonfires lit the shores on both the European and Asian sides of the strait, showing the camps of Ottoman troops. A scouting party sent by longboat reported that thousands of soldiers and civilians were throwing up earthen redoubts just below the city. Further away a few dim lights shone where Constantinople waited.

Duckworth had run one gantlet, but victory would require that he run another. There were Ottoman guns ahead and Ottoman guns behind.

The admiral paced the quarterdeck.

I couldn't sleep either; Astiza and Harry were so near! And in danger, since Von Bonin and Dalca were so close. Marines left on errands or to sleep, and eventually I was forgotten in my corner of quarterdeck. I belatedly realized that my cage door was open if I crept quietly away. I resolved to go for a cold swim to the nearest island and find a fishing boat to get me to the European shore. I'd report to Sebastiani and Selim and, with their permission, reunite with my family. At the very least I could send Astiza warning.

But first I had to grapple with our wicked cargo. Somewhere on board were Cezar Dalca and Lothar Von Bonin, and I couldn't believe the mission of either creature wasn't connected to my own. Best to settle our hash now. My rifle and horse pick were back in Constantinople, given that I'd arrived as a diplomat, so I quietly looked for a weapon. This wasn't an easy task since the marines carefully guarded all small arms to discourage theft or mutiny. I finally settled on a marling-spike, a two-foot long iron awl used to untie knots in the ship's massive ropes. It was a crude dagger, but serviceable. I also found a cleaver jutting from the gundeck where it had been used to chop a sailor's ankle free from an overturned cannon.

I crept back down to the orlop where I'd been chained, keeping out of sight of the powder magazine's weary sentries. The only light was that single lantern. The hold was silent as a tomb. Feeling I was probing the den of a bear, I took the lantern and crept forward to where Dalca was secreted. I listened. Nothing. I cautiously lifted the light. A door was open on a wood and iron box, but whatever it had held was gone. Had Dalca really been there?

"Looking for someone, Gage?" The Prussian accent was unmistakable.

Von Bonin's silhouette was blocking my way out.

"Some *thing* would be a better way to put it," I replied. I set the lantern down and put the spike in one fist, the cleaver in the other.

"Our passenger has an appointment in Constantinople with a woman who eluded him," the Prussian taunted. "It's been quite the exhausting journey for my new colleague, who is hungry as the devil. He needs restoration. That cannonball hole, however, made it easier for him to exit the ship to a partner's boat. Dalca best travels by water."

"Surely you don't trust that monster."

"I trust no one. You'd be wise to do the same."

"How did you two scoundrels get together?"

"Yes, who suggested our partnership? I'll let you ponder that one. I've trailed all of you for months, you know. The blustering prince, the mercenary brother, and the naïve American. Quite the clumsy cabal! Quite the bonfire you lit at Balbec! Since you risked everything to go into Dalca's lair, I decided there must be some value to Cezar. I watched his vermin flee the castle gorge and found the odd duke as a refugee on the Danube River, thirsty for renewal and quite rational about our plight. We had something in common, him and me: our desire for revenge. We sailed south from the Black Sea to the Aegean, and eventually sought alliance with the British. They think we're all going to share!"

"Share what?" How much did he know?

"Invincibility, of course. You're quite the bird dog, Ethan, pointing the way for your betters. Imagine finding the wooden idol that controlled ancient history. One of us is going to be very rich." His tone was mocking.

So I charged.

It was a mistake. Von Bonin's artificial arm swung up, I heard the click and snap of the mounted lock, there was a flash of powder, and suddenly a spout of fire stabbed from his prosthesis. The tube spewed flammable oil!

I jerked backward and fell on my back as flames shot over my face. The heat was terrifying. Then the dragon's tongue puffed out as quickly as it had flared.

"An ingenious improvement, no? Come get warm, Ethan."

I scrambled backward. "You madman. You'll set *Canopus* on fire."

"You fear my new appendage? Your aggression at Jelgava made the refit necessary. I pump oil and alcohol from a bladder, add spark from a flintlock strapped to my wrist, and cast flame like a sorcerer. Yes, that's right, back into that corner there. Easier to roast you."

"You'll kill us all!"

He jerked his head to indicate a leather bucket. "There's sand enough. I'll put you out, once you're cooked." He aimed.

I hurled the marling-spike and Von Bonin flinched and ducked. The flintlock sparked, but his jerk spewed the oil sideways and it didn't catch. I leaped sideways over a gaping hole leading to the bilge and caught a provision barrel that dangled from a counter-weighted block-and-tackle hoist. The cask swung in the dark, me riding it like a wild horse. Snarling, the Prussian yanked out a pistol with his other hand and tracked me.

"All pendulums come to a rest."

I pumped to swing even more, and then chopped at the tackle rope with my cleaver. Von Bonin cursed and triggered another geyser of fire, but I swung through it. So he risked a shot.

The rope parted. The barrel fell away back into the hold, bursting like an egg. The counterweighted rope catapulted me upward.

The Prussian's shot buzzed past my ankles. Now his gun was empty. I launched to the gundeck and landed on its planking. "Guards!" Where's a marine when you need one? My enemy bounded after me, dashing up a companionway ladder.

I looked wildly about. How to hold him off? I seized a bucket hanging by a cannon and hurled it at the Prussian's head. He dodged. I grabbed a ramrod with a woolen head for mopping out the muzzle and charged him like a knight wielding a lance.

Another gout of fire. I hopped back. "Help! Marines!" My ramrod had ignited and I weaved it like a torch, holding Von Bonin just far enough away that his puffs of heat pulsed without burning me. We fenced for advantage with fire. Cotton hammocks had been rolled and placed against the bulwarks to help contain splinters, and one of them flared up. Ropes and canvas began to burn. I had to put an end to this insanity; there could be gunpowder anywhere. "Fire!" I hollered.

I heard shouts on the deck above.

"Too late, Gage."

Then I spied inspiration. I'd retreated to a grog butt used to give sailors a drink after the battle, and a rum keg sat nearby. I hurled the flaming ramrod at Von Boning like a javelin, whirled to seize a cannonball, smashed the keg's top, and bowled the ball at my tormentor.

He dodged like a matador and came at me, eyes bright, lethal arm extended. My back was pressed against the water butt.

"See you in hell."

The flintlock flashed, and flame seared like a bolt of lightning.

So I tossed the contents of the rum keg straight at his face and threw myself prone.

Alcohol exploded. The air of the gundeck became a fireball. Von Bonin screamed. Suddenly it was him, not me, on fire. His hair flamed. His clothes erupted. He howled with fury and pain. His diabolical invention had backfired.

The Prussian ran, trailing fire that ignited tarred rope and cotton hammocks. The deck was becoming a smoky inferno. Sailors were tumbling down from the deck above, yelling and cursing. I ran after the scoundrel, pursuing a scarecrow of fire.

Von Bonin launched himself through the gaping hole in the hull of *Canopus* and, as fiery meteor, plunged into the dark beyond. There was a big splash.

I lurched to a stop and looked down. Foam marked his entry but there was no sign of my antagonist.

A midshipman pointed at me. "It's the American Jonah!"

"Saboteur!" Two marines raised rifles. "Arsonist!"

So I seized the cannonball I'd bowled and dived headfirst myself, crashing into the cold waters of the February sea.

As intended, the weight carried me thirty feet straight down. My eardrums squeezed. I released the ball and swam beneath the ship's keel. Every eye would be on the port side where I dove, so I cautiously surfaced to starboard near the weedy hull, gasping for breath and looking anxiously about. No sailor spied me but I didn't see Von Bonin, either. Had the burns killed him? I didn't feel that lucky.

I dove to swim underwater away from the ship, seeking distance and concealing darkness. No shots came. After fifty yards I struck out in a crawl for the nearest island. There I'd steal a boat to take me to Constantinople.

Disaster! But the shock of fire and chill water had cleared my head. Cezar Dalca was still at large. Lothar Von Bonin may or may not be alive. Both could reach shore. I had to make Astiza safe, and I knew just how to do so.

I was already composing a message. She and Harry must hide in the sultan's harem while I helped Sebastiani drive off the English.

Then I'd get Caleb and we'd destroy these monsters once and for all. It was time for the Gage brothers to put an end to our torment.

CHAPTER 33

Astiza

"We're in peril, priestess."

The worried sultana had curled up next to me on a sofa in her salon, she golden, me dusky, and yet of similar age and temperament. We both felt life had swept us along in adventures of great but unknown meaning. A fortuneteller in Martinique had told the child Aimée that one day she'd bear a king. I felt that I was always tantalizingly close to piercing life's veil of mystery that always seems to recede like a rainbow, finding our ultimate meaning.

"I don't feel imperiled here in your vast palace, surrounded by thousands of guards and soldiers," I said. I'd been invited to visit again, leaving Harry in the temporary care of a governess at the French embassy.

"The English fleet has fought its way past the Dardanelles

and is anchored at the Prince Islands," Aimée replied. "We haven't had word of your husband or his brother."

"I'd sense if something fatal happened to Ethan. It would strike my heart like an arrow. Caleb is presumably with the Turkish fleet. Selim and Sebastiani are working to mount more cannon on the walls of Constantinople. Surely such a great city cannot fall."

"Any city can fall from within." Although we were alone, the sultana's voice quieted. Did harem spies peer through hidden peepholes or listen through latticed windows? "For the English to get this far is a shock. The Janissaries may bang their cauldrons."

"Isn't it their duty to defend the city?"

"Their loyalty is only to themselves, and they hate and fear Selim. His New Army exposes their uselessness. He's taken advice from France and the French kadin, me. All this threatens the Janissary lock on power. How long will the sultan invite them to receive their pay if newer soldiers win the victories? The Janissaries forced Selim to appoint Hilmi as Vizier and Gelib as Aga, and both are reactionaries. They suspect me of being the whore who pushes Selim toward France."

"Some must appreciate you."

"My influence is exaggerated. The sultan turned to the West because he knows the Ottomans must change, even while some claim that change threatens Islam. Selim wants to *strengthen* Islam. But his enemies use religion against him."

"You think there will be a coup?"

"If we're defeated by the English or the Russians and the sultan doesn't take precautions, yes. I've tried to persuade him to move his regiments into the city to counter the Janissaries, but he fears civil war. Meanwhile trade has ceased and food prices are soaring because the enemy interrupts commerce. There's been another outbreak of plague, and the muezzins are calling the faithful to the mosques. The palace buzzes with rumors. Ministers are making alliances with both sides. As a woman I can't pretend to know all the plots being hatched. I only know we're in danger."

"You and the sultan."

"Me, the sultan, my son Mahmud, and you. If the Janissaries rise they'll put weak-willed Mustafa on the throne. Since I've always been close to Selim I bested Mustafa's mother as the new sultana, but she remains determined to overthrow me. Who knows what 'accidents' might occur when Janissary soldiers rampage through Topkapi? I'm draped with jewels, yet as vulnerable as a mouse under the shadow of a hawk."

"Can't Selim take steps to protect you and Mahmud?"

"Not without betraying fear and seeming weak. The sultan is determined to pretend all is well, lest people panic and soldiers desert. He thinks he can save the city and, by doing so, save himself. We women must hope he succeeds, yet prepare for the worst. That's why I've befriended you, Egyptian seer. I need magic."

"Magic!"

"You must enable us to disappear if peril comes."

"I'm a scholar, not a sorceress."

"You've been in many mysterious places and have secret knowledge no mortal can match. No, don't deny it, I see the wisdom in your eyes! You've been sent by Allah, Astiza, to help us in our hour of need. Somehow you must cast a spell of refuge, even while your husband tries to help with artillery."

I was taken aback. She was so earnest! First the tsarina wanted prophecy, and now the sultana wanted invisibility. Such faith people put in me, for so little reason! But Harry trusts me too, and in any revolt we might be swept up in violence and chaos. Where would we hide? The harem has hundreds of rooms, but wouldn't they all be searched? Every exit door was guarded against escape. Even if the black eunuchs let us flee, what were the chances of survival in a rioting Constantinople? Aimée in particular had a cascade of golden hair likely to betray her. Yet a spell? I knew no magic.

She was watching me expectantly. I pondered. The French embassy would be no guarantee of safety, either. There were only a handful of French soldiers to guard Sebastiani.

And then I remembered the story told by the Kizlar Aga. "At the entrance to the harem there's a domed anteroom with two mysterious closets," I said. "The chief eunuch pointed them out to me. Have you heard the legend?"

"That a naughty eunuch and naughty slave girl hid there and disappeared," Aimée said.

"What if the stories are true, sultana?"

"They are magical closets?"

"Not magic. Secret portals to a secret place. That's my suspicion."

"But how? Why?"

"Who knows? This palace is hundreds of years old. Many castles and manor houses have secret doors and passageways. We escaped through one at Jelgava last year. Perhaps a sultan built the closets for just such an emergency. If I could confirm my hunch, it might be just the magic you're looking for."

Now her eyes were bright. "Yes! We had a secret door in

my childhood home in Martinique. There was also rumor of a hidden corridor in the medieval convent where I was educated in France. Why not here in Topkapi?"

"The original secret has been long lost, but the closets remain. You must get me into one to investigate."

"Ah. Difficult. The eunuchs would not allow it, or if they did the secret would soon be shared all across the palace."

"Then I can't help you."

"Yet your request is not impossible for the bold." The sultana thought a moment and then smiled. "Come. I'll cause a distraction as you're about to leave and you can slip inside. If you find yourself trapped, pound on the door and explain you were foolishly curious about the old legend. The Kizlar Aga will scold you, but also think you a silly woman and throw you out. If you do find a secret way, come back in another visit and tell me."

"Secret passages are dark," I said. "Lend me a tinderbox and small lantern to hide in my robes."

"Of course. What fun to be conspirators!"

The charade worked. The sultana insisted in escorting me through the Court of the Black Eunuchs to the Place of Attendants beyond, and there bid me goodbye with kisses on both cheeks. I was ready to vanish when a eunuch startled me by pressing a sealed letter into my hands. "A message from the city," he said.

The sultana shook her head in alarm.

"I'll read it on the way home." Any note could wait.

As I stepped through the door to the Carriage Gate anteroom, Aimée pretended to fall. "My ankle!" Such a stumble was a calamity on par with an earthquake, for failure to protect the sultana from her own clumsiness might mean execution. Guards sprang to help, a cry went up for a doctor and litter, and I used the tumult to slip inside a closet.

"No, please, I'm alright," I could hear Aimée saying as I shut the door. "Just a tiny twist. Please, let me up. Where's Astiza? Did she leave? Yes, yes, it's sore. Can you carry me back to my quarters?"

The closet was full of guard cloaks and quite cramped. I used fire-steel to strike sparks on a sulfur match and lit my lamp. The rectangular box in a stone alcove seemed ordinary enough, with a wooden ceiling, door, and floor. I patted the surfaces, but they were far too solid for my meager magic. The door itself had no way to be opened from inside, so there was no escape without calling for help. I tugged on the coat pegs, but none was a lever. Maybe the story of the disappearances was just that, a story.

I dreaded having to call for rescue.

How had a slave girl discovered what I could not? I heard guard voices outside, complaining in Turkish and probably muttering about my impolite exit from their care. Then I heard the creak of the opposite closet door being opened and closed. The guards were not fools. They were checking.

I counted the tread of steps to my cubby, puffed out my lamp, and squirmed to the closet's end, squeezing myself as small as possible behind the rank of cloaks. The door swung open, dim light fell, and I pressed like wallpaper. I even brought back my feet.

"Hicber sey." Nothing. The door slammed shut, leaving me in darkness.

Even as it did there was a click where I'd rammed my heels.

The closet's wooden floor began to roll away as if on wheels. I gasped as I dropped to a second floor, six inches below the first.

The instant my weight hit this platform, it began to gently descend into the earth. It was completely black. Overhead, I could hear a snap as the primary closet floor stopped its recession and returned to position, concealing the platform I was standing on. Then this second floor stopped with a jolt.

I listened cautiously. Silence. No light. I smelled damp stone. I touched cobwebs and cold air.

Somewhere, something skittered.

It was several minutes before I dared strike a light. Ropes suspended my small wooden platform from the closet above and a tunnel led beneath the palace. When I stepped off the platform it ascended and clicked into place, higher than I could reach.

So there was no going back. At least I saw no bones of missing eunuchs or slave girls; if those truants had escaped then maybe I could too. I began to follow the featureless tunnel, calculating that I was heading vaguely east, away from the harem and towards the Bosporus Strait.

When I saw dim light ahead I snuffed my own lamp out and crept forward. The illumination was coming from an overhead grate. My tunnel had widened into a small crypt, filled with several Roman stone sarcophagi, but it seemed as forgotten as a sewer. I looked up. There was a much vaster room overhead, and a dome high above that. The meager light was coming from small glass skylights. I could make out weapons, robes, carpets, books, and metallic objects that glimmered and glowed.

My heart hammered. I was looking upward at the Topkapi treasury and what must be some of the most fabulous objects on earth. It was like the Peter and Paul vault. Life is circular, I tell Ethan.

There was no stair or ladder to the chamber above, and my own corridor ended at a blank wall. I was stalled in a crypt of the dead.

And yet why this passageway? The crypt was ancient and isolated, with no evidence of being visited. This was an old Roman passageway under newer Ottoman architecture, I guessed, its only air coming from that grate. And yet its dead-end had no logic, unless this wall was magic as well.

Once again I patted and explored. It took half an hour, me fearing discovery from the treasury above, but finally a wall stone pressed inward and a hidden door swung to reveal a darker chamber beyond.

This could have been an escape route for sultans. I stepped through, closed the hidden door behind me, and relit my lantern.

It was a repository of statuary and antiques cast off by the Byzantines and Turks. There were Roman shields and breastplates, ancient pottery, lead dinnerware, a chariot without wheels, and a litter without slaves to carry it. I counted a dozen statues of long-dead emperors. Here was the detritus of civilization too foreign to care about but too venerable to destroy. Bronze horses. More stone sarcophagi. Busts of great men no one remembered anymore. I fingered papyrus scrolls, Egyptian mummy cases, and bug-eyed pagan idols, all heavy with dust. The swords were greened bronze and pitted iron. The spear shafts had shriveled with time. Had the Muslim conquerors of Constantinople thrown down here images that Islam banned? Were these the lost treasure of Constantine the Great, who founded the city? Maybe relics of ...

Troy.

I lifted my lamp.

Athena stood sentry in a chamber corner, half-hidden behind a statue that I guessed was Poseidon. The wood sculpture was an unremarkable five feet high, its torso almost black from age—and yet, in some miracle of preservation, still in existence after three thousand years. Her features had eroded, the carved eyes almost flat, the nose just a snub, but she clearly stood proudly in gown and armor, one arm holding a shield. Was this modest statue the protectress of Troy, Athens, Sparta, Rome, and Constantinople: the Trojan palladium, the Trojan icon? Her spear had broken off to a blunt stub that jutted above her head. Her head wore a helmet. Were her powers lost? After all, the Byzantines had finally fallen to the Turks. Or perhaps the foolish Byzantines had put her aside, forgetting her history, and buried her down here with antiquity's debris. Perhaps the Turks had found her under Constantine's earthquake-toppled column, and, not knowing what she was, had stuck her away in the dark.

Or perhaps it was all hoary myth, as false as a fairy tale.

I came close. There was still power emanating from this carved fossil, I sensed, the same spiritual radiance I've felt from representations of Mary, Isis, and Sophia. Athena power. Female power. The power of the mother protectress, the lady lion. This wood held the spirit of the mother-gods worshipped since prehistory, when barbarians stared in wonder and terror at the cold night sky.

I touched the wood. It seemed to buzz and my fingers sprang away, lightly burned. Her worn wooden eyes were blind, and yet she looked at me. Looked *through* me. My breath came quick and shallow. I half-feared I'd go blind, but no curse fell.

I considered. Clearly the Ottomans no longer recognized the importance of this relic.

Which meant the palladium wouldn't be missed.

And at that, my fear and doubt slid away. Athena wanted liberation. Veneration. I touched her arms, the wood polished smooth by century after century of trembling and stroking hands. She felt warm, alive, and protective. I took faith from her serenity.

There's always a way out.

Pay attention to find it.

I snuffed out my lamp yet again, waited for my eyes to adjust to the dark, and listened and smelled.

The scent of the sea.

The dark allowed me to notice the dimmest of glimmers that emanated from behind a bronze warhorse. I crouched between its legs and spied a low passage that led toward the Bosporus. Some ancient ruler had prepared his wriggle-hole.

I measured the opening with my hands and calculated. Just big enough, perhaps, to squeeze through the Trojan palladium. Perhaps Ethan and I could drag her together.

An iron grate guarded the end of the tunnel but a lever inside released a latch. I pushed it outward and crawled into thick brush, invisible to anyone watching from the palace walls or the sea. Dusk was falling. Before I let go of the grill I jammed a stick to keep it from locking. Then I pushed through brambles to the water's edge and looked back. Topkapi Palace loomed. I'd already lost the precise spot of the tunnel grill, so artfully was it hidden. I looked out at the water. Few ships sailed because of the English blockade. Looking south toward the Sea of Marmara I could see a line of Turkish warships, beyond which were the threatening British. On the walls above I could hear the chants of sweating soldiers as they levered more cannon into position, readying for naval attack.

Could Constantinople fall to the English if it had the palladium?

Would we cause the fall if we took it?

I waited until full dark and cautiously made my way along the shoreline to a gate and the main city, hurrying to catch a ferry back to the French embassy. It was only when I was seated in the boat, finally certain I wasn't pursued, that I belatedly remembered the message pressed into my hands as I left the harem. I took it out and broke the seal.

It was from Ethan. My heart leapt, because I hadn't heard from him for two weeks. But then I read the brief words.

Cezar Dalca may be alive and roaming in Constantinople. If you are in the harem, summon Harry. And don't leave.

CHAPTER 34

Harry

I had a scary dream.

Pig Man was back. He was somewhere in my room, breathing hard in the dark. He wanted to find Mama and would use me to get her. There was a dark thing in the Pig Man's mind, and it throbbed.

The Pig Man is always unhappy, and always bad.

He wishes he could die, but he's afraid to.

He makes other people die instead.

In my nightmare I touched the dark thing in his head and it squirmed like a wild animal. Sunken eyes suddenly glowed like red coals. I had to fight! But then I woke up.

I was hot and shivery. At first I was afraid to peek from my covers, but then I remembered how Papa tells me to be brave and protect Mama. I finally looked. Pale light from the big city made my room shadowy.

Pig Man wasn't there.

He was *somewhere*, though. Somewhere near. I could feel him.

I wanted Papa, but he's off fighting.

So I decided to go to Mama's room. Sometimes she lets me in her bed.

I stood in my nightgown on the cold tile floor. My feet curled as I listened. There were dogs barking, and far-off sounds of lowing animals and grumbly wheels. Something smelled like spoiled food.

"Pig Man?"

There was no answer.

The house creaked and groaned.

"Mama?" It was too quiet.

I crossed my room to listen. Nothing. I opened the door. The hall outside was empty.

Sometimes servants sleep there, or creep quietly on night errands. Tall French soldiers stand guard. If they see me, they lift a pipe in greeting.

But nobody was there. I only felt Pig Man. I only heard my heart.

I was afraid to go out my bedroom and down the hall to Mama's room. But I made myself brave, counted to five, and rushed to open her door.

I stopped. What if the Pig Man was in there? What if he'd killed Mama?

Maybe I was still dreaming.

It was scary to go into Mama's room, but scary in the hall and scary to go back to bed. So I went in.

Something was in her bed. The something was very still,

and for a moment I was afraid Mama was dead. But I touched, and she was warm, so I scrambled in, my heart beating fast.

"Horus?"

"It's the Pig Man, Mama."

She bolted upright so suddenly that it startled me. She put a finger to my lips. "Hush. We have to listen."

I stopped snuffling. The big French house sighed in the wind. The dogs had gone quiet. I heard steps. Someone was coming.

"I got a note from your Papa."

Mama slid out of bed and listened at the door. Then she dragged a table and chest against it.

"Did you see our guards?"

I shook my head. "Everyone is gone."

She looked anxious but fierce. "Janissaries. Somehow they've gotten in. Bribed by Dalca. We have to leave."

Mama cracked the shutters of her window and peeked out at the big city. Then she ripped the blanket off her bed. "Horus, bring me the sheets." She began to tie them all together.

A candle burned but she snuffed it out. Shadows swelled in the corners.

I heard boots. The Janissaries wear bright red and yellow boots and tall, scary hats. They have long mustaches like pirates.

Mama hung the sheets out the window.

Someone tried her door. Men began to pound.

It was inky dark in the garden. I feared Pig Man was down there.

"*Açik kapi!*"

"Don't listen to them, Horus. Don't open the door."

Something heavy crashed against the door and it shook and wobbled the table. Light shone through cracks. It crashed again.

Mama clutched me so tight that I couldn't breathe. We swung into space.

CHAPTER 35

"The English have sailed into a sack, Ethan, and the way to get them out is to threaten to close the end. That's your job." I'd escaped *Canopus* and reported to the ambassador, but Sebastiani and the Turks wouldn't let me go to my family. I was ordered to complete placement of the bombards at the mouth of the Dardanelles to threaten the enemy ships. We had to frighten them into fleeing.

I couldn't explain my bizarre fear of Cezar Dalca, since that would entail explaining how I knew him and what he might have come to Constantinople to obtain. A monster in a warship hold? The story sounded absurd. I did warn that a Prussian agent named Lothar Von Bonin might be at large.

"But you set fire to him, correct?" Sebastiani clarified. We conferred at a Constantinople bunker with a new battery of cannon.

"Yes, but the Prussian jumped into the sea."

"Did you see him when you jumped as well?"

"No."

"Drowned," Sebastiani concluded. "I understand your concern, Gage, and certainly agree we must protect your wife."

"And son."

"But the best way to protect your family is to beat off these English bastards and solidify Selim's rule. Dash off a quick line instructing Astiza to stay with the sultana in the harem, which is safe as a bank vault."

"She said it was full of dwarves and eunuchs and scheming women."

"She told me it was more like a convent. You must not fret. Now listen, Turkish cavalry will escort you to Fort Sestos. The Sultan is stalling negotiations while our fortification goes forward. Once we threaten Duckworth with more of your genius, he'll be pressured to sail away. If this Prussian survived at all, he'll be alone and helpless."

"Von Bonin only has one arm and one eye and yet is the most tenacious villain imaginable. Better I remain in town, ambassador. I can help with cannon here."

"No, the big bombards were your idea and their placement has stalled since you left. You're needed at Sestos. No soldier gets to run home to his family. You're ordered by Selim himself to return to the Dardanelles."

So once again I was the tool of other men, hustled against my will back to the Turkish fort. More massive bombards were dutifully mounted. Patrolling British frigates brought warning to Duckworth anchored off Constantinople. It became obvious that the Ottoman government was stalling as its military position strengthened. I could imagine the English admiral pacing the quarterdeck, glowering at his predicament. The Turks were obstinate. Von Bonin, Dalca, and Ethan Gage had all mysteriously disappeared from *Canopus* after a fiery altercation. A trap was closing.

I was hardly the sole hero. It was eventually calculated that the Turks studded their waterways with 520 new cannon, including several of my bombards, and 110 mortars. The English ships had already been damaged. My brother's Ottoman fleet blocked the Bosporus.

And so, ever so briefly, we won. On March 1, 1807, Duckworth and Smith gave up their diplomatic bluster, weighed anchor, and set sail back through the Sea of Marmara to escape the chokepoint I'd help prepare.

This time the gantlet was worse than I'd experienced, and I was safely on shore to watch. The huge cannons were not quick, but there were enough to average a gargantuan cannonball every fifteen minutes, each concussive roar bringing frenzied cheers from the bombarding Turks. The English ships seemed to physically flinch when one of the powerful shots struck home. One 850-pound ball of granite sliced the mainmast of *Windsor Castle* in two, and British casualties were twice as high as when they'd sailed the other way. Total losses reached 254 for no diplomatic advantage. Sultan Selim had triumphed.

Adding to British frustration, Admiral Senyavin's Russian fleet finally arrived in the Aegean just as the English were retreating. Duckworth refused Senyavin's proposal for another try together. "Where were you a month ago?" The Russians were too late. The English had had enough. They set sail for Alexandria.

So the old cannon had worked, the Ottomans had won, Selim was saved, my wife was safe, and my new sinecure as French aide and Ottoman advisor in the opulent East was firmer than ever.

I allowed myself a moment's optimism. Maybe a different kind of title, and a different kind of palace, but fortune still seemed within my grasp. I was ordered by Sebastiani to remain on duty at the Turkish forts while being assured that my family was secure in the harem, out of reach of any enemy.

And then the pugnacious Senyavin blockaded the Dardanelles all by himself, daring the Turkish fleet to fight.

The danger in giving advice is that someday somebody might actually take it, and the Russian admiral had clearly remembered my vivid description of Admiral Nelson's victories a year and a half before. If he couldn't get the help of the English ships to run past the forts, he'd lure the Turkish ships beyond them into a Nelson-style melee. The Russian blockade once more threatened Constantinople with famine and now time was against the Ottomans. Admiral Pasha Seid Ali was forced to try to drive Senyavin away with a sea battle. I assumed Caleb tried with him.

The result was Turkish disaster. Senyavin in his flagship *Tverdyi* maneuvered his ten ships-of-the-line against Ali's eight, the Ottomans led by the gigantic 120-gun *Mesudiye,* or *Sultan's Majesty.* The Russian copied Nelson at the Battle of the Nile by pressing his attack as night was falling, and copied Nelson at Trafalgar by dividing his formation into two lines that split the Turkish formation like spears. He then proceeded to gang up on and destroy individual Ottoman vessels in a dark, pell-mell battle.

Wind and tide carried the fleets to within cannon shot of the Turkish batteries on the European side of the strait, but the ships were too entangled to risk using the bombards. We simply watched, with sinking hearts. By dawn, most of the

Turkish ships had either sunk or fled and the Russians used the chaos to get past my gantlet of guns. Once again, a foreign navy was in Marmara and could threaten Constantinople.

A Turkish vice admiral was beheaded for not obeying Ali's signals to fully engage, but the execution was little more than an act of despair. Ottoman victory in March had been followed by Ottoman fiasco in May, and still no wheat ships could reach the city. Where Duckworth's bold thrust had failed, Senyavin's remorseless squeeze had succeeded.

Had Caleb survived the battle? There was no word of his even being on board. Where was my brother?

Three days later I finally received new orders from Sebastiani. "Return to Constantinople at once. Riots have begun since the naval defeat, and triumph has turned to despair. The Janissaries are pounding their cauldrons. Revolt is finally at hand."

CHAPTER 36

Astiza

We were supposed to be safe, but our gilded cage is under siege.

Fires are burning in the city. We hear the echo of rioting crowds through the harem's thick walls. Eunuchs run this way and that without purpose. Some of the dwarves are weeping. Instead of lounging by the pools the women cluster in fearful flocks, repeating absurd rumors to each other. The mutes manage to moan.

We can hear the drumming of the Janissaries, rising against their masters.

They are rising against Selim and Aimée.

It was Aimée who first saved us. When Dalca's new henchmen began to break down our embassy door the night Harry came to my bed, we escaped out the window and fled to the harbor. I gripped a curved Turkish dagger to plunge into the monster's heart, but he didn't materialize. What I felt instead was the palpable presence of his evil, like a miasma.

I don't know what Dalca is, but he's no longer human. His spirit exudes malevolence and frustration like the odor of the damned. He desires, without knowing what he really wants. He lives without knowing why he lives, except that foul life isn't terrifying death. So he abides in misery, a bloated parasite that feeds on the innocent.

I almost smothered Horus as I clutched him to swing out the window. Every shadow seemed a threat as we ran down the lanes toward the Golden Horn. Every sound seemed a warning. But I was soon panting at my boy's weight, reminded again that he is growing up. He wriggled from my grasp.

"I'm almost seven."

Constantinople seemed suspended, waiting on events. Harbor shipping had stilled under the enemy blockade and the poor were starving. Disease had come back. Soldiers of uncertain loyalty roamed like gangs, extorting and raping. People hid inside, no lamps burned, and the city was dark. The palace was a distant dream across the water.

I stole a *kayik* and awkwardly began to row. The craft are as large as a longboat and almost impossible for a lone woman to handle, but Horus had no experience with oars. We managed to drift into the bay, ships ghostly, minarets silent, the city and its empire holding breath.

Behind us I could hear and see angry Janissaries spill down the embassy hill, shouting and waving swords. Where were our French guards? Had they been massacred? No, lured away somehow: I saw a cluster trooping tiredly back toward our embassy after some false emergency.

I'd no diplomatic protection, no country, no servant, no husband, and no advice. I heaved so hard at the oars that they popped out of the water and thrashed in the air like the legs of an overturned beetle. I wept in frustration.

The Janissaries leaped in a boat to pursue us. A foolish *kayik* owner rushed up to protest and was cut down by a scimitar. The soldiers wanted to catch and kill us. Or worse, bring us back to Dalca.

How could that cancer still be alive?

How could Ethan know it, and yet linger at the Dardanelles?

But then he assumed us safe in the harem. I'd been impatiently awaiting another invitation from Aimée so that I could report on the secret passage, but communication has been suspended by chaos.

I pulled again and managed to make headway, the current taking us out toward Seraglio Point. Harry watched the men striving to overtake us. "Row faster, Mama!" He paddled with his arms.

The water was black, reflecting a crescent moon. There were ghosts below its surface, I knew. When a harem woman misbehaves enough to be condemned to death, eunuchs sew her into a sack and row her to this spot, her muffled cries as piteous as a kitten's. I watched once from a balcony with a stoic Aimée, both of us rigid from horrified fascination. There's little ceremony. The eunuchs row a hundred paces, stop, stand, and heave the bag overboard. I could see the terrified woman's feet kicking before the bag splashed into the water. And that is that. It's said at least a hundred women were drowned over the centuries and are still down there, legs weighted, their sacks swaying in the current, longing for a opportunity to drag down their executioners.

The Janissaries rowed expertly, their craft like an arrow. Soon the pursuit would end, or rather something even more terrible would begin at Dalca's hands. How much had he paid them? Or what did he threaten?

But then another *kayik* darted from the palace shore. It was a royal boat with a dozen occupants. "Here comes help, Mama!"

I awkwardly turned toward potential rescuers. A race commenced, each side trying to reach us first. I thrashed frantically toward the palace.

The Janissaries almost won. I faced backward with the oars and so watched with despair as they remorselessly gained. Some of the cruel soldiers held long pikes, and others leaned from the bow with curved swords. Their features were swarthy in the night, eyes dark as sharks, grins cruel.

I pulled hard, gasping. They pulled harder.

They neared. A bowman reached for my boat's stern. One, I realize with horror, was holding a large burlap sack.

"Bad men!" Harry held up his small hands in a vain attempt to protect me.

And then the Janissaries recoiled as if from a viper. Their commander shouted a sharp, panicked command. Oars crashed into the water. Their boat lurched to a stop and then actually jumped backward. Soldiers ducked their heads in fear, not daring to even look at me.

No. Not daring to look at a harem boat.

I turned. Black eunuchs were rowing a palace *kayik* with Aimée and half a dozen harem women on board. The slaves were veiled but clearly recognizable by their finery and beauty. Their pillbox hats were jeweled. Their silks undulated in the night breeze. Their almond eyes were liquid. They were a forbidden fruit, never to be seen by mere mortals, much less addressed or molested. The Janissaries were terrified of them, or rather terrified to be in their presence. Their boat drifted backward as if it had bounced off a wall. Pikes and swords clattered to the *kayık's* bottom as the men crouched.

Aimée's boat thumped into mine. "I've been watching for you, priestess. I'd hoped you'd return with your secret." Black eunuchs plucked Horus and I like feathers and tucked us into their vessel. The boat I stole was abandoned. Before the Janissaries could restore their courage for more mischief we rowed quickly back to the palace, running up the hill to a harem gate.

And so we were saved by the inviolate harem. Horus and I were given a room where we recovered as best we could, listening to the grumble of guns and rumors of navies and battles. The English ships, it was said, went away. But Russian ones came and defeated the Turks, meaning no food would reach the masses anytime soon.

The sultan had not saved the city after all.

Riots broke out. Fires burned. Sickness burned just as fiercely. And then we began to hear the thud of spoons on Janissary cauldrons.

Ministers were sent to hastily distribute coins to buy loyalty. The viziers were torn apart. And now we hear gunfire and explosions. The rebels are storming Topkapi.

CHAPTER 37

Al that Sebastiani could tell me was that my wife and son had disappeared from the embassy.

"Apparently there was mischief," the French ambassador confessed. "Your family was asleep. There was a disturbance at the Kingdom of Naples embassy, my men rushed to help, and Janissaries broke into the mansion in their absence. When my men returned Astiza was gone, a rope of bedding hanging from her window. We can't get any official word. One story is that she made it to the palace in a boat."

"I told her not to leave the harem in the first place."

"Perhaps by the time she got your message she was already outside it," Sebastiani reasoned. "Perhaps she had to fetch your son. But now she's in and Topkapi has been cut off. Astiza told my wife Fanny that she wanted to await your return from Fort Sestos because of a secret she needed to share. But then she fled, the Russian fleet prevailed, the Janissaries grew restive, and I ordered you back here."

"Have you heard from Caleb?"

"No. The Turks complain he deserted when the English

ships arrived. They're calling him a coward. He didn't reappear for the Russian battle."

"Whatever Caleb is, he's not a coward. But it's also within his character to simply vanish." Or, I thought to myself, Dalca got him.

"I agree. It's as if everything is evaporating, including our diplomatic gains. What Napoleon achieves on land is always undone by defeats at sea." Sebastiani was frustrated.

"If Bonaparte can defeat the Russians in Poland then fortune might turn again."

"Perhaps. But it appears that victory will come too late."

We looked gloomily out at a paralyzed city. Smoke from a dozen arsons hazed the sky, the minarets looking like tree trunks in a forest fire. Drums rumbled dull warning. Gunshots and cannon fire echoed as Turkish faction fought Turkish faction.

"If they elevate Mustafa they might try to kill his half-brother Mahmud, Aimée's child," Sebastiani said. "They might even kill her."

"To elevate Mustafa they must storm Topkapi to overthrow the sultan," I said. "Which means no one is safe. Even if Astiza and Harry managed to escape to the harem, now I have to get them back out. But how?"

And get them far, far away from Cezar Dalca, I added to myself. This quest had been a misfire from the very beginning, destiny mocking my ambition and fate punishing me for greed. It was time to go somewhere new. Sebastiani had said the new French envoy to Persia, Claude-Mathieu de Gardane, was looking for his grandfather's treasure. Maybe he needed help.

"I can't get messages to the palace," Sebastiani said.

"Which means I need to break into the harem."

"Impossible."

"Not in a riot, with Topkapi overrun."

"It's madness. You'll become a eunuch yourself, Ethan."

"Or maybe my wife will know some magic." I winked. What secret had she wanted to share?

The ambassador smiled ruefully. "Will I see you again?"

"Events have swung against us, my brother has disappeared, and my family needs a fresh start." I shook Sebastiani's hand. "Take care of your own."

"*Adieu,* my friend. Your bombards worked despite my doubts."

"Until they didn't. Now Senyavin need only wait for Janissary victory and the Ottomans desperate for peace."

I retrieved my rifle, horse pick, and traveling clothes for Astiza and Harry. I couldn't very well march up the palace ramp as we had as diplomats, asking directions to the harem girls. So I ferried across the Golden Horn to the main city outside the palace and made my way uphill past the fish and spice markets. Ahead loomed the mass of the Grand Bazaar and beyond, like great mountains in a range, the high domes and minarets of Hagia Sophia and the Blue Mosque. Smoke drifted past their timeless serenity.

It was an eerie journey. The merchant stalls were shut, all commerce dead, and the few people I saw were furtive. Every door not already smashed by marauding mobs was firmly locked, and every shutter closed. Looted belongings were scattered on the street. Several corpses lay in dark corners and alleyways, gnawed at by rats and dogs.

I stayed out of sight as much as I could, taking the smallest lanes and sometimes climbing walls and trotting on rooftops to avoid Janissary patrols. I also saw troops of Selim's New Army, but they'd barricaded themselves in pointless positions and seemed too dispirited to battle their political adversaries. All the gun batteries along the shore had been deserted.

A great crowd heaved back and forth in the plaza between the vast bulk of Hagia Sofia and Topkapi's Imperial Gate. Thousands of Janissaries, wailing servants, political opportunists, and excitement seekers were milling as they debated whether to storm the sultan. A handful of frightened sentries looked down from the wall above. It didn't take a Napoleon to know that the rebels would attack as soon as they worked up their nerve. The mob would be my camouflage; I'd follow their tide into the palace.

My first step was disguise. I slipped into the blocky Byzantine church turned Islamic mosque, its rooms big enough to swallow battleships and its walls as solid as Gibraltar. Gold-tile mosaics of Jesus were coupled with inscriptions from the Koran. The interior was vast as a cavern, seemingly capable of forming clouds, and its columns were thicker than ancient trees. The monument was mostly empty, but a few Janissaries had taken the opportunity to drift away to sightsee or malinger. There are always soldiers secretly not anxious for battle—usually those who boast the most.

Hagia Sofia has dark corners and shadowy balconies, and I'd plenty of concealment to stalk a Turk my size. I lurked in an alcove, clubbed one with my rifle, and stole his clothes.

The tall hat and bright robe went over my own travel

clothes and I marched back outside. The agitated Janissaries were zealots in their frenzy, believing Selim's reforms had brought defeat from Allah, and I squeezed myself into the tightest, most excited mass of them I could find. Machiavelli advised to keep friends close and enemies closer.

The Janissary Aga Gelib who'd scowled at me in Selim's Throne Room was at the head of the crowd, I saw. He mounted a wagon to harangue us in Turkish. A howl went up at his incendiary conclusion. There was a crackle of gunfire, the sentries vanished from the wall, and the mob of unruly soldiers burst through the gate and surged into the first courtyard.

A warlike sultan would have met us with grapeshot. Selim was in his library, listening to flutes and composing appeals to reason.

The Janissaries fanned out, loyalist troops fleeing. Then the rebels charged the turreted Middle Gate. More shots were fired, a couple attackers fell, the crowd crashed against the barrier like a breaker on the shore, and someone's bloody head was displayed on a pike. Everyone roared approval. The gate splintered and I was caught up in a near-suffocating press of men boiling into the sacrosanct grounds beyond, briefly lifted off my feet in the press of agitated flesh. The Janissaries' eyes were wide with fear and hatred, emboldened and terrified by their own political blasphemy. The invasion rolled on toward the Gate of Felicity.

I struggled aside the mob and caught my breath, looking for a way to the harem. The second courtyard was an agitated sea of Janissary headdress and waving weapons. The rebels seemed determined to smash down the third gate and get to the Throne Room, and from there they would assault the harem and hunt for the sultan. Somehow I must outflank and get ahead.

As I looked for a way I spotted European clothes and focused. A Western agitator was urging on the rebels. I peered closer and got a new shock. Lothar Von Bonin was ahead of me in the press of soldiers, waving his prosthetic arm to urge the rioters on. He wore a Prussian uniform, burn bandages, and eye patch, and hung on Aga Gelib like a cloak. Lothar no doubt hoped the chaos and anarchy would give him the freedom to search for the palladium.

Well, if I'd failed to finish the vile devil off on *Canopus,* I'd do it now. All was confusion, and nobody was paying particular attention to me. I checked the priming on my rifle, snapped it to my shoulder as if aiming at a distant loyalist, and fired across the milling crowd to drop the bastard like a deer. Yet even as I did so, a Janissary soldier stepped into the way of my bullet and spun like a dervish instead.

Bloody hell.

Von Bonin whirled, looking for the shooter as I grounded my gun. All he saw, I hoped, was a sea of Janissary *börk* hats. Then he was lost, too, using the mob as protective cover. I had minutes to get ahead of him.

I ran left across the courtyard to the harem side of the palace. Reloading and then slinging my gun, I swung up onto a courtyard tree and used a branch to leap onto the top of a thick wall. I danced along it to where I could pull myself up onto the tile roof of a colonnade leading toward the harem. Some men cheered, thinking me a cheeky daredevil, and others cried sacrilege. Someone else, perhaps a eunuch guard, took a shot that missed by inches. A tile broke and clattered off the roof. I bounded up to a gable and scrambled out of sight. The sound of the mob I'd left was like the roar of the sea.

I looked behind. No other Janissary had dared follow.

The complicated covering of the huge harem was a labyrinth of domes, minarets, towers, skylights, gables, sheds, and chimneys, cobbled together over three centuries. To my right I could hear the rebels blasting their way into the sacrosanct third courtyard. Below in the harem were women's screams, eunuch shouts, and pounding feet as hundreds of frightened people churned this way and that. Directly ahead was a chimney. To hell with its swirling smoke!

I tossed off my plundered Janissary robe and hat, climbed to the chimney lip, dangled my legs, held my breath, and plunged. I skidded thirty feet down the hot chute and landed boot first in a harem fireplace. Hot! I kicked my way out, crouched, and brandished my rifle, smoking logs and embers rolling across carpets and marble. I was black with soot. Shrieking women scattered like squirrels.

I'd prefer to report that I encountered the standard Oriental fantasy inside the fabled seraglio, with voluptuous harem girls lounging by a pool in the erotic poses so vividly imagined by French and Italian artists.

Alas, their beauty was impressive enough, and certainly it was a crime to have all that pulchritude sold to a single sultan. But every woman I saw had all her clothes on and was wailing unattractively to little purpose. The girls recoiled as if I were a demon. Eunuchs stood uncertainly with scimitars and whips, dwarves crawled into cabinets, and deaf mutes covered their eyes at my devilish materialization.

The sultan was nowhere to be seen.

I seized a woman by the arm. "Aimée?" This particular female looked like a house servant of some kind, probably having lost her place in the royal bed because she was as old as I am. Fortunately, she understood my pronunciation of the name and jerked her head to get rid of me. No one was going to protect the French sultana.

I let the woman go and dashed in the direction she'd indicated.

"Aimée? Aimée?" My wife would be near the sultana. A eunuch loomed to block my way, scimitar held amateurishly at waist-level because these guards had never had to bully anyone more formidable than weaponless women. I impatiently clubbed him aside and charged up a flight of stairs, flinging open doors upon cowering occupants. Several more pointed, and finally I burst upon the right room.

"Ethan? Thank God!"

My wife was costumed in Turkish finery that took my breath away, given our lengthy separation. Yet I was glad I'd brought traveling dress. We'd be caught in an hour if she tried to escape in harem clothes.

She rushed to embrace me and stopped short in consternation. "You're black as coal!"

I, in turn, was transfixed by my first look at the mysterious beauty behind her. If my wife is the epitome of serene Mediterranean allure, Aimée was a northern flower, her hair a sunburst, her eyes sapphires, and her figure almost stupefying. No wonder she'd enthralled two sultans.

"Papa!" Harry hugged me despite the filth. "You're dirty." Harry was in a tunic, vest, and Turkish pants.

"Filthy as a chimney sweep," his mother added. She wrinkled her nose.

"Like Sinterklaas!" I winked. "Dropped from the sky like Athena."

"You're funny, Papa."

"It's my disguise." I turned to the stunning sultana. "Ethan Gage, at your service, Madame. Do you mind if I borrow a basin to get a little soot off, and then borrow my wife and son? Astiza, I brought traveling clothes."

Aimée was examining her own fireplace with interest. "A man can fit up there? Hiding from enemies?"

"In an emergency."

"I'll remember that, Monsieur Gage. You may have saved an empire by saving my son Mahmud."

"Crawling about is my specialty." I'm sure my grin was dazzling against the soot. Then I splashed in a wall fountain while Astiza and Harry dressed.

We heard the boom of a cannon and a rising cacophony of cries and shouts. The riot had turned to pitched battle. In the habitual stillness of the palace it seemed shockingly loud.

"Quick, the Janissaries will be here soon and Selim either caged or dead. How can we get out?" I put the question to Aimée, but my wife answered.

"There's a secret passage that leads under the palace."

"Can we get to it?"

"I'll escort you," Aimée said. "The eunuchs will still obey me."

"You and your son need to come too. When Selim falls—"

"No, I've changed my mind. Our place is here. The Janissaries will elevate Mustafa but he's a stupid man and won't last. Mahmud must be ready. And there's no place for me in the outside world. I'm no more fit to fly than a caged bird with clipped wings. I'll stay to see my son on the throne. There will be perilous days ahead, but perhaps your chimney trick will save him."

"Aren't you afraid for yourself?"

She shrugged. "I've no power without Selim. They'll humiliate me and then they'll ignore me." She grimaced fiercely. "Besides, a mother protects her young." She looked at Astiza. "But the Janissaries fear women of learning. They'll think your wife a witch."

"Best we hurry, then."

We trotted through the maze of the harem, windows giving glimpses of palace courtyards. It was slaughter. Ministers were being dragged to chopping blocks. Captured white eunuchs were being strangled.

We descended with Aimée to the dim quarters of the black eunuchs, the creatures cowering as we passed. Two intruding Janissaries suddenly burst upon us, as surprised by us as we by them. Each was holding a burlap bag.

They hesitated. I didn't. I shot the first and hurled the horse pick into the chest of the other, even as Aimée gave a small shout of horror. The soldiers tumbled, eyes wide with the shock of realizing they were already dead. I reloaded as our party stepped over the corpses. The pick I once more hid under my coat.

"Bad men," I explained.

"Yes, Papa. You should have brought my gun too."

"Maybe when you're older."

"Certainly not," Astiza said.

"You must disappear," Aimée moaned, looking at the bodies.

"You didn't see this, sultana. You never left your quarters."

We reached a guardroom where a particularly huge black eunuch with a pike hesitantly dared block us. "Are you leaving, Nakshedil?" The sorrowful question was addressed to Aimée. The slave seemed stricken.

For one, long, agonizing second, the French kadin looked toward the door just past him. Freedom was possible.

"Come with us," Astiza urged.

But the sultana's eyes dropped, she shook her head gravely, and took my wife's hands. "No. As I said, my place is here. Those men—those dead Janissaries—I have to keep their kind from my son." She kissed my wife. "May Allah protect you as you've protected me." Then she addressed the guard. "Kizlar, turn your head and let these people pass. I command that they are invisible."

And with that the eunuch stood aside, we went past him into an even smaller anteroom, entered a closet, and descended into the earth.

CHAPTER 38

"I came this way before," Astiza explained. "It leads to the Bosporus by way of the Ottoman treasury."

"The treasury, you say?" About time.

"The jewels are in rooms above this one and blocked by a grate, but don't worry about trinkets. I found more than a bauble." She stuck tinder and lit a small lantern. Harry relaxed at the glow. He had his family again, even if we were once again in a hole.

"You mean the Trojan relic really exists?"

"Come and decide."

The passageway ran under the muffled sounds of battle, which I hoped would preoccupy Von Bonin for some time. He was as hard to kill as I was.

"Surely a wooden statue can't have persisted—"

"It's so strange, Ethan. Why is there so little faith?"

"You mean in Greek myths? Fairy tales?"

"In the power of spirit."

"You have to believe in belief, I suppose. Franklin liked facts."

"There is more than one kind of lightning."

The boom of a cannon somewhere above interrupted our discussion. Harry jumped. "Papa, can we go home?" He meant the French embassy.

I knew we'd never return there; that our lives had once more taken an irrevocable turn. "We're moving to a better house." A fairy tale of my own, I feared.

"The Pig Man is back."

"We're going to get away from him."

Gray light beckoned. We came to a foul-looking crypt filled with old stone tombs. There, the tunnel ended. The grayness came from an iron grate above. Light throbbed from torches up there, and we could hear men shouting, shooting, and looting. I was momentarily transfixed, thinking of the wealth over my head. As unreachable as heaven.

"Not there, Ethan, here. Come, and tell me what you feel."

Come where? But then Astiza pushed on a stone and a hidden door opened to a storeroom beyond. We stepped through and she lifted her light.

Nothing glittered. The place was a menagerie of old statuary, the rubbish of empires. Discarded gods and forgotten men. All of it looked heavy and worthless.

"There."

And yet when I saw it, I felt a curious thrill. The Trojan icon, the statue of Athena, was in the storeroom's darkest corner, tucked behind a statue of a sea god and in many ways as unremarkable as a piece of driftwood. I was surprised anyone had bothered to keep her at all. The girl was slightly less than life-size; her goddess spear broken off and her features eroded. This was a sacred palladium?

But Astiza took my hand as if I were blind and pressed

my palm to the wood. It was smooth and dry, again like wave-polished driftwood, and yet I detected a faint resinous smell reminiscent of cedar. And there was more than that. Very faintly, so imperceptible that I could have been imagining it, the wood seemed to vibrate, like the feel of a kitten's purr. No, that's too strong—it was a simple sense of life in very old, very dead wood. A presence. An aura. A charge a thousand times more subtle than electricity. And yet my hand was warming.

"They've cast it away like an unwanted heirloom," I marveled.

"The Turks obviously don't know what it is. But someone persuaded them to keep it down here with the other castoffs. It's eroded and worn, but it has strange power."

"Wood that lasts three thousand years, through several empires?"

"Not wood. Not flesh. Not stone. Not steel. This is sky scratchings. Stardust. The clay of Adam. The goddess incarnate."

"Papa?" Harry tugged my leg.

"How could it still be the palladium from Troy, Athens, Rome, and who knows where else?"

"The legend is that Constantine buried it under his famous column, later toppled in an earthquake. I'm guessing the Turks rebuilt, found this when they re-erected the column, and thought it a pagan idol unfit for Islamic beliefs. Unsure why the Romans buried it, they stuck it down here."

"Papa?"

"So this statue is the Trojan palladium, the only object in the world that can make an empire invincible?"

"If you believe. Let it touch you back, Ethan. Admit it into your soul."

And it did touch me, the statue giving off some vague sense of potency and terror. This was older than mere wood. It was older than the oldest stones. It was primeval, meteoric. *It hardly mattered if the assertion by a possessed child was true,* Czartoryski had said of the Icon of Kazan. *Russian troops believed it true, and victory resulted, just like Joan of Arc.*

"Papa, look."

"In a moment Harry. So how do we take it? Will it blind us?"

"Not if it trusts our hearts."

"My heart?"

"Believe, husband. Then she'll protect you. She seeks restoration."

"You know that?"

"I feel that. There's a low tunnel we can drag her through, just over there." She stooped beneath a bronze horse to peer at an opening and pointed. "I escaped this way." Then her face became confused. "But it's dark." She crawled, reached, and slapped something solid. "Ethan, it's been bricked up!"

"Just since you were down here?

"It can't be, but it is. Why? How?" She crawled back.

"Someone is foiling us. Following us. Which means there's no way out unless we go back to the harem. Hauling a wooden statue with Janissaries running amuck."

"Papa!" Harry's tone was urgent. "There's a man."

I looked down. My son was looking up and out, to the room that held the old tombs. I followed his gaze and realized a shadow had fallen on the grate that divided this basement from the treasury proper. Someone was kneeling up there, listening. Watching. I raised my rifle and walked back.

And then a spout of fire came from down the iron bars, dazzling us with its light. Astiza screamed. I yelled.

I fired my rifle reflexively and the bullet ricocheted off the iron bars and bounced down amid us, whining like a hornet. I'd narrowly missed killing my own family. Now my weapon was empty and my dread complete.

Lothar Von Bonin laughed. "Oh, this is the best of days!" The grate, its lock apparently shattered, was thrown back. The Prussian peered down with his one good eye, the orb seeming to protrude from his face like that of a Cyclops. "You've led us to it like dogs. No, don't move—I'll roast you if you try!"

First he threw down unlit torches. Then a rope dropped and the seemingly indestructible Prussian slid down it. He'd doubled the line around the grating overhead and after descending he pulled the hatch down with a clang. The rope slithered free.

Von Bonin was burned all right, his skin blistered, but he stood as sturdily as I remembered from St. Petersburg. In fact, he seemed oddly renewed. The good eye was bright, his grin demonic. He aimed his prosthetic arm at us.

"That's twice you've missed me today, Gage. A sign from heaven, no?"

"I'd say hell. And the third time's the charm."

"I've been awaiting your arrival in this crypt. My spies bribed guards who told of a woman spotted by the Bosporus shore. It was easy enough to guess a sally port. But what was our priestess doing there? The aga gave me a few men to brick this chink in our defenses so no one else could investigate. I did so. I researched the old legends and palace plans. And Astiza lingered in the embassy in Galata, forlornly waiting for you, even as you tarried at the Dardanelles. Oh, I was impatient! Were we wrong to rely on our Egyptian seer? We had to chase her from her bedroom. A boat race made it convincing. A Janissary revolt flushed her into action. And her husband to the rescue, so I could have it all! My prize, and my revenge." He nodded at his own genius.

"You've trapped yourself with us," I said.

"We can't get back into the harem," Astiza added.

"Oh, I suspect we could if we shouted and pounded long enough. But the last thing I want is to retreat to that mob scene. Treachery. Revenge. Mayhem. Oriental madness. I like the quiet down here. Just the four of us, with a pagan idol and an unloaded gun."

"Where's Pig Man?" Harry asked suspiciously, like the bark of a small dog. "He'd better not hurt Mama."

Von Bonin looked at my son with distaste. "It was Cezar Dalca who told me the legends behind your Transylvania quest. At first I didn't believe it. The Trojan palladium? After all these years? But the Czartoryskis are mad for the past, and I've been feeding on their passion for a long time. I realized that there might be something to it if they believed. And Ethan Gage does have a knack for trying to take things that aren't his, does he not?"

"So do you."

"And what about poor Lothar? Consider my plight. Amputated. Burned. My Prussia caught in the middle of Europe. This statue could make us invulnerable, no? So justice prevails. Selim and Mahmud are being thrown into the Imperial Cage and Mustafa will rule. Aimée Nakshedil will become a scullery maid. No more Sebastiani. No more French. No more using the Turks to outflank the Russians. Napoleon was checked in February at the battle of Eylau, and when he abandons Poland and his Polish whore, we'll take back the Grunwald swords, too. All has changed in an afternoon, Gage: Your defeat and my victory."

My family had drawn up in a little trinity of fear. Von Bonin kept the stump of his arm stiffly poised as if he were a statue himself.

"You're certainly satisfied with yourself."

"I like to win. Now I have."

"Then let us go," I tried. "We'll slow you down."

"But our reunions aren't complete, I'm afraid, and I need brute labor. Surrender your rifle, Gage. Carefully, so I don't ignite your son. Come, come, hurry. Pouch and powder too."

"This is for a two-handed man, Lothar," I said as I gave up the gun, feeling the twitch of the hidden pick in the small of my back. "Take the statue. I'll help you boost it up to the treasury if you let my family go. You're right. I never should have crossed you."

Von Bonin glanced upward. "Do you think the Turks would let me stroll away with the Trojan palladium? That they wouldn't torture me to find out why I want weathered wood? I can't go that way anymore than you can. Nor can I let your family free when I'm its newest member. We're a fellowship now. All of you and me."

"After blocking our escape route," Astiza said.

"Yes. And no." He looked beyond us to the shadowy

statue of Athena. "I'm afraid your palladium looks heavy and is reputed to be quite dangerous to carry. People have been blinded. I'm already missing one eye and was grievously burned on the *Canopus*. I really can't risk further injury. Do you know what it's like to live in constant pain, the result of villains grinding on your amputated arm and hurling burning rum in your face? Most distressing. So the Gage family will carry the statue for me. I'll reload while you bring out the palladium. I do quite well with one hand, Monsieur Gage." Cradling the gun in the crook of his amputated arm, he rammed down powder and bullet with the other. "Yes, two ways to kill you now, fire and lead. Just a reminder."

We dragged out the wooden sculpture. It weighed about the same as a small woman. "Carry it where?"

"Every home needs water, including Topkapi. Pipes and sewers have underlain this peninsula for fifteen hundred years. Yes, we've been doing research, and our own quiet digging. It 's amazing what remains hidden to those who won't look, and available to those who do. The key to life is paying attention."

"Research? Who is 'we'?" But of course I guessed.

"The sarcophagus—lift the lid."

It was one of the old Roman tombs, sealed with a marble slab, and I feared we'd find Dalca lying inside. But instead of a body or bones we discovered the sarcophagus had no bottom. Heaving off he lid gave access to a dark, narrow well.

"Yes, down you go. We dug the connector after Astiza was spotted. We knew something was down here, pondered old maps, and made our coffin into a door. Appropriate, no? But when we got this far we didn't know where to go next.

There was nothing here. Was it all a lie? So we had to follow the Gage family. You found the palladium for us. Now, statue first, and then you two. I'll follow with your son."

I couldn't see a chance. He'd burn us if I shouted to the Turks. He'd shoot if I tried a tackle. We'd have to wait for the scoundrel to drop his guard.

It was a ten-foot climb down a crude ladder into blackness, me hoisting Athena down to my wife. We couldn't run away with Von Bonin holding Harry. We waited in the dark, fetid water lapping at our boots.

"Cradle the statue and back away. I'd hate to burn your boy." The Prussian herded Harry down and lit a torch. And yes, we were in another tunnel of damp stone with a skin of water on the floor. Our nemesis had slung my rifle across his back and tied the rope from his waist to a noose around Harry's neck, just like the keeper at Balbec. My son looked miserable.

"It's just for a little while, Harry," I said. "Be patient."

"Too much bad, Papa."

"All the more reason for us to be good."

Von Bonin snorted. Then he lifted the torch, throwing light down a long passageway that ran deep under the palace and city, perpendicular to the corridor from the harem above. This tunnel was Roman-straight, five feet high with finely fitted masonry. The adults had to stoop.

"Built by Constantine and likely lost, forgotten, and rediscovered more than once," Von Bonin said. "Crusader accounts mention it from their sack of Constantinople in 1204. Three days of murder, looting, and rape of their fellow Christians. This is why I can't take the pious too seriously.

In the end, it's every man for himself." He gestured with the torch. "Go, go. Carry the palladium between you."

"It's heavy."

"Do I care? Warn me if it blinds you."

That statue was awkward, but no longer hot. I felt no loss of vision; I suppose we had the luck of Odysseus. We carried Athena horizontally, the spear jutting like a stubby lance. It was tiresome labor in a tunnel at least a kilometer long.

"An old aqueduct or storm sewer, I'm guessing," Von Bonin said. "Not good to be down here when it rains."

At length the passage angled steeply upward, with stone steps to one side. "That's right, up! Ah, breathing hard, are you? Tiring for the pretty woman? Don't you dare put it down. This relic must be on the Bosporus before the rioting has ended."

Astiza and I were sweating, but I felt moving air.

"I smell a lake," Harry said.

"Clever little imp. Yes, almost there."

A lantern shone ahead, and I saw the glitter of water. We came out onto a stone quay and gaped.

We were in an enormous cave, except this was a cavity built by man. It was an underground reservoir, a vast, bar-rel-vaulted cistern with a brick roof supported by classical pillars, probably recycled from old Greek and Roman tem-ples. The cave floor was a dark lake, the columns rising out of the water like the trunks of a submerged forest. I quickly estimated a hundred of them disappearing into blackness, and supposed there could be hundreds more. The reservoir was as still and opaque as a pool of oil.

"An ancient Byzantine cistern, completely forgotten by

the Ottomans," Von Bonin said. "A reservoir to slake a city, but the old pipes filled and the old doors buried by rubble. Today's fools drop buckets down narrow wells and never think to investigate why their water is so plentiful. But we realized this was the backdoor to Topkapi Palace, and the only way to sneak out the statue. So now our reunion is complete."

"Reunion?"

"There."

And with sinking heart I recognized who the 'we' fully was. Watching us from a *kayik* was a huge, hunched form with sunken eyes darker than the limpid water. Cezar Dalca waited in a boat like Charon, helmsman to Hades. He was no longer grossly fat and immobile but cadaverous, starved, like a snake that hasn't eaten. His chest rose and fell as he stared greedily at Astiza. So he'd escaped his castle, escaped *Canopus*, and would escape Constantinople until he could crawl back down into some new lair, feeding on innocents and bloating like a leech.

Yet it wasn't Dalca who the source of my surprise and disappointment. Do all nightmares have to return? Life is not just circular, it's a treacherous, sucking whirlpool. Because there was a second person in Dalca's boat, a nervous seaman, a cursed acolyte.

"Hello, little brother." He sounded embarrassed.

"Caleb?" Astiza was astonished.

So my sibling had joined our archenemies, our rivalry complete. I stared in dawning realization. "How long have you been in league with each other?" It was Caleb, I remembered, who had mentioned some confederate in Dalca's castle. Von Bonin? It was Caleb who had suggested to Sebastiani that I negotiate on the *Canopus,* where I'd been imprisoned next to Dalca.

"You told me you'd let them go," Caleb protested to Von Bonin. "You told me Ethan would never know."

"I needed them to carry the palladium, imbecile. Did you think I could manhandle it with one arm? That I would risk being blinded? And what do you care? Their usefulness is at an end."

"You can't kill them! You promised not to!"

"Do you want your money or not? It's dangerous to let them live."

Caleb looked frustrated, but not shocked.

"You deserted the Turkish fleet," I accused.

"I had to, to get Dalca off *Canopus.* Lothar signaled, I came with a boat, and the Prussian said you'd never know."

"Von Bonin tried to kill me."

"As you tried to kill him, little brother. And yes, I betrayed you. You taught me that trick back in Philadelphia. We've all used each other, Czartoryski, Dolgoruki, Von Bonin, Izabela, and I. Things got out of hand. Lothar bargained with Dalca. No one was in real danger, not at first. It was a clever game. I've never had a life like yours, Ethan. I've never had a partner like Astiza. I'm not a bad man."

"Yes you are," Harry said.

"I bargained to protect you, nephew."

"Protect us!" Astiza protested.

"It's all calibrated—me missing Cezar when I shot at him at Balbec and pretending Ethan's gun misfired, you getting into the harem by befriending Aimée, Ethan locked away with the British. Dalca would never have mummified you, it was a performance to convince you the icon was real and to set you on course to find it. But Dolgoruki was impulsive and your husband relentless."

"You're not just a liar, Caleb," I said. "You're a fool."

"No, no, this is where it ends. We're going to sell the statue together, Lothar, Cezar, and me, to the highest bidder."

"A trinity of greed."

"Of necessity, as you ally with your own villains. Napoleon. Czartoryski. Sidney Smith. Ambitious men. Powerful men."

"You really think Dalca is going to let us go?"

"He promised."

The words hung piteously above the black water. How had Caleb's desire degenerated into insanity? How many missteps had he made?

"Put Athena in the boat," the monstrous boatman finally rumbled.

The sound of his command cut off Caleb's labored justifications. Dalca's desire was our ultimate reality now. His was the voice of pure evil, fundamental evil, the kind of evil Czartoryski had warned about, and it filled me with despair. What folly was my vain attempt at a title! I'd doomed us all. Cezar looked tall and stooped, like a gigantic mantis.

"Yes, hurry," the Prussian said impatiently. Dalca frightened even him.

We reluctantly handed the statue down to Caleb, who rested it on the thwarts while Dalca watched.

"We're going to take the boat, Astiza," said Caleb, who needed her forgiveness. "I'll leave you with your family. Go back the way you came and leave the palace after the riot has ended. Call for help in the treasury or the harem. The Turks won't care about you once the coup is complete."

"You're in league with Lucifer," she said.

"No, I just look after myself." He nodded. "And you, sister." And with that my brother raised his arms to lift two pistols from his coat, one pointed at Von Bonin and one at Dalca.

"What are you doing?" Dalca growled.

"Imbecile!" hissed Von Bonin.

"See, I'm protecting you," Caleb appealed to Astiza. "I used you, but only to get the statue." Then he addressed his conspirators, his voice unsteady. "From now on you answer to me, Lothar. You too, Dalca. This is the end of our revenge. We have the palladium. The Gage family goes free."

"Caleb, you can't trust these creatures," Astiza said.

"I never trust anyone." He confessed this while looking at me. I learned at that heartbreaking moment that despite the creed of forgiveness my brother had expressed so many months ago, nothing is ever entirely forgotten in this world. Remembrance plagues us. Revenge poisons.

"Hurry, retreat up the tunnel," he pleaded. "I'll hold them at bay."

"Yes, never trust," said the Prussian. "Dalca!" And as my brother jerked toward the boatman, his pistol swung wide of Von Bonin for just that fraction of a second needed. The Prussian ignited his arm with a click and a flash, and a jet of flame shot out towards my wayward brother.

Caleb fired blindly just as he was set on fire.

CHAPTER 39

Chaos erupted. Caleb roared, a human torch, and toppled backward into the water. I snatched out the horse pick from behind my back, coat tails flying, and swung at the man who'd ignited my brother. Dalca, with the speed of a snake and impervious to a bullet, snatched at Harry and chopped free the rope holding him to the Prussian. My wife screamed and leaped for her son.

My pointed pick first knocked away my rifle barrel that Von Bonin had taken, the gun going off harmlessly. Then I swung it to come down like a lightning bolt on the Prussian's head.

But the arc took time and Lothar was very quick. He stabbed upward to catch my chop, my horse pick jamming the nozzle hole of his prosthetic. Von Bonin howled from the impact against his stump, but he didn't fall. We locked like two stags with antlers, struggling on the edge of the reservoir. He couldn't eject more fire, and I couldn't free my pick. I seized his throat with my free hand while the Prussian clung to my empty rifle with his.

Dalca was snarling in pain. Was he wounded? I twisted

and saw Harry biting his hand while Astiza beat on his frame with her fists, her hair wild. The creature was half in the boat and half on the stone quay, trying to drag my son into the vessel, one of his hands held in Harry's jaws and the other yanking the noose around his neck.

My son was being strangled.

The distraction allowed Von Bonin to ram the barrel of my rifle against the bottom of my jaw, snapping my head back. I fell with the Prussian on top of me. Now he let go the rifle and seized my throat as I had his. His prosthesis twisted the pick, his stump using the weapon's leverage against me. Flammable fluid was pouring on both of us from the punctured flame-thrower. My ear rang with the narrow miss of the rifle shot.

"We followed you like breadcrumbs," Lothar gasped. "And now it's over." With a growl and heave he twisted the horse pick free of my grip, its point still stuck fast, its hammer jutting the other way. I tried to knee him, but was blacking out. I could hear Astiza and Dalca yowling.

"Harry." It was a croak.

Von Bonin lifted the pick suspended in his arm, aiming its hammerhead in order to brain me.

And then there was a spray of erupting water and the Prussian was knocked aside. Caleb! My brother was burned, soaked, seared with pain, and enraged. He bodily picked up Lothar, hurled him across the stone quay, and staggered after him. "You said you'd let them go!"

"Why aren't you dead?" The Prussian's hand was pumping the pick handle with his left hand to work the wicked point free from his stump.

Caleb lunged. The pick popped out and Von Bonin

turned it. The medieval weapon punctured my brother's chest with a ghastly thunk, splitting his breastbone. He grunted. The hammer end thudded against Von Bonin's chest. He gasped. They wrestled.

I dove at the boat where my family struggled. My leap knocked Astiza loose from Dalca's grip and we all tumbled, the boat rocking wildly as it pirouetted into the reservoir. Harry landed hard, but the monster had let go of the noose. The Transylvanian struggled up, swaying like a grizzly bear, pointed teeth barred, hurt, furious, his hand bleeding, my bloody son unconscious, my wife sprawled on the floorboards, me looking for some kind of weapon.

"Ethan! Athena's spear!"

Yes! The statue had its broken wooden stub. Even as Dalca pounced to wrap me with his arms, I aimed the palladium upward.

The spear shaft punched the hide of Dalca's torso. The monster's eye pits suddenly squeezed shut and his body writhed like a gaffed fish. Black blood spouted as the stake burrowed deep. His snarl changed to an oval of shock. And then he heaved backward, popped free of the stake, and with an agonized shriek crashed overboard with a mighty splash. There was an explosion of water and Dalca disappeared, sinking into watery blackness.

We drifted out among the columns. The water where Dalca had sunk began to steam and bubble.

Von Bonin and Caleb clutched and swayed on the stone quay, fighting for the horse pick buried in my brother's chest. "You weren't supposed to hurt them!" Caleb sobbed again, his flesh roasted red.

Then Lothar shoved, the pick sank deeper, and my brother

finally sagged. Von Bonin heaved him aside like garbage. Caleb sprawled. The Prussian wrenched the pick out of Caleb's chest, raised its hammer, and began bringing it savagely down on my brother's head, again and again and again.

Someone was mindlessly yelling, the sound echoing terribly in this underground cistern.

I realized it was me.

My wife clutched, urging me to sit down in the pitching boat. "Ethan, you can't help! It's too late! We have to get Horus away!"

Von Bonin, his frenzy spent, staggered away from my mutilated brother, the Prussian hideously spattered with Caleb's blood. His good eye rolled madly. He began frantically trying to load my rifle, clumsy and slow with one arm.

So we paddled with our hands, drawing away into the forest of pillars to get out of the light. The water was opaque and I feared that one of Cezar Dalca's massive hands would somehow rear from below to seize us. But perhaps the palladium had finally finished him. The spear stub was blackened and smoking. The steam where the monster had sunk was dissipating. The pool was still.

I realized there were oars in the bottom and we switched to them. Harry groaned, but stayed prone.

"Gage!" Von Bonin's cry of rage was a screech. We could no longer see him, and he could no longer see us. "Ethan Gage, I'll follow you to hell!" There was a shot, aimlessly pinging off a stone column. Now he'd have to load again.

Instead, the light on the quay abruptly went out. The Prussian must have taken the lantern and disappeared back into the tunnel we'd come through.

We scraped a pillar and drifted in shock. At first we seemed entirely blind, lost on our own River Styx. But then we saw the faintest glimmer across the vast cistern, and cautiously rowed toward it, our oar tips scraping the pillars. The light grew. At the far end of the reservoir there was a blush of illumination as faint as shallow breath. A sluggish current began to carry us.

"It's an outlet," I said. "An overflow. Dalca and Von Bonin planned to use it to carry the statue outside. The ogre can barely walk."

"Is he dead?"

"I'm not sure he was ever even alive. But he didn't like Athena's spear. That lance did more than just wound him."

"So she does have magic."

"Magic. Power. Punch. Poison. Don't go blind."

Now we heard the hiss of rushing water. "Ethan, this must drain the cistern when it fills too high from rain."

"How did Dalca drag the boat up into this place?"

Yet even as we asked we passed a ledge at water's edge and saw half a dozen bodies of Szekler workers. The henchmen had been used, and killed.

Like Caleb.

We scraped over the lip of the cistern and began sliding down a slimy ramp toward stronger light, like a toboggan in St. Petersburg. The few inches of water were just enough. We skittered out into a tiny underground harbor, a slippery stairway climbing from another stone quay to a door to a street above. Without knowing, no one would guess this outlet existed. An arch barely sufficient to squeeze the boat through led out to the Bosporus. We lay flat and floated through.

It was nearly dusk. Smoke drifted from Constantinople across the channel to Asia. The shooting had abated. We could see towers and minarets of the distant Topkapi palace, but the complex was dark. In the streets of the city, however, torches and lanterns lurched one way or another like agitated fireflies. Rebels and loyalists hurried this way and that.

Who would win?

We already knew. Sebastiani would have to flee because the Russian blockade and Janissary revolt had triggered Selim's fall from power. Aimée would try to try to save her son Mahmud from Mustafa, the new sultan, and perhaps hide him in a chimney. The Janissaries had once more triumphed. And we at last had our prize from ancient Troy, the protectress of empires stolen by Odysseus, exported to Rome by Aeneas, and safeguarded by Constantine.

Would it protect the Ethan Gage family?

The current and wind was carrying us southwest toward the Sea of Marmara, and for a while we drifted in exhaustion. Harry was breathing but unconscious, Dalca's blood in his teeth. My treacherous brother was dead from being unable to forget or forgive.

I was devastated. I'd failed to warn him of the implacable evil that Czartoryski had foretold. We'd treated each other as wary rivals when we desperately needed each other as brothers. Failure to trust had killed him and ruined me. I felt corrupted.

Harry moaned.

"I think Horus is sick, Ethan. Biting that monster poisoned him."

"We'll find a doctor."

"His illness is like Prince Dolgoruki's." Her tone was frantic.

"Maybe we can hail a ship." But from which side?

So now my boy was ill, my brother brutally murdered, and my career in tatters. I wouldn't be a prince in Russia or a vizier in Constantinople. I'd not have a palace, or even a home. I was the possessor of a worn chunk of ancient wood and perilous freedom. I was as cursed as Odysseus, spent and bitter.

Except that I already had my Penelope and Telemachus, I finally realized. My wife and son were here. And that was enough, I conceded, more than enough. We could go anywhere. Do anything. We could stop pursuing absurdity. To the devil with Vesuvius and palaces! Our journeys had become our destination. Self-reliance had become our fortune. Love had become our home.

The moon rose over Asia.

At some point I began to pull the oars and make for the distant Dardanelles. Current and wind pushed us, but the Hellespont that led to the Aegean and safety was still a full night and day away. Yet I relished the labor. The rhythmic pull quieted our minds. Astiza and I took turns.

We'd go to Italy, perhaps. Malta. Cordoba. We left the city's smoke behind and the stars wheeled. I landed at a village at dawn and managed to beg water and wine, which we dribbled on Harry's lips. No one knew a doctor.

We rowed on, Astiza fretting. The sun grew hot. The water dazzled. The Russian blockade kept the sea curiously empty of ships. We wearily passed all the way through Marmara and into the narrow, forty-mile-long strait of the Dardanelles, pushed by wind and current. The day was waning again as I spied the familiar forts of Sestos and Abydos. Even from a distance they looked curiously lifeless. Where was everyone? The Russian fleet tacked back and forth in the Aegean just beyond, blockading.

Harry began to stir, groaning.

"Give him more water."

Astiza did so. "He's starting to wake." Then, "Ethan, there's a galley."

I looked back. Following was a Turkish craft rowing furiously in the same direction we were, heading straight toward the Russians. The Turkish navy had been defeated, the capital was in new hands, the superior Russian fleet was lurking just outside the Dardanelles, and here came a lone ship hell-bent toward the enemy. What foolishness would bring Turks this close to peril?

My foolishness, of course. My enemy. My curse. I groaned, realizing what the ship was actually aimed at. "He's still after the palladium."

I looked over my shoulder, judging the distance to the blockading Russians. Past them, milky in the haze, far beyond the forts and their gigantic cannon on the Asian shore, I could see the plains of ancient Troy.

The very place where Athena had fallen from the sky.

CHAPTER 40

We rowed for Fort Sestos. If the Turkish garrison was still there, maybe it could protect us from the mad Prussian. Russian occupiers could do the same. The palladium might be confiscated, but what choice did we have? It was imperative to escape the Prussian.

The galley, several times our length and powered by a hundred oars, gained steadily. As it grew in size I realized that Von Bonin was in the bow, holding my rifle.

I leaned into the oars, watching him slowly load my gun, its barrel cradled in his stump, his left hand ramming the bullet down the muzzle.

He fired at very long range and yet a waterspout still kicked up just a few feet from our starboard side. Yes, he was a hunter, and a very good shot. He wouldn't miss when the galley drew nearer. I stroked faster.

Then the bastard actually waved. He was enjoying this.

How could we fight back? I thought furiously, and then remembered the green and blue shallows near the shore that I'd observed in the long days of sighting the old bombards. The colors marked rocks and reefs.

I craned my neck to look ahead. "Help me steer for that crabbed tree," I directed. "It may give us a chance."

Astiza pointed. We veered, my oars dipping faster than the galley's as I furiously rowed, and yet still our lead shrank against the larger vessel. I heaved at the oars. "Do you see a dark spot?"

"Almost there." She anxiously glanced behind.

Another shot. This one whined by like a hornet, splashing just ahead.

"Now," my wife said.

We passed over weedy rock. Our shallow *kayik* barely scraped, and then we were in the fortress shallows.

I looked toward the shore. Odd. I'd expect to see Turkish soldiers running down to the beach to intercept us. No one. "Where is everybody?"

Another shot, and this one clipped our gunwale. A splinter of wood flew past Astiza's cheek. She spat a curse, which shocked me. She was furious at this relentless pursuit. "Harder! We're almost there!" Then she threw herself on Harry.

I pulled, muscles popping. I could see Von Bonin vigorously reloading. The galley oars dipped and rose, flashing in the lowering sun in perfect synchronization. The vessel was aimed directly for our stern, gaining by the second. There was a steady drumbeat setting the oarsmen rhythm, an ominous boom-boom-boom that came across the water like the hammered cauldrons of the Janissaries. Its captain began shouting. Von Bonin hollered back. The captain cried angrily. Von Bonin gave a crude gesture. White foam marked the on-rushing bow where it cut water. The Turks were making a last desperate surge to catch us before we reached land.

The Prussian took aim. It was only a hundred yards now, and he couldn't miss with that fine Czartoryski gun. If he even just wounded me, it was over.

The galley hit the reef.

There was a tremendous crash and shock, the vessel's lateen mast snapped like a twig, and Von Bonin shot off the bow as if launched by a catapult. The rifle sailed lazily through the air and hit the water with a splash. The German did likewise several yards away, throwing up a spout worthy of a cannonball. Galley oars lurched, cracked, and tumbled, and a great cry of consternation and pain went up from slaves and crew. The front of the ship reared partway out of the water, the gash in its bow like a shark bite.

"Yes!" my wife cried.

We grounded beneath the fort.

Musket fire from the wrecked galley peppered the beach as we sprang out. Astiza hoisted Harry while I cradled the palladium under one arm and took an oar in the other, the load heavy and awkward. I had no other weapon. We struggled toward the earth ramparts where the vast cannon rested. I kept expecting a challenge or rescue, but no one appeared. We scaled a bunker, crawled through an embrasure where a bombard muzzle jutted, dumped the statue, and looked back.

The galley was in chaos. Men were in the water, clutching at broken oars. Others on board were shooting toward shore, the bullets plunking into the rampart. In another direction there was a Russian ship anchored just beyond the fort, in a shallow bay at the edge of the Dardanelles. Russian marines were getting into longboats to investigate the tumult.

"Has there been a plague?" Astiza wondered, looking at the empty fort.

"I'm guessing that Selim's New Army troops heard of his fall and deserted. The fort has been abandoned."

"Not by Lothar."

I knew the devil could swim, since I'd failed to finish him off on *Canopus,* and here he came with a respectable crawl even with his stump of arm. His flamethrower was disabled, his rifle gone, and yet he didn't hesitate. He must know we didn't have a gun, or we'd have fired back. But what was his weapon now?

He stood waist-deep and reached for it.

The bastard had kept his murder weapon, my medieval horse-pick.

My lance would be the oar.

I slid back down the earthen rampart of meet him, the Turkish fire slackening as Von Bonin emerged from the waves. He was breathing hard but grinning when he saw me gripping nothing but an oar of wood.

"At last you decide to fight, American? Pick against oar? I didn't think you had the courage. Will you fight me with one arm, too?"

"You told the British I didn't fight fair, Lothar. Remember?"

"Never too late to reform."

The wicked pick whistled as he twirled it overhead with his left arm, carefully advancing. The hammerhead was still matted with Caleb's blood and hair. He followed my eye. "Yes, a brutal antique you chose, Gage."

I jabbed at him with the oar blade and he parried with the pick. Both weapons were clumsy, and we staggered for balance on the steep shingle of the beach. I thrust, keeping him at bay, while he tried to circle, aiming to get on the uphill side and force me against the water.

"The Trojan palladium is far too important for an ignorant treasure hunter to possess," Von Bonin panted. "The world will thank me for taking it from you."

"But not Athena." I lunged again, deliberately striking him on his damaged prosthesis. He shouted. The pick came down in furious response and the oar blade sheered off, leaving a jagged edge of splinters. I swept this at his face, tearing a scratch and forcing him back.

But I'd lost two feet of advantage.

He was forcing me around.

"Ethan!" Astiza called. "Up here!" She threw a stone at the Prussian.

I swung the shaft of the oar like a club, Von Bonin ducking away to avoid being brained, and then I scrambled in retreat.

"Coward!"

I made for the embrasure where the clumsy bombard jutted. Von Bonin climbed right after me, swinging the pick but hampered by his lack of a second hand to grip the earth. I could hear Turkish sailors jeering at my panic. The pick point caught my jacket and tore it in two, momentarily dragging me downhill toward the Prussian. I twisted and clubbed him with the oar shaft on the shin. Von Bonin toppled. He raised the weapon to finish me but I threw sand and pebbles into his face, momentarily blinding his one eye. Then I kicked, making him skid. He brushed at his face, cursing in German.

I made it to the embrasure and climbed onto the cannon barrel to gain height. The pick clanged on old iron as my enemy followed. I rose to balance on the cylinder and danced, holding the broken oar, and now Von Bonin was up on the barrel too. We tottered. I thrust, he parried, and he tried to get inside my guard. I jabbed the shaft at his darting head and he minced backward, his one eye regarding me with hatred.

The Turks were screaming with excitement. The Russian marines were shouting from their boats.

"Find a sword or pike!" I shouted to my wife. Yet when I risked a look back she'd retreated to the butt of the cannon. Had she panicked? No, she wouldn't leave Harry. The boy lay unconscious and I feared he was dying.

My fury redoubled. I thrust again, too hard. Von Bonin twisted to let the broken oar pass his torso, and then he brought the pick down with all his force, knocking the wood from my grasp. I lost my balance and fell, sprawling painfully on the bombard.

But the force of the blow made the Prussian lose his balance too, and he toppled off the end of the gun, just catching himself on its lip to save a nasty fall to the beach. He hung awkwardly, his amputated arm wrapped around the curve of the cannon barrel, his good arm trying to grasp the muzzle without losing its hold on the horse pick. He was dangling over the mouth of the gun, his head just above the metal, wheezing but determined.

"You can't outfight me, Gage."

"But we can outthink you." It was Astiza's voice.

He sneered, lifting himself upward. "I told you not to get involved in issues beyond your grasp. I told you to leave it alone." But then he looked beyond me to where Astiza waited, and his eyes suddenly widened in fear. What had he seen? "Wait—"

Behind me, black powder hissed and whistled. I twisted to look. Astiza had struck a flint to oily cotton and touched fire to the cannon fuse-hole.

The Turks had left it loaded.

The Prussian's torso was still draped over the muzzle.

"No!"

There was a blast. I bucked from the jumping cannon as if it were a wild horse, pitched to the ground. The gun barrel recoiled as an eight-hundred-pound granite cannonball shot out in a sheet of flame and smoke. It disintegrated Von Bonin like an insect, his body disappearing in a cloud of smoke. As I hit the earth I could still see the shadow of the shot and his trailing remains hurtling toward the Turkish galley.

The explosion had cuffed my ears, but I could see the gaping mouth of sailors screaming.

Then the ball struck. The warship exploded in a thundercloud of debris. Wood, oars, men, and cannon tumbled in the air and rained into the sea.

A wave radiated out, breaking on the beach.

Dazed, I got to my knees. A triumphant Astiza threw herself beside me. "We got their boat!" I heard her dimly through the ringing.

My ears were bleeding, my body numb, my muscles trembling from exertion. I didn't care. My wife's shot had hit the grounded galley bow-on and split it open like a half-peeled banana, hurling yelling men into the water. The craft slid backward off the reef, filled with water, and sank.

There was a rumble of boot-steps behind and we turned.

A company of Russian naval infantry had rushed the empty fort and charged toward the cannon's eruption. Now they gaped as they saw a battered civilian, his exultant wife, and prostrate child. Beyond, frantic Turkish sailors were swimming for their lives, aiming for the shore well beyond the fort to escape Russian capture.

Half a dozen marines pointed muskets at us. A lieutenant shouted something in Russian.

I nodded, even though I didn't understand a word.

My ears still rang as I drew myself up as straight as I could, given my depletion, and addressed the officer in French. "At last you've arrived," I said, adding that edge of haughtiness that Russian soldiers expect. "I demand a meeting with my old friend, Admiral Dmitri Senyavin. Tell him that the American Ethan Gage is proposing to save Mother Russia from its enemies."

CHAPTER 41

"You realize, Monsieur Gage, that you're a wanted man in St. Petersburg?"

"I once was wanted as an advisor." I was standing stiffly in front of Vice Admiral Senyavin in the great cabin of his flagship *Tverdyi*. It had been more than a year since I'd seen him at that ball in St. Petersburg. Now the admiral's eyes were darker from the weariness of command, his great domed forehead giving him a professorial look as he frowned at me, as people are wont to do. His battleship's black paint was still pocked by the bright raw wood of recent Turkish cannonball hits, and crews were still hard at work repairing the rigging. Officers had told me the Russian fleet had lost more than eighty men in its victory over the Turkish navy.

"No," he said, "you're wanted as a criminal, which of course came as a great surprise after our friendship in St. Petersburg. I enjoyed our discussions of Nelson and was astonished to learn that you were apparently a Polish agent and notorious thief. The rumor is that you somehow broke into the Imperial Treasury at the Peter and Paul Fortress."

"One thing led to another."

"Which explains, I suppose, why you fled an Ottoman galley in a small longboat with your bedraggled family and an old wooden figurine?"

"People are always taking shots at me, admiral, a habit that leaves me as consternated as you. I'm the mildest of fellows, or would be if unfriendly people didn't get in my way. My son calls them bad men."

"There is no shortage of those in our world."

"I could still give the Tsar my military advice if it would square things with your government. Perhaps Minister Czartoryski could speak up for me?"

"Your Polish patron was removed from his position in February," Senyavin said. "Something about his dislike of Prussia and his pro-French leanings to favor Warsaw. Fortunes change quickly in St. Petersburg."

"A volcano, Adam called it."

"I suspect any advice you have for the Tsar will be far too late in any event. Russia and Napoleon fought a terrible winter battle at Eylau to a draw, and their armies are maneuvering for a final showdown even as we speak. By the time I returned you to St. Petersburg in chains, the French war will be either won or lost."

"The current French war," I said. "I don't believe either Napoleon or Alexander will regard any defeat as their final one."

"Aye, war never ends. But your wife is the fortune-teller, not me. My duty is to return you to justice, now that Providence has delivered you into my hands."

"Not Providence, admiral, but my own family's initiative." Since the Russian naval infantry had arrested us and taken the palladium to the Russian flagship, I'd quietly discussed with

Astiza what our real options were. I was a thief in St. Petersburg, and our allies in Constantinople had been overthrown. Aimée and her son Mahmud had reportedly been confined with Selim in the harem. If history held to its habits it was unlikely the deposed sultan would be alive very long, and Mahmud might be executed as well if he didn't find a good chimney to hide in. Both capitols were dangerous for us. So what choice did we have? Only to go on, as we all go on, bucked from the great bombard barrels of life and climbing on for the next catastrophic episode—yes, a bombastic metaphor, I admit.

I'd become somewhat philosophic about my devil's luck. As Princess Izabela said, I've traded treasure all my life for astonishing experiences, and that, perhaps, is my fate and fortune. What I wanted now was freedom, and the time and space to recuperate with my family. A ship's doctor had helped Harry regain some color but my boy was still ill and weak.

"The boy needs medicine from physicians wiser than I."

So I'd remembered the interesting tale of Claude-Mathieu Gardane looking for his grandfather's treasure in exotic Persia, while representing Napoleon as Sebastiani had done. Persia by repute has some of the world's greatest doctors. And it's not that far away after all, I decided.

"You're taking credit for becoming my prisoner, Gage?"

"This is not imprisonment but a mutually desired rendezvous, admiral. I'm offering you a brilliant trade. It does Russia no good to throw me into prison. I'd be costly to feed, would complain far too often, would confess anything you wish before a torturer even got started, and would pepper court nobles with petitions for sympathy and relief. Far better is the alternative, which is mutual generosity. I rowed to the Dardanelles with a gift to balance any wrongs I accumulated in St. Petersburg. I'm going to offer you, admiral, the one thing on earth that can save Russia from ever being conquered by Napoleon. I'll tell you what it is, but first I have a simple request. Forget you ever found me, take all the credit for our discovery upon yourself, become a hero when you return to the tsar, and quietly put me and family ashore on the plains of ancient Troy."

He looked at me suspiciously. "That's all you want?"

"To be forgotten. I've had all the renown I can take."

"What's this object you're offering?"

"The greatest prize of the Emperor Constantine, ignored by the Turks, lost to time, and resurrected by the Ethan Gage family. Have you ever heard of Odysseus and ancient Aeneas, the Trojan refugee who by legend founded Rome?"

"Of course."

"A gift from the sky, a sculpture of Athena, tied the fates of Troy, Rome, and Constantinople together."

"You're talking about that piece of junk wood?"

"Touch her before you say that. And ask yourself, what if this statue came to St. Petersburg or Moscow?" And I began to tell the unlikely story of the Trojan palladium, the curiously preserved statue that yes, had made even me temporarily invincible. I was alive, and Dalca and Von Bonin dead.

And so Senyavin put the palladium in the hold of his warship and deposited us on the shore of ancient Çanakkale, where Troy controlled the Hellespont. There are mounds of rubble on the arid plain, and I suppose one or more of them might mark where Achilles and Hector fought. I'd have dug about for a helmet or golden shield, but didn't have a shovel or the time.

I looked back at the longboat pulling away for Senyavin's flagship, wondering if I'd ever see Russia or Constantinople again. Would Athena disappear into the Peter and Paul Treasury or the storerooms of the Kremlin? Good riddance, I thought; the wooden girl was a world of trouble. But maybe she'd keep Tsar Alexander out of trouble as well, if she didn't blind anyone. And then we'd be square.

The sky was blue, the distant hills scrubby. Once more the Ethan Gage family was starting from nothing, except this time less than nothing, because Harry remained sick from our fight with Dalca.

"I'm still dizzy, Papa."

"That's because you're brave."

Perhaps my quest should not be for gold or jewels, but medicine.

"Now what, my love?" said Astiza, looking at the ancient landscape before us. Beyond was Asia in all its immensity.

"I've heard the Persians have good doctors," I said. "Treasure, too. The French embassy there is poking about, and surely they've heard of my service to Sebastiani. I think we should travel to Tehran and take in Isfahan, Khorasan, and the ruins of Persepolis—just to broaden our perspective."

"Always an exotic land." She smiled wryly. "What gypsies we are!"

"The journey has become our destination."

"And we're traveling to a better house," Harry reminded.

So yes we *did* have something, our love. It was good to be alive. "Our family is our home, son."

"Yes, Papa. But I'd still like a palace."

"Me too, if I'm being honest."

I took one of Harry's hands, Astiza took his other, and feeling the sun of Asia Minor on our shoulders and the dry dust of ancient Troy beneath our feet, we began to slowly walk.

HISTORICAL NOTE

The years 1806 and 1807 marked the summit of Napoleon Bonaparte's career. He defeated the Prussians at the battles of Auerstadt and Jena in 1806, the Russians at Friedland in June of 1807, and in July—shortly after the events of this novel—persuaded Tsar Alexander to sign the Treaty of Tilsit that temporarily forced Russia into French orbit. While the winter slaughter at the battle of Eylau in 1807 was a preview of Napoleon's grim struggles to come, he would dominate Europe for many years. It wasn't until 1808 that French embroilment in Spain began his long unraveling. Bonaparte would not face catastrophic defeat until 1812 in Russia, and be defeated for the final time at Waterloo in 1815.

The Trojan Icon is set in the period of Napoleonic domination, and its discussion of strategies between Russia, Prussia, Poland, England, Persia, and the Ottoman Empire is taken from history. The naval defeat of Duckworth's English fleet, the victory of the Russians under Senyavin, and the revolt of the Janissaries against Selim III all really happened. Some of the Turkish bombards described in this novel still exist.

Ethan's experience in the battle of Trafalgar was related in *The Barbed Crown*, and at Austerlitz in *The Three Emperors*.

While Mustafa was elevated to sultan, Aimée's son Mahmud overthrew him in an 1808 coup, becoming Sultan Mahmud II. He would go on to crush Janissary power and rule as an effective reformer until his death in 1839.

Most of the novel's other characters are real people, including Tsar Alexander and his wife Elizabeth, Alexander's mother and mistress, Adam and Izabela Czartoryski, the future Louis XVIII who would succeed Napoleon, Marie Walewska, Selim, Ambassador Horace Sebastiani, Admiral John Duckworth, and Sir Sidney Smith. Prince Peter Dolgoruki was indeed misled by the French at Austerlitz, was sent to campaign against the Turks, and died of a mysterious disease in late 1806.

More problematic is Aimée du Buc de Rivéry, the charismatic kadin who has been the subject of several novels and at least one movie. The idea that a French slave girl, cousin to Empress Josephine, was the mother of a future sultan has obvious appeal in the West. Unfortunately, historians regard Aimée as a charming legend whose existence has never been confirmed. Many stories do surround Mahmud's narrow escape and ascension to the throne in 1808, including a tale that he hid in a chimney or, alternately, escaped to the harem roof after a slave girl named Cevri Kalfa threw ashes in the eyes of his pursuers.

Lothar Von Bonin and Cezar Dalca are inventions, but the Grunwald swords and Trojan palladium are not. The swords were indeed rediscovered and delivered to Izabela's new Polish museum at the Temple of Sibyl, though historians have overlooked Ethan Gage's critical role in their recovery. Russians occupied Pulawy again during the November Uprising of 1830-31, and a parish priest hid the swords in his home. Their importance was slowly forgotten. The priest died in 1853 and Russian police confiscated the swords as illegal weapons. They were taken to a nearby fortress, where they disappear from history.

The palladium legend is as described, with the ultimate fate of the Athena statue unknown after its alleged transport to Constantinople by the Emperor Constantine. The Napoleonic era's abiding interest in ancient knowledge, magic, mysticism, archeology, and artifacts has been a consistent thread through the Ethan Gage novels, and is taken from history.

Poland has been in existence for more than 1,100 years, but has suffered frequent invasion, partition, and temporary extinction. Napoleon did have an affair with Marie Walewska and did constitute a Duchy of Warsaw in 1807, but the Congress of Vienna partitioned the country again after Bonaparte's fall. Despite periodic revolts, Poland didn't become an independent nation again until after World War I, only to be divided between Germany and Russia at the beginning of World War II. It was reconstituted yet again after the war, dominated by the Soviet Union, and has recently emerged free. Poland's geographic vulnerability and its struggle to exist is one of the great tragedies of history, but Adam and Izabela Czartoryski did keep alive the dream of Polish nationhood.

As for the Ottoman Empire, it dissolved after losing World War I while fighting on the German side. Britain and France redrew the Middle East into today's fractured states, with Constantinople-Istanbul remaining in Turkey. The Persia that Ethan refers to is modern-day Iran.

Catherine's Palace, the Winter Palace, the Peter and Paul Fortress, the palaces at Jelgava and Pulawy, and the Temple of Sibyl are all real places. Descriptions of Topkapi Palace and its harem are taken from history and personal visit—including the mysterious closets where a eunuch and harem girl vanished. The history of the ship *Canopus* and the accidental loss of the *Ajax* are as described in this novel.

As for Balbec, I leave it to readers to hunt for its foundations in the beautiful mountains of Transylvania. Follow old legends, odd stories, and the enigmatic clues of furtive and mysterious mountain people. Look for a place where thunder rumbles, mist swirls off high peaks, and bears rear up to indeed look like trapped, enchanted men.

ABOUT THE AUTHOR

WILLIAM DIETRICH is the author of twenty-two books of fiction and nonfiction. His New York Times bestselling Ethan Gage series of Napoleonic adventures has sold into thirty-one languages. The author's Pacific Northwest nonfiction has won the Pacific Northwest Booksellers Award and the Washington Governor Writer's Award. As a career journalist at the *Seattle Times*, Bill shared a Pulitzer Prize for coverage of the Exxon Valdez oil spill. Dietrich has been a Nieman Fellow at Harvard University and the recipient of several National Science Foundation journalism fellowships. He lives on an island in Washington State.

The author's website is www.williamdietrich.com.

Made in the USA
Middletown, DE
25 May 2016